5   23
STRAND PRICE
5 00

Novels by Carol McD. Wallace

Fly by Night
Waking Dream

Carol McD. Wallace

St. Martin's Press   New York

"Every Breath You Take" by Sting © 1983 Reggatta Music, Ltd./Illegal Songs, Inc. All rights reserved. Used by permission.

THE WRONG HOUSE. Copyright © 1994 by Carol McD. Wallace. All rights reserved. Printed in the United States of America. No part of this book may be used or reproduced in any manner whatsoever without written permission except in the case of brief quotations embodied in critical articles or reviews. For information, address St. Martin's Press, 175 Fifth Avenue, New York, N.Y. 10010.

Design by Basha Zapatka

Library of Congress Cataloging-in-Publication Data

Wallace, Carol.
  The wrong house / Carol McD. Wallace.
    p.   cm.
  ISBN 0-312-10579-7
    1. Marriage—Connecticut—Fiction.   2. Family—Connecticut—Fiction.   I. Title
  PS3573.A42563W76 1994
  813'.54—dc20   93-43649
                                                               CIP

First Edition: March 1994

10 9 8 7 6 5 4 3 2 1

For my father, William N. Wallace

Acknowledgments

My heartfelt thanks go to the people who helped me with *The Wrong House*. I am grateful for the research help provided by Nancy Casserley, Phil Cunningham, Don Kukuc, Juliet Packer, Gary Parks, and Moon Wallace. My agent, Lynn Seligman, and editors, Hope Dellon and Jenny Notz, provided moral support of a very high order. And I thank my husband, Rick, who gave me the idea in the first place.

1

As Hart opened the back door and stepped onto the porch, Margaret Harwood's voice followed him. "It's been in the same family for generations," she was saying. "I adore that kind of old-fashioned continuity. You just know they've taken good care of the place. You say you live in a Victorian house now?" His wife's response was muffled. "Well, I always tell clients it's hard to settle for anything else after you're used to that kind of gracious living. Now, out here"—Margaret Harwood's high heels tapped their way onto the porch—"is the nicest rose garden in Weymouth. Are you much of a gardener?"

Hart turned away from his examination of the porch foundation to catch his wife's reaction. Frances's garden in Chester was spellbinding, and she specialized in roses. Of course, Frances was too much of a lady to put Margaret Harwood in her place, but Hart, watching his wife's blue eyes scanning the forlorn-looking beds of roses in their little burlap tepees, could imagine what she would say about the real-estate agent on the long drive back to New Jersey.

He turned back to the porch, peering at a suspiciously powdery-looking spot where the steps reached the ground. Termites? Carpenter ants? There was so much to think about when you were buying a new house. This one was charming, a pretty little Victorian board-and-batten cottage with scrolled carving under the eaves. The rooms were smaller than the rooms in their Chester house, but nicely proportioned, with high ceilings, long windows, and a neat little fireplace in each one. What was more, two of the bedrooms had views of the harbor and Long Island Sound, which Hart thought of as a real drawing card. Still, aesthetics were one thing, practicality another. Hart walked up onto the porch, where Margaret Harwood was watching his wife examine the rosebushes.

"What about the wiring?" he asked.

"Rewired in the sixties," she answered, all efficiency. "They put in a new furnace at the same time. To be perfectly honest," she said, in a way Hart didn't much trust, "you may want a new hot-water heater."

Hart looked at Frances, who was now crouching and poking the frozen soil. "We don't use oceans of hot water," he said. "Can we get up to the roof?"

"I'm not sure," Margaret answered, with an insincere smile, "but let's try! We can probably get there through the attic." Hart looked at her tight knee-length skirt and the stiletto heels that were probably the reason why she wasn't cooing over the roses with Frances. He couldn't quite envision her clambering up ladders or onto the steeply pitched roof in that getup.

"Okay. I'll tell Frances." Hart crossed the lawn, noticing that the grass, even in February, seemed strong and springy. "I'm going up to try and get a look at the roof," he said. "Check out the gutters and slates."

Frances straightened up and glanced at the house. "Right. Okay. I'll be nosing around," she said, with a little smile. "It's a nice house, isn't it?"

Hart followed her gaze and looked at it. "Yes," he agreed. "You said that about the last one, too."

Frances's smile broadened. "Yes. And the one this morning. It's going to be fun to pick."

Hart nodded. "I'm glad. I like the views here. Is it a good garden?" He gestured at the roses.

Frances pursed her lips. "Pretty good. Unimaginative, but sound as far as it goes. There's a lot of scope for improvement."

"Good." Hart put his hands in his pockets and turned to head back to the house. Then he turned back with a little frown. "Could you live with that kitchen?" he asked. "Some of those fixtures looked familiar from my childhood."

Frances, who had crouched back down, looked up at him. "A new stove would take care of the worst of it," she said.

"You wouldn't want to redo the whole thing?"

"Not right away," she answered, then smiled slightly again. "Not if the roof had to come first."

Margaret Harwood, witnessing (without quite overhearing) this exchange, scented a sale. If it wasn't this house, 259 Shore Road, it would be the little mansard-roofed number on Elm Street. Frances and Hart Drummond were just the kind of people you could sell these old Victorians to. People who were older, probably retired, with the kind of money and time that it took to maintain a house like this. She'd taken a chance and shown them a modern house farther out Shore Road first thing in the morning, but it was not the kind of house that people like the Drummonds moved to Weymouth for.

Hart Drummond would have resisted the notion that moving to Weymouth was a predictable step—but in fact it was. The plan had been arrived at after several years of amicable discussion with Frances. When Hart retired from the New York law firm of which he was a partner, he and Frances would move out of the big Victorian house in Chester, New Jersey, where they had raised their two children. They certainly didn't need the space anymore, and it seemed silly to be sitting on an asset that had appreciated immensely since they'd bought it forty years earlier. They had thought about Florida, but after a couple of unsatisfying winters in rented condos in Hobe Sound and Palm Beach, they discarded the notion and decided instead to buy a year-round house in Weymouth, Connecticut.

Hart had discovered Weymouth when he was an undergraduate at Yale, exploring the coastline with young ladies from Connecticut College. In those days, before I-95 was built, Weymouth had the architecture of a prosperous nineteenth-century port and almost no economy at all. Decades of neglect meant that, although the Victorian houses were falling apart, there were relatively few twentieth-century eyesores. When the town was rediscovered in the 1960s by prosperous burghers from New Haven and Hartford, the gingerbreaded eaves and mansard roofs got tarted up and the local contractors got rich. But there was enough working farmland nearby that Weymouth didn't become precious. The grain and feed store really sold grain and feed. There was a very busy blacksmith and an active 4-H Club. And though the harbor had a rather good deep-water anchorage, there was no yacht club and most of the boats moored there were modest cabin cruisers or beamy old sloops. Along with a handful of manifestly expensive yachts, of course.

Weymouth, in fact, was a connoisseur's town. Most people rushed past on I-95 on their way to Madison or Old Lyme. There wasn't even a sign for the town on the Thruway; you had to hear about it by word of mouth. There were no shops to speak of; just a faintly dingy IGA store and a post office, and one pathetic boutique that tried to sell Battersea boxes and sandals with shells on them. There was a public beach, but it was rocky, and low tide exposed yards of mushy black mud that sucked at your ankles if you tried to walk out to the deeper water to swim. The only signs that the town was other than a simple New England village were the real-estate office installed in a lovely house in the center of town and the large proportion of Mercedes Benzes parked by the post office. Still, lots of the townspeople still drove pickup trucks. That was probably the detail that had decided Hart, who, in spite of his patrician background, education, and career, cherished a romantic view of The People. In Weymouth, although there would be plenty of citizens who read *The New Yorker* and watched the financial pages of *The Wall Street Journal*, there would also be plenty who watched the weather and fed their cows and hauled the milk to the processing plant. Hart felt that gave the town a balance. At the back of his mind he cherished images of profound conversations about the nature of Life, held among sacks of alfalfa seed. He would have hated to know that Margaret Harwood considered him a typical client.

Frances couldn't have cared less about The People, as long as she wasn't forced to live in one of their houses. What she liked about Weymouth (taking the *New Yorker* readers for granted) was the abundance of houses with what she thought of as "potential." As she and Hart drove back to Chester, she mulled over the competing appeal of the houses on Shore Road, Elm Street, and Main Street. She weighed the advantages of a mature rose garden, a harbor view, a pool, a sleeping porch, new wiring, a renovated kitchen, and proximity to the village.

"Do you think we'd actually sleep on that sleeping porch?" she said to Hart, interrupting a long silence.

"No," he answered promptly. "But we could glass it in and make a little"—he took a hand off the steering wheel to gesture—"boudoir or something for you."

"Mm," Frances said. "White wicker and chintz."

"Right. And plants. Orchids, maybe?"

"Oh, *orchids*," Frances said, dismissing them with the scorn of a dedicated rose gardener. "I don't know about orchids."

"What's the matter with orchids?" Hart asked, glancing over at her.

"Oh, I don't know," Frances answered evasively. "They're just a little—creepy. Anyway, it would take more than a sun porch to grow them. They need humidity. Which house do you like best?"

Hart looked straight ahead, thinking. "Of the Victorians? You know, I did kind of like that modern one we saw first."

"Oh, Hart." Frances sighed. "That house was impossible."

"I know," he conceded. "It was hideous. But I liked the views. Of the others, I think the one with the garden was in the best shape. Though I'm a little worried about that kitchen."

"Well," Frances said, "when we go back I'll look extra hard at the kitchen."

They drove back up to Weymouth two weeks later, with a spring-loaded measuring tape and notes on the dimensions of their furniture. It was a horribly busy day at Strong Harwood Realty; Margaret Harwood's partner was away and her dim-witted assistant had called in sick. "Look," she said to Hart, cradling a phone on her shoulder, "I never do this. But I'm so swamped: Can I just give you the keys and you look around by yourself? I hate to send you off alone, but I have a couple coming in an hour and I don't want to rush you after you came all this way. If you have any questions I'll meet you here afterward, okay? Don't tell anyone." The Drummonds were rather relieved at the prospect of seeing the houses free of Margaret Harwood's strong personality, so they accepted three bunches of keys from her red-nailed hand and gratefully left as two phones began ringing simultaneously.

The mansard-roofed house on Elm Street seemed just a little too "rickety" to Hart, and the house on Main Street was really too big, the Drummonds agreed. So they took measurements at Shore Road and Frances took notes on the varieties of roses and scooped up a bit of soil to analyze, since she was thinking about transplanting some of her best bushes.

When they got back to Strong Harwood Realty there was no one there. A note pasted to the door with a Band-Aid said "Back 2 p.m.," but it was already three-thirty.

"Should we wait?" Hart asked.

Frances looked at her watch. "We're going to hit New York right at rush hour, aren't we?" she said. "Do we need to talk to her face-to-face?"

Hart grimaced. "I'd sort of rather not. I think we can do it all by phone."

Frances shook her head. "It's really very slipshod. Do you think we can trust her to handle the closing? She seems amazingly scatterbrained to be running this business."

"It's the only game in town," Hart said, turning his back to the door and rattling the coins in his pocket. "And maybe Strong is the brains. We don't have to worry about the closing; I can keep her on track. Let's go have a drink in New Haven. Maybe even have an early dinner and wait out the traffic."

"That's a good idea," Frances said. "So you'll call in an offer next week?"

Hart nodded. "Right. What do you think we should do with these keys?" They looked all over the porch and, in the end, left them in the mail basket hung next to the front door, where they ended up staying all night since Margaret Harwood had had a flat tire on I-95 and never did make it back to work that afternoon.

So Hart made an offer for the Shore Road house, which was accepted after the usual dickering over whether or not the chandeliers would be left and when the closing would take place. Meanwhile, the house in Chester was put on the market and an offer for a very gratifying price was made by a young couple with

6

small children. In fact, the Drummonds stood to make so much money on the sale that Hart astonished Frances by suggesting they take the *QEII* to England for a little vacation before the move. It was so unlike Hart to be extravagant that Frances was shocked into agreeing, even though she felt she should stay home and worry about packing instead.

A minor hitch came up as they got ready to leave: The owners of the Weymouth house wanted to move up the closing by a couple of weeks, which meant that they wanted to close while Hart and Frances would be away. Hart got annoyed and tried to put the closing off until his and Frances's return. But the owners had to be in a new house and were intransigent. For a moment it looked as if the deal would fall apart, so Hart backed off. He would give his brother Pete power of attorney, and Pete would attend the closing. Frances said this made her a little nervous (Pete was the Drummond renegade, a bachelor inventor who made a lot of money designing electrical gadgets), but as Hart pointed out, what could go wrong? The worst of it was that they would own two houses for a couple of months.

So Frances and Hart steamed off to England on the *QEII*. They saw daffodils in the Cotswolds, lambs in the Lake District, and bought Hart a new tweed jacket in Edinburgh. When they got home they owned the house in Weymouth. Meanwhile the young buyers of the Chester house had had some difficulty getting a mortgage, so it was with great relief that the Drummonds agreed to a closing, though it would be early in June. It was later than they had hoped, but better than nothing.

Then one afternoon late in April, Hart had gone off to the city for a Yale Club dinner and Frances, taking a break from measuring furniture to decide what would go into storage, was leafing through some mail-order catalogs while she drank a cup of tea. There was some good-looking stationery in one of them, handsomely printed with just an address, very handy for either her or Hart to use in the new house. She pulled a pen from the Limoges beaker next to the phone and started to fill in the order blank. It would be nice to have the stationery waiting. She wrote down the address in the little squares provided in the order blank: "259 Shore Road, Weymouth, CT 06...." What was the zip code? Frances put down her pen. Drat. She considered putting the catalog aside and waiting until Hart got home—he would know. But she hated leaving anything unfinished. Anyway, it would be in Hart's file on the new house.

She found the file right on top of Hart's desk, with Strong Harwood's phone number scrawled on the cover. And inside, a letter from their lawyer, "Re: Purchase of 751 Shore Road, Weymouth, Conn." That was odd. A letter from the attorney shouldn't have the wrong address on it. Frances flipped through a few more papers. The contract was still at the lawyer's office, being bound with the other relevant papers, but there should be something else, maybe the engineer's report. . . . The engineer's report, which Frances had never looked at before, was for 751 Shore Road.

She sat down in Hart's desk chair, staring out the window at the long shadows on the lawn. This just wasn't possible. Maybe she'd had the address wrong. Maybe the Victorian cottage was 751 Shore Road. She put the engineer's report aside and started leafing through the rest of the file. At the very back, she found the original listing sheet from the real-estate broker, with a Xeroxed photograph of the cottage. At 259 Shore Road.

At that point Frances was still calm. She called Strong Harwood Realty. Margaret Harwood was out, of course. So was Mr. Strong. Frances asked the assistant very sweetly if she could look up the file for their purchase; could there be some confusion? No, there didn't seem to be. All the paperwork was for 751 Shore Road. And what did 751 Shore Road look like? Well, it was a two-story modern house with Swiss-style detailing, three bedrooms, three baths, maid's room, deck, waterfront property. . . . Frances felt a hollow sensation spreading from the pit of her stomach. She managed to get off the phone somewhat civilly and hung it up, staring at the receiver. The modern waterfront house on Shore Road. It just wasn't possible.

Frances tried to reach Hart at the Yale Club, but the man at the desk could only leave a message for him. She went through the file again and read the engineer's report carefully, wondering with growing rage how her husband, the meticulous attorney, had overlooked the report on the soundness of the "new redwood deck." Shouldn't that have made him wonder? How could he have done it? How could he possibly have bought the wrong house?

This was the point when Frances tried calling her children. She dialed Harry first. She was of the generation and class that naturally turned to men in a crisis, and Harry, even though he wrote soap operas for a living, had developed into a substantial and responsible man of property. Of course he probably wouldn't be at home, and he kept his answering machine on all the time anyway, a habit Frances deplored. The phone rang twice and she heard his voice saying, "This is Harry Drummond's answering machine. You know what to do."

"Harry, are you there? If you are I wish you'd pick up, it's your mother. Please call me when you get in if it's not too late, it's very important."

But of course he didn't pick up. Frances glanced at her watch. Eleanor would still be in the office. She dialed that number and heard the secretary's voice: "Mrs. Gray's office."

"Is she there?"

"I'm sorry, Mrs. Gray is in a meeting," came the adenoidal response. Frances felt a spurt of irritation that some undereducated teenager was obstructing communication with her daughter.

"Could you ask her to call her mother, please?" requested Frances in her iciest, most intimidating tone, and hung up. She called Eleanor's apartment next, skeptical about the secretary's efficiency.

"Hullo," said a very young voice in a rather muffled way. There was an audible swallow. "Sorry. Hullo," the voice repeated.

"Toby? It's your grandmother."

"Hi, Gran. Sorry, I was eating a muffin."

"At five-thirty? Won't that ruin your appetite?" said Frances reflexively. Her children had never had snacks after four P.M.

"No," said Toby, chewing again. "Mom's not coming home until eight tonight, so we're having dinner late."

"Well, would you ask her to call me after you and Simon are in bed?"

"Sure, Gran."

"Are you doing your homework?"

"Did it already. Simon and I are working on a new cage for Ramona." Ramona was the guinea pig, whose life was a series of architectural upheavals.

"Who's taking care of you?"

"Luz."

"Could I speak to her?"

"Sure. Bye, Gran." The phone clattered down and Frances could hear Toby yelling "Luz!" at the top of his lungs.

Footsteps shuffled toward the phone and a soft voice said, "Yes?" with a strong Spanish accent.

"Luz, this is Mrs. Drummond. Could I leave a message for Mrs. Gray?"

"Of course. You wait while I write?" The footsteps shuffled away. A drawer opened and closed; the footsteps shuffled back. "Yes?"

"Could you have Mrs. Gray call me when she gets home?"

"Yes, of course, Mrs. Drummond. I tell her. Thank you." The phone was hung up before Frances could reply.

Throughout this interplay Frances found herself becoming increasingly annoyed. Having left messages with a machine, an eight-year-old, a semiliterate housekeeper, and Eleanor's novice secretary, Frances had no confidence that her offspring would call her back. Hart, of course, was incommunicado: That was the whole point of places like the Yale Club. And in the meantime, what was she supposed to do?

She could call a friend, she supposed, but maybe there was some mix-up. It was possible (though she couldn't imagine how) that this whole thing was going to iron itself out. And Frances, even annoyed, was very loyal. If Hart had not, in fact, bought the wrong house, there was no point in making a fuss outside the family.

So Frances did what she always did in times of stress: She got busy. She pulled on her gardening gloves and put her pruning shears in a basket and set out to reform the privet hedge. (Which, as a result of her fierce snipping on that April evening, spent the summer looking weedy and abashed.)

The house in Weymouth might not have been so wrong if the house in Chester hadn't been so right. And the house in Chester would certainly not have been so right if Frances hadn't spent forty years tending it like a child. It was, to begin with, a house of great charm, tall and elegant with a mansard roof and a generous front porch. Everything about the house, in fact, was generous: the height of the ceilings, the languid curve of the staircase, the arch of the parlor doorway, with its mahogany pocket doors. There were eight fireplaces, five bathtubs with ball-and-claw feet, and a butler's pantry to die for. Over the years, the house had grown more and more beautiful. Miscellaneous suites of hand-me-down furniture from the twenties and thirties gave way to rather good American antiques. As Frances's and Hart's parents died, the butler's pantry filled with excellent porcelain and the little tables in the parlor sprouted the odd Louis XV snuffbox. Frances got to be an expert gardener, and every year there was a seasonal parade of brilliantly arranged cut flowers: violets, lilacs, peonies, roses. Especially roses.

Frances took enormous satisfaction in the house. As the children needed her less and less, she spent more time on what Hart vaguely thought of as "house things." She drove down to Winterthur a lot and discoursed expertly on the carved knees of Philadelphia chairs. She took an interest in charity show houses and studied layouts from *House and Garden*. Of course, her home was always on the Junior League house tour, and sometimes the awestruck comments of the visitors would echo in her head for days.

This was all, unfortunately, lost on her husband. Frances had grown up in a Philadelphia town house that could only be called gracious, but Hart's family belonged to the bleaker, New England sect of his class. Comfort was suspect, beauty a snare, unless found in the lines of a boat or a horse. Hart's childhood memories were of dark-green painted wicker and damp-smelling chintz sofas. His favorite chair was a cracked red leather club chair that Frances ruined forever when she had it reupholstered in tobacco-brown corduroy.

Hart loved Frances in his undemonstrative way and made a great effort to appreciate her handiwork. He learned the names of plants and pottered around the garden on weekends. He had always been clever with his hands, so he took a course on restoring antiques and performed a number of clever little repairs on injured chairs and tables. But the house, in the end, was her province.

It would have been very hard to leave, except that Frances had felt that 259 Shore Road was a member of the same family of houses. A younger sibling, perhaps. Another house to be loved and burnished into perfection. She had already begun imagining the changes she would make: a wide-striped wallpaper in the hall, pretty swagged curtains in the parlor, and, in time, depending on the state of the roof, a completely new kitchen.

But now, Frances thought, clipping savagely, that wasn't going to happen. They were going to live in a horrible modern house. A ticky-tacky box. A house so ugly that even Margaret Harwood couldn't find anything nice to say about it. Even as reason told Frances that they could always turn around and put it right back on the market, she entertained self-pitying visions of herself stuck in the kind of house she had always scorned. Shag carpet and TV aerials and shiny wallpaper in the bathroom, she thought to herself. A "rec room" in the basement.

As darkness fell she was still pruning away, angrier than ever.

Eleanor Gray leafed through the pink message slips on her desk as she loaded her briefcase to go home. She noticed the message from her mother and considered returning the call from her office, but it was seven-thirty and her car was waiting, so she stuffed the message into her pocket on her way out the door.

Ordinarily Eleanor took the subway home. She always left the office after rush hour, so the clattering, jerking ride uptown represented half an hour of quiet time to her. It was sacred, actually: She would go to great lengths to avoid colleagues headed in the same direction and spent the trip with her head buried in a novel. So when she got home, and the boys leaped on her as she opened the door, she had at least had a break. But tonight she'd had a late meeting, so she took a radio car home to dinner with the boys. She leaned back against the upholstery and shut her eyes as the driver careened up West Street, and tried not to think about the documents due at the end of the week, the enormous assessment for rewiring her co-op building, or Toby's passionate desire for a skateboard.

Eleanor Gray's entire life was a closely fought war against entropy. Sometimes the war took the form of a major pitched battle, as it had in the year following her divorce. Faced with the task of raising the boys and running her large West End Avenue apartment single-handed, she had, like any canny general, turned to mercenaries. Luz, a grandmother from Ecuador, lovingly bullied the boys when their absurdly expensive private school let them out after all too few hours in the classroom. Jadrancka, a Croatian electrical engineer with no English, cleaned and did the errands by some miracle of feminine resourcefulness and sign language. A market delivered the weekly food order, a personal shopper from Saks helped Eleanor select two new suits each season, and every month the rather imposing salary paid her by a Wall Street law firm only just met the bills. After almost five years, the big battle had been won. Life had a routine, and if Eleanor felt like the Red Queen, running to keep in place, she surely had nothing substantial to complain about. Many women did just what she did, she would tell herself, with a lot less money and no support system. Many women would be thrilled to have a good job, a nice apartment, two healthy boys, reliable help, a network of friends. In her dark moments Eleanor told herself as much.

The dark moments came when she felt overwhelmed, as she frequently did, by the little things. The guerrillas of entropy that kept loosing off fusillades of disorder. Late subways. Snagged stockings. A pregnant secretary. Simon's measles. A client who could meet her only on a Sunday. There was always something about her life that was out of control.

Like the way she looked. She never managed to get her hair cut quite often enough, and though she sometimes toyed with the notion of chopping it all off, she feared she'd then have to have it cut even more often. So she had a slightly unprofessional-looking mass of chestnut tendrils usually bundled into a knot. She was tall, which was a good thing since she was also fifteen pounds overweight. Exercise was clearly a good idea—for other people. Not something she personally could manage to fit in. She wore the same kind of mascara and blusher she'd worn at her wedding, and simply accepted the crows' feet deepening around her eyes. There was often something not quite right about her clothes: a button missing from her silk blouse, a slip that was a sliver too long, worn-down toes on her high heels. Snagged stockings yet again.

It sometimes crossed her mind that her air of dishevelment might be a professional disadvantage. In fact, it was just the opposite. More than one fellow attorney had been completely disarmed by her distracted air and slightly mussed-up look.

"If she didn't look as if she'd just gotten out of bed," one of them had complained following a will contest that he'd lost, "one would be inclined to take her more seriously."

"Or stop thinking about getting her back there," sourly replied his colleague.

Which would have reassured Eleanor immensely. For all her busyness, all her resolute cheerfulness, all her abhorrence of self-pity, she occasionally admitted to herself that she was lonely. And worse, that her loneliness was unlikely to be remedied. For what was missing was a man in her life. And what chance did she have, a plump thirty-eight-year-old mother of two, in a city where blond twigs of twenty-five were a dime a dozen? The obstacles to finding some pleasant masculine company (let alone another mate for life) seemed insuperable. Where was the time? How would she meet someone? Who would want her? Ever since her divorce, friends had attempted to set her up with eligible men, but they always seemed to freeze when she mentioned her sons. Or they were intimidated. (If only I weren't so *big*, she often thought.) Or it was all too obvious why they were still single (or single again). As in the case of the plastic surgeon who, within ten minutes of their meeting, was discussing her need for an eye lift.

It shouldn't bother her, Eleanor thought, as the driver pulled over in front of her building. She signed the chit and handed it back to him. Life wasn't perfect. That was what you learned by the age of thirty-eight. Nobody had everything. She had been married once, she had two wonderful sons. Whose voices she could hear the minute she got off the elevator.

"Catch her, quick!" Toby yelled.

"She went into the kitchen," Simon's higher voice piped up. "Quick, get her into the cupboards!"

Eleanor opened the door, put down her keys and briefcase, and picked up the mail from the hall table.

"Mom! Mom, Ramona's out again," Toby called. "Quick! She's coming your way!" And the waters of family life closed over Eleanor's head.

In the fuss over getting Ramona back in her cage and then getting dinner on the table and the boys to bed, Eleanor forgot about calling her mother until she finally got around to hanging up her suit jacket. It was ten-thirty. She sat on the edge of the bed and sighed. Her mother had also left word with Luz, but since she hadn't tried to call again, it couldn't be an emergency. Eleanor weighed her filial duty against her fatigue and decided to go to bed and call her mother first thing in the morning.

Harry got home at midnight and went to bed without listening to his messages.

Hart caught the last train to Chester and crept into his bedroom at one A.M. By which time Frances's sense of injury had blossomed until she was filled with a sense of self-righteous resentment. And she lay there brooding in the dark while her husband quietly got ready for bed, not wanting to wake her. He fell asleep quickly, reflecting briefly, as he often did last thing at night, what a fortunate man he was.

2

It was a soft morning in early May. In the Drummonds' garden, dew still frosted the primroses growing in the shade, but the sun was already warming the herb garden by the back door. The air had a vague, heavy sweetness from the last petals of the tulip magnolia, scattered in a decorous circle on the grass. Every few minutes another wilted blossom, weighed down by the dew, dropped off the tree and drifted silently to the ground.

In Weymouth, Connecticut, the air from Long Island Sound still had a crisp edge. The tiny waves slapped and sucked at the pebbly shore. In the boatyard the seagulls strutted on the dock while a dory with an outboard engine coughed its way out into the glassy harbor. From the water, the new leaves budding on the trees blended into a faint, mottled wash of yellow-green.

At the Vince Lombardi Service Station on Interstate 95 in Rutherford, New Jersey, the haze of exhaust blended with the industrial effluvium from Elizabeth, a few miles south. The air smelled richly of burning rubber and diesel fuel, while the smooth roar of traffic on the highway made conversation impossible. Which was something of a relief to both Frances and Hart Drummond as they carefully locked the doors of their Mercedes.

Wordlessly, they walked into the restaurant and separated, he to the men's room, she to the ladies'. In front of the mirror in the ladies' room, a pair of teenagers in black high-heeled boots and leather jackets were spraying their massive, disheveled locks into place. They eyed Frances in the mirror as she walked past, taking in her tweed skirt, her boiled-wool jacket, her Nantucket basket purse. Just as brazenly, she eyed them, and thought with relief that at least neither of her children had turned out like *that*.

When she came out of the ladies' room she looked around for Hart. The girls with the leather jackets had both bought large packages of peanut M&M's from a vending machine and were lighting cigarettes. For breakfast! thought Frances, more shocked than she had been by their spandex pants or their reflexively foul language. A toddler staggered past waving a bottle full of pink milk, and a ten-year-old girl with pierced ears ran after and caught her up, giggling. Frances's face softened and she walked into the restaurant, where she was surprised to see her husband's tweed-clad back at the counter. He turned and came toward her, holding a paper bag.

"What did you get?" she asked. Hart had never eaten fast food that she knew of.

"Coffee. I'm a little groggy. And I thought I'd like to try one of those breakfast croissant things you hear about so much on the television." He patted the bag gently.

"Oh, Hart," Frances said with a sigh. "They're so terrible for you."

"One won't hurt," he answered mildly. "Can I get you anything? Tea? Juice?"

"Not here," she said, turning to go back outside. "I may want to stop when we get past New Haven, but I'd rather keep going to avoid the traffic." She walked ahead of him to the car. He unlocked her door first and closed it carefully after her, a courtly habit he'd acquired from his father. The girls he'd dated had seemed to like it, though now he was usually hip-checked at the car door by his daughter and her generation, who were just confused by the gesture. Frances took it for granted. She sat still in the passenger seat while he unlocked his door and clambered in, holding his paper bag carefully.

"Could you punch that little hole in the lid for me?" he asked her, holding out the coffee cup with one hand as he pulled back onto I-95. Silently she accepted the cup and studied the plastic lid.

"There is no little hole." She held it out to him.

Eyeing an enormous tractor-trailer in his rearview mirror, Hart didn't see the cup. "Well, could you *tear* a little hole?"

She took the cup back and studied it again. Then, holding it gingerly in one hand, she reached behind the seat and extracted a pair of gold stork-shaped sewing scissors from her needlepoint bag and carefully cut a hole in the plastic lid of the coffee cup. She handed it back to Hart, who sipped from it. "Thank you. Perfect."

Frances didn't answer, but replaced the scissors in their bag and clasped her hands in her lap.

The traffic was already heavy, though it wasn't even seven. The highway was choked with immense sixteen-wheelers hauling the world's goods into New England, and Japanese cars each occupied by a lone commuter. As often as not their occupants were doing in their cars what Frances Drummond did in the privacy of her own home: brushing their hair, drinking coffee, filing their nails. One woman was expertly applying eye makeup with two hands, presumably steering with her knees. Soon, as the road narrowed to two northbound lanes, everyone halted. Hart put his coffee on the dashboard and, using one hand, began to unwrap his breakfast croissant. As he popped open its Styrofoam box, a smell of egg and bacon filled the car. Frances wrinkled her nose.

"Want a bite?" Hart offered it to her, and she shook her head.

"No. Thank you," she said.

"It's actually quite good," Hart said judiciously. "I think maybe next time I'll try those potatoes they sell."

"Oh? Is this going to become a tradition?" Frances asked with a manifestly false mildness.

Hart didn't flinch. "Well, even if we do find a house today, we'll have to make the drive a few more times. For the paperwork, and so on. Of course, you wouldn't have to come if you didn't want to."

"I think I'd better, don't you?" his wife said, again in a conversational tone.

He glanced over, but she was bending down to pull her needlepoint bag onto her lap.

A honk behind him drew his attention to the ten-foot gap between him and the car in front, so he eased forward and took another bite of his breakfast.

Frances had obviously not forgiven him, Hart thought. She'd been like this for days, ever since he'd come down for breakfast after the Yale Club dinner to find the real estate folder sitting on his plate.

Over and over he'd mentally rehearsed the steps of the deal, starting with his admittedly inexact offer on "the Shore Road house," telephoned to a distracted Margaret Harwood. Both houses had been on the market for the same price, but how could she *possibly* have thought he'd wanted the modern one? They'd had it out on the phone, in a conversation that verged on acrimony until Margaret, scenting another sale (after all, they still wanted to move to Weymouth), offered to halve her commission for reselling the Wrong House. If Hart had been at the closing himself, he would probably have caught the error, but Pete could hardly be held responsible; he'd just been there to sign papers. Having Margaret Harwood walk through the house before the closing had been careless, Hart supposed, but Pete was useless about house things. Eleanor had offered to stand in for her parents at the closing. Looking back, Hart realized, he should have let her. Eleanor was a trusts and estates attorney, she often handled real estate, she would have been perfect. And if she had even laid eyes on the Wrong House before the closing, she would have known it was not what her parents meant to buy. But Hart knew how busy his daughter was. He knew about keeping your billable hours at an acceptable level, and he hadn't wanted her to sacrifice a day in the office.

So here they were, back on I-95, trundling up to Weymouth to find another house. Of course, all of the houses Frances had liked originally were no longer available. But Margaret had airily assured him she'd "get them suited" before Memorial Day. "You won't even have to spend a night in 751 if you don't feel like it," she'd said. (She no longer called it "the Shore Road house," Hart noticed.)

This, of course, was real-estate agent hyperbole. They had to be out of the Chester house on Memorial Day weekend. Even if they found the perfect place on this trip, the negotiations and closing were bound to take a couple of months.

Hart sneaked a glance at Frances, wondering how she would react to that. If the past ten days were anything to go by, it was going to be a pretty bleak summer.

It wasn't that she'd exploded. Frances didn't explode. In fact, she probably thought she was being a perfect trouper about the house. But Hart knew, from the way her face froze when he told her that they couldn't back out of the purchase of 751, that she was upset. She never reproached him—aloud. She never told him he'd been an idiot—in so many words. But in the cryptic language of their marriage, a dialect of expressions and sighs and gestures, she let him know exactly how little she thought of him.

What Hart didn't realize was that Frances was trying. She was trying to keep her temper and trying to put a brave face on things. To be a good sport. But every now and then she lost control and bitchy little remarks spurted out in spite of all her efforts. The fact was that she was miserable at the thought of living in a horrible modern house, and she had no way of explaining this to Hart.

They had never been big on talking things over. In the days when Hart and Frances married, you didn't. You started life with a set of common assumptions and went on from there. You discussed the practical issues like where to live and whether to buy a new car. The eternal verities took care of themselves.

Not that the Drummonds didn't communicate. Over the years they grew attuned to each other. Accustomed. Hart had understood, for instance, that Frances's irritating thoroughness in arranging Eleanor's wedding was probably a way to face the emotional upheaval of marrying off her daughter. And he understood this without articulating it to himself. He and his wife, after all, belonged to a generation that lacked the vocabulary and the technique for that kind of casual psychological analysis. (Hart even disparaged it as "touchy-feely," once that term came into use in the 1970s.) Nevertheless, they instinctively grasped the emotional truths behind apparently unemotional actions. Harry, momentarily beguiled by Roland Barthes, even wrote a paper at Yale on the semiotics of his parents' cocktail hour. Though flippant, it was absolutely accurate. The height from which the ice was dropped into the glass, the vehemence with which the soda siphon was wielded, the placement of the glass upon the coaster all had their significance.

So of course now, stolidly sipping watery coffee from a Styrofoam cup in his immobile car on the New Jersey Turnpike, Hart interpreted his wife's silence in the spirit in which it was patently meant: recrimination.

The problem was that he didn't feel guilty. He had made a mistake. As a result of his mistake Frances was going to be inconvenienced for several months. But why couldn't she look on it as an adventure? After all, a house was a house. They weren't going to be pitched out on the street. The whole Connecticut coastline was for sale, and spending a summer in a modern house wasn't a matter of life and death. Frances was just being a little too rigid. Couldn't she relax and go along with things?

Of course she couldn't. Hart knew she couldn't. She didn't like adventures and she never relaxed. But Hart was angry, too. He was tired of being reminded that he was an incompetent. He was tired of her air of martyrdom. So he overlooked her native tenseness and ignored what had been gradually dawning on him for several months: the fact that she was profoundly unsettled by his retirement and the move.

The business of her husband's retirement had made Frances anxious right from the start. She'd practically pushed him out of the house to his golf games and committee meetings. When a little consulting work had come his way, she'd barely tried to hide her relief. Clearly, she was only comfortable when he came home at six o'clock wearing a suit. If he was in the house (or, as she would probably have put it, "underfoot") all day, she seemed perpetually surprised at his presence. She had announced defensively, on his first morning at home, that she wouldn't be making lunch for him every day. He had answered in mild surprise that he hadn't expected her to. And after the day when he'd unthinkingly eaten the leftover asparagus she'd intended for *her* lunch, he'd usually gone out for a hot dog at the local greasy spoon, where he soon made friends with the waitress.

Hart glanced over at Frances again, stitching away on her needlepoint. This was one of a set of twelve seats for the mahogany dining room chairs. They had been designed to harmonize with the Crown Derby china inherited from her grandmother, rust and gold and cobalt. She'd been working on them for three years and had only one left.

"What are you going to do when you've got those finished?" Hart asked.

"I don't know yet. I'll miss them," she said, holding the canvas away from her to see the whole design. "I was thinking about a rug, but I'm not sure I should get started on one. My eyes might not hold out."

"Are you having trouble with them?"

"No. But I'm getting to the age when people do."

"That's silly, Frances. Not to do something you want to do just because your eyes *might* give out. Anyway, you could get some of those nifty half-glasses."

"Well, I can't start on anything anyway until we get settled," Frances answered, starting to stitch again. "From what I remember, this isn't much of a needlepoint kind of house."

Hart felt his jaw tighten, and drank some coffee. End of thaw. It was going to be a hell of a summer.

The Drummonds' drive that morning was a long and nasty one. Even the bewitching air of a lovely May morning couldn't redeem the miles of truck exhaust, bone-jarring road surface, and shabby urban landscape. The Cross-Bronx Expressway was blocked solid by a jackknifed tractor-trailer that had spilled cartons of frozen chicken all over the highway. A bridge was being repaired in Westport. They hit Bridgeport at the peak of rush hour and the congestion continued for another hour, until they were past Branford. "Want to stop?" Hart had asked as they passed the New Haven Howard Johnson's. But Frances had looked at her watch and said, "We're due to see Margaret Harwood at eleven. I think we should push on."

Branford was the last place where commerce fringed I-95. The highway narrowed to four lanes, cutting through a more rural landscape. There were low trees just showing green, and open sky that hinted somehow at the water beyond. They turned off the Weymouth exit at a quarter to eleven. On the way to the real-estate agent's office they drove past 259 Shore Road. Hart noticed that Frances didn't even glance at it as they went past. Stiff upper lip, he thought, and momentarily admired her.

Margaret Harwood was talking on the phone at her desk and waved at them to sit down. Frances murmured something and went off to find the ladies' room while Hart tried not to eavesdrop on Margaret's conversation, which she punctuated with puffs of smoke from an incredibly long cigarette. Every time she moved (and she was a fidgety woman), her charm bracelet jingled. She scrabbled through the papers on her desk and handed a paper-clipped sheaf to Hart, saying into the phone, in her Georgia drawl, "Impossible, honey. There's nothing to rent this late in the season, not for love or money. . . . No, it looks like a good summer up here, all along the coast, but you might try Westerly. Sure I'll let you know, hon, but don't hold your breath. . . . Good luck!"

She hung up the phone with an emphatic tinkle from the bracelet and laughed. "She just decided a summer on the shore would be nice for her children! Money no object, she said. They usually go to the Hamptons, so she's used to high prices. You want to rent her your house and go to Europe?" She laughed and brushed a bit of ash off her fuchsia silk blouse. Hart noticed the buttons gapped open over her bust.

"Listen, I can't tell you how sorry I am about the mix-up," she went on, sounding insouciant rather than regretful. "But you know, things were so crazy around here that week." She looked down at her desk, which was buried in papers with a fine overlay of ash. It crossed Hart's mind that he should report her as a fire hazard.

"Never mind," he said, aware that he sounded a bit brusque. Well, why not? "What do you have for us to look at?" he asked, as Frances reappeared.

"Well, just a few houses," Margaret said, gesturing at the papers Hart held. "Say, would you like coffee or anything? How about a cup of tea, Frances? Sure you would. Annette, could you get Mrs. Drummond a cup of tea? Hart? Coffee? Okay. There's a nice little place north of Route 1 you might like. It needs some work, but the grounds are heaven. There's a stream and a pond and the most divine views. Then another house closer to town just came on the market. Great location. And I know you like the older houses, there's an eighteenth-century farmhouse, wait, here it is," she said, running a fuchsia fingernail across the listings. "Right, three bedrooms, three baths, new plumbing and wiring, oh, thanks Annette, listen honey, could you get me a muffin from Cindy's? Toasted corn, no butter? Got to lose some weight," she addressed Frances, "I hate you thin women, you've probably never been on a diet." She pulled a crumpled dollar bill from a Vuitton wallet lying in an open drawer, waved it at Annette, and went back to the listings. "Then there's another waterfront house, really lovely, maybe a bit big for you. Has a pool, though. So what do you think?" she said, standing up to leave without waiting for her muffin. "Shall we take one car or two?"

They took two. Hart and Frances could scarcely bear to be shut up in a car with the chattering, smoking, clattering, idiotic Margaret Harwood, and they wanted to be able to talk frankly about each house after they saw it. Not that they needed to say much, as it turned out. The farmhouse was dark and poky. The house on the beach was vast. The new place on the market ("great location") was a characterless 1920s bungalow, and the place with the pond ("needs some work") was barely habitable.

"It'll be better after the summer," Hart said to break the silence, as they drove back to town from the last listing. "People are holding on to get the rental income, and then they'll put things on the market."

"Do you really think so?" Frances asked. And there was a forlorn tone in her voice that made Hart soften toward her.

"Yes. I do. We'll find something. You said yourself there were a dozen houses in this town you'd be happy to live in."

"Yes, and apparently so are the people who own them!" she snapped, temper getting the better of her again.

"We'll get some lunch. You must be starving; it's past two." Frances just nodded, and Hart suspected she was on the verge of tears.

After a soggy clam roll eaten in silence, they drove back to Strong Harwood Realty.

"I'll just run in and get the key," said Hart, leaving the car running. Frances, lost in silence on the front seat, didn't even look up.

Margaret was on the phone again, but put her hand over the receiver. "Nothing you liked? Honestly I didn't think there would be. Listen, you just move into 751 Shore Road and we'll get you fixed up this summer. I'm expecting a couple of great things to come on the market soon. Then you can turn right around and sell 751. Listen, honey, in the end you'll get a free summer on the water out of this." She handed over the keys and waved her fuchsia fingertips. Hart, walking out the door, reflected how little a free summer on the water was going to console his wife.

The Wrong House was magnificently located. A short drive down Main Street (lined with old trees and several of the dozen houses Frances was willing to live in) brought you to Shore Road, which at its beginning was lined with one charming house after another. But just beyond the entrance to the marina, Shore Road turned north. To the right, between the road and the Sound, lay several acres of marsh and tufty grass, threaded with shallow tidal streams. Just beyond the swamp, marked by a bare aluminum mailbox, a driveway pierced a clump of eight-foot privet bushes. It didn't bother to wind picturesquely; it just dove straight and no-nonsense through overgrown shrubs toward Long Island Sound. When you came out of the bushes you were alone on a little headland, with water all around.

Hart brought the car to a halt and got out. Without waiting for Frances, he strode across the coarse mustard-colored grass. The breeze off the water was stiff, cutting right through his old tweed jacket. No doubt it would whip up into quite a gale. But what a view! Hart stood at the very tip of the point, looking down onto the barnacle-covered rocks below the seawall and straight out to the misty blue line that was Long Island. Closer in, dotting the Sound artistically, were a group of tiny islands, some large enough for a house or two, some little more than a rock with a topknot of beach plum bushes. To the right, the wetlands curved in a beige crescent toward the harbor, with a line of trees visible beyond. A line of buoys dotted the channel toward the harbor, where a toy lighthouse (the one portrayed on the Battersea boxes) stood guard on a breakwater.

On the left-hand side of the point where Hart stood, the rocks leveled out to sand. Treading carefully, he stepped off the lawn onto the highest rock and climbed down. The high-water mark was no more than six feet from the seawall. Hart looked at the wall for a moment, wondering how sound it was. Poured concrete; it must have been constructed along with the house. Should hold up for quite a while; that was one advantage of a modern house.

It was warmer down on the sand, sheltered from the wind. As Hart walked along the little stretch of beach, dry pebbly sand filled his shoes. Across this little cove he could see the town beach, an empty stretch punctuated by lifeguard chairs. And behind, another little point like theirs, with a much bigger house on it, and a brick boathouse with a jetty.

Of course we have our own little dock, thought Hart, and climbed up its ladder from the beach. He walked out to the end, admiring the sturdiness of the construction. There were several big cleats and another ladder leading down into the water, draped with sea lettuce. Hart lay on his stomach to look at the underside of the dock, wondering if barnacles ate away at wood. Did you have to clean them off docks the way you did off boats? He unfolded the jackknife that was always in his pocket and tried to scrape a few off. That wouldn't be easy.

But of course, it wouldn't matter, he thought, sitting back on his heels and wiping the knife blade with his handkerchief. They wouldn't be staying long enough to worry about barnacles.

As he got to his feet he surveyed the house. Through the big bay window he could make out something moving: Frances, examining her new home. Hart sighed. Better go in and face the music. Maybe the house wouldn't be as bad inside as it was outside.

For in truth, it *was* ugly. It had apparently been inspired by a Swiss chalet, which might make sense in practical terms (heat conservation, for instance) but here, on this breeze-washed scrap of Connecticut, looked ridiculous. Painting the shutters pink hadn't helped. Maybe to cheer Frances up he could offer to paint them dark green. The famous deck thrust out from the house at an angle, with steps down to the lawn. Half of the house's seaward facade was covered with half-timbering, another third with weathered shingles. The rest, ludicrously enough, was brick. There were two long window boxes beneath the big living room windows, both pink. The chimney was faced with big round stones; there were even boulders scattered artistically on the roof. Courage flagging, Hart walked across the deck and knocked on the Dutch door. No answer. There was a brass bell hung on an iron bracket by the door. Hart rang it. The house would be better inside. It had to be. He could hear Frances's footsteps inside, echoing. It was only for a summer, just a few months. The floor must be tile or something, the way Frances's shoes clattered on it. They could probably find a new house by September. Latches on the inside of the door clicked. Maybe they should look in Old Lyme or Essex. Pickup trucks parked by the post office weren't everything. The top half of the Dutch door swung inward. The westering sun, reflected off the water, flooded Frances's face in a beautiful golden light. She stood framed in the doorway like a Renaissance portrait, and fleetingly Hart admired the way the sun warmed her still-fair skin, brightening her clear blue eyes, gilding the silver hair that swept back from her temples. She was still, Hart realized with surprise, quite beautiful. And she was also, plainly, enraged.

"Can you get this damn door open?" she said, stepping out of the sunlight. "There seems to be something the matter with the bottom half."

Hart leaned over and tried the knob, fiddling with the lock, but couldn't make it open. Reluctantly, he climbed stiffly over it, regretting as much as anything appearing elderly and ridiculous in front of his angry wife.

She was standing in the middle of the room, every line in her body radiating fury. And as Hart looked around in wonderment, his heart sank. He had lived happily enough in Army barracks during the war, but this—this was going to be hard to take.

The room they were in was shaped like a big L, comprising both living and dining room. The living room portion had a double-height ceiling and two huge bay windows overlooking the Sound. Beneath the windows, logs had been halved to form window seats. The previous owners had left the cushions, which matched the full-length curtains: a rust and olive large-scale plaid, rendered in shaggy wool. The wall at a right angle to the water was dominated by a large boulder-faced fireplace with a kind of inglenook built of logs that matched the window seat. Cushioned in plaid, naturally. From the ceiling hung an immense chandelier made of antlers.

In the dining area the decorative scheme lurched into another gear. The ceiling dropped to eight feet and was plastered smooth. On the wall facing the water, two large mirrors were framed in pseudo-rococo cartouches and hung against pale blue metallic paisley wallpaper. The chandelier, hung unnervingly low in the center of the room, was Venetian in style, festooned with pink and gold and white blown-glass flowers.

Wordlessly, Frances pushed through the swinging half-doors (Western saloon style) that separated the kitchen from the dining room. Hart followed. "Oh, good heavens!" he exclaimed as Frances switched on the overhead fluorescent fixture. The floor was brick-patterned linoleum, the appliances turquoise, and the cabinets, floor to ceiling, had been painted a deep, shiny cherry red.

Beyond the kitchen there was a small powder room: fuzzy gray kittens frolicked on the walls with balls of pink and blue yarn, while the sink sported shiny curlicued taps. There was also a little utility room which, with its sedate orange-centered daisy wallpaper and grass-green indoor-outdoor carpet, was a relief.

The banister at the edge of the stairs was fake wrought iron, while the staircase wall had been faced with what appeared to be barn siding. Hart flicked it with a fingernail as he climbed the open risers and thought briefly of Frances's precious Oriental stair runner. He'd better start looking into more storage space.

The three upstairs bedrooms were more conventionally laid out, but still a far cry from Frances's taste. The one at the top of the stairs, facing the driveway, sported pink wallpaper patterned in ballerina motifs: tutus, toe shoes, dancers *en pointe.*

"This can be the guest room," Frances said in an icy tone.

The bathroom, which Hart just peered into, was avocado green. The next bedroom, on the same side of the hall as the ballerina room, had been given a hasty coat of white paint that didn't quite cover the black and white op art pattern of the paper underneath.

"This will be be my room," Frances announced, standing stiffly in the doorway. Hart glanced at her.

"But—the master bedroom?" he asked.

"*You* may want to sleep there. I will not."

Mystified, Hart crossed the hall into the third bedroom and understood instantly. There was an immense mirror on the ceiling over the bed. Frances Drummond would sleep bolt upright on a camp stool before she lay down under that mirror. At the moment it reflected the bare mattress left by the previous owners on the built-in platform bed, which was set into a mirrored headboard. Tentatively, Hart sat down and looked around. There was the water, on both sides of him; but there he was, too, a thin, freckled sixty-six-year old in wire-framed glasses and an old tweed jacket. He was distracted for a moment by the view, new to him, of the top of his head. His hair was holding up pretty well, he thought. The color wasn't much of anything, kind of dirty blond, but you couldn't see any skin through it, that was something.

His eyes turned back to the water and he sat for a minute more, hands loose in his lap, looking at the sunlight on the little waves. Sunrise would be beautiful from up here. He turned away to survey the rest of the room. It wouldn't be bad without the mirror. It was a big room, plenty of space for his desk in here. Yes, desk on that wall, and maybe his big club chair by the window, with a side table and a standing lamp. . . . He got up to check the baseboards. There was an outlet in just the right place. Of course, with the adjustable spotlights already on the ceiling he might not even need the standing lamp. He went over and pressed the dimmer switch by the door. As he'd guessed, the spots were trained on the bed. Well, dammit, why not? Apparently the previous owners had a good time in the sack. What of it? There was probably a Jacuzzi in the bathtub.

There was, of course, along with a bidet and two sinks and yards of brownish marble. He peed in the toilet with the marble-patterned seat and listened carefully as he flushed. Plumbing sounded good. He washed his hands: the water pressure was fine, though the dolphin-shaped taps would be tricky if you had soap on your hands. So what? It was a lark. He went back into the bedroom for a last look at the water, drying his hands on his handkerchief. To hell with Frances anyway. Of course the house was ugly, and it had been decorated in the worst possible taste. It wouldn't kill her to live in it for a few months. He turned off the spotlights and glanced around the room with a dawning fondness. In that moment, he and the house became allies.

Hart and Frances drove back to New Jersey in unbroken silence.

3

By the time she heard Harry's footsteps coming up the attic stairs, Eleanor had worked her way through about a quarter of the cardboard cartons that had accumulated in "her" portion of her parents' attic. It was a depressing experience. So far she had examined the contents of six boxes of old clothes and three boxes of books from college. She'd found nothing but drab, stretched-out turtlenecks, Fair Isle sweaters sporting mysterious stains, and half-read English novels. She'd been working steadily since eight A.M. and hadn't even touched the wedding presents or the boys' outgrown clothes, let alone the cartons marked RECORDS or MISC.

"How's it going?" Harry asked as he leaned down to kiss her. She looked up at him and noted, for the thousandth time, his mysterious band-box quality. Here she was, hair straggling down her neck, dust all over, wearing an old pair of sweat pants and one of her father's worn-out shirts. And there was Harry, impeccably handsome as ever, his tawny hair sleek, yellow polo shirt and khakis creaseless, though he'd just driven down from New York. At the end of the day he would still look immaculate; at the end of the day, Eleanor knew, she would look like a ragbag.

"This is hell. Why can't I ever throw anything away?" she asked. "I mean, why did I save this? The Salvation Army wouldn't take it, so why have I carefully preserved it?" She held up a blue terry-cloth bathrobe that was shredding at the cuffs and hem.

Harry hesitated. "You thought it would make a nice rag?"

Eleanor snorted. "What would I want with a rag? Jadrancka will only use Handi Wipes or paper towels."

"That's what you get for having a cleaning lady from a former Communist country," said Harry. "I think Milagros would like this for my silver. Could I have it?"

"Be my guest," Eleanor answered. "It would be nice to think that at least *something* had been worth keeping."

"That bad, huh?" Harry asked, sitting down. "Well, let me do some boxes. What's the system?"

"That pile is 'throw away,'" Eleanor said, gesturing at the largest stack of cartons. "That pile is 'keep,' and the pile in the middle is 'consider for tag sale if it passes muster with Mom.'"

Harry peered over at the "tag sale" pile, which so far consisted of a high chair and a pair of worn L. L. Bean boots. "You haven't gotten to the wedding presents yet," he stated.

"No. We could really just put those boxes directly into 'tag sale.'"

"Oh, no," her brother answered, standing up to select a box marked CRYSTAL from the untouched stacks. "It'll be like Christmas, looking through them. Can I do that?"

"Fine," Eleanor said, slitting the tape of the CRYSTAL box with a kitchen knife. Resting on top of the crumpled newspaper was an index card, listing the contents in her former husband's tiny, angular handwriting.

She handed the card to Harry, who studied it silently for a moment. Finally he asked, "Do you know any architects who aren't anal-retentive?"

Eleanor considered. "No. But even Jared's architect friends thought he was unusually . . . tidy. You realize all these cards were cross-referenced on a computerized list: what was in our apartment, what was here, who wrote the thank-you note. . . . I was so impressed. I thought my life might finally become organized."

Harry shot her a glance. "That should have been your first clue."

"Oh, come on, Harry," she answered, irritated. "I was madly in love. You know that stage, when any characteristic of the other person seems incredibly wonderful, like the fact that he only uses razor-point pens or never loses his temper?"

"Do I ever," Harry said ruefully. "My apartment is full of razor-point pens, metaphorically speaking."

"Oh, I'm sorry," Eleanor said, full of compunction. "Have you heard from Gretchen?"

"Yes. She's found a place, and she wants me to pack up her stuff and send it out. She doesn't think she's going to be back here for a while."

"But Harry!" Eleanor remonstrated. "I thought this was just a trip to find a place to live for the fall. What is she going to do all summer in Iowa City?"

Harry shook his head. "Apparently she found a great apartment, and they're much harder to come by in September, and everybody is so healthy and sincere out there, and she can't bear to pollute her lungs anymore with metropolitan carbon monoxide."

"Oh, Harry," Eleanor said. "I feel terrible."

Harry shrugged. "Yep. So do I. But she'll make lots of serious friends and walk around in her Birkenstock sandals and read Emily Dickinson and write me beautiful letters for a while, until she takes up with some strapping bearded fellow in a lumberjack's shirt who's writing an epic novel."

"So you're supposed to pack up her quilts and dried flower arrangements?"

"Right."

"If you want to do it next weekend, I'll bring the boys down and we can help you. And we'll take you out to dinner afterward."

"That would be nice," Harry said. "If you think Toby and Simon could be called 'help.' " He looked at the card in his hand. " 'Six snowball candlesticks,' " he read. "No, thank you. 'One three-dimensional star ornament.' No. 'One modern vase.' What's that?"

Eleanor was digging in the box, feeling for the largest newspaper-wrapped bundle. "Can I just say one more thing about Gretchen?"

Harry raised an eyebrow. "One. Carefully."

Eleanor nodded, peeling off the newspaper. "She took herself awfully seriously. Here it is." The paper fell away, revealing a large free-form vase with a very rough surface, as if it had been carved from a block of ice with a hammer.

"It looks like something left over from the Dartmouth Winter Carnival," Harry said.

Eleanor snorted. "Jared was so appalled. He wouldn't even let me put it in a closet in the apartment to bring out in case his boss ever came to dinner. When he left the firm over 'aesthetic differences,' I honestly think he was talking about the fact that Norm gave him such an ugly wedding present."

"Talk about taking yourself seriously!" Harry said, turning it around in his hands. "Say, maybe we should give it to Mom for the new house. It's modern."

"You wouldn't dare. Believe me, it's not a laughing matter. Last night at dinner she was moaning and groaning about the sea air and her French furniture, and the minute Dad suggesting putting her desk in storage she got up and left the table."

"Really?" Harry put the vase down. "She might as well have slapped him in the face."

"Well, she did come back with a pitcher of mint sauce. But that was just to save face. When she got up from the table, she sort of slammed her napkin down. And it was a good five minutes before she reappeared. Meanwhile, Dad sat peacefully eating his lamb as if nothing had happened. I even wondered . . ." Eleanor shook her head.

"What? Go on," Harry urged.

"Well, I got this strange sense—I even wondered if he was baiting her. You know, he looked kind of smug. As if that was the reaction he'd wanted."

Harry narrowed his eyes. "That doesn't sound like Dad. Things must have gotten really awful between them if he's egging her on." He looked down at his hands abstractedly and dusted the palms together. "It would be very unfunny if their marriage broke up over a stupid house."

"Yeah, well, it's more than a stupid house for Mom, you know that," Eleanor said, turning back to the boxes and cutting the tape on one marked RECORDS. "It's her persona or something. Remember how she used to call those ranch houses on Maple Drive 'ticky-tacky'? And now she has to live in one. It would be like asking you to go to Lutece wearing a baby-blue leisure suit or something."

Harry considered this seriously. "Unimaginable."

"Well, exactly! I'm serious. She doesn't have anything else. The house, the garden, the china, the furniture, her needle-point . . ." Eleanor shrugged. "That's it."

"Maybe it'll do her good," Harry offered. "She was getting awfully tied up in all that house stuff."

Eleanor sat back with a pile of albums on her lap. "Yes . . . she was. But things are so ugly between the two of them right now. I mean, basically she's making a lot of fuss about something that isn't a big deal; so she'll have to live in this terrible house for a summer, maybe six months. It's not earthshaking. But she's so pissed off at Dad. As if he'd done it on purpose. When, if it was really anyone's fault, it was that moronic Realtor's. And you know the way Mom and Dad are, they don't actually talk about stuff. So it's practically World War III between them and all they can say is, 'Do we have any mint sauce?' "

"Maybe they didn't want to discuss it in front of you," Harry suggested.

Eleanor shrugged. "Maybe." She started looking absentmindedly through the albums. "I don't know how they live like that. These must be yours: Jimi Hendrix? The Doors? More Hendrix. The Rolling Stones. These aren't mine."

"I never went through a hard rock stage," Harry reminded her. "You probably brought them home from college."

Eleanor slipped a record from its cover and said, "Oh, they're Jared's. Look: he always prints his name on the label. Hell, I guess I should get them back to him."

"Why bother?" Harry asked. "What would he do with a scratched old Jimi Hendrix album? Do you think Holli's a fan?"

"Do I think Holli would allow anything so vulgar to pollute little Samantha's ears? I'm sure it's strictly Mozart for the Gray household. Do you know, Holli won't even let Samantha watch 'Sesame Street'?" Eleanor shook her head. "That poor child is going to be a freak by the time she gets to kindergarten. I'm tempted to leave these with their doorman. Oh, look, Simon and

Garfunkel. James Taylor. These are mine," she said, pulling them out of the box.

"You're not going to keep them?"

"Well . . . Oh, Lord, Don McLean. You know, there should be an old record player in here somewhere; let's play them." She stood up and moved a couple of cartons, revealing a portable record player with attached speakers.

"Come on, they'll sound terrible," Harry protested.

"No worse than they did twenty years ago," Eleanor said. "Where's the live outlet up here?" She looked around, plug in hand, and spotted it beneath a window. "Okay. What would you like to hear? How about Joni Mitchell?"

Harry considered. "Isn't there anything a little more upbeat?"

"Early Beatles? I can't throw these things away," Eleanor said, looking at the *Abbey Road* album in her hands. "They're historic."

"No, they're not. Can you imagine how many copies of *Abbey Road* are in existence? That is completely worthless."

"Right. Thanks." She put it on the record player, and after a couple of preliminary scratches, "Here Comes the Sun" came from the tiny speakers. She listened for a moment. "Does take you back, doesn't it? All right. Back to work. Maybe we can finish the wedding presents before lunch."

"Maybe," said Harry.

As the morning wore on it got hotter and hotter in the attic. The dry, woody smell grew stronger until Harry got up and pried one of the windows open, letting in a slight breeze. Gradually the piles of boxes were shifted from one side of the attic to the other. The "tag sale" pile grew, increased by a Waring blender, a fondue pot, stacks of plates, cast-iron candlesticks, pottery pitchers, glass soufflé dishes, and an immense pewter platter in the shape of a fish. "The thing about upper-middle-class WASPs," Harry said, assessing the selection, "is that they're so incredibly *cheap*. If you'd married a nice Italian boy you would at least have gotten some cash."

"Yeah, and Mom making subtle nasty cracks for the rest of my life. Never mind. It's history," Eleanor said with a tight little smile, and got up to put on another record. But she got very quiet and stopped responding to Harry's comments about the contents of the boxes.

They stopped working around one and went down to make sandwiches, which they took outside to eat under the big maple tree.

"Hard to believe this is going to be somebody else's house," Eleanor said, sitting with her back against the trunk and gazing at the thick canopy of leaves above her. "Sometimes I wonder . . . I think about my memories of this house and I wonder if I'm depriving the boys of something by staying in the city. You know, riding your bike all around town, having little secret places in the woods."

"A tree house," Harry said.

"Mm-hm," Eleanor answered, and swallowed. "A tree house. I can't let the boys go outside alone."

"So why don't you move to the 'burbs?" Harry asked.

Eleanor took another bite, thinking. "It's partly logistics; a longer commute would mean I'd see them less. And also . . ." she looked over at her brother. "This is going to sound stupid. But I don't know how to take care of a house. You know, boilers and roofs and sump pumps. Or whatever. Dad always took care of that stuff. I don't know about it and I don't want to learn. At least now if there's a problem with the hot water I call Angelo. Or better yet, Luz calls Angelo and it gets fixed even faster."

"You're depriving your sons of an idyllic childhood in a healthy environment because you don't know the name of a good contractor, is that it?" Harry asked.

Eleanor smiled, but said seriously, "The money's a problem, too. Anything close enough for a practical commute would cost an arm and a leg."

"Oh, come on, El," Harry said impatiently. "You're a Wall Street lawyer. You can afford a house in Bronxville."

"Not with two children, on my salary alone," Eleanor said. "I know it sounds ludicrous, but you have to remember, I'm only a mommy-track associate, not a partner. And it costs a lot to run our household. I have a big mortgage. The maintenance is high.

There's Jadrancka, and there's Luz. And I really do need them both, because if there's nobody to clean, I can't spend any time with the boys. And Luz has to be around after school."

"Why can't they go to public school?" Harry asked.

"Oh, get this," Eleanor said bitterly. "Jared doesn't approve. Of course, because I make so much more money than he does, he doesn't pay any child support. But when I suggested public school he started muttering about his rights and his attorney and I just didn't have the nerve to fight him about it." Eleanor shrugged and picked up a maple leaf from the ground. "So I take the morning train and work my tail off and at my last review they suggested that my billable hours were a little low, Mrs. Gray, and honestly, Harry, I'm at my wits' end. There are no more hours in the day." She was shredding the leaf, picking at it savagely, and Harry noticed that her nails were bitten and the cuticles red almost down to the knuckle.

"I have an idea that might help," he said. "But I know exactly what you're going to say."

"What?" Eleanor said. "Try me. Anything's possible."

"How about letting Toby do some acting?"

"What?" Eleanor said, and dropped the leaf. "You've got to be kidding."

"Come on, eat your sandwich before the ants do," Harry said. "We still have a bunch of boxes to get through. I'll explain while you eat." Obediently, Eleanor picked up her sandwich and brushed off the bits of maple leaf that had fallen on it. "You realize that Toby is extraordinary-looking." Eleanor nodded, with her mouth full. "He is also very self-possessed for a child of his age." Eleanor nodded again. "Okay. One of the characters on my soap is about to adopt a boy who has just been orphaned. He was brought up by a deaf couple, so he doesn't speak, but he's going to learn to talk on the show, and anyway once he can talk he's going to turn out to be the natural son of a Ruritanian prince who has no heir—"

"Oh, come on." Eleanor groaned.

"I'm afraid so. I was reading *The Prisoner of Zenda* and got inspired," said her brother with a grin. "Listen, the network loved it. The producers are crazy about the idea of filming abroad, so we're negotiating to shoot in this little town in Hungary. Anyway, they're apparently having trouble casting the kid. Toby would be perfect."

"I hate child actors," Eleanor said flatly.

"Toby is an actor already," Harry said, just as flatly. "Whatever you say about it, he is."

Eleanor shook her head and clambered to her feet. "We'd better get back upstairs. I just can't see it, Harry. If nothing else, Jared would have a fit."

"Well, think about it," Harry said. "You'd have nothing to lose by having him read for it."

Eleanor looked down at him. "I know you want to help, Harry, but I seriously think it would bring out the worst in him."

Harry shrugged and got up. "Okay. It just seems like you're kind of in a hole."

Eleanor turned away from him back toward the house. "It's not that bad," she said over her shoulder. "I was just kind of whining."

When they got back to the attic, Harry said, "I need to take care of my boxes. Not that there's much there, but I just want to look through them before I put them in storage." He looked at his watch. "What time were you going back to the city?"

"I can pick the boys up at Jared's anytime before eight. They're going to have dinner with him."

"Tofu burgers?"

Eleanor smiled reluctantly. "No. Jared takes them to Jackson Hole and eats off their plates. Then he and Holli have their grilled fish and millet after Samantha's in bed."

"I'll give you a ride back, then, if we can be done by five."

Eleanor looked at the remaining boxes on her side of the attic, which were labeled 12–24 MOS. SUMMER, and 3T–4T, SIMON. "If I can't get this done by five it'll be nervous breakdown time anyway."

Harry turned to the cartons he'd stacked under the window and opened the ones that said PAPERBACKS. Within seconds he had forgotten about Eleanor as he scanned the spines of the books: *Tristram Shandy, Tom Jones, Pamela.* He lifted out the top row and soon had all the books out of the boxes in piles on the floor. *Don Quixote* could go to the tag sale. *Hablar Español*, why in the world had he kept that? *Vanity Fair*: he picked it up and riffled the pages. Becky Sharp was a great character. There was someone a lot like her on *Too Much Loving*; he put the book on the windowsill.

He had finished with the books and turned around to move the cartons to the "tag sale" pile when he noticed that Eleanor wasn't there. Some of the boxes of the boys' clothes had been opened and sorted through; there were piles of corduroy overalls and striped turtlenecks draped on the high chair, and three pairs of ragged sneakers on the floor. The next box opened must have been baby clothes, for a tiny green stretch-terry sleeve flopped out of it. Harry glanced at the stairs. She'd probably just gone down to the bathroom.

But ten minutes went by. He zipped through a box of old clothes. And a box of photo albums. He looked again at his watch and went down the stairs. Walking with a little emphasis, to warn her that he was coming, he went down the hall to what had been her bedroom. Where he found her sitting disconsolately on one of the twin beds, sniffling.

"It's okay, I'm just about done," she said in a strangled voice. "Done crying, I mean." She sniffed powerfully. "It was just . . ." Her voice trailed off and she started to gulp. On her knee she spread out a baby's undershirt, yellowed at the neck. "Oh, God, they were so *little*," she whispered. "And things turned out so wrong. I'm sorry, I'm being maudlin," she went on, in an attempt at her normal voice.

Harry sat down next to her and put an arm around her. "It's allowed," he said. "You're under a lot of strain."

"Still, it's no reason to break up over a drool-stained undershirt," Eleanor said. She held it up by the shoulders, then wiped her eyes with it. It was no bigger than a bandanna.

"Look, let's get this finished and we'll have time for a drink when we get back to the city," Harry said. "I'm just about done; I can help you with the clothes." He hesitated for an instant and added, "You know, El, you do a wonderful job. You probably don't hear this from one month to the next, but you do a great job with the boys."

Eleanor turned to him, face crumpling. "Oh, Harry. You're awfully nice to say so."

He patted her on the shoulder again. "Well, I mean it. They're nice boys."

"They are," Eleanor said, sitting up straight and rubbing her face. She stood up and straightened out the bedspread and the rumpled pillow. "Okay," she said, standing in the doorway. "I feel better." So Harry followed her upstairs.

"Now, look," he said, when they got back up to the attic. "Do we really need to go through these at all?"

Eleanor considered, then heaved a big sigh. "Yes. Some of the stuff is junk. And some of it I want to keep."

"What are you going to keep it for?" asked Harry, surprised. "Are you planning on having more children?"

"For my grandchildren," Eleanor said, with exaggerated dignity. "Of course I'm not going to have any more children. I'm thirty-nine years old and I haven't been on a date in five years. Let's get serious. But some of these things are very nice and I want to keep them."

"Okay," Harry said. "How will I know?"

"I'll pick them out of each box; you sort the rest for the tag sale."

They worked in silence for a few minutes, then Harry said, "You really haven't been on a date since you got divorced?"

"Yep."

"But Ellie . . ."

"You know what the statistics are. Listen, I'm lucky that I've even *been* married. And much as I moan about it, I'm lucky I have the boys. Look at my friend Sophy. Or Martha. Or any one of dozens of women."

"I guess," said Harry, unconvinced. "There seem to be a lot of shoes here for just two children."

"You're awfully sheltered in your bachelor existence," said Eleanor, carefully folding a velveteen blazer. "That's how many shoes two children grow out of in five years. Nobody'll buy them; put them in the throw-out pile."

"How long has it been since you had a vacation?" Harry asked, piling the shoes on top of a ragged sweatshirt.

"We went to Disneyland last year, remember?"

"No, *you*. By yourself."

"Me? Oh, umm . . . well, it wasn't a vacation, but I spent a night in the Village with Sophy last fall. It was great."

"Well, why don't you take some time off?"

"Oh, come on, Harry, how would I do that? Here, this is mostly in pretty good shape," she said, pushing a box along the floor.

"Doesn't your firm give you much time off?"

"Sure, but what about the boys? What would I do about them? Besides, I like to spend time with them. I don't feel that I see them enough as it is."

"Yes, but surely you fantasize sometimes about going someplace alone. I mean, when you read the travel section of the *Times*, don't you ever imagine going to those places?"

"I don't read the travel section, Harry, because it is so unlikely I will *ever* go to one of those places."

"Okay, but if you could," Harry persisted. "If you could go anywhere for a week by yourself, where would you go?"

Eleanor sat back on her heels, considering.

"Just imagine the kids were somehow taken care of," Harry went on. "You used to love Renaissance art so much. You could do a little driving tour in northern Italy. Vicenza, Verona, Parma . . . And the food! You could eat really well, too. I had the most incredible meal in Parma two years ago," he said dreamily.

"It would be lovely," Eleanor agreed, with a faraway look in her eyes. "But I think I'd rather have a week in Venice and pass on the car. I'd just wander around and look at pictures and eat and look at more pictures and eat some more. And never wash a dish or make a bed or read anything more serious than a guidebook."

"Well, then," said Harry, more briskly. "How much vacation time do you have left this year?"

"Four weeks, including what I can carry over from last year,"

Eleanor said, coming out of her reverie. "But it doesn't matter, Harry, the kids *aren't* 'somehow taken care of.' "

"One thing at a time. What about your work? Can you really take that vacation time? Without creating chaos in the office or getting fired or something?"

"Yes, but—"

"Could the boys stay with Jared?" Harry asked, ignoring her objection.

"Not a chance. The carpets in that apartment are white," Eleanor said, as if concluding an argument.

Harry was silent for a minute, carefully folding a small raincoat. "I'll take them."

Eleanor just looked at him. "You're out of your mind."

"No. You'll have to work around my schedule. But I can take some time off in June or July. Mom and Dad will be in the new house. Maybe I'll take them up there."

Eleanor was still staring at him. "You don't know how to take care of children," she protested.

"They're not babies. They can tell me when I'm doing something wrong," Harry said, a little offended. "It's not as if I'm going to have to change diapers or anything."

Eleanor was silent for a moment. "I can't afford it," she said.

"You don't even know what it would cost," Harry countered. "You're trying to think of excuses not to go."

"No, I'm not." He looked straight at her, and her eyes fell. "Well, maybe I am. But I still can't see it."

"I just think a real vacation would be good for you," Harry said. "You know the boys would be fine with me. Your office can spare you. You deserve a treat and it really isn't impractical."

"I'll think about it," Eleanor said, but that wasn't enough for Harry.

"No, Eleanor. I'll call you with the dates in a couple of days and then if you don't get right on the phone with your travel agent, I will."

Eleanor looked at him with eyes welling. "I guess I can't protest anymore."

"No."

"Well, what can I bring you as a present?"

"I could use some wineglasses," Harry said. "From Murano. With twisted colored stems. You can carry them back on the plane and curse me every time you kick them."

"Hardly likely," Eleanor replied. "Venice, huh?" She smiled as she opened the next box.

4

A few hours later Harry was back in his apartment, with his copy of *Vanity Fair* and Eleanor's old blue terry-cloth bathrobe. Though he hadn't confessed as much to Eleanor, his heart sank whenever he walked in the door. The apartment didn't seem to belong to him anymore. It would probably be a good idea to get Gretchen's "quilts and dried flower arrangements," as Eleanor had put it, boxed up and sent to Iowa. As it was, Harry found them almost unbearable to look at.

It wasn't so much that he'd really thought he and Gretchen would marry. Maybe at first, when they'd only been going out for a few months and they spent a lot of exhilarating time talking about movies and books and agreeing about everything—then, Harry had to admit, he might have been making vague assumptions about a rosy, limitless future discussing the merits of the latest Salman Rushdie novel. Gretchen had been an assistant at one of the Condé Nast magazines. She spent half of her salary on good shoes and two-hundred-dollar haircuts, and lived in a dreary studio apartment in Queens. She devoted her weekends and nights to writing attenuated short stories that she sent off, with fruitless determination, to every literary magazine in the country. Harry had found the combination charming: the worldly life during the day, the life of art at night. After she moved in with him, it was possible for Gretchen to take fiction-writing classes in Manhattan after work. She was also promoted, having discovered a knack for writing fashion captions.

Looking back, Harry thought things had started to fall apart when Gretchen began wearing her long blond hair in braids. Harry was observant, and he believed that details had meaning.

In this case, the silky plaits hanging down Gretchen's back (or occasionally, when she was really feeling militant, pinned around her head like a caricature of a farm girl) signaled her growing contempt for her milieu. Her entire style changed. She gave up caffeine and drank rose-hip tea. She bought a hand-thrown mug (one, not two: another detail not lost on Harry) to drink it from. She discovered Indian print fabric, having been too young for it the first time around.

Then she applied to the Iowa Writers Workshop. She announced this to Harry with some pugnacity, as if expecting resistance. But by this time Harry was beyond resisting; he was only sad. The thing about Gretchen was, she spoke his language. They understood each other. Their minds worked the same way. They noticed the same details in a movie, a picture, a landscape. Harry had thought that was what you built a relationship on. And if it wasn't, what was?

But what made it worse was Gretchen's parting lecture, about how Harry was wasting his talent writing for soap operas. He had sold out, she claimed. He'd become accustomed to living in luxury, he took no risks, if he were truly an honest artist he would strip down his life to the essentials and mine his psyche for the gut-wrenching novel Gretchen assured him was "in him." (Her short stories had become much less attenuated under the influence of a Columbia writing teacher.)

When Gretchen (who was supposed to be on his side) told him he was a cynical luxury-loving idler, it was a real betrayal. And it revealed to him that she had misunderstood him all along.

He did like luxury, that he conceded. His apartment (before the quilts) was a serene renovated loft in the west twenties, all Biedermeier and silver silk. He loved good clothes and ate out whenever he felt like it. He drank good wine, bought hardcover books, and liked to have his sheets ironed.

But he was not cynical. At first, Gretchen had tried to persuade herself that Harry wrote soap operas because he was experimenting in a truly popular storytelling format. When she finally had to relinquish this notion, she assumed that Harry was exploiting his talent in a form he despised, simply because he craved the money he could make.

The truth was that he enjoyed his work. He had a great deal of respect for a genre that entertained millions of Americans daily. He loved manipulating the characters, and he had a priceless facility at inventing plots. To Harry, writing the story line for a year's worth of episodes was as much fun as a marathon gossip session, and this relish showed. In the industry, Harry was highly respected. He had won several Emmys and was, at thirty-two, one of the youngest head writers in the business. The ratings of *Too Much Loving* had been climbing steadily since he'd come on board.

But in the end, Gretchen hadn't taken him seriously. And that was probably what hurt the most. It was bad enough that his mother was still waiting for him to settle down and get a "real" job. It was bad enough that Eleanor, seven years older than he, occasionally still condescended to him as her "baby" brother. But when even your girlfriend considers you a lightweight, Harry thought, you have a problem.

He sighed as he looked around the living room. He unhooked a wreath of twigs from the wall nearest him and tossed it onto the kitchen counter. Maybe he shouldn't even wait until the weekend. There was nothing like a feeling of accomplishment to dispel depression. But he was due at dinner downtown. And dinner with George Sinclair would probably be as bracing as purging his apartment of Gretchen's knickknacks. Leaving the wreath on the counter, Harry went off to take a shower.

George Sinclair was one of his newer friends. Harry had wandered into George's first one-man-show at a 57th Street gallery and had gone back, liking the huge, technically adroit historical paintings. He had finally bought one, a detailed depiction of the assassination of Empress Elizabeth of Austria. The dealer had taken Harry down to George's studio, where he had also admired the portraits he saw on the walls. The friendship had blossomed from there.

The two men had a great deal in common, including the fundamental point that, having been brought up in very conventional households, they had chosen unconventional careers. They both read a great deal, though George preferred history to fiction. They liked the same kind of movies, and were interested in wine. Harry especially enjoyed the great pleasure George took in life—and George's love life was as hapless as his own.

For George, having reached the age of thirty-five, was ready to settle down. He was a man created for domesticity. He cooked, he cleaned, he ironed his own shirts, he loved doing laundry. "At heart," he had once told Harry, "I think I was made to be a petit bourgeois housewife in nineteenth-century France." But in spite of his good looks, his charm, and his positive hunger for commitment, George had been unable to find a wife.

When Harry appeared at his door that evening, George let him in wearing an apron and said, "I'm basting. I'll be right with you," then disappeared into the kitchen. Harry, hanging his jacket on the brass hatstand by the door, followed him, looking around appreciatively as he always did.

George also lived in a loft, but it was the very opposite of Harry's precious space with its bleached wood floors and matched settees. George had twenty-five hundred square feet of raw space that was still all but raw. The ceiling receded into darkness, with pipes and the sprinkler system and the occasional kite or bicycle emerging from the gloom. At one end of the loft he had built a log cabin, complete with windows and a door, that he used as a bedroom. At the other end, behind a set of folding screens, a Victorian plush sofa and a massive sideboard flanked an oak dining table, while a peg-boarded wall, a butcher-block counter, and old restaurant fixtures comprised the kitchen. In between the two areas of civilization was the expanse George needed for his paintings.

He worked as neatly as he did everything else. The finished canvases stood in racks on one side, the stretched, prepared canvases on another. The paints and brushes were all ranged in perfect order in shelves and drawers that George had built to house them. Other shelves were lined with books, and one expanse of cork had been covered with sketches, postcards, business cards, maps, and menus. Finally, a rolltop desk stood on a dais, so that George could do his paperwork standing up. The desk shared the dais with a massive Gothic revival chair draped in red velvet. When he could persuade his friends to pose, he sat them in the chair and executed portraits in the swaggering style of John Singer Sargent.

The smell of garlic and roasting meat had met Harry at the door, and when he walked into the kitchen George was just finishing basting four Cornish hens. Harry perched on a stool and watched George painstakingly drizzle fat onto a tiny drumstick. "I couldn't decide what to drink," George said, "so there's a bottle of Stag's Leap chardonnay in the fridge, and a nice little Chinon over there on the counter. Your choice."

Harry looked speculatively at the hens. "Did you marinate them?"

"Yes. In soy sauce, with garlic and honey. And juniper berries. May turn out to have been a bit much," George answered, closing the oven.

"Let's have the chardonnay first," Harry said, sliding off the stool to open the wine. "How was your week?"

"Mixed," George said, unwrapping a log of goat cheese. "Mixed," he repeated, nodding. "I got a job."

"What do you want a job for?" Harry asked, frowning as he poured wine into two glasses.

"To pay the bills," George answered calmly. "We can go sit down; they won't be done for a few minutes." He led the way to the sofa, carrying his wineglass and the plate of cheese and bread.

Harry followed, sitting in the wicker basket chair at an angle to the sofa. "Hard times?"

"Hard enough. I must be getting old." George sighed. "My father's lectures about health insurance finally sank in."

"So what's the job? You're not waiting tables."

"Teaching," George said, leaning over to press a wedge of goat cheese onto some bread. "Teaching art at an extremely expensive, extremely stuffy boys' school on the Upper East Side. The boys call me 'Sir.' It's very odd. I can't decide if I like it or I hate it."

Harry frowned. "I didn't know you taught."

"I didn't either. But the man who taught art at this place apparently dropped dead in the cafeteria one day and the father of one of the boys has bought a couple of my paintings and asked André if I might be interested in the job. So André, a true dealer at heart, is trying to charge me ten percent of the salary!" George shook his head. "He has such nerve."

"They can hardly be paying you much," Harry said.

"No. But it's only part-time."

"Still, how will you have enough time for painting?"

"No more movies for the next few months. No dinners out. And no Edith." Edith was the current girlfriend, a tiny, humorless Eurasian dancer who had been pursuing George ever since New Year's Eve.

"How do you feel about that?" Harry asked, studying George's face.

"You sound like a shrink," George said, grinning, and stood up. "Mostly I feel relieved. Stay put, I just need to baste the little birdies once more."

When he came back, Harry asked idly, "What school are you teaching at?"

"Place called Avalon. Right next to the river. It's hell to get to," George added.

"Have you met a boy named Toby Gray?"

"I'm not sure. What does he look like?"

"Blond hair, blue eyes. Handsome, in a child-model way."

"Oh, yes. Third grade. Precocious little kid. Told me he wanted to do his still life in black and white."

"What did you do?"

"Told him if he could get enough different tonalities into it he was welcome. And left him to it. His canvas looked like a slushy sidewalk when the class was over, but he's probably got some surprise up his sleeve."

Harry laughed. "Probably. He's my nephew."

George looked at him, and laughed in turn. "No wonder. He looks just like you. Birds are done. Let's eat."

It wasn't until an hour later, when the birds had been reduced to bones and the bottle of Chinon had been opened, that Harry said, "You said the week had been mixed. Which part is good and which part bad?" He folded his hands to listen, eyes gleaming with interest.

George leaned back in his chair. "I wish we belched in the West. Or did something ceremonious to express satisfaction. I don't really know. Edith . . ." He sighed and swallowed some wine. "She was a mistake, of course. I mean with Gretchen"—he gestured toward Harry—"at least you thought there was a future to the relationship. Gretchen's smart, and if she'd been halfway human you'd be married now." Harry started to protest, but George went on talking. "With Edith, I always knew I was being a cad. But she was so damn aggressive, and I kept thinking I'd straighten things out with her next week, so . . . I guess having her out of my life is a good thing. Do you want coffee?"

Harry answered, "Sure. But I'm in no hurry."

"I'll just put it on." George got up and took the plates with him into the kitchen. When he came back he sat down again and said, "I'm very discouraged. You know, sometimes I think my father was right after all and I should have sold insurance. The problem is, all the women I meet think I'm incredibly hip because I'm a painter, and they all expect me to stay up till four A.M. and dance at clubs. Meanwhile, all I want to do is have a good dinner, make love, and go to sleep at eleven so I can get up and paint in the morning. And all the women who want to live like that want to do it on Park Avenue, with trips to Bottega Veneta sandwiched in."

"I know what you mean," Harry said a little bleakly. "I know there are lots of single women out there; all I have to do is listen to my sister talk about them. But why are the right ones so hard to find? This is New York. They have to be here somewhere."

"Why don't you have your sister set you up with someone?" George asked. "If she knows so many eligible women."

"She's seven years older than I am," Harry answered dismissively. "I don't think many of her friends would be all that interested in me."

"You'd be surprised," George countered. "I think people aren't as rigid about women being younger anymore. Is this Toby's mother, then? Wait a sec, I'll get the coffee."

Harry raised his voice as George clattered around in the kitchen.

"Right. Eleanor. I spent the day helping her clean her stuff out of my parents' attic. She has a helpless streak." Harry leaned forward to snuff out a candle that was sputtering wax onto the table. "She was married to a very uptight passive-aggressive architect. You know the type; never said no, then one day told her he was leaving her. Said he felt stifled. Which was news to her. She'd just had Simon, Toby's brother. Fortunately she's a lawyer, so she makes some money. She manages the kids and the job, but somehow getting a bunch of boxes out of the attic was too much for her. I found her crying over a baby undershirt," Harry finished.

"I think that's sweet," said George, setting down the tray with the coffee cups.

"Well, it was pretty pathetic. Anyway she's going to return the favor next weekend and help me send Gretchen's stuff to Iowa City."

"What? Gretchen's not coming back?" George asked, startled. "You want me to go out there and drag her back by her pigtails?"

"No," Harry said wearily, stirring his coffee. "But maybe I'll buy another one of your pictures to put where her log cabin quilt was."

George ruminated for a minute. "I don't think I have anything exactly that shape—but I'm working on one about the Defenestration of Prague—it'll have to be taller than it is wide. You know, the guys are going to be tumbling out the window." George gestured. "It'd look great over a bed. Or you know what else?" he went on, full of enthusiasm. "I'm going to start learning to fresco. Why don't you let me do a fresco for you?"

"Fresco? Why?" Harry asked. "It's so different from oil."

"I know," George said. "It makes me a little nervous. See, André's negotiating a commission for me to do a mural of Venice for a new Italian restaurant in your neighborhood. It doesn't actually have to be fresco, but I'd like to try it. And I can practice on your wall. Actually, I'm going to Venice for a research trip. André wangled that out of the owners."

"First Eleanor, now you," Harry said. "Maybe I should go to Venice, too, to forget my sorrows."

"What do you mean?" George asked, pouring more coffee. "You want more?" he gestured with the pot.

Harry shook his head. "El needs a break; she hasn't had a vacation from her kids ever. So I talked her into going to Venice for a week, while I take care of the boys. And now you. Where are you going to stay?"

"I don't know," George answered. "Apparently the expenses won't run to the Gritti Palace, so I'll probably end up in some damp *pensione*. I was going to stay with a friend, but his wife just had a baby."

"I know a really nice place," Harry offered. "Not damp. Right on the Giudecca Canal, so you can have a water view, but it's not too noisy or expensive. It's mostly Americans."

George shrugged. "That doesn't matter. Listen, I feel so lucky to be going."

"Let me write this down for you," Harry said, getting up to look for a piece of paper. He walked over to the desk, passing a huge shrouded canvas on an easel. "Is that the Defenestration?" he asked, while he wrote down the address.

"Yes," George answered, following Harry. "But it's not ready to be seen. Here's a sketch." He lifted a sketch pad off another easel and showed it to Harry.

Harry looked at it. "I don't think for over my bed. . . ." he protested. "I'm not sure how soundly I could sleep with these guys suspended in midair over my head."

"That's the idea," George said. He looked at what Harry had written on his desk. "Pensione Inghilterra. It sounds perfect. Very respectable, no backpackers . . ."

"Exactly," Harry answered. "Nice retired couples or honeymooners who can't afford the fancy hotels. Actually, I gave the address to Eleanor, too. There's a chance you might be there at the same time. You should keep an eye out for her."

"I will," George said, nodding. "Will I recognize her? Does she look like you?"

"Not much," Harry answered, heading back to the table. "She's tall, big. Big-boned. Like you. Generously built. She thinks she's fat, but a hundred years ago she would have been just perfect. Lots of hair, kind of a mess, but some people might think it's attractive. It's brown, her hair. Green eyes. Sort of perpetually rumpled-looking. I always want to tweak her collar or pull her slip up, but that's me."

"Well, I'll know her if I see her," George said, following

Harry. "Let's sit on the couch; these chairs aren't all that comfortable. Would I like your sister?"

"Oh, I think so," Harry answered. "But you know what, maybe it would be better if you didn't mention me. I mean if you do meet her."

"Sure, fine," George said, shrugging. "But why?"

"Oh—it would be nice for her to get away from everything, her family, her kids, her job, New York. . . . If she knows you're a friend of mine, she might, I don't know, feel less free."

"Well, we probably won't overlap at all anyway," George said. He looked at his watch. "You know, I meant to suggest this earlier: do you want to try to catch the last showing of that new István Szabó movie? We can make it if we hustle."

So they hustled and by the time Harry got home, he was too tired to be depressed about his love life.

5

The next few weeks were hell for Frances. Getting ready for the move was not the problem. She had always found solace in being busy, and in a way she welcomed the complication that the Wrong House brought. They could no longer simply put a few things in storage for the children, move everything else to Weymouth, and be done with it. Now all the inlaid furniture, certain rugs, the dining room table, their Chinese headboard, most of the good china, and almost all of the books were going into short-term storage. And Frances decided that since they were getting involved with storing things, they should keep other items: Eleanor's twin beds, Harry's bunks, the loveseat from the kitchen. It would have been simpler just to leave them for the tag sale, but Frances's reaction to stress was always to elaborate matters.

So her days were filled with lists and measurements and a scheme of different-colored tags. But even the constant bustle and focus on detail (Should the brasses be removed from the little Louis XV table? Would this be a good time to have the Hepplewhite chairs reupholstered?) couldn't distract her for long from feeling miserable. The prospect of moving in a few weeks to what she privately thought of as "that horrible house" lay like a black cloud on every moment of the day. She woke up to a sensation of gloom and could not shed it. As she moved around the Chester house being efficient, every decision she made saddened her. Her attempts to imagine how this bureau or that chair would look in Weymouth only made her feel worse. Day by day, as the moving date neared, her conviction grew: The whole plan was a terrible mistake.

She dreaded the move and felt cut adrift. But at the same time, she felt she was behaving badly. She should have been able to adapt, to simply accept a few months of life in a house she didn't care for. Frances knew she shouldn't be making such a fuss.

So she tried not to fuss. She didn't tell anyone about her disappointment or apprehension. In truth, she had become something of a loner since the children had grown. Though she had many friends, she had no real intimates. She had never been the kind of woman who sat over a glass of iced tea and complained about her husband. It simply wasn't in her to call her friend Joan Failey and say, "I'm angry, I'm anxious, I don't know what I am going to become in that house." For what was at stake, though Frances didn't have the insight to realize it, was her notion of herself.

Frances was not accustomed to self-examination. But Harry and Eleanor, discussing their mother, diagnosed the problem instantly. "She's having an identity crisis," Eleanor stated.

It was a Saturday night and Harry had come over for dinner. He and his sister were lingering at the dinner table while Toby and Simon watched *Kindergarten Cop*.

"I know. Though you might have thought she'd be a bit old for it," Harry answered.

"You're never too old for an identity crisis," Eleanor said with conviction. "It was bad enough when Dad retired and she didn't have the house to herself anymore. But now that she won't even have that . . ." Eleanor paused and shrugged. "What is she going to do, learn surf casting?"

"I know. Hard to imagine," Harry conceded. "And she's so particular about houses, too."

"Right. She's going to cringe every time one of her friends sets foot in the place," Eleanor said. "And with people she doesn't know it's going to be even worse. She'll worry that they think the house represents her real taste."

"But it's only for a few months," Harry said.

"True." Eleanor sounded unconvinced.

"Dad thinks the whole thing's a great adventure," Harry said, fiddling with his napkin ring. "He keeps talking about 'a summer at the shore.' "

"As if he were a Fresh Air kid who'd never seen water that

didn't come out of a fire hydrant," Eleanor added. "Of course he's thrilled. He gets to picture himself communing with nature on his lonely peninsula. There's just nothing fun for Mom in the whole arrangement." She stood up, stacking the plates. "I don't know, she's hard to be around these days, but I kind of feel sorry for her."

"She'll cheer up when they find a new house," Harry said.

Eleanor stopped on her way into the kitchen and looked back at her brother. "Yeah, but they have to get through a few months in this house first. And the way things are going . . ." She shook her head and pushed through the swing door. Harry picked up his glass and followed her.

"What do you mean?" he asked as she rinsed the plates and loaded them into the dishwasher.

She turned off the water and faced him. "Am I nuts to think they would divorce over this?"

Harry stared at her for a moment. "Totally," he stated. "People don't get divorced over such stupid things. Or no, they do. I take that back. But Mom and Dad won't."

Eleanor just stared at him, with a worried expression on her face.

"Look, El, it'll be okay," Harry said, patting her on the shoulder. "You and I might not manage our relationships the way they do. But we have to give them some credit for having gotten along all these years."

Eleanor sighed. "I don't know. I've never seen them like this. She snaps and he gloats and I'm sure they haven't talked at all about how terrible she feels."

Which was true. Frances and Hart had never talked about such things. There was no need. Hart knew his wife was unhappy. But what was he supposed to do, beat his breast and tear his hair out? It was less than kind, he knew, to flaunt his anticipation of the move. But every time he relaxed and thought Frances had gotten over her snit fit she would remind him, in the politest possible way, that he was a boor and an oaf and her life was in ruins. Or something to that effect. And he was tired of it.

What Hart didn't realize was that Frances was really trying. She believed that somehow, if she could remain civil and feign equanimity, everything would work out. She would attempt to be cheerful as well as competent, and from time to time she fooled her husband, if not herself. But all the time, anxiety and anger were simmering away, and sometimes they escaped in little bursts of nastiness (however polite) that only made her feel worse afterward. She was tired of it, too.

The move itself went as smoothly as these things ever do. The movers had been in the house for days, packing crystal and china, wrapping the legs of Frances's little French desk, taking the red-tagged things to long-term storage, the green-tagged things to a short-term warehouse, gently dismantling the chandeliers. Frances moved among them with her clipboard, pitching in wherever she was needed, and Hart had to temporarily abandon resentment for admiration. Frances, for her part, felt more cheerful than she had in weeks. She had accomplished a great deal, and she was able, for a change, to think well of herself.

As the two of them sat on the terrace on the last night, eating chicken salad off paper plates, Hart said, "I don't know why I should be surprised, but I am astonished how much work this all is."

"We haven't done it for forty years," Frances reminded him mildly. "And we've accumulated a lot since then."

"Well, I have to hand it to you. I've never seen such organization in my life," Hart said. "I wish you'd let me help a little more in planning it."

Frances looked at him in surprise. "Really? Well, if you want to take over dealing with the movers, I'd be delighted. I'm convinced they think I'm a witch. I know they sigh and roll their eyes every time I walk into the room." She was right, of course; they did.

"Fine, sure," Hart answered, then said after a pause, "You know, leaving here makes me very sad." He looked over at Frances. "They've been good years."

She met his glance and nodded. "I know. Me, too." And when Hart reached out his hand, she put hers in it. It was an olive branch, and it made her feel a little better. They sat there for a few minutes, looking out on the lawn where their children had learned to walk, where the tent had been pitched for Eleanor's wedding, the lawn they would never see again. Then the gnats began to whine in their ears and they went inside.

The next day, the hostilities resumed over the matter of the master-bedroom ceiling.

While Frances had been organizing the move, it had been Hart's job to ready the new house. They had agreed to do a minimum of work, since they would put the house on the market immediately. But Frances had certain requirements. The red kitchen must be painted white. (It took six coats.) The indoor-outdoor carpet in the downstairs maids' room had to be replaced. The op art and ballerina wallpapers upstairs must disappear, Frances wasn't fussy about how. The swinging saloon doors into the kitchen and the rococo mirrors in the dining room were also removed, but Hart stored them in the basement in case the next buyer wanted to put them back. The chandeliers (so carefully written into the contract) stayed, and on consideration Frances decided she could live, for the space of a summer, with the hideous olive and rust curtains and cushions in the living room. She left the barn siding on the stairway up to Hart.

Though she didn't mention the mirror on the ceiling of the master bedroom, Hart knew that he'd have to get rid of it. Most of the work he had done himself, camping out in the house for a few days at a time. But he needed professional help to remove the mirror. As it happened, the contractor recommended by two sets of friends was at his Florida house and wouldn't be back in Weymouth until mid-June. Hart decided he would wait and be sure the job was done right. Meanwhile, he repainted the shutters and window boxes dark green and as a goodwill gesture went to a nursery to buy a flat of white impatiens and laboriously transplanted them into the window boxes, where they would wither (though he didn't know this) in the direct sun.

On the day of the actual move, Frances left Chester early in the station wagon packed with clothes, bedding, pots and pans, and staples for the kitchen. Hart waited until the movers left and closed the house, then drove the Mercedes up, reaching

Weymouth late in the afternoon. The movers were already there, and Frances was directing the placement of the furniture.

What Hart noticed first when he walked in the door was the sofas. They were upholstered in a cheery pink and blue hydrangea print and they looked, in that rustic living room with its antler chandelier and plaid curtains, like Barbara Cartland in the Wild West. The pine kitchen table, meanwhile, looked like the Wild West in a Barbara Cartland novel, poised under the flowered Venetian chandelier.

Footsteps were thumping and sliding upstairs, and Hart realized that one feature of the house they hadn't thought about was its noisiness. The insulation between floors was apparently none too generous. He opened the turquoise refrigerator idly and saw that Frances had already managed to stock it with Bitter Lemon and beer, eggs, bread, apples, lettuce. She was a wonder, he had to admit, pouring Bitter Lemon into a glass (which he found in the first cupboard he tried). It was too bad about the barn siding, he thought, running his finger along it as he walked upstairs, but he'd pried back a little and discovered the studs beneath it. Damn! A splinter. Hearing voices from the former op art bedroom, he poked his head in.

"Yes, that lamp there, and there should be room for the night table between the two beds," Frances was saying. She turned when he came in and did something she'd never done before. She looked at the top of his head, and broadly, as if playing for the back mezzanine, let her eyes travel down his body, ending at his toes and returning to the finger with the splinter that he had just reflexively put in his mouth. Without thinking, Hart straightened up, wiped his finger on the pocket of his khakis, hid his glass of Bitter Lemon behind the doorframe. Frances continued to look at him as if her eyes were knives and she were filleting him for dinner. "So glad you could join us," she said. "When you've recovered from your drive perhaps you could see to the things in the front bedroom. I've had your desk put in there."

Hart nodded. If Frances had been watching him (or in a mood to notice), she would have seen a bland, inscrutable look replace the instant's recoil that was his response to her greeting. He walked across the hall, whistling "The British Grenadiers," and set to work shifting furniture around. He had noticed, as he was supposed to, that one of their bedside lamps was on the night table in the op art room. And the other was in what he thought of unconsciously as his room. Where the offending mirror still hung from the ceiling, reflecting the king-size bed.

They had dinner that night at the pine table, surrounded by the ice-blue metallic paisley wallpaper of the dining area. Outside the Dutch door, the Sound had flattened to a glassy gray in the sunset calm. The sky had taken on a remote, pearly tone, flushed with coral where it met the horizon. The islands floated like tufts of dark foam between the sky and the water. The waves made a quiet, regular hushing sound, like a giant animal's breath. As Frances came out of the kitchen carrying two plates of Stouffer's Chicken Divan, Hart turned to her and said, "Isn't it just beautiful?"

Frances put his plate in front of him. "I suppose so." She sat and began eating. There was a long pause.

"All in all, I thought the move went very well," Hart said. "You did a tremendous job organizing it all."

Frances raised her eyebrows in response, but didn't answer.

Hart put his fork on his plate with a little emphasis and it clattered onto the table. "Would you care to tell me what you are sulking about?"

"I am not sulking," she said, eyes blazing, jaw tight. "I am *tired*."

"Nonsense, Frances. You may very well be tired, and I can't blame you, but you're behaving like a child, so why don't you just spit it out. Why are you so angry?"

She hunched a shoulder and took a sip of wine. "Nothing."

Hart took off his glasses and rubbed his face with both hands. "Okay. You're not angry, you're just tired. Then maybe in the morning, after a good night's sleep, you'll be able to tell me what I have done wrong *this* time."

"If you can't figure it out for yourself, I could hardly tell you," she answered. "I think I'll go to bed now. Would you mind doing the dishes?"

"Not in the least," Hart answered, staring into the middle

distance. He sat where he was, stoically forking in chicken and broccoli in the bright light from the Venetian chandelier while Frances took her barely touched plate into the kitchen.

When he went upstairs forty-five minutes later, he noticed that the door of the op art room was shut. The master bedroom was empty, the enormous bed made up, sheets taut and untouched, spotlit and reflected in the ceiling mirror. Hart closed his eyes for a second and walked across the hall, knocking on the closed door.

"Come in."

His wife was sitting up in one of the twin beds, reading *Mapp and Lucia*. She looked up at him defiantly.

"What is going on here?" Hart asked wearily. "Why are you sleeping in this room?"

"I told you I would not sleep in that room while that mirror was on the ceiling," Frances answered. "It's still there. So I'm here."

"Would it help if I told you that the contractor who I want to help me with that mirror is in Florida and is going to come take it down in a couple of weeks?"

"Not particularly," said Frances.

"Oh," Hart answered, nodding as if she were being perfectly logical. "In other words, I sleep alone until the mirror's gone."

"That's right," agreed Frances. "I think I'm going to turn my light out now."

"Oh. Well. Sweet dreams," her husband said, and stalked across the hall. She had to get out of bed to close the door.

In the middle of the night, when she woke up, Frances had no idea where she was. The square of light at the window was in the wrong place, she was in a tiny narrow bed, and her husband's warm bulk was nowhere to be found. Then she remembered and settled herself to go back to sleep, still angry.

Eleanor and Harry came to visit the next weekend. Jared was taking the boys to East Hampton and Eleanor took the Friday afternoon off so she and Harry could leave New York early. As they drove up to the house, Harry looked at the sweep of the view and said, "It seems to me they got a lot for their money. This is pretty staggering."

Eleanor agreed, a bit reluctantly. "It's completely unlandscaped," she pointed out.

"I kind of like the wildness," Harry said, parking the car. "My, this house really is ugly." He sat for a moment looking at it through the windshield, and got out. "Can't wait to see inside."

Frances was out, so their father gave them an oddly neutral tour. Not "This is the living room, can you believe those curtains?" or "This is the living room, isn't it a swell view?" but "This is the living room. This is the dining room. This is the kitchen."

"Harry, you're going to be in here," he said as they peered into the maid's room off the kitchen. A cot stood wedged against the wall, with a tiny chest of drawers next to it. "Oh, fine," Harry said, putting down his duffel bag on the braided rag rug. "Is there a bathroom down here?" Hart pointed to the door of the downstairs bathroom, with its perpetually frolicking kittens.

As they walked up the stairs, Eleanor's flowered skirt snagged on the barn siding. Everyone paused on the stairs, waiting silently as she bent down to detach it. Nobody mentioned the folly of paneling an interior wall in a high-traffic area with old, splintery wood. Nobody mentioned how hard it might be to live with. And nobody said anything as Hart showed them the master bedroom, with his desk and reading lamp, the guest room where Eleanor would sleep, or the former op art room, where Frances's needlepoint and water glass by the bed trumpeted her occupancy. But as their father preceded them down the stairs, Harry and Eleanor turned to look at each other.

Later, sitting on the end of the dock, Eleanor said, "It doesn't look good."

Harry, with his eyes shut and his face lifted to the last of the afternoon sun, answered soberly, "Nope. I was all ready to suggest a big party for their fortieth anniversary. I thought it might give Mom something fun to think about. But I'm not sure they'll feel much like celebrating." Out in the Sound a Boston

Whaler puttered by. Harry sat up and watched it, shading his eyes with one hand. "Bet he gets a great view from there," he said.

"Mm," Eleanor said, still preoccupied by their parents. "I mean, exactly *why* are they sleeping in different rooms?"

"Well, either she's colossally pissed off at him and this is how she's punishing him, or there's something about the master bedroom she doesn't like," said Harry, still watching the boat.

"Like what?" Eleanor said, hoping Harry would come up with an explanation that would assuage her worry.

"Oh, El, it could be the morning light or the fact that the toilet runs or that the mattress isn't hard enough. And I'm sure that kinky overhead mirror drives her nuts. Maybe," Harry went on, "she's so annoyed at Dad, so irritated with him, that she just can't stand physical proximity to him anymore."

"Lovely," Eleanor said dryly. "It's enough to make me glad I'm divorced."

"Listen," Harry said, suddenly turning to his sister. "Let's give them a Whaler for their anniversary."

"A what?" Eleanor asked, confused.

"A Boston Whaler. One of those." Harry pointed to the little boat out in the Sound. "They could have a lot of fun with it."

"Wouldn't it be incredibly expensive?" Eleanor objected.

"We could get one secondhand," Harry told her. "And, El, you know I make more money than I can spend. You can just chip in what you want."

Eleanor looked at him sharply. "That's very sweet, Harry. But—" She paused for a minute, trying to assess her objections. "It would be more of a present for Dad," she said. "Mom wouldn't enjoy it very much."

"She might, though," Harry answered. "What I'm thinking is, maybe she could be won over. If she liked the boat or learned to fish or something. If she acquired a new skill. And it would give them something in common."

Eleanor stared at him suspiciously. "You're plotting, Harry. Mom's not some character on your soap. You can't make her pick up a fishing rod just by wishing it."

"I know, but it might work," he protested. "Look, here she comes."

Harry and Eleanor both turned toward the house as their mother came out the Dutch door and walked across the dock. As she looked at them her heart softened. They looked so young sitting there. They might have been teenagers sitting on someone's dock in Watch Hill, surreptitiously letting their cigarettes drop into the water at her approach. In fact there was something about the way they whipped around and stopped talking that made her think—well, of course they'd been talking about her. They'd seen the bedrooms. They'd figured out that she and Hart weren't sleeping together. She felt suddenly very weary as she sat down next to them on the dock. For a moment she considered explaining. Harry was so observant, he never missed a trick anyway. What would happen if she just told her children: "I'm furious at your father. He thinks only of himself. Sometimes I think I'm completely irrelevant to him." But the force of habit was too strong. It was unnatural to complain about Hart to anyone, let alone to his children. So she merely said, with an attempt at a smile, "You two look like a Ralph Lauren ad, sitting here."

"Well, Harry does," Eleanor amended. "It's quite a house, Mom."

"Isn't it, though?" Frances answered with a tight little smile. "Your father thinks it's nifty."

"But you don't," Harry stated.

Frances glanced back at the boulder-strewn roof. "Not exactly," she said, with creditable smoothness. "It's not quite what I had in mind."

"Does that make it worse?" Harry asked, ever quick to probe emotions.

Frances looked at him sharply. "What do you mean?"

"Well, the fact that you had the right house picked out. It must be disappointing," Harry said, in an encouraging tone.

But Frances wouldn't be drawn into agreeing. She glanced around and said brightly, "Oh, Ellie, what a pretty skirt. Is it new?"

Eleanor looked down and tucked a fold of the skirt under her leg. "Not really," she said, disconcerted. "You know, this really is a beautiful spot. You guys should have a party while you're here. It's a perfect place for it."

"You must be joking," Frances said, a bit coldly.

"Well," Eleanor plunged on, glancing at Harry, "I mean the house is awful, but you could do something outside. Some kind of anniversary party."

"El's right," put in Harry helpfully. "Have everybody out on the deck or the lawn. I'm sure it's gorgeous at sunset. You could have a huge cocktail party."

"But we hardly know anyone here," Frances objected. "Most of our friends are in Chester."

"No," Harry countered. "Not when you think about it. The Eberhardts are here, and the Faileys are in Madison, and the Davises in Essex. Clara Henschel would probably be here by then; I think she opens her house on June fifteenth."

"And the Strakers would come from New York," Eleanor went on. "And us, of course, and Tom and Lucy Whittall, and Uncle Pete."

"You can't ask people to drive three hours and just give them drinks," Frances protested, drawn into the scheme despite herself.

Harry shrugged. "Make it a buffet. Something simple. Chili. I can come up early and help."

"Oh, no." Frances frowned. "You'd have to do something a little more substantial. Not chili in June, for a fortieth anniversary. Maybe poached salmon."

"Okay," Harry said, catching Eleanor's eye. "We'll do poached salmon, dill sauce, maybe some cucumbers. Asparagus should be cheap by then."

"And strawberry fool for dessert," Frances said, envisioning it all. "That's easy enough to do and it looks nice."

"Look, here comes Dad," Eleanor said as Hart walked stepped onto the dock carrying a small tray with beer bottles and a glass of wine on it. "Doesn't he look just like a waiter at the Yale Club?"

"Well, not exactly," Harry said. "Dad, we're planning your

fortieth anniversary party," he announced, without letting anyone put a word in. "A buffet on the deck for fifty of your very best friends."

Hart, handing Frances her wineglass, shot a startled glance at Harry. "Oh?" he said. "And when is this going to be?"

"Late June," Harry answered smoothly. "What's the exact date, the twenty-third? The Saturday after that. Does that sound all right, Mom?"

In fact, it didn't. The whole idea was anathema to Frances. Why invite fifty people to see this ghastly place? "I don't know, Harry," she protested. "After all the work of the move."

"I'll be here to help," Harry said.

"It would be fun," Eleanor chimed in.

"I think it's a splendid idea," Hart added.

There didn't seem to be any graceful way out of it. "Well, why not?" Frances said with a sigh.

6

Entertaining had never come easily to Frances. She did it often, she did it well, but it always entailed hours of planning, pages of lists, and a certain impatience with Hart's casual disregard of domestic details. She was a hostess of the old school, insisting on lots of flowers, real glasses and china, crystal canisters of cigarettes, fresh boxes of wooden matches in porcelain matchbox covers. All of this, in the Chester house, had merely added a level of festivity to an already refined setting. In the new house, every detail that had been standard in Chester managed to look more out of place. The silver candelabra, placed on the table in the dining area, demonstrated that the Venetian chandelier was tacky. In the living room the two chintz sofas, facing each other with a coffee table in between, huddled together against the tastelessness of the boulder-faced fireplace wall and the hideous curtains. There was no sensible place to put the bar, so Hart had to drape a damask tablecloth over a pair of card tables next to the fireplace. The flowers, which Frances had arranged to look like a spontaneous gathering from a phenomenally well-stocked meadow, somehow looked like a funeral arrangement from FTD when she placed them in the living room.

"My God, I hate this house," she muttered to Eleanor as she put a stack of gold-rimmed plates on the table in the dining area. "Everything in it is wrong. Do you know that? There is not one single feature of this house that I like."

"Oh, come on, Mom. It's a gorgeous night; everybody will spend the whole time on the deck."

"Until they're eaten alive by the mosquitoes," Frances said bitterly.

"You've got the citronella candles, and Harry sprayed out there three times. And we've got five bottles of Cutter's. It'll be fine. And you look great."

Though she would have liked to object, Frances knew this was true. She had gone to New York to shop for this occasion and had bought an immensely expensive, beautifully cut dress in periwinkle blue silk. With it she wore her grandmother's triple strand of pearls with the diamond and sapphire clasp, and her mother's matching pearl bracelets.

"Thank you, dear," Frances said, and leaned over to kiss her daughter on the cheek. "So do you."

Eleanor raised her eyebrows. She had never had the confidence in her looks that Frances and Harry shared, and could never quite believe compliments. "You don't think it's too dressy? Or too wintery?" She had put on what she thought of as her party dress, bronze taffeta with a full skirt and a low neck. An unusually frank saleswoman had talked her into buying it four years earlier by pointing out that it made the most of her shoulders and camouflaged her hips. The bronze color brought out the chestnut in her hair, and Harry had often admired the way the dress made her look like an expensive Belle Epoque courtesan. This he didn't tell Eleanor.

"Mom!" shouted Toby, skidding into the dining room. "Can you come help Simon with his tie?"

"Inside voices, Toby," said his mother automatically.

"Can you help Simon with his tie?" repeated Toby, in an ostentatiously modulated voice. "Those plates are pretty, Gran."

"Thank you, dear. You look very handsome."

"I know," said Toby artlessly. Eleanor had insisted that her sons wear white pants and button-down shirts for the party and she thought, looking at Toby, that he was the most attractive child she'd ever seen. "So will you come, Mom?"

"Can you spare me?" Eleanor asked Frances.

"Yes, of course," Frances said, turning to her list and checking off "plates." "Where is Hart?"

"Upstairs getting dressed," Toby answered. "Splashing bay rum all over the bathroom."

"Toby!" expostulated Eleanor, but Frances only nodded absently and asked, "Do you remember where we put the silver sauceboat?"

"In the second cupboard on the right under the sink," Eleanor called back from halfway up the stairs.

"It's not Simon," Toby whispered stagily as they reached the second floor. "Harry and Granddad can't get that mirror down." He knocked importantly on the master bedroom door and Hart peered out, then beckoned them in and shut the door behind them.

Inside the bedroom was a scene of barely suppressed chaos. A dropcloth on the bed was littered with chips of paint and plaster. Simon, wearing nothing but his Mickey Mouse underpants, was sitting on the dropcloth pretending to drill holes in the mattress with a screwdriver. Harry, in an immaculate white shirt and steel gray linen pants, was up on a tall stepladder, squinting into the space between the mirror and the ceiling. Hart, in his party uniform of blue blazer and bow tie, went to the bottom of the ladder and peered up, ignoring his own reflection peering back anxiously at him from above.

"As far as I can tell, it's *welded*," Harry said.

"Oh, come on," Hart answered disgustedly.

Harry reached a hand in farther and tried to jiggle something. "Well, you can get up here and feel for yourself, but I honestly think it is. It's like a giant hook and eye, welded shut."

"Christ on a crutch!" Hart exclaimed. "Why in hell would anybody do that?"

"They wanted to be able to relax during their bedtime fun and games," Harry suggested, descending the ladder. He lifted his tie from his father's desk chair and slipped it around his neck.

Simon looked up from his drilling, intrigued. "What kind of games do people play in bed?"

"Monopoly," Eleanor said hurriedly. "Simon, please go put your clothes on right now. And wash your hands and face first."

"Okay, Mom," Simon said, sliding off the bed and walking away slowly with the screwdriver held in front of him like a torch.

"So now what?" Harry asked, looking up at the mirror while knotting his tie.

"It's probably sturdier than anything else in this whole damn house," Hart commented. "But we've got to get rid of it somehow."

"Why?" Toby asked.

"Gran doesn't like the way it looks," Eleanor put in quickly. "Toby, the guests are going to be here any minute. Can you go make sure Simon is really getting dressed?"

"Oh, okay," Toby said, reluctant to leave what he sensed was a crisis, though his mother was clearly holding out on him about its true nature.

"Well, we can't get it down," Harry said flatly.

"Then we have to hide it," Hart said. "Your mother doesn't want her friends to see it and the contractor who was supposed to take it down yesterday called this morning to say that he was still in Florida but his son-in-law might get over here this afternoon to do the job. Needless to say, he didn't."

Harry shot a glance at his father and said to Eleanor, "Mom's exact words were, 'If Clara Henschel sees that mirror, I will never live it down.' "

Eleanor stood with her hands on her hips, studying the mirror. "Clara Henschel is a lot more broad-minded than Mom gives her credit for. It's Joan Failey she should be worried about," she said. "How can we hide it? It's enormous."

Harry looked at his watch. "Dad, you painted the kitchen, didn't you? Is there any paint left?"

"You're going to *paint* it?" Eleanor said. "It'll look ridiculous."

"I know. It's going to look like some weird acoustic baffle or something, and the paint won't really adhere to the mirror. But maybe it will confuse people. And what else can we do? It's a quarter to six."

Hart interrupted. "I think Harry's right. I have some white latex left over. Unless you think we should use the green from the shutters."

The three of them stood silent, imagining the mirror painted dark green. "White's bad enough," Harry said, unknotting his tie again and handing it to his sister. "El, do you have something I can put over my hair? And Dad," he said as his father started to leave the room, "don't forget a small brush for the edges."

"I know, I know." Hart's voice receded as he went down the stairs.

An hour and a half later, the party was in full swing. The long driveway was lined with discreet foreign sedans. The noise of fifty confident, well-bred, well-fed pillars of the community drowned out the rhythmic hush of the waves and spilled out across the scrubby grass. Inside the house, a local teenager in a clip-on bow tie tended bar very competently while his mother and his sister emptied ashtrays, washed glasses, and passed silver trays of cheese straws and hot artichoke dip. Toby and Simon, now wearing their school blazers and ties, squirmed through the crowd, shaking hands here and there where they couldn't evade grown-up attention and pestering the bartender for maraschino cherries. Pairs of men, and those women who clung to flat heels even in the evening, ambled across the lawn to the dock. One enterprising geriatric even went out on the rocks with his cane, but Eleanor was dispatched to bring him back before he could slip on the seaweed and break a hip.

The deck was hugely popular. Retired stockbrokers propped their behinds and their drinks on the broad railing, gesturing expansively at the Sound, talking about yacht clubs and property values. Meanwhile, their wives took tours of the house.

Frances had wondered, in the days before the party, exactly what line she should take about the house. Pretend it was all right? But all of her friends would know it wasn't. Permit herself to express some irritation with Hart for having bought the wretched place? It was tempting, but she couldn't envision it. Not at a party, not with so many people there. Not on her fortieth wedding anniversary. In the end, she settled on rueful relish: "Isn't it ghastly, can you *believe* the taste?"

This tack involved special attention to the dining room chandelier (which interfered a bit with the help, but Frances always apologized when she got in their way), the kitten wallpaper in the downstairs bath, the window seats and curtains, and the barn siding on the stairs. "Upstairs isn't as bad," she said over and over again. "Hart took down the ghastly wallpaper in the bedrooms. One of them made me absolutely dizzy, it was so bad! Have you got a drink? Oh, excuse me, I must talk to . . ." She let her guests go upstairs by themselves. It did occur to her to wonder what Hart had finally done about the mirror, but as she was on her way up to look, a fuse blew in the kitchen and she got sidetracked.

The guests who did go upstairs (where, after all, there was a bathroom one might legitimately need to visit) didn't find much to look at. Frances had unobtrusively moved her things back into the master bedroom, though anybody who looked in the closets (as some women, of course, did) would realize that all her clothes were in the bedroom across the hall. Really the only odd thing was the strong smell of paint in the master bedroom and that streaky slab over the bed.

"That doesn't look much like Frances," said Lucy Whittall to Joan Failey, gesturing at the ceiling. "Do you think it's supposed to be some kind of modernist reference to a canopy bed?" (Lucy was a docent at the Metropolitan Museum and never let anyone forget it.)

"I don't think it knows what it's supposed to be," croaked Joan in her cigarettes-and-whiskey tenor. "Hope they don't suffocate in paint fumes tonight. Too bad Hart couldn't get the painting finished a little sooner." She moved over to the window. "Still, it's a view to die for."

"Hmm. It looks like a late Kensett," mused Lucy. And she added, on a more practical note, "I'd be a little frightened here in a storm. I wonder what their insurance is like."

"They'll be gone by hurricane season," predicted Joan, whose house on the water in Madison had been flooded more times than she cared to think about.

"Oh, really?" Lucy asked, turning to go back downstairs. "Have they found something else?"

"Not that I know of," Joan answered, "but that was the original game plan. Once . . . you know. They realized," she said, with an indeterminate gesture that made her gold bangles clatter.

"Realized Hart had bought this monstrosity, you mean," Lucy said, poking the barn siding at the top of the stairs. "Honestly, how anybody could," she said, shaking her head as she went downstairs. It wasn't clear whether she meant panel a stairway with barn siding or buy the wrong house.

Frances had just sent another group upstairs when she glanced out the front door and saw an immense gleaming Bentley trundling up the drive. She put her glass of wine down on the bar and, smiling, went outside.

A short, bowlegged man in a chauffeur's cap slid down from the high front seat of the Bentley and opened the back door. "Hello, Mr. Parker," Frances said to the little man. "How are you? Did you have a good winter?"

"Pretty good, thanks, Mrs. Drummond," the chauffeur answered. "You need some help in there, Mrs. Henschel?"

"Yes. Damn bracelet's hooked on my dress. Frances!"

"Yes, Aunt Clara," Frances said, poking her head into the cavernous interior of the car. "What can I do for you?"

"Can you unhook this thing? Hate to snag the lace; it's real Chantilly." She pronounced it with a perfect French accent.

"Here, scoot over into the light a bit," Frances said, bending over the two-inch-wide platinum-and-diamond bracelet that circled Clara Henschel's tiny blue-veined wrist.

"Easier said than done, dear."

"Wait . . . there. I've got it. Can you get out by yourself?"

"Well, now that you're halfway into the car, why don't you give me a good tug?" Clara said, holding out her hands.

Frances obliged, and Clara finally emerged from the car in a cloud of black lace and tulle.

"What a dress, Aunt Clara!" Frances said, kissing the older woman on the cheek.

"Chanel," Clara said succinctly. "Not Lagerfeld, either. One of Mademoiselle's. Put on my best bib and tucker for you and Hart. My lord, whoever built this house ought to be shot," she said, taking a step toward the house. "Let me have my stick, Parker."

"Is your arthritis bad?" Frances asked, offering an arm for Clara to lean on.

"No, but it's a useful prop at a party," she answered, accepting the thin malacca cane with the carved ivory head. "Snag a waiter, trip a buffoon, pound the floor for emphasis. In the unlikely event that I can't make myself heard," she added.

Clara Henschel had spent ninety-two years making sure that she was heard and that she got what she wanted. She had been a great beauty and had married the son of a robber baron (who died), a French aristocrat (whom she divorced), an immensely successful songwriter (who divorced her), and finally a dry-cleaning millionaire who enjoyed ill health—and her occasional visits—in Palm Beach. She had been a great friend of Frances's mother, and was in fact Frances's godmother. When the mother had died, she had transferred her friendship to the daughter, although Frances still held her slightly in awe. The Drummond children adored her and visited her often at her splendid New York town house. Clara claimed that her only interests in life were gossip and meddling in her friends' lives, and like much that she said, this might have been partly true. She adored parties, and particularly relished sitting in a corner with a presentable young man (which by now meant anyone under fifty), flirting outrageously and spreading slanderous rumors behind a ring-decked hand. Or a fan, if she was feeling very Louis XV.

"My, my," she said as Frances helped her through the door. "Looks like a . . . You know, I don't know quite *what* it looks like," she said. "They've made the most of the view, though. Got to hand them that. Why don't you settle me down here"—she pointed at a sofa with her cane—"and send me Harry with a strong martini? I'll make you give me a house tour a little later." Harry couldn't be found, so Eleanor appeared with the martini and settled down next to the old lady, whispering in her ear.

Harry and Eleanor had argued over exactly how to present the boat to their parents. Eleanor, who hated public fuss, was all for driving it over early one morning and leaving it tied up on the dock with the keys in the ignition. But Harry overruled her. He wanted a little more drama. So it was agreed that he would slip away from the party, drive to the municipal marina in the next cove where the boat was moored for the night, and drive the boat back over to appear in front of the house with a flourish before the sun set. He devised a huge calico frill for a cleat on the bow, and at the last minute Toby and Simon, bored with the grown-ups' chatter, went with him to the marina.

Dinner had just been served, and the guests were all settled with their plates of salmon and asparagus. Hart sat next to Aunt Clara, listening to a startling story about a prominent Broadway playwright who was trying to buy a house next to the Henschel "cottage" (with ten guest bedrooms and a five-car garage) in Fenwick, up the coast. Frances, after prowling around one last time to be sure everyone was comfortable, put a morsel of salmon on a plate and pulled a little Sheraton side chair into a group that included her husband's best friend Tom Whittall and smoky-voiced Joan Failey. The roar of the conversation had died to a more polite "don't talk with your mouth full" hum when Eleanor, standing on the deck, heard what she thought was an outboard motor. She stopped talking and cocked her ear.

"What?" asked her Uncle Pete, who was, as he'd told Eleanor, loving the sight of "all these stuffy stockbrokers in a house built by an architect tripping on magic mushrooms."

Eleanor said, lowering her voice, "I thought I heard a motor. It's a surprise. We're giving Mom and Dad a Boston Whaler for an anniversary present."

"What for?"

"Uncle Pete! For fun! So they can putter around on the water," Eleanor hissed. "Look! here they come!"

And indeed, around the point came the little boat. Toby and Simon were standing in the stern, waving maniacally and jumping up and down, while Harry, looking incongruous in his Armani suit, steered in a graceful curve toward the dock.

"Um, Mom?" Eleanor said, sidling through the crowd to her mother.

"What?" Frances answered, turning around in her chair. "What is it?"

"Come on," Eleanor said. "Come outside. It's a surprise." She took her mother's arm and urged her out the door, and beckoned to her father from across the room. "Come on, Dad!" she called. "It's a surprise!"

The guests all put their plates down and stepped out onto the deck or the lawn. Clara Henschel, left in the living room with the teenage bartender, said imperiously, "Young man, please help me outside. I must see what's going on."

There, at the end of the dock, stood Frances and Hart, with Eleanor between them. The water was at midtide, so the boat floated several feet below the dock, and they had to bend down to talk to Harry in the boat. Their voices could not be heard from the house, but their gestures were as clear as pantomime. Hart was grinning and turned to his wife with evident exhilaration. Frances, with a hand on her pearl necklace, was clearly dumbfounded. "She's wondering what the hell she's going to do with a boat," came Clara Henschel's voice, and several people watching the group chuckled. Harry boosted Toby and Simon up onto the dock, where they jumped and pranced with glee. Hart bent down to check that the bowline was cleated securely and held out his hand to Harry, who had to clamber a bit awkwardly onto the dock. For an instant, the family group closed. Frances leaned forward and kissed her son. Her daughter moved closer, arm around her mother's waist. Then Hart took his wife by the shoulders and kissed her gently on each cheek. They turned and walked up the dock toward the house, with the boys racing before them.

As one, everyone on the deck and lawn started to clap. A few snuffles were heard, and a few eyes surreptitiously wiped. Clara Henschel said to the bartender, whose arm she was still clutching, "Is there any champagne?"

"Yes," he answered, "but I wasn't supposed to serve it until dessert."

"Never mind. Now's the moment. Get the other ladies to help you. If you get in trouble, blame me," she said, and pushed him off. So by the time Hart and Frances stepped back onto the deck, glasses of champagne were thrust into their hands and the Yale element was calling out, "Toast! Toast!"

Hart looked at Frances, who only shrugged her shoulders. So

he climbed up onto the broad deck railing. "Harry? Where's Harry? Harry, come here and hold on to your old father. I'm afraid I'm going to tip over backward," he said. "Eleanor, Frances, you, too. We're all in this together." There was a pause as they slipped through the crowd to his side. He said, in the silence, "I don't suppose you'd like to stand up here, too, Frances?" and added, when the laughter died down, "Never mind, she's got her own pedestal." He paused again, scanning the faces in front of him. "You know, I did have a few clever words tacked together to say, but I really am just—incapacitated."

"Spoken like a true lawyer," called his brother Pete from the back of the crowd, and Hart had to pause again for the laughter.

"All I can say is thank you. Thank you to our friends, for coming here tonight. Thank you to our children, for this splendid surprise"—he waved in the direction of the boat—"and above all, thank you to Frances, for forty wonderful years." Still holding Harry's hand, he jumped down from the railing and put his arm around Frances, who was blushing. He kissed her again on the cheek, and when her arm went around his waist, Hart felt obscurely satisfied. Surely that would placate Frances. After all, he'd just announced in front of fifty people that—what, that she was important to him. That he was fond of her. Whatever. He couldn't have put it more plainly, and she seemed to understand. Hart squeezed Frances's shoulder and grinned at the crowd. Joan Failey, who had watched the whole thing with a sharp eye, raised an eyebrow and said to Lucy Whittall, "Well, maybe the closet space in the master bedroom is inadequate." Lucy Whittall only said "Who knows?" and sat down again with her plate of salmon.

After that the noise got even louder. Up to that moment the evening had been a sound success, a pleasant evening spent among good friends. But after Hart's little speech, it took off into that special, memorable realm of really wonderful parties. Every conversation seemed inspired. Pairs of women sat down on the deck, forgetting their party dresses, and shared terrible secrets about their children's failures. Joan Failey and Tom Whittall walked out to the end of the dock to look at the boat, and Tom reminded Joan of that night on the dock in Darien a million years ago before either of them was married. Joan smiled mistily and let him nuzzle her neck for a moment before she pulled away. Five men who had been in the Whiffenpoofs forty-five years earlier stood in a little group on the lawn singing "You've Got to Put a Nightie on Aphrodite" in surprisingly creditable harmony. Uncle Pete told Eleanor she looked ravishing and she said, "Oh, come on, Uncle Pete," then slipped away to put the boys in bed. Frances, with a champagne glass in hand, finally relaxed, and when someone congratulated her on how comfortable she'd made the house, said, "I'm beginning to think we should have kept it just as it was, every horror in place, and charged admission!"

"Well, it's time for me to be going," Clara Henschel said, "so why don't you show me right now? Spare no details."

"The first thing you have to imagine," said Frances, helping Clara to her feet, "is that the shutters and window boxes were all painted pink. Pepto-Bismol pink. And the kitchen was fire-engine red," she went on, "and there were Western-style swinging doors into the kitchen. . . ."

"Pity you didn't keep them for your grandsons," Clara put in.

"And have gunfights over the breakfast table?" Eleanor said, coming down the stairs. "They're in the room on the end, if you want to avoid getting trapped into an endless good-night conversation," she added, as Frances and Clara started up the stairs.

"Stay away from that wall," Frances said. "The rustic touch won't do the Chantilly any good." She was beginning to wonder what Hart had done with the mirror. What if he hadn't been able to get it down? What if people had been looking into that room all night? And seen that huge, obscene mirror hung over the bed? The bed she—theoretically, at least—shared with Hart? What would they be thinking?

"No, I can imagine," Clara said. "I don't really know why I'm bothering to climb these stairs anyway. It's just nosiness about other people's houses."

"We've disguised the worst of it up here," Frances answered, genuinely anxious now. "Hideous wallpaper." They peered into the bedroom she had been using, which was now strewn with Eleanor's clothes. "I don't know why I spent so many years yelling at Ellie to put her clothes away. It seems to have been a complete waste of breath," Frances said, with undue irritation.

"Never mind," Clara said, crossing the hall. "She's a good girl. Got to find her another husband, though."

"Hush, Aunt Clara, the boys are still awake!" hissed Frances, as they walked into the master bedroom.

"Oops. Sorry," said Clara unrepentantly. "I forgot. I need to sit for a moment," she said, perching on the side of bed. "Stairs were a bit ambitious. Grand view you get from here," she went on. "Do the waves keep you awake? Every time I come up here I can't sleep for the first week or so. The water seems so insistent. And then when I get back to the city all I can hear is the taxis and the sirens. Sometimes I wonder why I bother keeping up the cottage except that Gus loved it so much and I think Parker likes to get a chance to drive on country roads. His hearing isn't so good, which is probably a boon. . . ."

But Frances wasn't listening. She was looking at the mirror over the bed, which Hart hadn't removed.

It was the only thing she'd asked him to do. She'd done her best to give a civilized party in this heathen house, and all he'd had to do was get the damned mirror off the ceiling. She hadn't nagged—she had a dread of nagging. But he knew how important it was to her. And all he'd done was slap a coat of paint on it.

Now all her friends had seen it. They'd probably known right away what it was, in spite of the paint. And suddenly Frances felt the tears start hot in her eyes. She tried to blink them back, but she couldn't control her face, she could feel her mouth pulling into a grimace, and, ignoring Clara's ongoing monologue, she ran into the brown marble bathroom. She pulled the door closed behind her and sat on the edge of the bathtub with her head in her hands, weeping.

Another woman might have been frankly angry. She might have thrown a hairbrush at the bathroom mirror, or sworn roundly at her absent husband, Clara Henschel or no. But

Frances had never been very successful at anger, and it always sneaked up on her. She could sulk or cry, but not rage.

And once she'd begun, she couldn't stop. It wasn't just the mirror. It was the whole awful thing, the lovely little house they'd lost, the ghastly place they had to live in now, Hart's callousness about how much she hated it, the frustration of trying to give a party there, having all her friends see that awful mirror. Frances gulped and mopped at her eyes with some toilet paper, and the tears welled up afresh with each new thought.

Clara tapped at the door. "May I come in?"

Frances sniffed. "Of course. I'm just blubbering away in here."

Clara stepped into the bathroom, closing and locking the door behind her. "My!" she exclaimed. "How unpleasant. Brown is such an odd choice for a bathroom." She leaned on her elegant stick and looked at Frances.

"Is Hart being odious?" she asked.

Frances sighed and got up to look in the mirror. "The worst thing about being so fair-skinned is that everybody knows when you've been crying," she said, and dabbed at her eyelashes. "I don't know if Hart's being odious. I think he is, but apparently he doesn't see it that way."

"I think a cold washcloth might be better," instructed Clara. "That's a mirror over the bed?"

Frances obediently ran some cold water over a washcloth. "Right. And I've been after him for weeks to take it down. Weeks. I even . . ." Her face disappeared behind the washcloth.

"Oh, I know, dear. Raoul had one at the hunting lodge. Once I put my foot down it only took him three days to arrange to have it moved. It took four men. Give Hart the benefit of the doubt. In case he deserves it." Frances snorted from behind her washcloth.

Clara sat down on the lid of the toilet. "Do I gather the house is the problem?"

"You do," Frances said. She took away the washcloth and her eyes looked piercingly blue. "Aunt Clara, just how much nonsense do I have to put up with?"

Clara swung her cane. "You know, dear, much as I love to interfere, I don't think I can tell you that. You and Hart have always played your cards very close to the chest." She thought of something. "He's not playing around?"

Frances looked startled. "Goodness, I don't think so." She thought for a minute and repeated, "I don't *think* so. How would I know?"

"You'd know," Clara said succinctly. "After forty years, you'd know. So there's that to be thankful for." Outside, someone rattled the doorknob. "Just a moment," Clara sang out. "I'll only be a minute longer. You'd better powder your nose, dear, and get back to your guests."

Frances reached for her powder compact and sighed. "Oh, hell," she muttered, examining her pink nose. "I guess I'll have to stay outside in the dark for a while."

"You'll walk me to the car and have a nice long chat on the dock with Hart's brother Pete," Clara recommended. "He's always thought the world of you, even if he does seem like a fool. Maybe he can cheer you up."

And that was how it happened. Even Pete's persiflage couldn't take away Frances's bleak, defeated feeling, and she was sure Harry noticed her red-rimmed eyes, but everyone else seemed oblivious as the party sparkled on. No one was more oblivious than Hart.

7

A week later, Eleanor flew off to Italy and Harry brought the boys to Weymouth. On his first morning there, Toby came downstairs in his surfer shorts, poured himself a bowl of cereal, and planted himself at the table on the deck, where Frances was eating her toast. It was already a beautiful day. The air was perfectly clear, and cool enough so that Frances, sitting in the shade, had a sweater over her shoulders. There was sufficient breeze to shatter the blue surface of the water and tweak at the pages of *The New York Times*. Toby, hunched over his Cheerios, watched his sharp-edged shadow on the deck. He put his hands behind his head and horns sprouted on his shadow-head. He waggled them experimentally, then said, "So, Gran, let's take the boat out to one of those islands today."

Frances looked at him over the pages of the paper. "What's your grandfather's game plan?"

"He's taking Harry and Simon to some museum," Toby said disgustedly, watching the shadow of his spoon drip shadow-drops of milk back into his bowl.

Frances watched him, but didn't say anything. She did not, in fact, know how to drive the boat. She hadn't even been out in it, though several times when Hart wasn't at home she had walked out to the end of the dock to look at it. Once she had even climbed down the ladder to get into it. She had sat there for a few minutes, bobbing gently, examining the steering wheel and the funny little windshield and the heavily varnished bench you sat on when you drove. It didn't really do much for her.

She had been living in the house for a month now. Every now and then Frances mentally tested: Was she getting used to it? Did she, perhaps, hate it any less? There were a few—a very few—good features. She had always scorned the idea of a "deck"; a deck was a place where you barbecued hot dogs and drank funny-tasting sodas and watched bowling on TV. But it had turned out that she and Hart ate most of their meals out there. It was really quite pleasant, she conceded: the fresh air, the sound of the water, the magnificent view. It also meant she didn't have to look at the hideous wallpaper inside.

The master bedroom, too, had its advantages. Three days after the party the contractor had finally come and, with much to-do, removed the wretched mirror. Frances, watching carefully, noticed that it took a blowtorch, a hacksaw, and three burly men wearing wide leather weight-lifting belts to carry it, in a gingerly way, downstairs. When the contractor's truck drove away, Frances moved her things back into the master bedroom. Hart did not comment, but turned to her that night in bed and let her know he had missed her. The brown marble bathroom was ghastly, but it *was* nice to have two sinks.

But there was nothing for her to do. She cooked the meals, naturally, and did the laundry and dishes. Mrs. Wilucki came in to clean. In Chester, Frances had always polished the silver and washed the procelain knickknacks herself, but most of them had been stored, so that task was removed. There was no garden. There was a garden club, and she'd gone to a meeting, but that had only occupied a couple of hours. She had had lunch once or twice with friends and driven down to visit Clara Henschel, but time hung heavy on her hands. So why not explore the islands? she thought, with a sudden rush of resolution. It wasn't the kind of thing she usually did. But neither was living in a house with a deck.

"All right," she said to Toby. "I'll just get Granddad to show us how to drive the boat before he goes to the museum. And you'll have to wear a life preserver," she added.

"Oh, Gran . . ." Toby objected.

"Don't even try it," Harry said, coming out onto the deck with a cup of coffee. "I know that look. She means business."

She did, of course. If a thing was worth doing, it was worth doing well. She paid close attention to her driving lesson and to Hart's warnings about unmarked rocks. She packed lunch and basted an unwilling Toby with sunscreen. She pored over one of Hart's charts to decide which islands would be worth visiting. Just before eleven she and Toby drove away from the dock rather professionally and headed out into the Sound.

As she opened the throttle and the boat slapped over the waves, Frances's brow smoothed out. Feeling competent always cheered her up. The salty air rushed past, whipping the ends of the scarf she'd tied over her hair. The sun glittered fiercely on the water, so bright she had to squint. She nudged the steering wheel an inch and the boat responded, leaving a curve in the wake surging behind. The shore fell away, looking like the landscape for a toy train.

Farewell Island was their goal. It was one of a group of islands owned by the state, one of which even had picnic tables and barbecue pits and a couple of outhouses. Farewell was the smallest, with a sandy beach where Toby and Frances could pull the boat ashore and have their picnic. Hart had showed Frances how to tip the engine up out of the water, and she felt masterful as she cut the engine a few yards from shore, watching the sandy bottom loom up through the cloudy water.

"Look, Gran, fish!" cried Toby, looking down.

"Minnows," she said, watching them dart aimlessly in and out of the boat's shadow.

"Can we catch them?"

"You can try," she said, clambering to the bow as the boat's bottom grated against sand. She climbed cautiously overboard, landing in knee-deep water. "Come on. We're here."

She fixed the anchor and pulled the boat a bit farther out of the water. It was surprisingly light, she thought, tugging a little more to haul it over the high-water mark. Toby threw his towel onto the sand and waded back into the water, intent on the tiny flickering fish.

Frances settled down in the sand to watch him, thinking she should have brought a book. It was amazingly quiet. The beach was sheltered from the wind so the waves just licked at the sand, and the beach plum bushes behind her merely quivered in the occasional breeze. The sun was strong enough to dry her legs very quickly. She leaned back on her elbows, closing her eyes.

She could hear Toby splashing in the water, and the raucous call of a seagull somewhere to her left. The sun baked into her, warming her very bones. It was peaceful. Hart would like this secluded little spot. But he wouldn't be lying in the sand. He would be up on his feet, exploring the island, looking for evidence of habitation, poking in the remains of a campfire, picking up remarkable pieces of dried seaweed or dingy pebbles striped with veins of pure quartz.

Frances shook her head at the thought that Hart was just like Toby. It was one of the things she'd always liked about him: his energy and enthusiasm. "He keeps busy," she would say indulgently to her friends when they remarked on the fact that he had joined the board of a new charity or built new steps for the back porch.

But now that busyness (which once she had matched, in her own sphere) was annoying. Hart adored life in the new house. He swam every day, no matter what the weather. He dug for clams at low tide (unsuccessfully, for the most part) and puttered around in the boat. He kept the birding glasses at hand and gloated over unusual sightings.

She didn't share his enthusiasm. They had already had one night when the wind screamed around the eaves and Hart went down to the dock at three A.M. to make sure the boat was secured bow and stern. She hated the narrow little kitchen with its one silly window over the sink. They had moved the sofas three times without finding a really comfortable way to furnish the living room. She'd snagged her sweater untold times on the stairs. It just wouldn't do.

They hadn't discussed moving, though. After their one depressing tour with Margaret Harwood, they hadn't seen any more houses. They'd been so busy, getting ready for the party and now with the boys here, Frances told herself. But somehow she felt she couldn't bring up looking for a new house. She'd tried. She'd thought and thought about how to do it: just drop it casually into conversation, or exclaim over an ad in the real-estate section of the *New Haven Register*, or announce one morning, over coffee, "Hart, I can't stand living here anymore!"

But whatever resolutions she made on the subject in private, she couldn't carry them out.

"Gran, look!" Toby called out. He scampered up to her holding out his sodden baseball cap, which contained three frantic minnows, dashing fruitlessly from end to end of the cap, desperate to swim away.

"Well done," Frances said. "And now what are you going to do with them?"

"I'm going to build them a water city," he said. "First I'll dig a big pond for them, and then I'm going to dig some rivers and canals. Want to help?"

"Yes, of course," said Frances, so they went down to the water's edge and started to dig.

Eleanor, meanwhile, was reveling in the water city of Venice. From the moment her plane landed at Milan and she walked by the airport coffee bar, she had been in a trance. It might have been jet lag and fatigue: she'd had to work until midnight the three nights before she left. But added to that was her sense of liberty. All the way over on the plane she had reveled in the fact that she could do exactly as she pleased. For the first time in years, she read a novel for three hours straight. Didn't have to give her airline peanuts to one of her children. Monopolized the window.

But it was the smell of the coffee that really transported her. She turned aside from the stream of passengers going to claim their bags, and propped herself at the counter. Ordered "un caffe." Drained the bitter little cupful. Smiled, without noticing the sidelong glances from the businessmen next to her. Waltzed off to get her luggage.

Her dazed state lasted for hours, and afterward she could only remember odd details about her first day in Venice. Her first glance of the city, hovering surrealistically on the surface of the lagoon. Seaweed on the steps leading down into a canal, undulating in the gentle wake of a gondola. Opening the window of her room in the Pensione Inghilterra, letting in the watery light reflected from the Giudecca Canal. A conclave of cats wreathing around a wellhead in a piazza. The first taste of the risotto she had for lunch. The vast white bulk of a cruise ship on the San Marco Canal, sliding by in the gap between two buildings. The whir of video cameras inside San Marco.

That was the only way, later, that she knew she'd been to the Basilica. She remembered nothing else about it, or about wherever else she'd been. She had spent most of the day just roaming, speaking to no one but the odd waiter. She was completely unaware of herself, Eleanor Gray, attorney and mother. She was just a pair of eyes, a pair of ears, watching and listening and smelling and tasting and feeling, beneath her feet, the old, worn paving stones of the Venetian alleys and bridges.

But by late afternoon, the trance was wearing off. She became conscious of fatigue, and the ground felt unsteady, as if she'd just disembarked from an ocean voyage. She turned back to the *pensione* to take a nap.

It was easy enough to find, just a few doors down from the church of the Gesuati on the Zattere. The setting sun glowed through the film of cloud, tinting the white marble facade of the church of the Redentore across the Giudecca Canal. The café next door was busy, the tables full of tourists reviewing their days, comparing postcards, rewinding film, easing feet out of their shoes. At the table closest to the door of the *pensione*, a man held a sketch pad on his lap and drew rapidly, looking not at the paper but at the severe symmetrical lines of the Redentore across the water.

As Eleanor drew near, the artist put his pencil down and propped the sketch pad up straight to assess his work.

Eleanor paused, reaching into her bag for her room key, eyes on the sketch. Involuntarily, she smiled. Looked at Palladio's church planted on the silver water. Looked at the sketch, delicate and elegant. Shook her head and smiled at the artist in simple pleasure. "It's lovely," she said, without even thinking to speak Italian.

The artist smiled up at her and looked back at the sketch in satisfaction. "Yes," he said contentedly, "it's very hard to make an ugly drawing in Venice. Do you think I should wash it? Color?"

Without pausing to wonder why this stranger was asking her advice, Eleanor said seriously, "Only if you're sure you won't ruin it."

He reached absently for the wineglass on the table and studied his drawing. "That's always the risk. Still, I think just a blush. . . ." He bent down to open the box of paints on the ground beside him. Eleanor noticed suddenly that he was young and quite attractive.

"Well, good night," she said, grasping her key. "And good luck."

He glanced upward from his paint box. "Good night," he said. His gaze met hers and held it. He smiled again, a small, sweet smile. "Thanks."

For some reason Eleanor felt herself blushing as she went up to her room. And George Sinclair, following her with his eyes, wondered why Harry hadn't mentioned that his sister was incredibly alluring.

By the next morning the jet lag was gone and Eleanor was ready for some serious sightseeing. At college she had been an art history major, and some of her happiest moments with Jared had been the vacations in their early marriage, when they went from museum to art gallery to monument, discussing line and brushwork, iconography and composition. So she went down to breakfast in the waterfront dining room with her guidebook in hand, plotting her itinerary. Maybe San Marco first thing, before the hordes, then a quick spin through the Doge's Palace, then a cup of tea at Florian's. Waiting for her coffee to come, Eleanor glanced around the room. The guests at the *pensione* were, as the name implied, mostly British, with a sprinkling of Americans. Young women just released from their their foreign study programs, a pair of honeymooners, a pleasant-looking foursome in their sixties. Not many tables for one. There was a man sitting by the windows, obviously a professor in his seersucker jacket and bow tie. Eleanor craned to see the cover of the book propped against the breadbasket. Drab olive cloth. Probably Ruskin, she thought. Or a vintage Baedeker. In the far corner of the dining room sat a couple with a little boy. About four, she thought, admiring his silvery blond hair and pale skin. He was studying the waitress, whose voice Eleanor could hear across the clatter of coffee cups and quiet breakfast-time voices: *"Che bellissimo ragazzo!"*

Eleanor thought with a pang of Toby and Simon. Would they have liked Venice? Could she imagine them sitting quietly in this dining room, looking forward to a day of paintings and buildings and sitting still? Hardly. They were much better off with her parents and Harry, messing around in the water, building forts, and catching fish. But maybe she could talk to that little boy later.

As she looked up to see if her coffee was on the way, she saw the artist from yesterday standing in the doorway. He hesitated for a minute, scanning the tables, and she watched him. He was awfully attractive. Not really handsome; his features were a little too craggy for that. Too much nose, too much jaw. All a little larger than life. Thick, strong blond hair. Tall, too. Well over six feet, and sturdily built. It was obvious now why she'd spoken to him in English automatically. He could be nothing but an American in his white cotton shirt and khakis. She wondered how old he was; too young for her, that was sure. There didn't seem to be a woman in the dining room who would quite match up. Or a man, for that matter. Maybe the academic by the window? But no; as she watched, the tall man's eye lit on an empty table for two, and he threaded his way between the tables to reach it. Hurriedly she turned her eyes to her *Blue Guide* as he walked past, conscious that she'd been staring. His girlfriend (he wore no wedding ring; she'd noticed that much the day before) was probably still getting dressed.

But he opened up a folder of papers and by the time Eleanor had finished her rolls, no one had joined him. Which was odd because in Eleanor's experience, men who looked like that inevitably had mates. Thin girls in black with lots of hair or blondes with headbands and big earrings or other young men in starched shirts. Eleanor dismissed the thought of him and went upstairs to get her big shoulder bag for the day's expedition.

It was a surprising day for Venice, clear and dry. There were still puddles between the paving stones where storekeepers had hosed off the street. Eleanor paused on the Accademia Bridge, looking up the Grand Canal to the gray domes of Sta. Maria della Salute, and watched the water of the canal sparkle where the morning sun sliced through the shadows.

In the Piazza S. Marco the pigeons pecked busily in the cracks between paving stones, scavenging for leftovers from the banquets the tourists fed them every day. Eleanor paced slowly to the middle of the piazza, admiring the way the rhythmic procession of arches on either side led the eye so insistently to the confection of domes and spires and arches at the end. Men with briefcases cut purposefully across the corners of the piazza behind her, while a scattered line of pastel-clad sightseers began lumbering toward the Campanile, where someone was waving a bright orange flag. It was time for serious tourism.

Eleanor was an earnest tourist. Inside San Marco she examined statues and paving stones, studied her guidebook, and scrutinized the difference between the medieval and nineteenth-century mosaics. She admired the Pala d'Oro and, with waning enthusiasm, the reliquaries in the Treasury. Then she gave herself a rest at one of the tiny tables at Florian's before starting on the Accademia.

It was probably too much. By eleven-thirty she was looking at a massive Tintoretto with a touch of irritation that had its roots, she recognized, in low blood sugar. There was no point in disliking paintings just because she was hungry, Eleanor thought. Better to come back when she was rested. Looking at her floor plan, she realized that she was halfway through the museum anyway, as close to the exit as to the entrance. So she walked briskly onward, glancing for future reference at the Guardis and Bellinis and Tiepolos. She dimly remembered, from a trip with Jared, a room full of saints on gold backgrounds. There, on the right. She peered in. It was a big room, maybe a former chapel. She walked along one wall, scanning the panels hung against it. Saints. Madonna. Baby Jesus. More saints. The label said "Bartolomeo Vivarini, Polyptych: Nativity and Saints." The irritation resurfaced. *Which* saints? Who was the bald guy in black and white? That was Peter with the keys, obviously, but what about the man holding the model city? Why couldn't they tell you these things?

She turned abruptly for the door and backed away, startled, from the back of a white shirt that was six inches away from her face. Somehow, putting her hand out to avoid bumping into the man from the *pensione*, she jostled his arm. He dropped the manila folder held under his arm and the sketch pad and the pencil, and Eleanor felt her face flaming again as she stooped to pick things up.

"That was incredibly clumsy," she said in a resigned tone, as if she'd been talking about a dancer's unsuccessful pirouette. "Here, do you have everything?" She held out the folder and the sketch pad.

"Yes, I'm sure I do," he answered easily, riffling through the loose pages in the folder. "None of it's priceless anyway." He brushed a little dust off the sketch pad and turned it to show her. "See: your basic saint." He gestured back up at the Vivarini polyptych. "Do you know who he is, by any chance? I'd like to . . ." He took his pencil and rapidly drew a curling banner beneath the stolid saint's feet, then wrote "Saint" in archaic letters in the banner. "Give him a name," he finished.

"Well, that one I think is Saint Peter," Eleanor offered. "Because of the keys."

"Of course, the keys," he agreed, and wrote "Peter" in the banner. "You don't happen to know about the lovely lady with the palm branch?"

Eleanor looked closer. "I know the palm branch means she's a martyr, but that doesn't help much. Sorry."

"What about this one over here?" He gestured to a freestanding panel in the middle of the room. "The one with that iron thing?"

Eleanor grinned. "That's Saint Lawrence and that's his barbecue. That's how he was martyred."

"He was barbecued?" The man was standing in front of the panel drawing quickly, eyes flickering from saint to page and back.

"More or less. I think the story goes that halfway through he said to the men who were doing it 'Gentlemen, I fear the other side is not yet well roasted,' or words to that effect. Of course, he's the patron saint of short-order cooks," she added, relishing the tale.

"Really?" His eyes slid over to look at her, unnoticed.

"Well." For Eleanor, that was often a sentence. It meant *Don't take me literally*. She shrugged a shoulder, which amounted to the same thing.

He seemed to understand. "Do you know any more of them?"

"Um. That's Barbara with the tower, and Catherine with the wheel," Eleanor said, conscious that she was showing off, but enjoying it. "And the one in the animal fur is John the Baptist."

"Oh, right," he said. "How do you know all this?"

"I was an art history major about a million years ago," she said, "and it stuck."

"So was I," he said ruefully, "and it didn't."

"Well, it's hardly useful material," she pointed out.

"It has its points," he said. "For instance, old San Lorenzo here might come in very handy for me. I'm designing frescoes for a restaurant in New York. What could be more appropriate than the patron saint of fast food?"

"Don't quote me on that," Eleanor said, alarmed.

"No," he agreed. "My name's George Sinclair, by the way."

"Eleanor Gray," she said. There was an awkward little pause as they adjusted to this new stage of acquaintanceship. George felt Eleanor withdrawing, starting to step back and mutter something about "see you later," or "must be going."

"I did ruin that sketch," he said, to keep her standing there.

"You did? Oh, I'm so sorry. What did you do to it?" She was relaxing, distracted again.

"Spilled a glass of wine all over it," he said. "Got the color just right and then, splash! it's covered with mediocre Chianti. I never learn," he went on, folding up his sketch pad and gesturing toward the door. "Are you . . . ?"

"Yes," she said, falling into step with him, but still, he sensed, wary. "My eyes are pretty well stunned for the moment."

"Always a problem in Venice. It's very important to allow time for rest. I take a lot of naps when I'm here."

"You do?" Eleanor had never heard a man admit to sleeping during the day.

"Yes. The light's not so good after lunch anyway," George said, unruffled. They had reached the entrance of the museum. "Which way are you going? Would you have lunch with me?" The minute he'd said it he questioned his judgment. It had been an impulsive invitation, but now that he had started talking to Harry's sister, he didn't want to stop. There was something so beguiling about her. Something about intelligence she didn't mind showing, and a physical magnetism she seemed unconscious of. But now she looked startled, and likely to bolt. He went on, pretending that he hadn't noticed her alarm. "I know a very good little restaurant near here that does a wonderful fritto misto for two that I can't manage on my own. Of course, you may not like seafood," he finished.

They were standing outside the Accademia, in the little square in front of the bridge. The sun was beating down directly on the café that sold pizza and ice cream in four languages. Eleanor hesitated, looked around. She took a deep breath and felt annoyed at herself. Why was she so jumpy about a man asking her to have lunch with him?

"That sounds nice," she said temperately. And added, to make up for her lack of enthusiasm, "I love fish."

As they walked to the restaurant, Eleanor tried not to feel uncomfortable. Lunch. It was only lunch with a fellow tourist. An isolated incident. It didn't mean they had to have lunch together every day, or share breakfast tables at the Pensione Inghilterra. It was just lunch. Everybody has to eat. In New York she wouldn't have thought twice about lunch with a man she barely knew. But those lunches, eaten in a suit with a briefcase by her side, Eleanor considered practically business (to the occasional disappointment of a lunch partner who had something more frivolous in mind). Even as she scolded herself, Eleanor recognized the source of her discomfort. The encounter seemed casual, free of significance. Here she was with a chance acquaintance, strolling through the Venetian streets, admiring an iris blooming from a crevice in a wall, lightly discussing the clientele at the *pensione*. But they weren't having lunch to discuss the vagaries of a certain probate ruling or the complexities of the tax code. They were having lunch because—there was no way for Eleanor to avoid the thought—this man seemed to enjoy her company and want more of it. This was a situation that Eleanor had avoided ever since her divorce.

It hadn't been conscious. She had never set out to close herself off from romantic involvement. In fact, she sometimes wondered why it was that no one ever seemed to see her as anything besides an attorney or a mother. In truth, this was the defense she had unconsciously chosen. She could fulfill the responsibilities of those two roles only if she avoided the distractions and weaknesses of love affairs.

But here she was in Venice, alone. Neither attorney nor mother. Faced with an attractive man who seemed attracted to her.

Of course, she was being ludicrous. Even to think that he had anything in mind . . . It was pathetic. Thinking that this man had some kind of romantic agenda, just because they were having lunch together! Eleanor scorned the very idea. She was at least five years older than he was, anyway. It was nonsense. And she tuned in to his story about the time he'd been in Venice during a major flood.

It was, fortunately for George, a story he'd told often and one he could recite with very little concentration. Because as he paced along beside Eleanor, carefully not looking at her, he was planning his next move.

George owed his great success with women to several factors. His looks, attractive but not intimidating, always helped with the initial approach. His open charm put everyone at ease. But his trump card was an almost uncanny sensitivity. He could read tones of voice and shades of movement, even in near-strangers. More than one woman had accused him of reading her mind.

He was certainly reading Eleanor's. And reading, furthermore, between the lines of what Harry had said about his sister. "It would be nice for her to get away from everything," Harry had said. "If she knows you're a friend of mine, she might feel less free." George glanced sidelong at Eleanor, who was clearly not listening to him. Free for what? Free to have a little fling? A little extracurricular romance? It wasn't what Harry had said or even meant, consciously. But George wondered. What else had they been talking about that night? Gretchen and Edith, and Eleanor's leagues of unmarried friends, and women with younger men. One thing was sure, Eleanor looked like a lot more fun than Edith, even if she was, at the moment, awfully tense. She walked along beside him, fading in and out of the conversation, focusing now on him, now on some private argument she was having with herself. As they crossed a bridge she was jostled by a flock of running boys and stumbled. George put out an arm to steady her, and she all but flinched.

"It's just along here," he said to distract her, pointing to a tattered awning tangled with a flourishing grapevine. And he resolved, at that moment, to see if he couldn't get Eleanor Gray to unwind a little bit.

They both would have said lunch went well. There was a table in the courtyard, right next to a trickling fountain inhabited by a family of turtles. The waitress remembered George and asked him (fortunately in idiomatic Italian that Eleanor didn't catch) about the last woman he'd been there with. The wine, on an empty stomach, relaxed Eleanor. George managed to keep the conversation on interesting and completely impersonal topics. He felt Tiepolo was decadent and tried to explain to Eleanor why Tintoretto was superior. He discussed the technical difficulty of fresco painting and his own misgivings about his upcoming fresco commission in New York (omitting his plans for her brother's bedroom wall). Eleanor quizzed him about his career and he managed to avoid suggesting that she visit his studio in New York. Mentioning any thought of future meetings New York, he intuited, would be a mistake. They ate the excellent fritto misto, and George noticed with approbation that Eleanor had no squeamishness about the little bits of calamari that looked like tentacles. (Edith had been a strict vegetarian.)

As they waited for coffee, George stretched out on the rickety folding chair and studied Eleanor. She was watching the turtles pursue their inscrutable turtle business in the moss of the fountain. Shadows from the grapevine shifted and flickered over her white blouse, while the sun caught her bare arm, resting on the tablecloth. George looked at the freckles on her arm and the milky, private stretch above the elbow as it disappeared into her sleeve. He had a sudden strong urge to reach out and touch that skin, just the inside of her arm, with the back of his finger, the way a parent strokes a baby's cheek. He looked around for the waitress and drained his wineglass.

"We had turtles, growing up," Eleanor announced. She looked up, nothing in her eyes now but friendly interest. "They were prettier than this. Green and yellow. I never liked to hold them, though, because of the way their little claws felt on my hands."

"I know the ones you mean. We had big brown box turtles because I grew up in the country. We'd find them by the side of the road and make homes for them, but they always got boring after a few weeks, so we'd take them back to the lake." George glanced up at the waitress who delivered his coffee, and looked back at Eleanor. "Once you get used to the way they hide in their shells, they aren't all that interesting."

Eleanor smiled at the waitress and stirred her coffee. "No. I think maybe it's the idea of being a turtle: you know, bask in the sun, take a little dip, bask some more." She yawned behind her hand. "A little nap in the sun sounds so appealing. I haven't really adjusted to the time zone yet."

"You should go back and sleep for a little while now," George suggested. "Then by tonight you'll be on Italian time."

"Yes, I think I will," Eleanor said, bending down to get the map from her bag. "Now, which way should I go?"

"I'll walk you back," George offered. "I was going to go out to the Lido for a swim and my bathing suit is in my room." He gestured for the check.

"Well, that would be a help," Eleanor confessed, "since I don't even know where we are."

"Here." George leaned over, removing the map from her hands and refolding it. He spread it out in front of her and pointed. "And this is where the *pensione* is." He pointed again.

"So we go like this," Eleanor said, tracing the route with a finger.

"No," George said, and without thinking, took her hand to show her. "We'll go this way, by the Ca'Rezzonico."

It was a mistake. It was a tiny unconsidered gesture, but for Eleanor it was still too much. Cheeks flaming, she pulled her hand away, then tried to pretend she was straightening out the map. Fortunately the waitress arrived with the check and diversion.

Eleanor pulled out her wallet and craned over to see the bill. She pulled out two ten-thousand-lire notes and put them on the tablecloth. "That looks about right," she said, and George could hear the echo of countless business lunches in dark restaurants near Wall Street. It was prosaic, completely unromantic. George didn't like it. But he let it pass. If splitting a lunch bill would calm Eleanor down, he'd split the bill. So he put down his ten-thousand-lire notes and stood up, waiting while Eleanor stuffed the map back in her bag.

They walked peacefully back to the *pensione*. Eleanor was rather pleased with herself. She'd had an enjoyable lunch. There'd been no fuss over paying, which eliminated any uncomfortable obligations. She was going to take a nap. The early-afternoon light would glow against the shutters and the shipping noises from the Giudecca Canal would float up gently and she would drift off into a deep sleep.

She and George got their keys at the desk and started up the wide staircase. "Do you take a vaporetto out to the Lido?" Eleanor asked, to be polite and avoid the vacuum of silence.

"Yes," George's voice came from behind her. "The water isn't very clean, but I love to sunbathe." They reached the second floor and turned along her hall. "My room's at the end," he said.

"This is me," Eleanor paused outside her door. "That was fun. I hope you don't get sunburned." She put the big old-fashioned key into the lock and turned it.

"Wait," George said. "I have a favor to ask. Do you think—" He paused and looked down at the key in his hand. He felt awkward and was suddenly aware of the difference in their ages. "Could I draw you?" He looked back up and met her eyes.

For the second time in an hour, Eleanor blushed. She could feel the color rising and flooding her cheeks, and the consciousness of it made her embarrassment worse. Her hands went to her throat in an old gesture of disclaimer. "Me? Draw me? I don't think . . . What for?" she stammered.

George shrugged. Because I like the way your jaw meets your throat. Because the hair springs away from your temples. Because I think under that gauzy skirt you have the body of a goddess. Because you are going to lie on that bed in the heat of the afternoon alone. "Because," he said, "you have interesting features."

Eleanor raised her eyebrows. "I do?"

"Uh-huh," George said. "And I'd like to see if I can catch the blue lights in your hair."

"Blue lights?" Eleanor said, pulling forward a lock of hair and frowning at it in puzzlement.

"Yes," he said. "You don't have to decide now. I'll be downstairs having a drink between six and seven. Just come and tell me. You're swaying on your feet; go sleep." And he gently turned her around and urged her through her door before striding down the hall to fetch his bathing suit.

8

Eleanor slept. The sun crept around and turned yellow, then golden. She muttered and flung out an arm, then sank back into the pillows. George, returning sunburned and salty from the Lido, couldn't resist pressing his ear to her door. He heard her cough lightly and imagined opening the door and stepping in, but continued down the hall instead to take a lukewarm shower. By six o'clock he was back downstairs with his sketchbook. At six-thirty, Eleanor came and sat down opposite him.

She felt wonderful. She'd slept profoundly, the kind of deep cushioned sleep she remembered from pregnancy. When she woke up she simply stretched and lay in bed for a while, watching the reflected sunlight from the canal flickering silently on the shutters. She dressed and brushed her hair, thinking about the "blue lights." Then, picking up her bag, she went out for a stroll along the Zattere.

The brilliance of the morning, surprisingly, had held. The long shadows on the pavement were dark and solid, the details on the Redentore's facade perfectly clear. Eleanor walked, looking at the water, marveling at the way it slapped against the edge of the pavement. Just—water, then sidewalk. It seemed so incongruous, such an odd juxtaposition. In America there would have been all kinds of safety regulations and barriers with slats no more than two and a half inches apart lest babies get their heads stuck. Eleanor looked at her watch and turned back toward the *pensione*. It was a wonder that Venetian children weren't constantly falling into the drink.

As she walked back along the Zattere, Eleanor considered George Sinclair's proposition. When he'd made it, she had been taken aback. She hated thinking about her appearance. She hated having pictures taken or having her hair cut, all those minutes in front of a mirror with nowhere else to look. But she was powerfully curious. If he drew her, what would the drawing be like? Would he capture or reveal qualities she hadn't guessed at? Like the "blue lights," only psychological?

And so, when she sat down opposite George in the café, her first words were, "Why not?"

"Why not what?" George asked, startled. Had she read *his* mind? For he had been sitting with his wineglass, mapping out various avenues of approach. A dinner together, Piazza S. Marco at midnight, holding hands? Or maybe music? A box at La Fenice and a kiss during a Puccini aria? A drawing session that turned into love in the afternoon? Why not?

"I'll pose for you," Eleanor said, a little shyly now. "If you really want." But suddenly it seemed a little less simple. She had forgotten, walking along the Zattere, how compelling he was. Very male. Virile, Eleanor thought wryly, was the word the romance novels would use. She noticed for the first time the gold hair on the backs of his arms and glistening at his throat where he'd left the buttons of his shirt undone. And he was big, solid. Jared, who was fine-boned, had weighed less than she did. It always made her feel like a cow. George Sinclair could probably pick her up and throw her over his shoulder. Not that she'd want him to, Eleanor told herself hurriedly. She said, "You don't want to do it now, do you?"

In reply, George, now in tune with her, held up his sketch pad. "Have a drink and talk to me and don't think about what I'm doing."

"That's likely," Eleanor answered tartly. "When you're sitting there going scratch scratch scratch and telling me not to move my mouth."

George waved at the waiter. "I don't go scratch scratch; I'm using pastels. And you can move your mouth as much as you want. I'm not painting your portrait for the Royal Academy," he said. "Do you want to drink this? It's a Bardolino, pretty dry. Or white wine?"

"No, that would be fine," Eleanor said, now nervously eyeing the box of pastels George placed on the table. Even as he asked the waiter for another glass of wine, he was selecting his color, a russet brown.

"I don't think I've seen a box of pastels since I took studio art in high school," she said, fascinated. "Could I look at them?"

"Sure. Here," George said, tearing a piece of paper out of the middle of the pad. "You draw too."

"I can't draw," Eleanor said, as if he'd been stupid.

"You don't have to draw a picture *of* anything," George answered patiently. "Just play with the colors. Here." He pushed the box into the center of the table. "They feel great on the paper. Just laying the color down, the way it strokes the page. And they're so responsive, you get such a range of texture by pressing hard or like a feather."

Eleanor reached out for the box. It wasn't new: some of the sticks were worn halfway down, and the lining of the box was covered with flecks like confetti where the pastels had rubbed off. But the colors were sorted carefully from brown at one end to black at the other, shading through red and orange, yellow to green to blue and purple, just like a rainbow.

"You're very neat, aren't you?" she said, selecting a stick of fuchsia that had never been used. It had a pleasant cool powdery feeling. "And you don't much care for hot colors." She took out a pristine tangerine stick and a parrot green one.

"Matisse I'm not," George said, watching as she drew the corner of the green pastel across her page. The waiter put down her wineglass unnoticed. George shifted his chair around to get a better view of her neck. "Do you ever wear your hair up?" he asked abruptly.

Eleanor looked up, startled. It sounded vaguely creepy, like the kind of question an obscene caller would ask.

George, drawing, was unaware. "If you could just knot it somehow, I could get the line of your neck. . . ."

"I thought it was my hair you wanted to draw," Eleanor said a bit sharply.

"That was before you bent over so gracefully," George responded, with half his mind on the paper before him.

It was the only kind of compliment Eleanor trusted. "So gracefully," as if it were a matter of incontrovertible fact. He wasn't even aware of what he'd said. He wasn't being sweet or charming or trying to make time with her. He was concentrating on his drawing and the line of her neck. She bent down to her bag on the ground beside her and pulled it onto her lap. Somewhere, floating around the bottom, were some hairpins or combs or something. Her fingers closed around a lipstick, her little camera, a toy car, a Tampax, a subway token, a throat drop, and four of the fat tortoiseshell hairpins she bought at Caswell-Massey for a small fortune. She placed them on the table and put her bag back on the ground.

George reached out and took one, fascinated. "These are *wonderful!* I've never seen such beautiful hairpins." He held one up to the light. "Are they real tortoiseshell?"

"Probably not," Eleanor said, both her hands raised behind her as she twisted her hair. George hurriedly turned a page over and sketched the outline of her arms, thinking of Degas and Mary Cassatt. "Isn't real tortoiseshell illegal or cruel to endangered species or something? They kind of remind me of Mary Poppins or some sadistic German fraulein in orthopedic shoes," Eleanor went on, picking up another one and thrusting it into the coil on the back of her head. "But they're the only thing that holds my hair." She reached over and picked up the last one. "Which there is far too much of anyway," she finished, shoving the last pin through the knot and confirming with her fingers that it felt secure.

"It amazes me the way women can do things like that," George said, flipping back to his first drawing. "Put their hair up without looking. Braiding, too." He shook his head. "It's all I can do to tie my sneakers, and women can braid their hair at the backs of their heads just by touch."

Eleanor picked up the tangerine pastel and drew a broad line on the page, then examined the sharp corner she'd just worn down. "Men shave, though."

"Shaving's not an accomplishment, it's a chore," George said, happily tracing the line her neck resumed as she drew.

"Well," Eleanor said. "Tying a tie."

"Anyone can tie a tie. I bet you can tie a tie," George said. He switched colors, dextrously picking out a well-worn umber.

"True."

"And a bow tie. Or a black tie. In fact," George said, looking up, "I'm willing to bet your mother always ties your father's tie when he wears a tuxedo."

Eleanor laughed, picturing her father and mother standing before the mirror over the fireplace in the Chester living room, Frances in navy blue lace, Hart in the boxy old tuxedo he'd bought at Yale. Hart would stand in front with Frances behind, peering over his shoulder to make sure the ends of the black silk bow tie were even.

"Can you tie a bow tie?" she asked.

"I make a point of it," George answered. "But it's always crooked and I end up tweaking it all night." What really happened was that women straightened it out for him, but he didn't feel it would be tactful to say this.

"You could always untie it at a given point in the evening," Eleanor offered. "Like Tom Jones."

"And unbutton my shirt to my diaphragm as well," George said. "But what would I do with my studs?"

"Give them to some young lovely to hold," Eleanor suggested. "Though tuxedos do have enough pockets for any number of studs."

"And young lovelies tend to have no pockets at all," George said. "Not that I wear a tuxedo often," he added, anxious to correct her image of him. If there was anything he wasn't, it was the kind of man who spent his evening dolled up with young blondes in skimpy party dresses. It seemed important that she know this.

"Oh, of course," Eleanor said gravely. "Being an artist. Black turtlenecks and bars on Avenue A at two A.M."

"Not even that, I'm afraid," George said, though he'd seen his share of bars on Avenue A under the influence of Edith. "There. That's a start." He tore off the top sheet and showed it to her.

Eleanor took the page proffered across the table. It was not, somehow, what she had expected. She'd thought to sit there for a while, and at the end there would be a . . . *picture*. Something that was recognizably her, in her green linen dress, possibly with the Redentore sparsely indicated in the background. She took a sip of wine, not noticing that George had already turned over the next sheet of paper and was drawing again.

It wasn't what she had expected, nor was it a view of herself that she ordinarily saw. And yet there was something about it. It really was just a picture of the line of her neck, and her hair, swept up, and her ear. But she knew it was her own. She recognized it the way you recognize yourself, with a start, in an oddly placed mirror. It was a beautiful little drawing but at the same time completely matter-of-fact. It said, "This is what this woman's neck looks like. It happens to be beautiful, but if it were not I would show that, too."

It occurred to Eleanor that George Sinclair was a very good artist, and any tendency she might have had to patronize him because he was younger than she was evaporated.

They sat there for about half an hour. George drew isolated parts of Eleanor and showed her each drawing as he finished. Her arm resting on the table, her feet in their sandals, her hand curled around the wineglass. He did not flatter her. Her feet, she commented, looked like the feet of a peasant in a Brueghel (which was a bit unfair), and there was something a little unnerving about the abrupt foreshortening of her hand and arm in the wineglass drawing. But they were brilliantly done. There was no clumsiness in any of them. Eleanor was quite sober when George shuffled them together and put all the pastels back in the box.

"That wasn't so painful, was it?" he asked.

"No. But I do feel odd. You're very good, aren't you?" she asked. "Seriously."

George looked up and his eyes met hers. "Yes. I'm a good draftsman," he said. "It's my great gift. I'm not so good at color. I have to work much harder at it."

"Still," she said, draining her glass. "I'm very impressed."

"I'm glad," he answered simply, and tucked a few folded lire bills under the base of his wineglass. "I have to run; I just noticed the time." He stood up and paused. "Thank you very much," he said.

"You're welcome," she responded, and watched as he sprinted into the *pensione*. The waiter came over and deftly scooped the money into his pocket, leaving a few smaller bills and some coins. Eleanor looked at them and at the sheet of paper in front of her, streaked with fuchsia and parrot green. Then she stood up and shouldered her bag, heading off in search of some dinner, wondering about George Sinclair.

George's hasty departure hadn't been planned, but it was a master stroke. Eleanor wondered over and over again, as she ate her pizza and listened to chamber music at the Palazzo Falier, what it all meant. Over and over again, she caught herself thinking about him and was annoyed. She gazed up at the ceiling where a clumsy nineteenth-century (she judged) hand had attempted to suggest the clouds of a Tiepolo and managed only a barrage of undercooked meringues. She stared at the woman in front of her, who bobbed her head to the music and whispered during the adagio sections. When the concert was over she strolled back to the *pensione*, eating an ice-cream cone on the way, and wondered if she would see George Sinclair the next day. She watched for him at breakfast and mentally rehearsed the friendly but detached greeting she would give him. When he didn't appear, she went off to the Scuola San Rocco and tried to appreciate Tintoretto properly, but failed. Returning to the Accademia, she lingered in front of the pastel portraits by Rosalba Carriera, studying the highlights and layers of color. Pastel, she concluded, was not really George Sinclair's medium.

By midday she had worked herself into a tizzy. She would catch herself imagining another encounter, maybe another sketching session, and tell herself brutally that he must have a girlfriend in New York. She would mull over bits of their conversation and remember that she was almost forty. She looked for him in the crowds and laughed at herself for it. Finally, sitting exhausted on a chair at the back of SS Giovanni e Paolo, Eleanor faced up to herself. She was developing a crush on George Sinclair. She was strongly attracted to him and her imagination, without any encouragement at all, was barging along inventing scenarios of a romantic Venetian interlude. It wasn't stopping at sketching sessions and having lunch: it was suggesting lengthy kisses on arched bridges as the water lapped below, those strong-looking hands— Never mind, Eleanor told herself. She stretched out her legs and rubbed her face. The immense space of the church dwarfed her and she felt weary. She closed her eyes and let her head hang back. The verger, shuffling by, wondered if she was feeling faint and he was going to have to launch into the silly routine of slapping cheeks that he had to perform almost daily at the peak of summer. But she hitched her bag firmly onto her lap and, relieved, he ambled over to the Bellini polyptych, where the lights seemed to be out of order again.

It was all so depressing. This was what you got, Eleanor told herself, for letting your imagination get out of hand. George Sinclair had no doubt really wanted to eat fried fish for lunch. And draw her damned neck. The memory of that instant when he took her hand after lunch surfaced, but Eleanor brushed it away. It hadn't meant anything. If you went through life reading attraction in that kind of thing, you'd be in trouble. Like this: sitting in the back of a church full of masterpieces, mooning about some artist who was six or seven years your junior. And as Eleanor had been irritated the day before by her shyness toward George, now she was annoyed by her interest in him.

"Grow up," Eleanor muttered, heaving herself to her feet. He hadn't even suggested another meeting, she told herself savagely. She was being ridiculous again.

If another day had gone by before she saw George, she would probably have had her feelings under control. She had had the upper hand over them for so long. Another day of quashing her wayward imagination and telling herself how old she was would have restored her defenses. She was, in fact, well on her way as she stood at the vaporetto station on the Grand Canal. It was what passed for Venice's rush hour; several boats stopped at her station without having room for more than one person, and she wasn't quick enough to get on board. She used the time wisely, standing in the glowing sunset haze, scolding herself and making stern resolutions about blitzkrieg sightseeing. She actually had her head in her *Blue Guide* when the next boat pulled up and a hand reached out to help her on board. A strong hand. Tanned, with golden hairs on the wrist and arm, and a Timex watch worn face inward. She had a sinking feeling as she looked up and closed her guidebook, and let the hand haul her onto the boat. It pulled her between a pair of gray-suited businessmen to a tiny space in the center of the boat's cabin, where George stopped, facing her. As the driver increased speed, Eleanor stumbled. George reached up and steadied himself with a hand on the ceiling.

"Just hang on to me," he said, "if you feel unsteady. You look tired. You were standing there drooping on the dock, like a plant that needs water."

"Long day," Eleanor said, "and I thought I'd never get on a boat, they were all so full." Someone behind leaned steadily against her, pushing her forward. She tried to brace herself and push back, but had to take a step toward George.

"I'm sorry," she said, pulling on the shoulder straps of her bag and trying to stand up straight, "someone behind me is— Oh!" A foot had come down hard on her instep, and she gasped. To her left, a beige suit wormed its way to the stern. She swayed and caught George's arm. "Damn!" she said, reaching down to assess the damage. Her instep was tender, and she could feel tiny patches where the skin had been broken.

"Are you okay?" he asked, raising his voice over the din of the motor as the vaporetto picked up speed. The arm she'd been holding was around her shoulders.

She nodded, straightening up. People pressed against her on every side, swaying with the boat's slight roll. George didn't move his arm. His hand was at the back of her neck. The thumb, only the thumb, moved softly upward until it met her hairline. All around them the chatter went on, in German and French and American English. The boat's motor chugged slower as it neared the next station. Eleanor didn't feel she could look George in the face.

As the boat came to a halt, he put his other arm down. It came to a rest very naturally with a hand on her hip. Eleanor took a deep breath. The crowd shifted and jostled. An enormous knapsack jammed into her back, squeezing her closer still to George; chest to chest, thigh to thigh. As if they were dancing.

She could see, inches away from her eyes, an artery throbbing in his neck. Then his hand brushed the hair aside from her ear, and she heard his voice say, "Excuse me, I need to kiss you." And before she had time to think, his mouth was on hers. Not urgently. It was a gentle, friendly kiss. With a hint of something else in reserve.

Then the boat pulled away from the dock. Eleanor's eyes flew open and she looked up at George, astonished. "What was that all about?" she said, without thinking.

George smiled a little sheepishly. "I'm sorry. I've been thinking about you all day and then to have you materialize like that and you were so close to me . . . I'm sorry," he repeated. "Well, I'm not, really."

Eleanor looked around the boat. Out the window the facades of the Grand Canal were slipping by. The sky was almost white, tinged with apricot. She could smell whatever it was that George used, aftershave or something, just faintly.

"I . . ." she began, but couldn't think of what to say. She lifted his hand from where it rested on her hip. It was warm and dry. She touched the fingertips, where the nails were clipped short. There were a few hairs on the backs of the fingers. "At least you don't have sweaty palms," she thought, then realized she'd said it out loud.

"And if there were ever a time for sweaty palms . . ." George agreed, and leaned over to kiss her a bit briskly on the forehead. "The crowd should thin at this stop." And indeed at the Rialto Bridge enough people got off so that they could actually move aft and stand at the stern rail. It was very noisy outside. George considered putting his arm around Eleanor again, but decided against it. After all, she hadn't reacted, one way or another, to his kiss. She might be appalled, think he was some horny lout, not much better than a pervert, getting his jollies in a crowd. But George didn't think so. There had been great promise in the way she took his hand.

They got off the boat together at the Accademia stop and turned toward the *pensione*. George waited for Eleanor to say something.

They had reached the little Campo S. Agnese before she

turned to him and said, "I don't know what I'm supposed to say. Or do. Or anything."

"Well," George said, "I don't think you have to say or do anything. I mean, there it is. I find you enormously attractive and I would like to go to bed with you right this minute, but that's not, I mean . . ." He trailed off.

"It's not exactly the same as a friendly acquaintanceship," Eleanor pointed out mildly.

"No," said George.

"And we just met," stated Eleanor.

"Yes," said George.

"You know," said Eleanor, "this is going to sound ridiculous, but I don't even know how these things are supposed to happen anymore."

"Well, we could go up to my room," suggested George, a little surprised, "and put out the Do Not Disturb sign. . . ."

"That's not what I mean," said Eleanor. "I mean . . ." She paused for a long time. They had reached the Zattere. They turned and walked toward the church of the Gesuati. "I don't know what I mean."

"I do," George said. "I think. Usually people hop into bed first and talk afterward. If they talk at all. Is that it?"

"Yes," Eleanor said, relieved. "Let's sit down for a minute." She sat on the white marble steps of the church, and George settled down next to her. "This all seems so unusual."

"I think you could say it's unusual," George agreed. "But the etiquette of sex has always been a mystery to me."

Eleanor didn't answer. A pair of seagulls whom they'd disturbed resumed patrolling the pavement. A loud thump inside the church behind them seemed to indicate a door being locked.

"Look," said George finally. "I don't want to talk you into something you don't want to do. But could I urge you not to think too much about it? Look," he said again, and gestured, "look at how beautiful this all is. It's a dream. Couldn't you just go along with it?"

Eleanor sighed. A damp little breeze lifted a curl from her

forehead. What, she wondered, would she regret more afterward? Sleeping with him? Or saying no?

There was no question. Without a word, without even looking at him, she put her hand in his and leaned against him.

"It'll be okay," he said, kissing her on the temple. "I promise."

9

It was, as George had said, a dream. They walked hand in hand back to the *pensione*, Eleanor only faintly aware of the usual gathering in the café, the barges hooting on the canal, the recurring breeze that swirled her skirt around her legs. She didn't notice the carefully impassive face of the man behind the desk as they asked for their room keys. She floated along up the stairs, willing herself to think only of sensation, George's hand against hers, but as they reached the landing she felt herself hanging back, hesitant.

So did George. "Cold feet?" he asked, turning toward her.

She nodded and dropped his hand. "I can't do this," she said, shaking her head. "I just can't."

George looked down at her, patient. "Right this minute? Or ever?"

"Right this minute. And maybe not ever."

"Well, look," he said reasonably. "Could we talk about it? Not standing here in the hall?"

She looked up at him gratefully. He wasn't furious. He wasn't going to stamp off down the hall in a huff and avoid her for the rest of the week. He was at least willing to listen to her qualms. "Sure." She nodded and turned to open the door to her room.

George stood while she put down her bag and opened the windows, letting in the breeze to tease at the curtains and bedspreads. She paused for a minute, watching a man down below throw a stick for his dog, then sat on the bed with her feet up.

"This is very awkward," she said with a sigh. "I'm too old for this kind of thing. Sit, it makes it worse when you loom over me."

George hesitated. Sit where? Next to her on the bed? To put a reassuring arm around her? Or on the rickety-looking desk chair, to make it all seem cool and detached? He compromised, perching on the end of the bed with his hands in his lap.

Eleanor leaned back against the pillows and closed her eyes. How could she possibly explain? There was no way to put all her doubts and fears into words. She hadn't slept with anyone since Jared left. She was unsure about her power to attract. She was uncomfortable in the long-forgotten role of temptress. She was acutely aware of her size-twelve hips.

"You know," remarked George, "I do understand that this is all a bit hasty." He paused, considering what to say. In all of his experience with women, he had never found himself in this position. With Eleanor, as with all shy women, he would have used a tactful approach. A comfortable, friendly prologue, the subtlest intimation of desire, a gradual seduction. To put it bluntly, he wouldn't have expected to get her into bed until Thursday at the earliest. But here it was Monday, and his cover was blown. He looked over at Eleanor and found her eyes on him, full of wary intelligence. And the instinct that so often guided him prompted a confession. "I want to go to bed with you. I was even planning how to go about it. But I hadn't planned to be so . . ." words failed him for a moment and he gestured helplessly. "I guess I jumped the gun," he finished.

He fell silent, and without thinking laid a hand on her leg, stretched out on the bed next to him. He stroked the skin, feeling the faint bristle that indicated she must have shaved her legs just a few days earlier. He had a fleeting image of Eleanor nude in the tub, bending over an outstretched leg, another Degas. He put his hand back in his lap, discouraged. This whole thing didn't seem to be going well.

He was annoyed at himself. In just two days Harry's casual suggestion that he "keep an eye out for" Eleanor had taken on a life of its own. His interest in Eleanor, piqued at the Accademia, had deepened into fascination. He was attracted to her in a way that was unfamiliar and a little unnerving.

Physically, he thought Eleanor was magnificent. He had never had a taste for the slender, well-tuned bodies that were so fashionable in New York. Edith he'd found actually scrawny. Eleanor had curves you could subside into. She had oceans of hair and a kind of languid unhurried grace. He had always hankered after the kinds of bodies you saw in Baroque paintings. And here, lying on the bed in front of him, disguised in a rumpled green linen dress, was a splendid example. He could just imagine Eleanor on canvas, dressed in nothing more than a string of pearls, with perhaps a swath of golden satin draped artistically over her pubis. And Cupid leering behind her.

Besides, she was smart. George's several previous girlfriends had been so dull that he'd begun to suspect cynically that boredom was a necessary corollary to sex. Harry had given him grief about this, and George had complained about how hard it was to find an intelligent woman in his milieu. But Eleanor wasn't boring.

By the end of their lunch together, he wanted to take her to bed. Repeatedly. And talk to her a lot in the interim. And ask her questions. He would have loved to ask about her job, to get a glimpse of the highly competent professional she must be. He had to stifle the urge to ask her about her sons, because he wasn't supposed to know they existed. He wanted to spend his spare hours with her. So he worked out a little scenario of seduction (to put it bluntly). A dinner, an afternoon on the beach, a good-night kiss, and so on.

And then, standing next to her in the vaporetto, with her hand on his arm, a sheen of moisture on her collarbone, her breasts visible when she bent down to nurse her injured foot—he'd lost it. Her proximity, the quasi-intimacy forced on them by the crowd had simply overwhelmed him and he had abandoned all his caution to gratify a momentary whim. Which had, he reflected sourly, been provocative rather than actually gratifying. Kissing Eleanor on the boat had only made him want her more. But he might have scared her away for good. George looked down and found he was cracking his knuckles.

"The best-laid plans?" said Eleanor. She put her head to one side and added, "You know, it is such a *relief* that you're being so honest. Can I make a suggestion? Could we just go back to plan A? I mean, I know what you have in mind and in principle I'm all for it." She fell silent and steeled herself for a confession of her own. "I would like to sleep with you." She looked at him steadily. "But not yet. I just met you yesterday. I have nothing against the idea of a little Venetian idyll, but—"

George broke in, smiling. "I'm old enough to appreciate deferred gratification," he said. "Do you have plans for tonight?" She shook her head. "Good. We'll have dinner together. Shall we meet downstairs around seven?" She nodded again, with a smile of her own. George stood up. He bent down, with one hand on either side of her shoulders. He kissed her gently, and at some length. When he broke away she was breathing faster, and she didn't move as he left the room, except to follow him with her eyes.

Harry, meanwhile, wondered if George had actually met Eleanor. And if he had, what had ensued. He had in fact begun to regret suggesting that George look out for Eleanor. He had mentioned his sister thinking that George might provide a little amusement for her. But what he didn't want was his sister providing a little amusement for George. It had been weeks now since George had broken up with Edith, weeks of painting and teaching and little else. By now George was sure to be horny as hell, Harry thought. And Eleanor—well, Eleanor cut loose in Venice might be a sitting duck. Harry had seen George operate. He had observed and envied George's gift at making women feel singled out. And if George chose to turn his charm on Eleanor, could she possibly resist?

The problem was that Eleanor was so vulnerable, Harry thought. So precariously balanced. George could take a little Italian fling in stride, put it in place next to the fine meals and magnificent pictures that made for a pleasant vacation. But Eleanor, who hadn't had a date in five years—how could she not take sex seriously? Harry told himself he was being fanciful—plotting, as Eleanor herself would have said. Maybe he didn't have to worry. George was so much younger than El. Maybe she'd automatically adopt a maternal tone with him and treat him like a larger version of Toby. Maybe they hadn't even met. The chances that they were getting involved, he told himself, were extremely slim.

Harry got up and walked to the window. It was a foggy day. A dank white shroud had dropped over the Sound. The outlines of the end of the dock were blurred by the mist, and everything dripped. The house was quiet. Frances and Hart had taken the boys to Groton, where someone Hart knew from Yale, now a retired admiral, was going to show them around the submarines.

Harry was surprised that his mother had chosen to go. She couldn't have cared less about submarines and had never made a secret of her dislike of this particular classmate, whom Hart still called, in unguarded moments, "Porky." The nickname had its roots in some undergraduate uncouthness, which Frances maintained had not been completely outgrown. She surely hadn't gone for Hart's company. Whatever detente had flickered the night of the anniversary party had since frozen over into strained civility. His parents, Harry realized, were delighted to have their grandsons visiting because this meant they didn't have to talk to each other. Now it occurred to him (correctly) that by going to Groton Frances was being conciliatory.

Hart, too, had been startled. They had been at the dinner table the night before, discussing which car to take, when she calmly said, "I'd like to come, too." Hart looked across the table at her in surprise. No one else noticed her tiny nod, and certainly no one saw the relaxation of the lines around Hart's mouth, for he opened it right away to shovel in a mouthful of stew.

Now, trailing along behind the menfolk in the cramped, stuffy quarters of the submarine, Frances was having her regrets. It had seemed like a good idea last night, when she'd proposed coming along. Maybe she wasn't making enough of an effort to share things with Hart. Maybe they could reconnect somehow if she took an interest in what he was doing. So here she was, fighting claustrophobia and pulling the muscles in her neck as she tried not to yawn. The boys, of course, were thrilled. They quizzed Porky (whom they called "Admiral" with gusto) endlessly about battles and torpedoes. Simon was disappointed that there were no windows to see the fish, but Hart had suggested stopping at the Mystic Aquarium on the way home. Belatedly, he glanced back at Frances to confirm that they could. She shrugged. Why not? It had to be more interesting than this.

And besides, the boys would love it.

Hart was in his element with his grandsons. He had time for the most rambling of Simon's stories or the most penetrating of Toby's questions, and he was inventive about entertaining them. He hadn't spoken to Porky Creighton in years, but the boys had been arguing about boats and within minutes of Toby's mentioning submarines, Hart was on the phone to Groton.

Hart had been that way with their children, Frances remembered. He'd built wonderful creations for them. A tree house, a thrilling rope swing. A puppet theater. He was particularly good about accepting each child on his or her own merits. It was obvious, of course, that he had a soft spot for Eleanor, who in some ways was really like an elder son, following in his footsteps. But he'd supported Harry's unconventional career choice with enthusiasm. If only he'd been a little more responsive to his wife lately, Frances couldn't help thinking bitterly. It didn't occur to her that the children's needs had always been obvious, while she went to some lengths to hide her own.

Finally, the tour was done. And Frances felt her good intentions were being rewarded when Creighton looked at his watch and said, "I'd love to show you all around a little more, but I'm afraid I've got to be off to the doctor's." So amid honest exclamations about how fast their bodies were falling apart and false declarations of intent to "get all four of us together, I know Gloria would love to see you," they parted.

The boys sat in the back of the car, silent. Toby's mind was full of heroic seamen and evil black-painted enemy subs. Simon wondered if you *could* make a submarine with windows, and set about designing one in his head.

In front, Frances rolled down her window as they pulled out of the parking lot.

"Do you want the a.c.?" Hart asked.

"No, fresh air."

Hart nodded. A minute or two went by. As they pulled onto I-95, Frances rolled her window up.

"Porky Creighton's an amazing bore," Hart remarked.

Frances, staring straight ahead, smiled slightly. At least they could agree about something. "He certainly is," she said. "Shall we try to find a place to eat at Mystic?"

The morning after the vaporetto incident Eleanor woke up with a feeling of immense anticipation. She was aware of the excitement before she could analyze its source. But in an instant, she remembered. George. She couldn't help smiling. It was just such a heavenly feeling. She would see George today. He had some sketching he needed to do in the morning in the Scuola San Rocco. She was going to Ca'Rezzonico. But they were going to meet in the afternoon and go to Torcello. Then spend the evening together.

Dinner had been—"piquant," as George put it. Some of the time she actually forgot about the afternoon. George had quizzed her about becoming a lawyer when she was so interested in art, had gotten her to talk about why she loved the law, which was one aspect of her life Eleanor was uncharacteristically reticent about. Trading confidence for confidence, George talked about being an artist in New York, about his friends and college classmates making huge sums of money while he was still living in a rented loft with no assets beyond a three-month supply of blank canvases.

"My mother," he confessed, "keeps wondering when I am going to become respectable. My father talks a lot about Wallace Stevens."

"They all talk about Wallace Stevens," Eleanor said, shaking her head. "Next time, mention T. S. Eliot. Didn't working in a bank give him a nervous breakdown?"

"Did it? My father will never know the difference. I'll try it."

"Do they come and see you often?"

"They do, to give them credit," George answered. "They enjoy a little taste of *la vie de bohème*. And my branch of bohemia is not very scary."

"Where is your loft?"

"Reade Street. Tribeca. Lonely at night, but safe."

"Oh, sure, I know where that is. My office is nearby. Isn't there a store that sells glass eyes for stuffed animals on Reade Street?"

"Right," George said, smiling. "With little trays in the window, brown and green and black, and a stuffed otter."

"Are you sure? I could have sworn it was a fox, with one foot on a branch and its tail stuck out behind."

"No, that was several years ago. It's an otter now. I live right across the street from it. You should come and see me."

"I don't know," said Eleanor, suddenly somber. "I have a feeling this is just a shipboard romance."

George was silent for a moment. "I know. But it doesn't *have* to be." And he took her hand, and just the contact of his palm on hers made her throb, in all the private places.

They kissed on the way home, of course. Necked, actually, if you wanted to be crude. Lying in bed the next morning, Eleanor grinned to herself, remembering that stumbling stop-and-go progress. Once, as George pressed her against the parapet of a bridge, Eleanor had gasped, laughing, "This is such a cliché!" and George muttered into her neck, "Clichés get that way for a reason." But as they got closer to the *pensione*, the kissing got more temperate. As their beds (and Bed, Eleanor thought) loomed nearer and nearer, they were careful to turn down the heat. They actually parted at Eleanor's door with a quick kiss, but it was the quick kiss of two people who don't dare linger.

Eleanor would have slept with him right then, George thought. He stood at his window listening to the water lap against the pavement. She would have slept with him, but it seemed better to wait. He wanted desire to overwhelm all her reservations. Because if she had any beforehand, they'd come back in triplicate afterward. Reservations and remorse, George knew, nearly always surfaced the morning after. And he didn't want Eleanor to feel remorseful. He wanted her to look at him afterward with clear-eyed satisfaction.

As for himself, he could wait. Barely. His fuse, as he put it to himself, was getting shorter and shorter. It was all very well deferring gratification. But if Eleanor didn't succumb soon he was going to have to take matters into his own hands. As it were. He had grinned inwardly at his pun as he got ready for bed, and dreamt several extremely erotic dreams.

When they met on the Fondamenta Nuova the afternoon after their dinner, Eleanor was wondering about the wisdom of the trip. The previous day's mist was consolidating into a brutally humid heat wave. Even at the edge of the lagoon the air was perfectly still, and Eleanor felt a tightness at the back of her neck that was going to creep upward and flower into a stunning headache. She glanced around to see if there was a store nearby that might possibly sell sunglasses. Even some touristy straw hat might be better than nothing. Still, she couldn't whine, Eleanor told herself. Here she was, about to get into a boat to cross the Venetian lagoon on a languid afternoon with an extremely attractive man. Who appeared on cue, hurrying toward her. Eleanor's heart lurched and she forgot about anything as prosaic as a hat.

It might have been an awkward moment. Their relationship was so tenuous, yet so intense. How do you greet a man with whom, though you don't know him very well, you intend to sleep? Give him a peck on the cheek? A pat on the back? Resort to shifty glances and shuffling feet? George seemed to feel no embarrassment. He put one arm around her and kissed her firmly on the mouth, then leaned back and said, "You look a little peaky; did you sleep last night?" With his arm still around her.

Eleanor could only smile. "I did. It's just the heat. Did you?"

George grinned. "Nope. Restless dreams. Tossing and turning. All your fault. Do you want to do this tomorrow morning instead? It might be a little cooler." He looked at the crowd waiting for the boat. "It might be less crowded, too. On the other hand, the breeze out on the water might be pleasant." He gazed out over the water, which glistened, flat and slick. "If there is a breeze."

Eleanor hesitated. "We're here," she said. "I hate changing plans. Let's go."

So they got onto the ferry with the crowd and set off across the opaque blue water of the lagoon. The sun beat down on the bits of debris that floated past: a leaf here, a branch there, a bit of orange peel. The peach-colored walls of the cemetery, restraining the dense twisted zigzags of black-green cypress trees, slid past on the right. The ferry docked at Murano, exchanging one load of tourists for another. Eleanor and George sat still, shoulder to shoulder, Eleanor leafing through his morning's drawings.

"It's interesting," she finally said, as the ferry pulled out toward Torcello. "You copied the figures?"

"Right. Neck craning. I did wonder a lot about what kind of scaffolding might have been rigged for the painters in the first place."

Eleanor nodded, not really listening. "The figures are beautiful," she said. "So it must be the colors that put me off."

"What?" George asked, lost.

"Tintoretto's colors. I like looking at the figures and the composition, so it must be the colors, his palette, that I don't like. They always look murky to me."

"You probably don't like Rembrandt, either," George said, a bit nettled. "You probably like Fragonard better than Rembrandt."

"Come to think of it, I do," Eleanor agreed happily.

George shook his head. "That's a very damaging confession. Anybody with pretensions to culture is supposed to rank Rembrandt above Fragonard."

"Yes," said Eleanor, "but I don't have pretensions to culture. I'm just a lawyer who never gets inside a museum from one year to the next, so I'm allowed to be light-minded. Or wrongheaded. Or whatever." She leaned back and closed her eyes. "But as a professional artist, you probably have to pretend you like Braque. And prefer all those dark, tortured macho painters. Even if you secretly wish you were, oh . . . Ingres." She smiled with her eyes shut and George's amusement deepened. She was very close to being right. Also, Edith had never heard of Fragonard or Ingres.

When they got to the dock at Torcello, George suggested hanging back to let most of their fellow passengers go ahead.

"Half of the charm of this place is its emptiness," he said. "It's almost deserted in the right season. I came out here in January once, in the fog, and I had it to myself. It was great."

Eleanor looked at the neat brick path leading through tufty grass and thickets of bushes she couldn't identify. Already the voices of the crowd were lost. The ferry had turned around on its way to Burano, and they were alone on the landing stage.

The spires of Venice floated on the horizon, a strip of filigree parting the great blue expanses of sky and water. Other islands lay on the water, which was punctured here and there by clumps of grass or reeds. To Eleanor the silence, the boat vanishing into the blue, the wet weeds, and the heat were oppressive. The sun beat down from straight overhead and she felt as if it were driving her into the ground. She turned to George, who was staring at the water. "Let's go. I need to get out of the sun."

He turned immediately, concerned. "Of course. Do you want to get inside? There's a little place where we could get a drink. I don't know how cool it would be—"

"No, let's go on," said Eleanor. What was a little unease or discomfort? Certainly no reason to skimp on sightseeing. She was on the island of Torcello, there were a church and a cathedral to be inspected, and a case of the heebie-jeebies or a little headache was no reason not to take in the sights. She might never come back here. Better to press on regardless, as her father had always said when the temperature dropped below zero on the ski slopes.

They took the path alongside a little canal. There were few real trees, just tall bushes with their lower branches dipping into the water. A man rowed by standing up, with his long oars crossed in front of him. A few birds twittered. Amazingly, there was no one else in sight. Eleanor could even hear their shoes scuffing the neatly laid bricks of the path. She glanced up at George, who was gazing around almost fiercely, taking it all in. As they came around a bend, the tall square tower of the cathedral appeared, rising stark from the greenery. Eleanor shaded her eyes to look at it.

"Mostly eleventh century," said George. "There was quite a thriving town here. Nobody knows why it was abandoned."

Eleanor looked around. A russet stucco house rose next to the path a hundred yards ahead. "People live here now?"

"A few families, I think. It's not completely wild. There's a Cipriani inn here, too, run by the same people as Harry's Bar. We'll go right by it."

"Oh, well, that's a comfort," said Eleanor dryly.

George looked down at her. "You don't like it?"

Eleanor paused, walking on. A narrow arched bridge spanned the canal ahead of them. It had no handrails; anyone could trip and fall off it into the canal below. Why was she so obsessive about Venetian water safety? "I don't know," Eleanor said at length. "It's a little spooky."

"Spooky," echoed George with satisfaction. "It is, isn't it? And you haven't even seen the mosaics. The Madonna in this church is the saddest Mother and Child I've ever seen."

Oh, great, thought Eleanor. Spooky *and* depressing. But she didn't say anything, merely followed George to the cathedral, hoping it would be cool and gloomy.

It was neither. It was quite bright for a romanesque cathedral. Admirably bright for examining mosaics. The Virgin and Child loomed high on the apse wall, with the mother's dark eyes staring out into space and her elongated hands clasped around the Child without seeming to touch him. Eleanor looked around for somewhere to sit. The headache had moved forward, crushing against her temples. The soft sockets of her eyes felt as if they were being squeezed from inside her head. Her fingers found the throbbing artery in her left temple and rubbed it, pressing the pain back into her skull. Her left eye started to stream.

George had moved to the front of the church and was fiddling in his canvas bag for the ever-present sketch pad while he looked up at the saints and angels floating on the apse. As Eleanor stood rubbing her face blindly, a tall man with a video camera, walking backward as he filmed the *Last Judgment* mosaic, slammed into her. She closed her eyes against the wave of pain and, without hearing his halfhearted apology, walked out of the church to the porch, where she slid to the stony ground with her back against the wall, feeling ridiculous.

Eleanor didn't like to think of herself as the kind of person who got migraines. Ill health was unpopular in the Drummond family. If you felt "under par" (Hart's term) you withdrew to your room until you could "behave attractively" (Frances's term) again. Complaining and being coddled were both out of the question. So when Eleanor had her first serious headache when she was at law school, she kept on going to lectures and classes until she threw up in the bushes and had to go to bed, where she slept for two days. The infirmary had given her a prescription with instructions to take a dose when she felt a migraine coming on. Though she had kept the prescription refilled over the years, she had never been able to remember to carry the pills around. Even now, crouched on the pebbly ground with her hands pressed to her face, Eleanor didn't know if she had packed the damn things. Who would have thought she'd get a migraine here? It was a vacation. Stress-free. Maybe it was the heat, or the sun, or the vibration from the ferry. It didn't occur to Eleanor that meeting George was relevant.

He found her sitting there ten minutes later, with her palms pressed to her eyes. "Are you all right?" he asked, squatting down next to her with a hand on her back.

"Not really," Eleanor said, controlling her voice, which was dangerously close to wobbling. "Can you look in my bag and see if there's any aspirin?"

He pulled her straw bag onto his lap and sifted through the contents, just as she had two nights earlier. He found, as she had, the toy car, the lipstick, the hairpins. "No aspirin," he said, leaving his hands inside the bag for a moment. Touching her wallet and camera and hairbrush. Things she touched every day.

"Okay. I think I'd better go, then," Eleanor said from between her hands.

"What is it, a headache?" George asked. He set her bag on the ground and smoothed the hair back from her forehead. "We shouldn't have come. I'll take you home."

"No, you stay," Eleanor said, but of course she didn't want him to. She couldn't imagine how she would get across the lagoon and back to the *pensione* by herself.

"No, no," George said, soothingly. "You can't get home alone like this."

"Well, I don't think I can," Eleanor said, lowering her hands and turning to him. "I appreciate it."

George didn't move for a moment. He sat there looking at her pale face. There was a greenish tinge to her skin, and faint purplish circles under her eyes. He couldn't know it, but this was as vulnerable as Eleanor Gray was ever going to get. To ask for his help, to accept it without demur, would have been impossible for Eleanor with her usual defences of competence and intelligence in place.

It broke down the barriers. She let him lead her to the landing stage and didn't object when he hired a water taxi to skim across the lagoon directly to the Zattere. She barely looked up as the taxi cut through the city to the Grand Canal, but sat leaning back against George's chest with her eyes shut. As they disembarked she handed him her wallet, but he tucked it back into her bag, which he pulled onto his shoulder.

"That probably cost about two hundred dollars," Eleanor said, given strength by the fact that she was within hailing distance of her bed.

"We'll settle it later," George said, handing her onto the quay while the taxi bobbed in its own wake. "You need to sleep." And he hustled her upstairs and tucked her in bed with a cool washcloth over her eyes and a glass of orange juice wheedled from the café next door. He found some Tylenol with codeine in his shaving kit (left over from the recent extraction of his wisdom teeth) and gave her one of them, promising to come back and see how she was doing in a few hours. But Eleanor barely heard him, having retreated to sleep.

When she woke up she felt as if she was floating. She lifted the washcloth from her eyes and saw the white sheet pulled over her body, the glass next to her, and George, sitting with a book on his lap in the room's one chair. She smiled at him. Her headache was gone. Instead she felt light-headed, a little shaky, and euphoric. There was George, putting a marker in his book. The afternoon sunlight raked through the shutters. She could feel her hair, loose around her on the pillow, sliding over her shoulders. She looked around for a place to put the damp washcloth and stood up to take it into the bathroom. She splashed some water on her face and inspected herself in the mirror. Still pale. She splashed water onto her collarbone and held her wrists under the faucet for a minute. Delaying tactics.

When she walked back into the room, George was still sitting in the chair, the book on his lap, watchful and silent. She sat down on the corner of the bed nearest him and held out a hand.

George took her hand, smiling slightly, and put the book on the floor. Then he sat on the bed next to her and kissed her.

They didn't talk. Eleanor groaned slightly when his thumb first brushed her nipple and she felt a warm echo of sensation between her legs. George let out a deep sigh when he lay down next to her, skin against skin the length of their bodies, and she reached down to touch him. They tried to spin it out. They broke apart, panting, more than once. Eleanor sat up and ran a hand over his chest, tracing the hair as it grew inward toward his breastbone, and down along his stomach, in a darkening line. Another time she pulled away from his mouth, closing her legs and sliding down the bed to kiss him behind the ear. Finally he pulled away from her hand to whisper, "I can't wait any longer, I'm sorry," and she lay back to take him.

There was a moment's hesitation, and she opened her eyes to see where he was, then relaxed again as he entered her and urgency overcame them both and the pulsing warmth exploded into a tingling flood that expanded outward, leaving her limp.

George stirred first, kissing her neck and then resting his head on her shoulder. Beneath her hands, she could feel his heartbeat gradually slowing. "Do you work out?" she asked, feeling the definition of the muscles in his shoulders and back.

"Every now and then," he muttered into her hair. "But I'm usually too lazy." He breathed deeply. "I don't want to move. I want to stay here forever." He closed his eyes and burrowed his face into her neck, then lifted himself off her and sat up. He padded into the bathroom and came back to find Eleanor lying exactly as he'd left her, with a small smile on her face.

"Now I know what the Mona Lisa was smiling about," he said, sliding an arm between her shoulders and the pillow. He ran his other hand over her ribs, beneath her full breasts, smoothing her skin. "Listen, I hate to be vulgar, but I hope we'll be doing this again and again in the next few days and I'd be happier if we—well, if we weren't completely dependent on Italian, um . . . prophylactics."

Eleanor looked up at him, startled. "I didn't really think . . . I mean, I knew you were putting a condom on, but . . ." She sat up, momentarily disturbed. "Lord, that just shows you how out of it I am." She looked down at George, sprawled on the pillow. "We're supposed to have a little conversation about our sexual past, or something? And then you tell me in a soothing tone that you've been monogamous for twenty years, but offer to use a condom anyway?"

George smiled and pulled her down next to him. "Something like that. Only I haven't, so we skipped that part."

Eleanor shook her head. Then she turned to George. "I guess I was so carried away by passion that I forgot to worry about it."

He pulled her closer and said, "No need for flippancy, my girl."

Eleanor smiled into his chest, then lifted her head as a new thought occurred to her. "So wait a minute. How come you just happened to have a condom handy?" She sat up again, and this time pulled the sheet up with her. "Have I just slept with the kind of stud who never travels without what I believe is called 'protection'?"

This time George sat up, too. "Eleanor, stop popping up and down like a jack-in-the-box. You're supposed to relax once we've actually taken the plunge." He put his arms around her. "I am not the kind of stud who never travels without protection, okay? I bought those things here. Now can we lie down again? It's customary, you know."

Eleanor sighed, but allowed George to draw her back down to the pillow, where she nestled against him. "I'm sorry," she said. "This whole thing has made me a little jumpy."

"I know," George answered, stroking her hair.

"So how did you know what to ask for?" Eleanor asked. "I

mean, I don't want to belabor a point, but I'm very—flattered. It must have been a lot of trouble."

"And mortification," George added, sliding down the bed so that he was face-to-face with her. "Because after I finally explained to the pharmacist what I wanted, with everyone in the place listening, he said I couldn't have them without a prescription. I have a feeling he was just torturing a tourist; that can't be possible. But I couldn't go through the whole rigmarole again in another drugstore." Eleanor was trying not to giggle. "So then I got a friend of mine to get them for me. It turns out they're not even Italian; they were made in Yugoslavia."

"Wonderful," said Eleanor. "Iron Curtain condoms."

"The Iron Curtain doesn't exist anymore."

"Neither does Yugoslavia, if it comes to that. I wonder what the shelf life for a condom is?" Eleanor shifted onto her side. "Just out of curiosity—when did you buy them?"

George ran a hand down her back. "This morning," he said. She nodded, watching his eyes. "But," he went on with a little smile, "I started *trying* to buy them on Monday. If that's what you wanted to know." Her smile told him that it was. "In fact," he went on, wondering if it was wise to tell her, "I started thinking about sleeping with you right after we had lunch that day."

"Do you sleep with every woman you have lunch with?" Eleanor asked, still smiling.

"Only if she has special qualifications," George said, and went on to show her, explicitly, what a few of those qualifications were.

George had had his doubts about the carnal approach. He had been uneasy ever since the episode on the vaporetto when his eagerness had become so apparent. But luck was on his side yet again. Eleanor had no trouble believing that a man might find her an interesting companion. That side of George's attraction to her she understood. What floored her, and won her over, was the fact that he *wanted* her. Thirty-nine years old, fifteen pounds overweight, crow's-feet and stretch marks and all. He found her alluring. Seductive enough so that now, half an hour after they'd made love, he wanted her again. So Eleanor closed her eyes and let his hands rove over her. And she took him inside her and went with him, over the edge again.

10

That was Tuesday. Tuesday was another damp day in Weymouth, and Harry drove the boys to the massive Stop & Shop in Old Saybrook to see if they could buy a Monopoly set, then took them to lunch at Pat's Kountry Kitchen, where they gorged on chocolate walnut pie and Toby teased Simon for talking to the stuffed bears that formed part of the decor.

On Wednesday in Venice, Eleanor and George went to Peggy Guggenheim's museum, where their increasing pleasure in each other was consolidated by the fact that neither much cared for Mrs. Guggenheim's art. George needed to do more sketching, but apart from his two hours in the Accademia they spent the whole day together. He moved his shaving things and toothbrush into her room.

In Weymouth the weather improved. Harry took his mother and nephews out in the boat and Frances, somewhat to her dismay, caught her first fish, a small bluefish that she refused to look at after Harry discreetly unhooked it. Even Hart, the would-be Man of the Sea, didn't feel up to gutting the fish, so they wrapped it in tinfoil and threw it away.

On Thursday Eleanor and George took a trip up the Brenta Canal to see some of the Palladian houses built by Venetian nobles to escape their fetid lagoon in summertime. The Drummonds all got rather sunburned and went to see the summer's hot juvenile film, a road movie about two eight-year-olds on skateboards. Hart and Simon fell asleep, Frances wished she'd brought her needlepoint, and Harry mentally invented a new villain for the next season of *Too Much Loving*. Toby loved every minute of the film and wanted to sit through the next showing.

On Friday Frances gathered up her nerve and suggested to Hart that they look at some new houses. He answered, "Let's just ride out the summer here, shall we? It's not so bad, is it?" Since he was tying a fly at the time (his newest hobby), he didn't notice the cold look she turned on him, and he attributed the consequent slamming of the upstairs bedroom door to a gust of wind off the Sound. Thus he was somewhat bewildered when she refused to play bridge with him and Harry that night and pretended to be asleep when he came to bed after an hour of gin rummy.

By Friday Eleanor was getting alarmed. She awoke early, lying next to George, and instantly felt a thud of regret. Two more days. George was lying on his back, sleeping neatly with his mouth closed and his hands clasped over his chest. Eleanor turned onto her side to look at him, and slid an arm over his rib cage. He felt warm and solid. His chest rose and fell quietly.

The night before, he had mentioned the future. "Why shouldn't we see each other in New York?" he had asked. And she hadn't really been able to tell him. The boys, of course: but the boys wouldn't mind that much. Toby, with the terrifying precocity of a New York child, had already asked her why she didn't have a boyfriend. Time, simply fitting George into the schedule, was an issue; but Jared did take the boys every other weekend. Eleanor allowed herself to fantasize for a moment. She and George could meet at the Metropolitan Museum on a Friday night. Take Toby and Simon to South Street Seaport. They could even shop together. Sometimes Eleanor felt terrible pangs when she saw couples in the supermarket on Broadway, calling out to each other "Honey, we need coffee filters," or "Shall we have tortellini tonight?"

But it didn't feel real. It didn't feel possible. She could imagine walking back into her apartment, hugging her sons, chatting with Harry as they surged around her with news and complaints and demands for her undivided attention. She could imagine walking into her office and leafing through her pile of pink message slips, or having lunch with one of the associates who would tell her all the office gossip. She couldn't imagine waiting around for phone calls from George Sinclair.

She didn't have the time for it. She didn't have the strength for it. Lying next to the man who for the last four days had shown her kindness, consideration, humor, and lust, she began to panic.

Eleanor would not have been able to put it into words, but she realized that the fragile balance of her life was in danger. In the years since her divorce, her defenses had formed themselves and one of the most important was her view of herself as sexually undesirable. It allowed her (though she had no idea of this) to ignore flirtatious remarks. It meant that when a man who'd been chosen for her at a dinner party asked her out for lunch, she automatically attributed his interest to some business motive. The possibility of romantic or sexual intrigue she automatically blocked out.

But George had shattered that defense. Eleanor had abandoned herself to his unfeigned desire. Worse. Worse, she had to admit. She liked George. She had even—better to admit it, she thought bleakly—toyed with the idea of marrying him.

She closed her eyes and tried to think clearly, raking her hair back from her face with her fingers. There were really two problems. One was the issue of trying to integrate George into her life. The second was really a question. How far could they go together? The word *love* flickered into her mind and she shut it out. She sighed and rolled onto her back.

"You don't have to decide everything at once," George remarked quietly.

Eleanor looked over at him, startled. Mind reading again?

"You're lying there huffing and puffing and rolling around as if you were on a bed of nails. Listen, sweetheart, I know something's troubling you. Can you tell me precisely what is the problem?"

"I don't know," Eleanor said, shaking her head. "It's just that shipboard-romance feeling. It's so easy here, it's a strange place, I have no responsibilities, nobody knows me."

"Let's take things one at a time," George said, propping up a pillow behind his head. "But we have to be honest with each other. All right?"

Eleanor looked at him doubtfully.

"Ellie," he said, in a voice that was close to a whisper, "I don't know exactly how you feel, but this is too important to me to be sloppy about. "Okay?" She nodded. "Okay. First. Is there anything about me that is going to embarrass you in front of your friends or family?"

Eleanor looked down. At length she said, "Your age. My age. The discrepancy."

George nodded. "I wondered if that was worrying you. But you know, five years is not a big deal. It's not exactly cradle-robbing. What about the fact that I'm a starving artist?"

At that, Eleanor smiled. "No."

"What does that smile mean?" George asked suspiciously.

"It means that if my friends—particularly my unmarried friends—saw you, they'd be green with envy."

"Oh," George said, mollified. "Good."

"What would your friends say?" Eleanor asked him, fiddling with her hair.

An image of Harry floated in front of George's eyes. "Oh, the artists would hardly notice. In fact, I'm not sure anyone would notice. That you're older, that is. I think most of my friends would be . . ." He paused. "Delighted at my good fortune."

Eleanor, who had been picking at the hem of the sheet, looked up at George. When their eyes met he smiled at her, the warm smile that she found so reassuring. But there was something: something in George's tone of voice, or maybe it was the stilted turn of phrase. She had only known George for a few days, not long enough to be sure. But it sounded as if he was being evasive. If not frankly lying.

But he was the one who'd asked for honesty, Eleanor told herself. How could she not take him at his word? So she put the sheet down and said, "I'm also worried about the boys."

George nodded. "Of course. And I think, from what you've told me, that Jared might give you some grief."

Eleanor shook her head. "I doubt it. You know, we're all very civil to each other. We sit around chatting in their white living room and go to each other's children's birthday parties."

"I think he'd be jealous," George said. "I think he would tell you—as nicely as possible, of course—that he was concerned about my influence on Toby and Simon, a younger man, bohemian lifestyle, do you take them down to his loft, dangerous part of town, weird friends, and so forth. Which would really be all about wondering if he hadn't made a mistake in leaving you."

"Oh, come on," said Eleanor, half laughing. "Since when are you a shrink? I mean, now that you mention it, I can imagine all that stuff about you being a bad influence. That makes perfect sense. But not because he regretted *leaving* me."

George looked at her. "Eleanor," he said, with complete confidence, "any man would regret having you vanish from his life."

At this Eleanor collapsed into his arms, laughing but flattered. George started to kiss her and one thing led to another and the last of the Iron Curtain condoms met its fate. After which it was time for breakfast and George and Eleanor dressed, both aware, in the backs of their minds, that they had left the biggest issue undiscussed: the extremely delicate question of how serious they were about each other. Which was a pity. Because George had meant to tell Eleanor he wanted to marry her.

Hart came slowly to the realization that Frances was still angry with him. Saturday morning started at an ungodly hour when the lawn man arrived with his ride-on mower at seven and started circling the house in a cloud of blue exhaust. By the time Hart had given him hell and told him to come back later, Toby was awake and wanted to go out in the boat. So Hart, seeing that nobody else in the house seemed to be up, took Toby to the marina in the next cove, where they had breakfast in a little hut that dispensed oily coffee and greasy doughnuts along with bait and gasoline. When they got back to the house, Simon was awake and trying hard not to cry about being left out of this expedition. Finally, when Harry had been hauled out of bed (for he could sleep through any amount of commotion) to take Simon to breakfast, Hart found his wife in the kitchen, perched on a stool by the phone with the yellow pages open in front of her and the phone cradled against her ear. Hart leaned over and saw the heading: "Real Estate."

He held out a white paper bag, soiled in spots where the cinnamon doughnuts he'd brought his wife had rubbed against the paper. "Brought you some doughnuts," he said.

Frances waved them away but didn't say anything.

"It's only eight-thirty," Hart said. "You won't get any answer at this hour."

She shrugged and hung up. "I'm forced to believe you're right," she said. She picked up her coffee cup and slid off the stool, preparing to leave the room.

"Why are you calling Realtors?" Hart asked the back of her neck.

She turned around. "Hart," she said in an irritated voice, "you shouldn't have to ask that question. I hate this house. I want to move out. You don't seem to be interested in finding a new place. Fine. I'll do it. But I wish you'd stop nagging me about it." Which was hardly fair, as he had simply asked once, politely.

"I see," Hart answered, stung. "I thought you were beginning to enjoy living here. But since I'm wrong, and since you want to take things into your own hands, I won't stop you. Just don't expect me to help you." He put the bag of doughnuts down on the counter. "And don't expect me to like what you choose by yourself, either," he said, with a viciousness, a biting rage, that astonished him. He pushed past Frances and, grabbing the car keys from the wrought-iron hook by the front door, slammed out the door.

Hart's colleagues and friends had often said of him that he was a slow burn. It took a great deal of provocation to make him blow up. When he finally did get angry, it was a brief flaring explosion in which he sometimes did or said regrettable things. He had once or twice hurled fragile objects across a room. He had called a first-year associate in his law firm an idiot. He swore mightily in a sand trap at a Main Line country club, and offended the bishop who was part of his foursome. But the rage faded fast and he made gracious amends. The only lasting damage done by his temper was to a Sèvres saucer that Frances had treasured. But ultimately, he'd even been able to replace that.

Now, driving rather too fast along the road that crossed

Route 1 and went north into the farmland, Hart ruminated. The problem was, he was still annoyed. Living with Frances this summer had been like living with a cactus. Every time he backed into her he got stuck, Hart thought, pleased with his analogy. And now, just when he thought she'd begun to cheer up, she started getting all excited again about a new house. Couldn't she relax and enjoy life, and they'd look for a new house after Labor Day? No, she could not, Hart thought with indignation. She had to be a martyr and do the job herself. Well, fine. Let her. Let her find out that it was not all that easy to buy a house. Let her find out about financing and mortgages and closing dates. Let her negotiate points and rates with a moronic bank officer. At this point, Hart relented. Better not, perhaps. When it came down to planning a financial transaction, he'd better step in. And so his plan formed. He'd keep an eye on Frances. Maybe contact real-estate agents himself, get them to let him know when she was interested. And when it came time for the difficult part, the financial part, he'd step in. Satisfied with this notion, Hart started looking around for a place to turn the car around and drive back through the rolling green fields to the Wrong House.

But Frances, in this case, was right. Summer *was* the time to look for houses. Owners put their homes on the market in June on a lark, to see what kind of offers they got. They slapped some paint on the shutters and put a couple of pots of hydrangeas on the front porch and didn't mind Margaret Harwood trooping through in the middle of the afternoon when they were sipping lemonade in the shade. By September, many of the summer people would be bored with it all. They would move back to Hartford, taking the hydrangeas with them to put in the ground, and take the house off the market because they didn't like having strangers in it when it wasn't occupied. Frances, who had no experience whatever in the real-estate market, knew this by instinct. It stood to reason. In a town like Weymouth houses would look their best in summer. And besides (though she hadn't thought of this in time to tell Hart) she could evaluate the gardens better when they were in bloom.

When Hart had interrupted her on the phone, she hadn't meant to get annoyed. To her it seemed perfectly logical to start looking for houses without him. She even felt silly that she hadn't thought of it sooner. It wasn't the idea of doing it on her own that bothered her; it was Hart's lack of consideration. It was as if she had said to him, I know you prefer all-cotton shirts but I don't feel like ironing this summer so why don't you just wear polyester for a few months. Itchy. Uncomfortable. Vaguely humiliating. Frances smiled a little sternly and said out loud, "This house is like a hair shirt to me."

Toby's head popped up from under the deck, where he and Simon had been excavating a massive tunnel. "What's a hair shirt, Gran?"

So Frances explained about saints mortifying the flesh, and Toby, commenting about the weirdness of some people, went back to his digging.

Eleanor and George had two errands that had to be done on Saturday. They had to renew their supply of birth-control devices. Eleanor teased George by saying she wanted to watch as he asked for them, but she ended up standing outside the pharmacy in a patch of sun, watching as the neighborhood housewives bought vegetables from a boat moored on a narrow little canal. When George came out carrying a paper bag she opened it inquisitively. She pulled out a squat green tube and examined it. "Spermicide," whispered George, trying not to be overheard by the pair of teenage girls looking at postcards by the door of the drugstore.

Eleanor turned the tube over. She looked at the fine print and raised her eyebrows. "I don't think so," she said. "I mean, it may be spermicide. But I don't think I want to use it. Do you know what any of this stuff is?" She handed the tube to George. He squinted at the minute green writing.

"No."

"Can you read a single thing on that label?"

"No," he admitted.

"Right." Eleanor took the tube back and unscrewed the cap. She sniffed it and wrinkled her nose. "For all we know, it's dandruff shampoo," she said.

"Well," George said, bending over to smell the tube, "the pharmacist did say it was . . ."

Eleanor screwed the cap back on. "If we were in Switzerland I'd do it," she said. "But you know the Italian attitude toward birth control. Doesn't Italian spermicide sound like a joke?" She looked up at him and added, "It's not that I don't trust you," she added. "And I appreciate your being so careful. But we're doing fine so far. Here, I'll take that." She took the bag from his hand. "You did get"—she looked around and lowered her voice—"the other things?"

George nodded. "This guy wasn't difficult at all. And at least I knew the word for them, from the last batch," he added with a grin.

Eleanor smiled back and put the bag and the tube of mystery goop into her shoulder bag. "Now let's do the glasses."

So they went off to a shop at the back of the Piazza S. Marco to pick out Harry's wineglasses. George privately resolved that he would return and order an extra dozen, also for Harry, also in thanks.

It was a hushed, pretentious shop. The gray carpets were very thick; the mahogany counters glistened. Behind each counter was a full wall of display space, ingeniously lit from behind. There were two tall chairs set at the counters, upholstered in muted Fortuny brocade. A magnificent chandelier hung from the ceiling but shed only the most tasteful, restrained light on the merchandise. A slender girl with blond hair and a black velvet headband offered her help in perfect English.

"I'm looking for wineglasses," Eleanor said, "with colored stems."

"We have these," the salesgirl said, setting a tall goblet on the counter. "Rhine-wine glasses. With the traditional green stem."

Eleanor picked up the glass, noticing how fragile the small round bowl felt. "Actually I was looking for multicolored stems," she said. "You know, one blue, one pink, one lavender . . ."

The salesgirl nodded and reached high on a shelf. Eleanor, noticing that the stems were straight, said, "I'm sorry—twisted. Twisted, multicolor stems."

The salesgirl nodded. "I'm sorry, we don't have anything like that. We have this—" She placed a glass with a straight lavender stem on the counter. "In sets of six, each one a different color. We also have"—and she turned away to lift another glass from the display case—"this. Also in sets of six." The last glass was quite spectacular. Its stem was formed out of a braid of glass, each strand a different pale color. Pink, lavender, coral, and yellow wove in and out, in and out, ending in a tiny knot at the bowl of the glass, which was very pale pink.

Eleanor hitched herself onto one of the chairs. "Oh, dear," she said. "This is going to be harder than I thought. Harry specifically asked for twisted stems, but . . ." she picked up the glass, gently stroking the braid of color. "This may be a bit much. Harry's taste is sort of minimal." She put it down and picked up the Rhine-wine glass. "Do you have these with twisted stems?"

George, who had been admiring the chandelier, stepped closer. "He already has Rhine-wine glasses," he said without thinking, then shut his eyes. Wincing at what he'd just said.

There was sudden silence. Eleanor heard a tiny clink as the salesgirl placed another glass on the counter. She turned around to look at George.

"He what?" she said blankly.

George's face was suddenly flushed under his Lido tan, but he looked straight at Eleanor. "Harry already has Rhine-wine glasses," he repeated. "Let's go. I'll explain." He seized her by the wrist and said to the salesgirl, "I'm sorry, we'll be back later," as they went out the door. But she, having seen any number of emotional scenes acted out over her counter, polished their fingerprints off the glasses and replaced them on the shelves, mildly regretting what had looked like a promising sale.

George and Eleanor stood in the arcade outside the shop. In front of them the piazza stretched out toward San Marco, filled with its tourists and pigeons. The sky was milky, covered with high clouds that held no threat of rain. George still grasped Eleanor's wrist, and he pulled her away from the glass shop into a doorway, where he leaned against the tall polished door and took a deep breath.

For a long time afterward, Eleanor would remember that door. It had a huge shiny brass knob right in the middle, at chest level. On the door frame to the right was an incongruous modern buzzer system labeled G. SADAR, AVVOCATO above a small lighted button. The wood was coffee-colored and highly varnished. George stood against it and clasped both of her hands.

"I know your brother," he said. "He's a good friend of mine."

Eleanor watched him, absorbing this information. George was a friend of Harry's. She thought immediately about his hesitation that morning. "What will your friends think?" she had asked. No wonder he'd hesitated.

Eleanor's mind moved quickly. He was a friend of Harry's. If she'd known that when they met, she would not have gotten involved with him. Harry's friends always seemed young to her, just as Harry was inescapably her baby brother.

Looking at George now as he anxiously scanned her face, something struck her. "How do you know? I mean, how do you know your friend Harry is my brother Harry?"

For the first time since she'd met him, George seemed ill at ease. He looked across the piazza, as if the Campanile were going to provide him with inspiration. Finally he look back and said baldly, "Because he set us up. Sort of. He thought I would like you. I mean, it wasn't anything more than that. I wasn't sure you'd be here when I was. But he told me to look out for you. Just in case we were here at the same time."

"He set us up?" Eleanor was repeating. Something occurred to her. "Did he give you the name of the *pensione?*"

George nodded.

Her eyes narrowed. "Did he tell you when I was going to be here? Did you plan that together?"

"No," George said, relieved. "I tell you, it was just a casual thought on his part. And then he even said . . ." but he broke off, putting his hand to his mouth.

Eleanor grabbed his wrist. "What? He said what? I can't *believe* you two sat around talking about me! What did he say?"

"Stop," George said, trying to ease her fingers off his arm. "He just said I shouldn't mention him. That was all."

"All!" Eleanor said with scorn, flinging his hand away and turning to face the piazza. "I can just imagine it now. That little—" she spluttered, searching for an epithet, "*asshole!* 'Why don't you go to Venice when my sister's there, she'd be an easy lay!' I'd like to strangle him!" she said matter-of-factly, turning back to George. "Or myself," she added. "What a moron. What a naive, sentimental moron I've been. What a credulous sucker."

"Eleanor, it wasn't like that," George said sternly. "You can't honestly imagine that's how Harry talks about you. He just thought we'd enjoy each other. And he thought you might take me more seriously if we didn't meet through him."

"Take you seriously," Eleanor said bitterly. "My God, do I feel foolish. When were you planning to tell me? When we got back to New York? Or not even then, probably. Lord, I might never have found out." She turned around and started to stalk across the piazza. George went after her, easily catching up with his long stride.

"Look, El, I knew you'd be angry. Can you please tell me one thing?"

"I don't know why I should," Eleanor snapped over her shoulder.

"Are you mad because I'm Harry's friend? Or because I didn't tell you I was Harry's friend?"

Eleanor just tightened her mouth and shook her head. Then she reconsidered. She wheeled around so fast that George almost bumped into her. They stood near the entrance to the Basilica, not far from a man selling sacks of birdseed. The crowds milled around, buying, selling, gaping, photographing. "I'm not exactly sure. I'm too mad to think clearly. But I know that I am particularly offended by the fact that you and Harry sat around and discussed me and made plans for me and you acted on them as if I were some dumb doll. And I'm furious that I fell for it. *Furious!* And I don't want to see you again." Eleanor tried to turn and walk away, but her path was blocked by a man wearing a placard of Venetian masks. George grabbed her arm.

"I know you won't listen now, but maybe you'll remember this. I meant no harm. I like you, Eleanor, I'm fond of you, I mean well. I wanted to keep seeing you." The man with the placard had passed, and Eleanor, seeing her moment, pulled her arm free and ran, dodging the vendors and tourists, toward the Piazzetta. "I'm starting to love you, damn it!" George called, running after her.

In response, Eleanor stopped. "Why on earth should I believe that?" she puffed, fumbling in her purse. "Here," she said, thrusting the bag from the pharmacy into his hands. "Save these for the next gullible spinster you find. And leave me alone."

So George did. He stood there in the Piazzetta, watching Eleanor's back weaving through the crowd until it disappeared. And planning, already, how he could get her back.

$$\left(\mathbf{11} \right)$$

On the Sunday morning when Eleanor was to return from Italy, Harry drove back to New York with Simon and Toby to air out Eleanor's apartment, sweep away a bit of the dust, and sort out the accumulated mail. In Weymouth, Frances stripped the beds and surveyed the refrigerator, hefting the milk carton to gauge how full it was. She sighed. Not enough to get by. She'd have to go to the market. As she began writing out her shopping list, Hart moseyed into the kitchen.

They had not had a private moment together since Hart had slammed out of the room the morning before, but Frances knew her husband wouldn't refer to his angry words. And neither would she. "It's so quiet without the boys here," he commented, setting his coffee mug in the sink. "I'm glad *I'm* not going to New York today. It's going to be hotter than hell there."

"Mmm. Does *salade niçoise* sound all right for dinner? I don't think I can bear to turn on the stove," Frances said, counting the eggs on the refrigerator door.

"Fine," Hart answered. "Do you want me to go to the store?"

"No," Frances answered, "I might as well stock up. Is there anything we need?" She always asked this, as a matter of routine courtesy.

"No," Hart answered, as he always did. "The milk seemed a little low," he added helpfully.

"It's on the list."

"All right, then," Hart said cheerfully, "I'm going to sit here with the newspaper and enjoy the silence."

Frances raised her eyebrows at nothing as he left the kitchen, and opened the freezer to see if they needed butter. Ten minutes later she left.

When she pulled back into the driveway nearly two hours later, Hart came out to the car to meet her. As she opened the trunk to reach for the bags of groceries, Frances looked sharply at him. Hart rarely helped her unload the car unless she asked him to lift a bag of charcoal. She thrust a bag into his arms and said, "What is it? What's the matter?"

A bunch of celery sticking out of the top of the bag was pressed against his cheek. For a moment Frances thought he looked like a wary animal, peering furtively out of some jungle underbrush. "Umm . . . the phone rang while you were gone."

"Oh?" Frances said, tugging on the bag that contained the frozen food. "And?"

"Um, it was Margaret Harwood."

Frances backed slowly out of the car. "And what did she want?"

"Well," Hart said, brushing the celery leaves out of his mouth, "she wanted to come over here. For a drink. Tonight. To show somebody the house."

A vertical line appeared between Frances's eyebrows. "She what?"

Hart sighed and repeated it. "She wanted to come over here for a drink tonight. Before dinner. She has some guy with her, I didn't quite catch who it was, and she wanted to show him the house."

"As a client? He's a client of hers and she's showing him a house that's not for sale?" For an instant, hope flashed through Frances. "You haven't put the house on the market, have you?"

"No!" Hart answered, affronted. "Why would I do that? No, she said something about wanting to show him the view; I don't know, Frances, you know her, she just talks over you. I never got a word in edgewise. They're coming over around six."

Frances stood still for a moment, staring at her husband. Of course he hadn't put the house on the market. He liked the damn thing. And now Margaret Harwood was descending on them with some unknown man to show him the view. "I hope she's not planning on making a habit of this," was all she said, and turned back to walk into the house.

"I'm sure you can find some way to discourage her," Hart said cravenly, after which he felt it would be prudent to spend the afternoon on the boat.

Outright rudeness was not in Frances's repertoire. But neither was a convincing show of warmth in the presence of people she disliked. The result was a kind of chilly cordiality that the faint of heart found rather terrifying, and it was this meticulous courtesy that greeted Margaret Harwood early that evening.

Of course, Margaret Harwood was anything but faint of heart. She bounded out of a long, low dark green Jaguar and astonished an unwary Hart by kissing him on the cheek. Frances forestalled this by holding out a hand and casting a swift glance at the orange and fuchsia caftan her guest was wearing.

"How *are* you?" Margaret cooed. "Y'all are so kind to let me bring Guy over here, breakin' in on your peaceful Sunday and all, but— Oh, I haven't introduced you yet, this is Guy," she said, drawing forward the man who had emerged from behind the steering wheel of the Jaguar. "He's a *surgeon*." He was a small, slender man in his early fifties, dressed as if for a 1920s yachting party, in a blue blazer and pale yellow trousers and a silk scarf around his neck. His jet-black hair was slicked back with what Hart thought of as "some kind of goop."

"Awfully kind of you, I do appreciate it, lovely place you have here," Guy said, so quickly that it sounded as if he were stuttering. "Magnificent view, awfully lucky, do any fishing?"

"Yes," Frances answered, breaking into the flow of sentence fragments, "why don't you come in?"

Margaret seized Guy's arm as they entered the house and whispered something in his ear. Hart and Frances, following them, exchanged a glance. "What can I get you to drink?" Hart said, with a hearty note that rang untrue to Frances's ear.

Margaret swung around to face him. The caftan swirled around and Frances thought she heard a sound like bells. "Could you by any chance make me a *gimlet?*" she asked. "I'm normally a white wine girl, but my Lord, it's just been so hot today, a real drink sounds so appealing."

Hart looked nonplussed. "Do we have any lime juice?" he asked Frances. "I have a terrible feeling we're out of it," he added. "There was a bottle in Chester, but I don't think—"

"No," Frances said, checking the refrigerator door. "We don't seem to. I remember thinking it wasn't worth moving all the opened bottles of things we never used. I'm so sorry."

"It's a pretty bare-bones selection," Hart said, opening the cupboard that served as a liquor cabinet to reveal ranks of bottles. "Just the basics."

"Oh, well—any Dubonnet?" Margaret asked.

"I don't know," Hart answered, crouching to look at the bottles in back. "Ellie sometimes drinks that stuff, there might be . . . Aha," he said, pulling a bottle forward by its neck. "Oh, it's red vermouth. Would that do?"

"Mmm," Margaret said, "I'm sorry to be so difficult. Maybe I'll just have a gin and tonic."

"Fine, fine," Hart said, relieved. "Guy?"

"Scotch, please," Guy answered, clasping his hands behind his back. "Just a splash of water."

"Why don't we go out to the deck?" Frances said, picking up a bowl of olives. "There's at least a breath of air out there."

As Margaret and Guy followed her, Frances noticed Guy covertly examining the living room. "Splendid chandelier," he said when they sat down.

"Oh? The glass one in the dining, um, room?" Frances said.

"No, well, I mean, yes, of course, that, but actually I was talking about the antler chandelier. It's quite remarkable."

"Isn't it?" Frances answered dryly.

"Guy is a collector, too," Margaret said. "Isn't it just heavenly out here? What a gorgeous spot. You must be enjoying it. I see you have a boat, isn't that fun!"

"Oh, yes, terrific, fishing," Guy put in. Frances noticed that his hands shook dramatically.

"And what kind of surgeon are you?" she asked him politely. "Do you practice in New Haven?"

"Yes, yes," he said, nodding. "Thoracic. Chest, you know."

"Ah," Frances said, appalled at the idea of this nervous man poking around inside anyone's chest.

"Have y'all thought about a pool?" Margaret broke in. "You've got plenty of room for one."

"No, we haven't," Hart answered, appearing with the drinks.

"Why would we want a pool with Long Island Sound right out there? I've been swimming almost every day this month," he added proudly, distributing glasses.

"Aren't you just *something?*" Margaret said, patting his knee as he sat down next to her. "Isn't that water awfully *cold* sometimes? Anyway a pool would add to the value of the property," she went on, without waiting for Hart's answer. "You could put a nice free-form one right over there." She pointed to the lawn in front of the house. "Unless you're saving that for a garden for Frances," she said, picking up the glass Hart had placed in front of her. "Thank you, this looks wonderful."

"It's not really a good spot for gardening," Frances said repressively. "It's very windy and there's a lot of salt in the soil and the air. Even the grass is weatherbeaten."

"Well, then, there you have it! A pool. I know a wonderful pool man, I think I might even have his card in my bag, oh, I left it in the car, Guy, would you mind . . ." She turned to him and actually batted her eyelashes.

"Oh, no, of course, not at all," Guy muttered, and got up with alacrity.

"Really, that's all right," protested Frances, "we're not thinking about a pool; you don't have to bother."

"Not at all," Guy said, and surprised them all by vaulting a bit stiffly off the deck and jogging around the side of the house to the car.

"Isn't he *divine?*" Margaret whispered before he was out of earshot. "And such a gentleman. I've never dated anyone with such marvelous manners before. You'd never believe how we met—at a gas station! It was one of those self-service places, and you know I have never really managed to figure out how to do that, and he was so helpful. So how are you liking the house? Settling in well?"

"No," said Frances baldly.

"Yes," Hart said at the same moment. He shot a look at his wife. "Well, you know how it is, I don't really notice my surroundings that much," he explained a bit lamely. "And I'm loving being on the water."

"But you've done such lovely things with it," Margaret

protested to Frances. "I have to admit, the decorating wasn't really my style, but you've made it look so . . . fresh, and . . ." She paused, clearly casting around for an adjective. Frances waited, watching as Guy jogged back over the lawn. "Charming!" Margaret said, with a tone of discovery. "It's just charming. In fact, I'd really love to see, if you don't mind, oh, thank you, Guy." She turned as Guy appeared at her side, panting and proffering a small beaded purse. "Frances was just going to show us around the house."

"I think Hart will, if you don't mind," Frances said firmly. "I have a bit of a headache, and I'd rather just stay out here in the fresh air."

"Oh, of course," Margaret said, standing up. "Guy, you're a doctor, can't you do anything for poor Frances?"

"No, really," Frances said, waving away the mere notion of the nervous surgeon laying a hand on her. "I'll be fine."

She could hear their voices inside the house as she sat there, watching the water. There was not, in fact, a breath of breeze. It had been humid and still all day, with a heavy gray haze hanging low in the sky. The water had an oily sheen, with faint streaks of purple and yellow in the ripples. She looked at her watch, conscious of hunger, and resolved that she wouldn't ask Margaret and Guy to stay for dinner if they sat there until nine o'clock.

She had a bad moment when they came back out to the deck and accepted fresh drinks, but Margaret said immediately afterward, "We're going up to Essex for dinner, but we have time for another quick one." She watched Hart vanish into the kitchen to get the drinks and said in a dramatic aside to Frances, "Now, listen, hon, if you really don't like this house, you just let me know. We'll put it back on the market and have it off your hands in no time! And I am just sure I could find a terrific new house for you. *Real* discreetly, if you know what I mean," she said, and patted Frances's hand.

Frances said stiffly, "We haven't really settled on what we're going to do," and pulled her hand away.

But later, as she set the table for dinner and Hart brought the glasses inside, she said, "Did you mean that about me looking for a house?"

Hart looked up from the sink. "Sure. Feel free."

Frances folded a napkin and nodded. "All right." She set a fork down next to it. "Let me ask you something," she said, looking Hart in the eye. "Was Margaret Harwood wearing bells?"

Hart shook his head. "I didn't see them, but I heard them. She's really something, isn't she?"

Frances nodded. At least that was settled.

As Eleanor walked into her apartment building, she felt a surge of anticipation. At least she would see the boys soon. Ever since the plane had landed, she'd felt anxious and eager, wishing she could cut through customs and the traffic and just be at home. Just be at home, hug the boys, get back to normal. Forget about George. A blip, that was all he was. Some kind of blip on the radar, an aberration. Something to put behind her and forget. As fast as possible. Eleanor humped her bag into the elevator and pressed the button for her floor. Simon and Toby could certainly be counted on to edge out any regretful memories. But as she put her key in the lock, she didn't hear the voices she expected, the "Mom!" and the quick footsteps as Simon ran down the hall to greet her. The apartment, when she opened the door, was empty.

A note on the hall table, in Harry's handwriting, read "Gone to the supermarket. Back soon." Eleanor kicked the door closed behind her and hauled her suitcase into her bedroom. A banner hanging over her bed said WELCOME HOME MOM in unsteady lettering. Mail-order catalogs and bills lay in a slippery stack on her desk. Eleanor stepped out of her shoes and went down the hall into the boys' room, where their duffel bags lay on the floor with clothes bursting out of them. Simon's balding, lumpy bear peered out of one of them, and Eleanor pulled it out. She put her arms around it, stroking it for a minute. In her cage at the end of the room, Ramona the guinea pig scrabbled at her bedding, which needed changing. Eleanor gave the bear a last pat and placed it carefully on Simon's pillow.

She wandered into the kitchen and opened the refrigerator, more out of habit than out of want. The whole apartment was eerily quiet. Even the street below was empty when Eleanor peered out the kitchen window. Like Sleeping Beauty's castle after everyone had been put to sleep, she thought. It was unnerving. Where was everyone?

Eleanor yawned and looked at her watch. It was only four-thirty. Eleven-thirty in Italy, she calculated. Her mind flinched away from the thought of George Sinclair, probably still awake in his bedroom at the *pensione*. She would not think about George. Better instead to make a pot of coffee and start to unpack. As the coffeepot began to gurgle and hiss, she went back into her bedroom and, noticing the blinking light on the answering machine, unthinkingly pressed the play button. And just like that, George's voice filled the room, as clearly as if he had been there. "Look, I'm sorry. It wasn't what it must have looked like to you, that was why I didn't tell you right away, I wish you had let me explain. Only you probably wouldn't have listened." There was a pause, so long that Eleanor wondered about the connection. "Oh, hell," George's voice came back, just as she was about to press the rewind button. "Here I am daydreaming on a transatlantic phone line, wondering how I could have been more tactful. Or something. Oh, Eleanor, please don't give up. I won't give up." Then the line clicked and the beep sounded, and the machine rewound the message while Eleanor stood there with tears pouring down her face.

It felt like a knife. Hearing his voice like that, unexpectedly. Wounding. Eleanor stood rigid, willing her sobs to stop. It wouldn't do. It wouldn't do, she couldn't cry. This was not the way. She sniffed, and scrubbed at her eyes with the heels of her hands. The boys would be back in a moment; they mustn't find her crying. She would *not* be affected by George. It was behind her. A fling. An episode. An interlude. She went into the bathroom and blew her nose on a handful of toilet paper. A romantic interlude, she told herself firmly. With a beginning and an end. That was the only way to look at it.

By the time Harry came back with the boys, Eleanor had herself under control. She had drunk some coffee, taken a shower, and started a load of laundry. She burst into tears again when Toby and Simon threw themselves into her arms, but told them it was because she was so glad to see them. For her brother she had only a searing glance and the stiffest of thanks. Which might have puzzled him if George Sinclair hadn't wakened him in the middle of the night with an agonized phone call from Venice. So Harry vanished tactfully, wishing he had never uttered her name to George Sinclair.

By the time Eleanor finally got her excited children to bed, she was so tired that every third breath was a yawn. Too tired to unpack, too tired to think. She was grateful for this. In fact she spent the next few days doing everything she could not to think about George. When people asked about her trip, she said it had been marvelous, and changed the subject. She threw herself into her work, mentally exaggerating the urgency of a few routine matters to keep her mind from wandering. One night after the boys were in bed, she dragged her old manual typewriter out of the closet and clumsily tapped out a scarifying letter to Harry, berating him for, as she put it, "pimping" for her. She poured all of her anger and pain into it, read it over once, then burned it, standing over the kitchen sink and dropping it when the flames reached her fingers.

She was so busy attempting to exorcise the pain that she gave little thought to its source. On the face of it, Eleanor was overreacting. With the kindest of motives, her brother and his friend had practiced a little subterfuge. But Eleanor's reaction went well beyond the anger of the deceived, or even the pain of the thwarted in love. Without realizing it, she was mortally offended. Harry evidently thought she was so unattractive that she couldn't find a man unless he set her up with one. It was her brother's implied estimation of her personal charms that cut Eleanor to the quick and lent heat to the anger that she was trying to defuse in harmless ways.

It was all calculated. She knew exactly what she was doing. Time, Eleanor knew, would dull the worst of what she felt. She was realistic. This was nothing compared to the divorce. She could weather it, but there were ways to make it easier. Keeping busy was important. So was maintaining your self-respect. Revisionist thinking helped, too, but this Eleanor was not able to manage. It would be simpler, she thought, walking home from the subway one evening, if she could only convince herself that it *had* just been a fling. Lighthearted. No strings attached. *La dolce vita* and all that. If she could only pretend she hadn't fallen for George Sinclair like a ton of bricks.

Eleanor paused outside the big Korean market on Broadway. There were tall stalks of sunflowers for sale next to the white plastic buckets of tulips and daisies and carnations. She reached out to touch the dark brown fuzzy center of one. It might be nice to bring some flowers home. But the stalks of the sunflowers were so long and their heads were so big. What would she put them in? That hideous vase that Harry had made her give away would have been just about right, Eleanor thought wryly. Her eye fell on a hunk of watermelon, brilliantly red beneath its plastic wrap. She picked it up. The boys would like that better anyway. As she went inside to pay, her thoughts returned, as they so often did against her will, to George. She sighed, fishing in her purse for her wallet. It was hard to know what was the worst part. The mortification? She still felt such a sense of *shame* about it. She felt she'd been so eager, so pathetic in her willingness to fall for the guy. She shuddered just thinking of it and pushed a dollar across the counter to the clerk. "No, no bag, thanks," she said, accepting her change. She tucked the watermelon under her arm and left the store.

The regret was pretty bad, too, Eleanor thought as she headed up Broadway. And there was something more that she didn't even want to face, some further hurt that her thoughts flinched from. She felt in the bottom of her purse for her keys, glad to be near home. She'd made it through the week. Nothing unseemly had happened. She hadn't burst into tears in a meeting or shrieked (more than usual, anyway) at her sons. She'd get over it, get over the embarrassment and the anger and the regret. She might even be able to face Harry in a few more weeks.

Eleanor stopped at her mailbox and pulled out the usual dispiriting assortment of things for sale that she didn't want to buy and bills for things she *had* bought. As she stacked the mail on top of the watermelon, something fell to the floor. A postcard of Venice lay faceup on the old circular tiles of the lobby, and Eleanor froze, feeling a sudden, physical shock. It was an old photograph, a sepia print of the Piazza San Marco underwater. Eleanor knew who had sent it even before her hand reached out very slowly to pick it up. On the reverse it said only, "I think of you all the time," in a neat italic hand. It bore an Italian stamp and an illegible postmark. She turned it over and looked at the front again. It had the amazing stillness of those early photographs. The fantastic outline of the basilica was reflected in the water with amazing clarity. A single pigeon in the sky was a small blur. Eleanor drew a deep breath and slipped the card into her purse, aware that her hands were shaking. What the hell did it mean?

What it meant, although she had no way of knowing this, was that she had seriously shaken George Sinclair.

George was an extremely pleasant man. He was honest, and he worked hard. But where women were concerned, his history was a bit complex. He was very attractive and enjoyed and understood women. He had had a series of substantial monogamous relationships, all of which had ended at his impulse. To put it simply, George Sinclair had never been dumped before. A less reasonable man might have been offended or piqued by Eleanor's treatment. A vainer man might have turned against her to salvage his wounded pride. But one of George's most appealing traits was that he took criticism well. He learned from his mistakes. He was, moreover, extremely practical. He spent his three remaining days in Venice sketching and preparing for his commission, and thinking about Eleanor. He thought about her intelligence, her sense of humor, her courage. And he decided not to give up. There must be a way to win her over.

But somehow, he wasn't sure what it was. Flowers and a letter? Pleading on the telephone? She could ignore a letter, hang up the phone. George thought about this, leaving his studio the morning after he came back to New York. Could he bear it if

Eleanor hung up on him? He walked slowly down the big dusty staircase to the ground floor. To hear Eleanor's voice, anger in it, possibly disgust? He flinched at the thought. No. He couldn't do it. It had been bad enough when she left him in Venice. He just couldn't bear to invite that again. Not yet, at least. Maybe in a few days he would feel braver.

He closed the heavy front door and turned left toward Church Street. Across the street was the store that sold glass eyes, with the stuffed otter in the window. Dodging a delivery van, George crossed to take a closer look. The otter was lying on its back, clutching a dusty shell to its chest, while its other paw held a rock. Its fur looked dry. In front of it, several dozen small boxes displayed glass eyes of all kinds and sizes, from tiny solid black spheres to an unnervingly lifelike blue human eye that glared at George from a nest of cotton.

George could see movement in the shop, and on impulse he went in. He came out five minutes later with a pair of green glass eyes on little steel loops, like fancy leather buttons. They looked as if they might belong to some kind of furry tubular animal like a mink or a ferret. On the way uptown to meet his dealer, George bought a small padded envelope. He tore a corner of paper from his Venice sketch pad and wrote on it, "To keep an eye on you." Then he stopped by the post office and mailed the package to Eleanor, who received it three days later. George hadn't really thought about what kind of reaction he was trying to elicit. It never occurred to him that his unconsidered gesture might be considered creepy, or even threatening. If anything, it had been a visual metaphor for the strong protective feelings he had toward Eleanor. It was a tribute to their innate compatibility that Eleanor took the oblique message in the spirit in which it was meant and slipped the eyes into the change purse of her wallet.

The oppressive heat held all that week, crushing the entire East Coast in humid misery. Gas station attendants kept bottles of Gatorade on top of the pumps to swig from between customers. The beaches were almost too hot to bear. Movie theaters did stunning business. Frances Drummond wished several times daily that she drove an air-conditioned car.

She had begun the week with the best of intentions and a genuine resolve to avoid bitterness. Hart wasn't interested in finding a new house. Fine. She would take matters into her own hands. She certainly hadn't anything better to do. She would start, she told herself, by exploring. Getting to know the other towns on the coast. There was a lot to see between New Haven and the Rhode Island border. In fact, why stop at the border? Maybe Newport was a little far from New York, but it had attractions of its own. First she would drive around and visit new towns. Then, with a better grasp of the surroundings, she would call real-estate agents.

Or so Frances told herself. She thought of it as doing her homework. She would not acknowledge, even to herself, that she was stalling. Somehow she just couldn't dial the telephone and announce to a real-estate agent, "My name is Frances Drummond and I am looking for a house." In fact, since the Saturday morning when Hart had found her on the phone, she hadn't even tried.

So here she was, roaming the outskirts of New London. Driving through a network of streets named by some Anglophile real-estate developer: Avon Road, Berkeley Lane, Cornwall Circle, Devon Avenue. Looking with mild horror at the regular rows of what real-estate agents called "Cape Cods" or "raised ranches." Wondering if she would ever see an acceptable house again. And searching for Gloucester Street, where an open house was being held at what the ad in the newspaper called a "spacious elegant 4BR Georgian" with "eat-in kitchen, marble baths, 3-car garage." It wasn't that she thought it would be the right house. But she did think it would be good practice.

Frances was relieved when she got to Folkestone Way and saw that the development stopped. The tiny quarter-acre lots gave way to a stretch of meadow that ended in trees half a mile away. Elm Avenue lost its purpose and began to curve in a languid arc. Frances noticed a sign that read DEAD END. And on the right, her destination was obvious. There was only one house on Gloucester Street.

If Frances had had more experience, she could have placed the house at a glance. It was the last hurrah of a contractor with delusions of grandeur. When the development had gone up after the war, municipal light and water had been extended as far as Gloucester. But the market had slowed, and the last batch of little houses weren't built. The rest of the tract was auctioned, and in the mid-1980s a young builder, dreaming of splendor, had bought the land on the cheap and put up a house he was prepared to build in multitudes for upwardly mobile young professionals. Who, alas, never turned up. The house had been on the market for a year, the price steadily dropping. It was listed with every real-estate agent in eastern Connecticut, and on that Saturday morning in July there was one young man with blow-dried hair standing languidly in front, squinting in the bright sunlight and smoking a cigarette.

As he spotted Frances, hesitating in the car with the engine still running, he threw the cigarette into a weedy yew and hurried toward her. She sighed and cut the engine. It would have been just too rude to drive away.

"Are you here for the open house?" he asked eagerly as she got out of the car. "My name's Jim Fusco, I'm with Shoreline Properties, how are you?"

Frances shook his hand and shaded her eyes to look upward at the "Georgian" facade. It was a tall two-story house with a Palladian-style door that looked as if it might have come out of a mail-order catalog. The front was faced with multishaded brick, but the rest of the house was white clapboard. (Hart would have identified it at a glance as aluminium siding, but Frances merely thought it seemed oddly regular.) Four extremely thin pillars supported an extension of the roof over what might have been considered a veranda, though you couldn't even fit a camp chair on the flagstone beneath it, Frances thought as she walked inside.

"Would you mind signing our book?" the young man asked. Frances noticed that he seemed extremely hot in his dark suit. It was one of those hazy days when the cicadas buzz incessantly and your hair sticks to your scalp. "And here's a listing sheet," he said, giving her a piece of paper with a picture of the house on it and a descriptive paragraph beneath. She glanced at it and tucked it into her purse.

156

"The owner is willing to sell furnished or unfurnished," the young man said as Frances gazed around the living room. There was an enormous pastel-hued silk screen of some birds of paradise over a fake fireplace. A butterfly-patterned fabric swarmed over a vast sectional sofa. Floor-to-ceiling curtains and several small cushions on the turquoise armchairs were also made of the butterfly pattern. A big vase held fronds of pampas grass dyed coral and turquoise.

"And do you have a family, Mrs. . . . Drummond?" the young man said, reading her name from the book.

"Yes," she said absently, looking out the window at the back of the houses on Folkestone Way. Quite a few of them had laundry hanging from those old-fashioned drying racks that looked like giant inverted umbrellas.

He stared at her, surprised. She looked awfully old to have kids. "Would you care to see the bedrooms? Or do you want to look over the downstairs first?"

Frances turned and looked at him. Poor boy, she thought, what an awful job. He must be so bored. The house was impossible, of course. But she might as well let the salesman do what he was supposed to.

They walked around the first floor, Frances glancing politely at the "gourmet kitchen" and the "gracious dining room" that was papered down to the outsize egg-and-dart chair rail in a startling maroon and yellow stripe. Next to the kitchen phone was a copy of *People* magazine, lying open to a feature on Cher. The young man closed it hastily. The upstairs rooms were notable only for the number of dead flies Frances noticed on their windowsills. One had been furnished as a study, with heavy dark bookshelves and a huge swivel chair pulled up to a rather small drop-leaf desk.

"It's awfully quiet, isn't it?" Frances said as she walked down the stairs. Their footsteps clattered in the house's silence.

"Oh, yes. Extremely quiet. And Elm Avenue isn't a through road, you know, so there's lots of privacy," the young man said earnestly.

"And where do you live?" Frances asked him, without knowing why.

"Me?" he asked, startled.

"Yes. Do you live in New London?"

"Um, yes. Near the river. In a mother-in-law. It's nice," he said. "Handy."

"Mmm. Well, I don't think this is for me," Frances said, glancing upward at the asymmetrical modern chandelier in the front hall. "Too quiet. Thank you."

"Not at all. Thank you for coming, Mrs. Drummond," he said. "If you'd care to tell me what kind of thing you're looking for, I'd be happy to see if we—"

"I don't think so," she said, opening the front door to the blast of heat. "I don't really think so."

Though she'd only been in the house for a few minutes, a surge of hot leather-scented air met her when she opened the car door. As she backed out of the driveway the young man stood on the narrow veranda waving, and Frances wondered how soon he would be able to take off his suit and tie and take a cool shower.

When Hart asked Frances that night how she had spent the day, she made a vague answer about going for a drive. She was also careful to crunch up the listing sheet and squash it way down in the kitchen garbage, next to the coffee grounds. For some reason she didn't want Hart knowing what she was up to. But he had taken the boat out for a long trip and seemed more interested in telling her about the enormous jellyfish he'd seen that he thought was a Portuguese man-of-war.

When the phone rang, Harry knew who it would be, so he picked up the receiver and just said, "Yes?" in what he hoped was a discouraging tone.

"It's me," George said. "Any news?"

"No," Harry said flatly. "No news. What news would there be?"

"Well, that Eleanor has decided she can't live without me and wants you, as a go-between, to set up a reconciliation between us."

"Oh, that kind of news," Harry said. Putting his feet on his desk drawer, he turned a page of the script he was working on.

Listening to George these days didn't require much concentration.

"No, huh?" George sounded crestfallen. "Listen, I'm having trouble working. Can we get together?"

"To do what?" Harry asked. "Talk about Eleanor some more? George, I have a job. I have a script to straighten out. I have this beautiful but troubled heiress who's pregnant with triplets by her illegitimate half-brother and our sponsor is a little curious to know what happens next, so I need to sit here at my desk until those adorable babies are happily adopted by the heiress's long-lost twin sister, okay?"

"Lunch?"

"No. You know I don't eat lunch when I'm working."

"Dinner?"

Harry sighed. "Something tells me you're going to hound me me until I say yes."

"I am," George said apologetically.

"All right. You can cook," Harry said. "Eight o'clock." He sighed and turned down the volume on the answering machine.

Eleanor had been miserable since getting back from Venice, but Harry hadn't been particularly happy, either. Over and over he'd reproached himself for trying to interfere. He knew that he was blameless, that his casual suggestion to George about meeting Eleanor had been well meant. But the result had been disastrous.

Harry was, by nature, empathetic. It was the easiest thing in the world for him to put himself in someone else's situation. This made him a good writer, a gratifying son, a sympathetic friend. And, at the moment, a very regretful brother.

He hadn't needed to see Eleanor's ravaged face to realize that his casual plans had gone awry in Venice. George had gone straight from the Piazza San Marco to the post office to call his friend Harry, waking him in New York at five A.M. with an incoherent account of romance gone wrong. So when Harry brought the boys back to Eleanor's apartment on that Sunday night, he had expected trouble. He felt that he deserved the bitter, withering glare he received as he walked in the door.

He had apologized and left as quickly as he could, aware that

Eleanor was too angry and hurt to listen to him anyway. Then, because such things came easily to him, he went home and wrote her a note affirming the innocence of his motives and his chagrin at having caused her pain. He finished, "When you stop being mad, please call. I want to tell you how much I enjoyed the boys." Then he waited five days to send the note, because Eleanor tended to nurse a grudge.

He still hadn't heard from her. An exploratory phone call to Frances ("What did El say about her trip? Did she have fun?") revealed only that she wasn't confiding in her mother. A clandestine conversation with Toby ("How's your mom?" "Oh, fine. You know, Uncle Harry, that kite you bought me broke") exposed only the incurious egotism of childhood. Harry realized he was turning pages without reading what was on them, and looked at his watch. Fretting. Fretting wasn't going to get any work done. If he was worried about Eleanor the thing to do was to find out how she was and then get down to work. He reached for the phone book. Maybe Eleanor had confided in her friend Sophy. Blackburn, Blackburn, Blackburn; there it was, Blackburn S. on Charles Street.

"Good morning," a brisk voice answered the phone. Sophy was a freelance art conservator who worked at home. Harry, who had never been to her apartment, imagined her in a bright north-facing studio.

"Sophy, this is Harry Drummond."

"Oh." The brightness went out of the voice.

"I know," Harry said, sympathetically. "I hate myself, too. Look, Eleanor won't talk to me. How bad is she?"

A big sigh came from the other end of the telephone line. "You know, Harry, men like you can be awfully dense sometimes."

Harry, in actual fact the least dense of men, merely nodded humbly and said, "But who could have known?"

"Known what? That Eleanor was very vulnerable? You're her brother, you're supposed to know stuff like that. Just a minute, there's the kettle." The phone clattered down. After a very long pause, Sophy came back. "I mean, suggesting that she'd be an easy lay for this guy!"

"It wasn't like that!" Harry protested. "El's so touchy! I just thought they'd *like* each other. You know what I said to him? All I said was—"

Sophy cut him off. "You know, I'm not really interested. Your sister is deeply depressed, okay? I'll tell her you called."

Harry shrugged as he hung up the phone. He remembered now that he'd never much liked Sophy anyway. She always struck him as a little strident. Still, "deeply depressed" didn't sound good. Deeply depressed. He wondered how depressed. Having trouble waking up in the morning? Weepy? Unable to laugh at jokes? Catatonic? He tried to imagine Eleanor catatonic. No. The thing about El was, she had a lot of determination. She wouldn't give up. He envisioned instead his sister grimly carrying out her responsibilities, listening carefully to clients, patiently chivvying the boys through their daily routine, allowing herself the occasional luxury of a good cry. And, clearly, the odd heart-to-heart with Sophy.

Like many of Harry's imaginative visions, this one was completely accurate.

$$\left(12\right)$$

Ⅰn the middle of July came a day Eleanor had been dreading for some time. She had to go to a meeting at the Surrogate's Court in Queens.

Trusts and estates law generally concerns highly complex matters that are achingly boring to everyone but the participants. It was part of Eleanor's success as an attorney that she enjoyed both the more abstract areas of her work, such as devising arcane ways to shelter her clients' money, as well as the more personal moments. Nobody had a better manner with her clients. Eleanor was respectful, soothing, and sympathetic, while always radiating competence. Old ladies adored her. But there were some aspects of her job that even Eleanor despised. Handling an executor's account of his administration of an estate could never be considered interesting, she thought. Haggling over that account was even worse. And it was the culminating insult to have to haggle in Queens.

But a pleasant old Viennese lady in Forest Hills, Mrs. Gast, had left a substantial estate to her three children. Unfortunately, the executor, an irritating real-estate lawyer whom Eleanor knew slightly, had neglected to file a federal estate-tax return when he should have. He then further neglected, it seemed, to open any letters from the Internal Revenue Service, with the result that the estate had been obligated to pay thousands of dollars in penalties and interest on top of the substantial tax. Eleanor's clients, the Gast children, were objecting the the executor's characterization of the penalties and interest as mere "miscellaneous expenses" of the estate's administration. A meeting had been arranged with the executor's lawyer and the clerk of the Queens County Surrogate's Court to discuss the executor's excuse for failing to file the the tax return when it was due. It meant a morning that would be at once boring, confrontational, and supremely inconvenient.

So on a sweltering Wednesday morning Eleanor walked into her subway station and, with the misplaced confidence of the regular mass transit passenger, assumed she knew how to get to Queens. It was only when she was sitting in an E train, leafing through her papers, that she realized she had gone too far. In fact, at the train's current speed she was going to be in Long Island by nine A.M.

Muttering to herself, she moved down the subway car to find the map. There were only half a dozen people in the car, since it was quite obviously going the wrong way, Eleanor thought. Who the hell went to Forest Hills (for that was the next stop) at eight-thirty in the morning?

"You lost, miss?" The man sitting next to the map looked up at her and cracked his gum. He had on a beige pin-striped suit and a maroon tie. "You need some help?"

Eleanor stood up straight, trying to peer at the map without bending over and letting the man look down her blouse. He stood up in a friendly way. She noticed that he was wearing extremely large golden—but not gold—cuff links. He was also unusually short.

"I'm trying to get to the courthouse," she said, leaning toward the map again, but this time clutching the neckline of her blouse.

"Oh, yeah? You an attorney? Yeah, you look like an attorney," he said, standing back. "Me, too. Howard Thaler," he added, sticking out a hand. "Nice to meet you."

"Oh, umm, Eleanor Gray," Eleanor said, distractedly shaking his hand and turning back to the map. She reached out to trace the blue and orange line that would take her back toward Court Square. Only it wouldn't, apparently. It didn't stop there. How the hell did people get to the court, anyway?

"No, you don't want the E train. What you do is, the next stop?" Howard reached out and poked Forest Hills. "You get out, cross the track, get on the inbound G train. It's a little slower, it's your local, not your express. But it drops you off right at the courthouse."

Eleanor looked. She was due in the clerk's office at nine. "How long would that take?" she asked doubtfully. "Wouldn't it be better if I took the E or the F? I'm in a hurry."

"No," her new friend said, with complete confidence. "It lets you off on Ely Avenue. Now, for a guy like me, that's fine. I walk. It takes me seven, eight minutes. For a nice-looking lady like you, I wouldn't recommend it. You don't want to take any chances, you know? Gum?" He held a stick of Juicy Fruit in her direction.

"Oh. No, no thanks," Eleanor said. She turned back to the map, trying to gauge how far it was from Ely Avenue to the courthouse. "There seems to be one of those underground passages," she said. "It can't be that far."

"No," he said, standing up again. "No, take my word for it, you want the G train. Now tell me, what's a lovely lady like you doing at the courthouse? C'mon, sit down." He sat and patted the seat next to his. "You're not going to tell me you're a criminal lawyer? Nah," he said, crossing his legs at the ankle. Eleanor noticed he had fancy socks with a design that climbed up his leg from the ankle. "You're too much of a lady for that, I can tell. I'll bet you're some kind of fancy corporate lawyer, am I right?"

"No, actually, I usually handle trusts and estates," Eleanor said.

"No kidding!" he answered. "Me too! And some other stuff," he went on expansively. "It's a small firm, you wouldn't have heard of it, a full-service firm." He nodded to himself. "We handle pretty much everything. I try not to do much of the criminal stuff myself. You gotta watch yourself, you know?"

Eleanor nodded vaguely, wondering where he was going to get off and hoping it wasn't going to be Forest Hills, with her.

"Say, listen, what time you going to be finished at the courthouse? We can have lunch. Here, here's my card," he said, holding it out like the stick of gum. "I'm sure we've got lots to talk about. You want to meet on the steps around one?"

"I'm sorry," Eleanor said, with huge relief, "I have to be back at my office for a meeting." The train was slowing down. She stood, picking up her briefcase.

"Well, listen, give me your card, I'll call you," he said. "We could get together. I can come into the city. You know, have dinner on Columbus Avenue or something."

"I'm sorry, I don't have any cards with me," Eleanor said. "Anyway, I'm married. Good-bye, thank you." She nearly leaped onto the platform at Forest Hills. As she scurried up the platform, she could hear a voice behind her calling out: "You oughta wear a ring, lady!" Then the warning tones sounded and the train whooshed out of the station.

She oughta wear a ring. She ought to wear a ring, Eleanor thought, sitting on the inbound G train watching an F train streak by on the express track.

When Jared moved out she had taken off her ring. No husband, no ring. Simple as that. And, as Sophy had pointed out, if anyone ever got interested in her, she didn't want them being scared off by a gold band. Not that that had ever happened.

But suddenly, ever since she'd come back from Venice, Eleanor felt besieged. It was the strangest thing. People who had always seemed like the most polite and sexless of colleagues were—there was no other way to think of it, they were making passes at her.

Eleanor was very careful about things like that. She had always been scrupulous not to perceive sexual interest where none existed. So why, now, was it being thrust in her face? The counter man who poured her coffee every morning tried to hold her hand when he gave her change. A young cabdriver with a Russian name and a poetic-looking photograph on his ID placard had invited her to have dinner with him. She'd noticed lately that one of the younger associates seemed to have an awful lot of questions that only she could answer, and he seemed oddly slow to grasp her explanations. A recently divorced partner had invited her to spend an afternoon on the yacht he kept moored at City Island, adding in a meaningful way, "It would be so nice to have some time alone with you."

To all of these overtures Eleanor responded with polite and puzzled negatives. But she was beginning to wonder. Was it her? Was it the phase of the moon, or something in the city water supply? Was the whole world sex-crazed? It wasn't exactly the kind of thing she could talk about with Sophy, since Sophy tended to moan about not having had a date in over a year. If she hadn't been so mad at Harry she might have asked him. As it was, Eleanor was bewildered and beginning to feel beleaguered. Couldn't all those men just leave her alone?

Eleanor would have been horrified to know what was behind what she thought of as "all those rampaging hormones," because it was actually a change in her. In what she was starting to think of as her previous life, before George, she had given off an aura of brisk capability. A firm handshake, a cheerful voice, and complete concentration on the matter at hand (whether her grip on a cardboard cup of coffee or a tricky clause in a trust agreement) had served to repel masculine interest. That was Eleanor's disguise, and it went far to cloak the helplessness and occasional forgetful vagueness that her family welcomed as a relief from Eleanor the Efficient. And the hint of vulnerability that sometimes made men curious about what Eleanor Gray was like without a suit on.

But she had changed. There was no getting around it, since she'd come back from Italy, Eleanor had lost some of her focus. The young associate fancied that she spent a lot of time, well, *looking* at him. Watching him. (Though sometimes he wasn't sure she knew he was there at all.) One of the partners had been astounded when she came to him and asked his advice on a really rather routine matter. She had listened to him with flattering intensity, her eyes never leaving his face. As she left his office he noticed that her hair seemed to be coming undone. When he pointed this out to her she thanked him and pulled out the pins as she walked down the hall, shaking her head to loosen the knot. He decided later that this was extremely unprofessional, and was glad it had happened after six o'clock.

On the one hand, Eleanor's super-professional demeanor had been slipping, and men especially noticed. On the other hand, her confidence had been shaken, and she was paying attention to people in a new way. Eleanor wasn't naive, but she had decided long ago to take people at their word and let *them* worry if she wasn't getting the message. (Jared, who delighted in the significance of the unspoken, had found this extremely irritating.)

But George had changed that. In spite of herself, Eleanor had mentally replayed every moment of their time together, trying to understand it. What if his motives had been innocent? Had she been wrong to fling herself away from him? If she had let him explain further, could she ever have believed him? Did he think of her, in fact, as an easy lay? Or had he really fallen in love? It was torture, turning this over and over in her mind. What did the postcard mean, or the glass eyes? Was George someone she could trust, or not? Had he really meant what he said? Did anyone?

Suddenly Eleanor found herself listening, and wondering, aware of what Harry would certainly have called the "subtext" of most of her conversations. This made her jumpy. It was as if she had suddenly tuned in to a new frequency on the radio. She didn't like realizing that her secretary Teresa was bored with her job, that Sophy resented Toby and Simon, and that about a third of the men she came in contact with were entertaining carnal fantasies about her. She might have found this flattering. Instead, she was appalled. Life was complicated enough without having to fend off the Howard Thalers of this world. As the G train pulled into the station at Court Square, Eleanor felt a sense of relief. The Gast will business was going to be tricky. But at least it was purely business.

Alas, it wasn't Eleanor's day. As she strode through the echoing hall of the courthouse, she tried to brace herself for unpleasantness. Some coolness about her arriving late, some ostentatious examination of watches and muttering about having to be back in the office by ten. Tight-lipped statements about the onerous obligations of the executor. Nitpicking about the irresponsible unpunctuality of "the beneficiaries' attorney" (Eleanor herself).

When she opened the door to the clerk's office he looked up from his desk with the expected expression of annoyance. And the other person in the office leaped to his feet. Eleanor felt her face go wooden. Professional conflict she had expected and could handle. Charlie Winter, very possibly, she could not. Before she could stop him, he rose and put a hand on her waist and planted a kiss on her mouth, murmuring, "Nellie, what a surprise!"

When she had married Jared, Eleanor's past was anything but lurid. There had been a serious romance in college, a fling one summer on Nantucket, and Charlie Winter. Whom she preferred to forget. Charlie Winter, the rake of Yale Law, who had flirted with and flattered and wooed the studious Eleanor, protesting his undying lust and sincere affection, until on a warm May night just before graduation she finally gave in and let him seduce her. After which he had dropped her, as she'd anticipated. And here he was, in a clerk's office at the Queens County Courthouse, handsomer than ever and leering like the vampire in a Grade-B movie. "Nellie," indeed!

Eleanor gave him a chilly little smile and dropped into the seat that was waiting for her. "How nice to see you again, Charlie," she said. "It's always so pleasant to work with old friends. Have you been out West?"

For a moment he looked confused, then fingered the bolo tie around his neck and glared at her. "No, honey, I'm a slave to fashion," he said. "Surely you know that by now."

It was not a productive meeting. Charlie was representing the executor, and seemed extremely ill-acquainted with the facts of the account. He kept referring to the "Guest" estate. Eleanor couldn't stop rolling her eyes in disbelief as he produced a string of halfhearted excuses for the executor that were only a step better than the old "the dog ate my homework" line. Within ten minutes the clerk was as fed up as Eleanor. With a meaty harangue about incompetence, carelessness, and near-criminal inefficiency, he demanded to see, within two weeks, cogent reasons why the executor shouldn't pay the IRS's penalty. Charlie didn't even bother to get out an appointment book to note the date, and seemed completely unconcerned at what amounted to a tongue-lashing from the clerk. But he always had had a hide like a rhinoceros, Eleanor reflected sourly as she left the clerk's office.

"That was painless, wasn't it?" Charlie asked her, striding down the hall next to her.

"Not for your client," said Eleanor, slightly shocked. "It could be expensive for him if he ends up paying the penalty."

"Oh, Russ can take care of himself," Charlie said breezily. "You going back to the city? I'll give you a ride."

Eleanor looked at her watch, and sidelong at Charlie. She shrugged. "Yes, I'll come with you."

When they left the building the sunlight on Queens Boulevard was searing. Charlie pulled a pair of black-lensed sunglasses from his jacket pocket and said, "I'm parked over here." As they walked toward the parking lot, Eleanor noticed that he had on cowboy boots. His car turned out to be a black Jeep convertible. As she clambered up into the front seat, she peered into the back and felt satisfied when she saw a baseball cap sitting on the backseat.

"How about some fresh air?" Charlie said and, without waiting for her answer, began to take the canvas top down. Of course, Eleanor thought sardonically. The open-air effect for the rugged trek on the Long Island Expressway. Charlie stuck the baseball cap on his head (Eleanor noticed it had a Y on it: trust Charlie to make sure everyone knew he'd gone to Yale) and pulled out of the parking lot with a squeal of rubber.

He was a terrible driver. That figured, too, Eleanor thought, as he changed lanes in front of an oil truck without signaling, then gunned the engine through a changing light. Eleanor put a hand up to her hair and felt the wind pulling it loose from the knot. She was going to get back to the office looking like a witch.

"I see we have no fear of moving violations," Eleanor said in what she recognized as a prissy tone of voice.

"Hey, what do you bill? Two hundred an hour? Time is money, sweetie. Gotta get you back to the salt mines, right?"

"I guess so. What about you, Charlie? Where are you practicing now? And where have you been for the last fifteen years?"

"Mmm, here and there," Charlie answered, turning around to assess the traffic behind him before cutting across three lanes.

"Did some work in South America for a while. Then Japan, but I didn't like it. Too uptight."

"I guess your personality was a little strong for the Japanese, huh?" Eleanor said.

"Yeah," Charlie said, accepting this as a compliment. "And I got tired of being the tallest person in the room all the time. So I came back here and I'm angling to get into entertainment law. I'll probably end up on the Coast."

"That seems like a good place for you," Eleanor said mildly. "How does representing Russell Berk fit in?"

Charlie turned to grin at her. He probably believed he looked like Jack Nicholson, Eleanor thought. "I am a member in good standing of the New York State Bar, Miss Drummond," he said. "And I do not feel I should discuss my client with you."

"No, fair enough. God, I wonder if I should hand this over to someone else, now that you mention it," Eleanor said.

"What, just because we're old friends?" Charlie said. "Well, a little more than old friends, huh, Nellie? So what have you been doing for the last fifteen years? How come you're not married?"

"I was," Eleanor said in what she hoped would be a discouraging tone.

"Didn't take, huh? Some guys don't know when they're lucky. Yeah, I got married, too. Not a good idea. And let me tell you, the Argentine divorce laws . . . Boy, I thought I'd never get out of Buenos Aires alive! Here we are."

Eleanor looked around her. "Here" was not Wall Street. Instead, Charlie had pulled the Jeep up to the edge of a little strip of green facing a river. Eleanor's sense of the geography of Queens was as foggy as any Manhattanite's. But looking at the gleaming angled top of the Citicorp tower across the river, Eleanor was sure of one thing: they were still in Queens. "Charlie, where are we?" she turned to ask him.

"Astoria, darlin'," he said, and put an arm around her shoulders. "We're taking the scenic route back to the office." And then, to Eleanor's astonishment, he leaned over and kissed her.

"Charlie Winter!" she exclaimed, pulling away from the hand

that had found its way into her hair. "What is this? A little petting session between clients? What about your billable hours, Charlie?"

"I never let business interfere with pleasure," he said, pulling out a hairpin. "Relax, honey, it's just your old friend Charlie. I'm just so happy to have you in my life again. God, you're so beautiful!" he said, and leaned over to kiss her again.

"Oh, for Christ's sake!" yelled Eleanor. And before she knew it, her right hand, all by itself with no prompting from her conscious mind, had slapped Charlie across the face.

"Ow!" he shouted, straightening up. He took his hand away from her neck. "Something tells me you mean business, honey." He rubbed his cheek thoughtfully and looked at the hairpins he was still holding. "Guess you'll want these back."

Eleanor sat completely still, horrified. What had come over her? To *hit* someone; she'd never hit anyone in her life (except Cindy Morrell in an eighth-grade play). Mutely, she accepted the hairpins and slipped them in her pocket.

Charlie sighed. "You know, darlin', your life would be a lot more fun if you would just lighten up." He started the engine and reversed the the Jeep in a wide arc.

Eleanor looked around. They were driving between rows of apartment buildings. There were tight lines of cars parked like strings of beads on either side of the street. Little kids on tricycles followed mothers with strollers. It was still before ten A.M. Ahead, she could see a stoplight and a busy commercial street.

"I'll get out here," she said, as Charlie coasted through a stop sign.

"Don't be dumb," he said, without looking at her. "I'll drive you back. We can still be friends."

"No," Eleanor said tersely, afraid she was going to cry. "I'll take the subway. Stop, Charlie!" The light turned red just as they reached it. She grabbed her briefcase and opened the door.

"You didn't used to be this tight-assed," Charlie shouted, leaning across the passenger seat. Eleanor, so close to tears now that she didn't dare speak, slammed the door of the Jeep and fled.

She paced along the street gripping her briefcase, with tears pouring down her face, hoping nobody would notice. What an asshole! What an incomparable jerk! Could he really be that self-satisfied? Was it possible that anybody could be so full of himself? Had she really hit him? Eleanor shook her head and scrubbed at her face with the heel of her hand. She could feel, at the back of her head, her hair bobbing with each step. She stopped walking and pulled out the two remaining hairpins, combing out her hair with her fingers.

Now what? After this hellish start to the day, what? Eleanor looked around. She was standing on the corner of Astoria Boulevard. Ahead, the elevated tracks of the subway spanned the horizon. *Some* subway. Some line that nobody she knew ever took, like the 7 or the R. Eleanor heaved a deep sigh and crossed the street. It was not a good day for taking a stroll dressed in business clothes. Everyone else, all the people doing their early shopping, parking strollers outside fruit stands or coming out of coffee shops with little paper bags—they all had on shorts or sleeveless dresses. Eleanor could feel the dampness around the waistband of her suit, and her hair hung like an unwanted blanket on her shoulders.

A few yards ahead, a thin young woman wearing a cropped shirt wrestled with the iron shutter of a storefront. As Eleanor watched, the woman managed to shove it upward until it retracted completely. Photographs of composed-looking models with extremely short hair were taped onto the shop window. As Eleanor passed by, she met the blank gaze of one of the models. Through the window she glimpsed knotty pine paneling, several big plants, and three hairdressers' chairs facing a mirrored wall. Without an instant of hesitation she grasped the door and entered the store.

"Can I help?" asked the girl with the cropped shirt. It barely covered her breasts. Her dark brown hair was very thick and stood out from her head in an artful tangle of stiff curls. Eleanor noticed that her stomach was extremely muscular. "Could you cut my hair?" she asked.

"Sure," the girl said with a grin. "That's what I'm here for. You want to put on a gown? I gotta finish opening up." She handed Eleanor a leopard-printed smock in some slippery fabric and pointed to a curtain at the back. "Dressing room's back there," she said. "I'll be right with you."

In five minutes Eleanor was seated in a chair, wearing the robe. She looked at herself in the huge mirror and barely recognized her own haggard face.

"So how much do you want taken off?" asked the girl, pulling a pair of enormous shears from a drawer in front of Eleanor. "An inch or so? Your ends need cleaning up," she said, examining a handful of Eleanor's hair.

"No," Eleanor said with determination. "I want it short."

"How short?"

"Short," Eleanor repeated, gesturing. "Like those pictures in the window. Really short."

"Oh, the androgynous look," the girl said, nodding. "Like Annie Lennox."

"Yes," Eleanor said, not caring to admit that she didn't know who Annie Lennox was.

"Okay," said the girl. "You wanna watch, or not? Sometimes when I take a lot off, people don't like to see the first cut."

"I'd rather not," Eleanor answered, relieved at the option. So the girl spun her around with her back to the mirror. The first snip, at the lobe of her ear, sounded incredibly loud. "You wanna keep it?" the girl asked, holding out the hank of hair she'd just cut off.

"No," Eleanor said with a shudder, and watched as the hair fell to the floor. It didn't look like hers anyway.

The girl wasn't chatty. After a few minutes she said to Eleanor, "You got a lot of hair, you know that?" But she kept quiet after that. The pile of hair on the floor grew. Eleanor felt more and more air around her neck, her jaw, her ears. Every snip of the scissors, every lock that fell on the leopard-print robe, made her glad. Once, when the girl left to answer the phone, she ran a hand over the back of her neck. It felt soft, like a newly clipped poodle. She touched the top of her head. There was a little more hair there. She ran her fingers through it. Not much more.

It took almost an hour. Eleanor sat there with her mind determinedly blank. She pushed out of her consciousness all thoughts of work, George, the children, Charlie Winter, Harry, how she was going to get back to her office. She concentrated on the sound and the feeling of the scissors. Snip, snip, snip. Like meditation: your mind is empty, snip, snip, snip.

"Okay," the girl finally said, sliding the scissors back into the drawer. "You're done. I haven't cut so much hair off anyone since my sister went into the convent. You wanna see?"

Eleanor nodded, and the girl spun the chair around. Strange new breezes caressed her neck and ears. When she'd walked into the shop, she hadn't consciously *decided* to get a haircut. She just wanted to get rid of it. The stuff was hot, it was troublesome, she was sick of it. On some unreasoning level she had assumed that, with short hair like the girls in the photographs at the front of the shop, she would also acquire similar features. A straight nose, high cheekbones, and a firm jaw. Irrationally and unconsciously, Eleanor had assumed that a haircut like the ones in the pictures would give her the confidence the models seemed to exude. Maybe even, if she was lucky, magically turn her into a new person with no problems.

But as she looked at herself in the mirror Eleanor realized that she had made an enormous mistake.

On top, her hair was about two inches long. Long enough to stand up. Not long enough to lie down. Above her ears, it was shorter. Eleanor turned to see better. Thank God, not so short that the skin showed through.

"You can style it different ways," the girl explained. "A little mousse, you can get some more height on top. Or comb it forward, you know, for a softer look around the face." She brushed the hair forward into spiky Liza Minnelli bangs on Eleanor's forehead. "Whaddya think, you seem kind of shocked."

Eleanor raised her eyebrows at herself in the mirror. Yep, they moved. It was her face. Hell. She turned to the girl. "It's fine. It's just going to take some getting used to."

"You want me to style it a little more?" the girl offered.

"Um. No, thanks," Eleanor said. She ran her fingers through the bangs, brushing them aside. "It's fine."

All the way home, Eleanor was sure people were staring at her.

She peered at her own reflection in the subway windows. As the Broadway local neared her neighborhood, she began to feel self-conscious. What if she ran into anyone? What would they say? What would she say? She practically sprinted from the subway station to her building. Mercifully the doorman was rattling around by the mailboxes and the elevator was at the first floor. Eleanor managed to get into her apartment without being seen.

She dropped her briefcase on the bed and called her office. "Teresa, it's Eleanor. I'm at home," she said in a faint voice. "I've got a migraine. No, I'll be all right. No, I can't take any calls. I'll call in when I'm better. Maybe this afternoon. Right, bye." Then, standing in front of the mirror on the inside of the closet door, she dialed her brother's number.

"Harry? It's Eleanor. Can you come up here? Something awful has happened. I've cut off all my hair."

When he got Eleanor's call Harry thought she was just being melodramatic, but he was so glad to hear from her that he got in a cab and went right uptown. When he saw his sister he realized that the haircut was disastrous.

She answered the door wearing linen shorts and an old polo shirt. "Come into my bedroom," she said. "I've got the air conditioner on in there." Harry followed her down the hall, eyeing the back of her shorn head with pity.

"It's pretty bad, huh?" she said, sitting on the bed. In the bright sunlight from the window Harry assessed the extent of the damage.

"It's a very . . . extreme cut," he said carefully. "Maybe a little young for you."

Eleanor looked up at him and made a noise. He couldn't tell if it was a sob or if she was laughing. "Oh, Harry, you are sweet. Thank you for coming up here. Especially when I've been so mean."

"You haven't been mean," Harry said, moving a pile of magazines off her desk chair. "You've just been pretending I don't exist." He sat down at her desk and started fiddling with a paper knife.

"Yeah. Well, if I'd seen you I would have been mean. Harry, what am I going to do?"

"About what? About George, or about your hair?"

Eleanor kicked the closet door shut and leaned back on her pillows. "Let's start with the hair."

"With the hair, brazen it out. What else is there to do? I mean, wear a wig?"

Eleanor rubbed her hand over her head. "I feel like an ex-con. No, don't tell me. If I look like one I don't want to know it."

"It'll be cool," Harry offered. He thought for a minute. "And easy to take care of."

"What are the boys going to say? What are they all going to say at work?"

"Ellie, they probably won't say anything," Harry told her. "Do you know anyone who's rude enough to tell you they hate your hair? When you walk in, there's going to be a shocked silence, that's all."

"Jared will say he hates it."

"Right. Well, to hell with Jared anyway." He paused. "George will be heartbroken."

Eleanor turned over and lay with her face in her pillows. "Oh, God. Harry, I don't think I can talk to you about George," she said in a muffled voice. Her arm reached out to put a pillow over her head. "Please."

Harry spun the desk chair around once and then spun it back. "Okay. But am I acquitted? I talked to Sophy, you know. She's convinced I was trying to sell you into white slavery or something."

Eleanor removed the top pillow. "You know Sophy overreacts sometimes," came the response. "I don't blame you. I'm not mad at you anymore. I can't afford to be."

Harry spun around again. "But what about George?" Eleanor's arm reached out. "No, leave the damn pillow there, El, I get the point. He's crazy about you, you know. But I know you think I've interfered too much already. I won't say anything else. Listen, I have to get back to work. Now that I've seen you aren't actually suicidal, anyway."

"Yeah," Eleanor said, rolling over. "I'll live. I mean, I am beginning to see the humorous side of this." She looked up at the ceiling. "And the thing is, hair grows."

Harry got up. "Yup. Hair grows. It'll look better soon. To be honest, I think all that long stuff was a little dowdy anyway."

Eleanor got off the bed to walk Harry to the door. As they stood there in the dark hall, he said, "Why'd you do it, anyway? I mean, what inspired you?"

Eleanor thought about Charlie Winter and the man in the subway and didn't think she could explain. "I don't know, Harry, I was so hot."

He knew she wasn't telling him the whole truth, but he let it go at that.

Eleanor got up enough nerve to return to her office that afternoon. The reaction was as bad as she'd feared. As she got off the elevator a group of associates fell into stunned silence when she walked by. Teresa only said "Mrs. Gray!" in a shocked tone of voice. Even her best friend among the partners said doubtfully "Well, I bet it's cool" when she saw Eleanor's cropped head.

It was, in truth, a ridiculous haircut. First, it made Eleanor look more than usually pear-shaped. Her long hair had at least balanced the somewhat lush proportions of her figure, but now she seemed pinheaded. In a suit she appeared as if the wrong head had somehow been attached to her shoulders. And in the businesslike world of pageboys and bobs, Eleanor now looked like a freak. At meetings, when she met people for the first time, Eleanor saw them carefully wipe the surprise off their faces when she introduced herself.

Simon said it looked like fur. Toby explained kindly who Annie Lennox was and brought a borrowed CD home from day camp to show his mother. He thought the haircut was a great improvement and suggested she consider dyeing a bit of it orange. This made Eleanor very anxious that Toby was heading into a punk phase, and she began to think up reasons why he couldn't pierce his ears.

The only person who welcomed Eleanor's extravagant gesture was George Sinclair. He was jubilant when Harry told him.

"Don't you see? It's a desperate measure!" he crowed. "At least she's feeling *something*. Think of it, Harry, widows who hack off their hair in ritual mourning! Nuns about to take the veil!"

"I don't know why that should reassure you," Harry told George sourly. "Maybe Eleanor's swearing off men completely."

"That's fine as long as she doesn't swear off me," George said. "How does she look?"

"Like a little shorn sheep," Harry said. "I have to get back to work now, good-bye."

George hung up the phone and crossed to his desk where he pulled a sheaf of postcards from a pigeonhole. He leafed through them, finally selecting a David portrait of Empress Josephine. "Where did you get your hair cut? I must have a lock to wear next to my heart," he wrote. Should he call Harry and find out? Could he really . . . No, it was a little ridiculous. Still, it hurt George to think of Eleanor's gorgeous mane being swept out to sit in some landfill on Long Island.

13

While Eleanor moped and Harry fretted, while Frances drove more or less aimlessly up and down eastern Connecticut, Hart was in heaven. He had always been a quick study. Energetic and intelligent, he could pinpoint and absorb the essentials of new material in a very short time. This facility had been invaluable to him as an attorney. In the months between retirement and moving to Weymouth, Hart had been more or less adrift, without a focus. But when he settled into the Wrong House, his focus presented itself. Hart began acquiring the Lore of the Sea. Or more precisely, the Lore of Eastern Long Island Sound. He bought nature guides and navigational charts. He ordered an immensely expensive pair of birding glasses and hid the bill from Frances. He mooned over fishing rods at a sporting goods store in Old Saybrook and crouched on the rocks at the town dock in the next cove, communing in a taciturn way with the men seated on upturned buckets. He examined the contents of tide pools and ate a raw mussel he had scraped off the rocks. It tasted nasty, though he was reluctant to admit this.

When Harry and the boys had appeared in the Whaler on the night of the anniversary party, Hart was overjoyed. He had wanted a boat, but didn't think he dared suggest the acquisition to Frances. Here, a gift they could not turn down, was his dearest desire. Overnight his image of himself was transformed. He was no longer a retired corporate lawyer from New York. He became a waterman. He read elegiac accounts of fishing families whose livelihood was dying out. He joined the Shoreline Conservancy group and volunteered to handle any legal work they might have. He bought a duck-billed hat and a splendid fishing rod.

He was gone from morning until dusk. He would bundle his

charts and rod and bottle of sun goop into the boat and go chugging off right after breakfast, waving automatically to Frances without looking back. (He didn't realize that she rarely watched him.) He puttered up and down the coastline, putting into unfamiliar harbors, nosing up creeks, circling islands. He had adventures. There was the day he ran aground up a creek near Lyme and had to get out and push the boat off the mucky bank. Fortunately nobody saw him clambering clumsily back aboard, though Frances made a face at the rank hems of his khakis. (He bought a canoe paddle to keep in the boat after this.) One afternoon as he was coming home he hit a submerged rock. Fortunately it only damaged the paint on the hull, but he carefully inked in its location on his chart.

Hart's self-absorption during this period was almost complete. He was never less than courteous to Frances, and he always made a point of asking her how her day had gone, without questioning what she had done. He commented appreciatively on the meals she made for him, and acquiesced in any social plans like dinner at Fenwick with Aunt Clara. But Frances, with her faculties sharpened by idleness and self-pity, often felt that a robot with good taste in clothes would satisfy Hart's needs as well as she could.

So she acted like one. The early part of the summer had been miserable for everyone, Frances acknowledged that. Sniping at Hart only made her feel like a bitch, and it didn't seem to get his attention in any constructive way. So Frances did the only thing left to her. She shut down completely. Well, not completely. She presented a calm face to her husband and did his laundry and cooked his meals. She listened (or pretended to listen, which Hart seemed to find equally satisfactory) to his tales of adventure and derring-do behind a seventy-horsepower engine. She read the real-estate ads assiduously, and drove around.

The days were long. Often, from the time Hart left to the time when he came home, she spoke to no one besides a gas station attendant or a waitress in a Friendly's on the Post Road. She drove, and looked at the exteriors of houses, and drove some more.

And although she didn't know it, this was good experience.

After her discouraging visit to the open house in New London, Frances concentrated on reconnoitering. She would read real estate ads in the newspapers and map out her route, then casually drive by each prospect. Sometimes she would see four houses in an afternoon, zigzagging up or down the coast from one town to the next.

She didn't set foot in a single one, but she learned a lot. She discovered how to read a neighborhood. What kinds of cars were parked in the driveways? Did the lawns look well cared for? Were there tricycles toppled over on the grass? How big were the lots? How uniform the houses? Prewar development, or postwar? Soon she could guess from the name of a street whether the house would be old or new. Anything on a "drive" or "lane" or "circle" had been built since the 1950s. And she learned to decipher the real estate lingo. The grandiosities of "luxurious" and "spacious." The euphemistic "cozy" and "needs work." The cryptic initials like WBF and c/a/c. She even began to discern between ads where all the words were spelled out and the sellers who restricted themselves to real estate shorthand.

It wasn't exactly fun, but at least she was occupied. And one day she made a discovery that made her life more bearable. She had stopped for lunch in Old Lyme on her way to look at a house in East Haddam. Walking back to the car, she passed a drugstore and remembered that she and Hart needed toothpaste, so she went in. It was a big store, the kind that carries children's toys and folding beach chairs as well as aspirin and dental floss. There was a big display of books and magazines by the door and as Frances walked past, she stopped to pick up a book that had fallen from the rack. She glanced idly at the cover. "Heroic fantasy in the tradition of Tolkien," claimed a line of bold type over the title. An armor-clad woman with long auburn braids brandished a sword at a green dragon, while some kind of spotted large cat (an ocelot? a jaguar?) clung to the dragon's wings. The title, *Lironia's Deeds*, blocked out the sky in slightly bulbous golden type. Frances turned the book over curiously and read the copy on the back. "Reared from childhood by a band of querls (the holy cats of Sindon), Lironia has come of age and seeks her heritage. Her startling powers of sword and sorcery, however, entangle her in a deadly struggle with the ice lords of Ranorth. In claiming her past, Lironia may mark the future of Sindon for ages to come."

Frances turned the book back over to reexamine the woman with braids. Powers of sword and sorcery, indeed. Now that she looked closely she could see that the sword seemed to be emitting some rays (the apparently desperate artist had fallen back on yellow lines like the sunshine in a child's drawing). The cat had blue eyes and a tail like a bottle brush.

Frances weighed it in her hand, considering. She knew who Tolkien was: Harry had gone through a Tolkien phase in his early teens, and Frances had glanced at the books in curiosity. She dismissed the tales of orcs and elves as typical boy stuff. But the redhead here, with her armor molded around breasts and her feline sidekick, somehow looked like more fun. Frances put the book on the counter along with her tube of Crest and sat down to read it that night after dinner, while Hart attempted to tie a particularly complex fly.

She had never been much of a reader. She had plowed through selected classics in a dutiful way in college and amassed quite a collection of cookbooks and gardening manuals over the years. But reading novels for entertainment had never appealed. She never seemed to have time, they put her to sleep, they were about unattractive people. Harry tried to keep her up to date by buying her each year's Booker Prize winner (assuming, correctly, that contemporary American fiction would strike no chord in Frances Drummond's heart). Each year she began and then abandoned the latest brilliant British confection, and the White Flower Farm catalog remained her favorite bedtime reading.

But *Lironia's Deeds* was something new. Lironia herself was refreshing. She stood no nonsense from anything she met, human or otherwise. (Otherwise seemed to predominate.) Bede, the querl who accompanied her on her quest, had the perverse nature of many a housecat, but rescued Lironia from several tight spots, including, in the first chapter, an attack by animated icicles. Frances particularly enjoyed Lironia's magic gifts: she could make fire (a great convenience in a country threatened by ice lords) and change her size, though not her shape. Frances read half of the book in one sitting and came to a little stiffly when Hart announced that he was heading off to bed. "What's that you're reading?" he asked, glancing at the garish cover.

"Oh, some nonsense I picked up in a drugstore," she said, looking at the book with detachment.

"Fun?"

"Well, yes," Frances said. "It is. I guess I'd better come to bed, too." But it was all she could do not to finish the book and find out how Lironia was going to vanquish the ice lords and save Sindon.

She finished Lironia the next day and drove the forty minutes to Old Lyme to buy up the three other fantasy novels on their shelves. One of them was a mistake: in her enthusiasm for the new genre Frances hadn't distinguished between the various veins of fantasy and bought what the publishers called "A titanic clash between the forces of the ages," which seemed to be largely about gravity and physics and barely had any people in it at all.

So two days later Frances drove down to New Haven and stocked up at Waldenbooks, carefully studying the cover of each book to make sure it was one of the tales of magic that she really liked. She visited the Weymouth Library and discovered the ranks of Anne McCaffrey novels. She even checked out *The Fellowship of the Ring*, but found Tolkien a little dense and dry compared with his imitators. The White Flower Farm fell under the bed and wasn't missed.

So life fell into a pattern in the Wrong House. Each morning Hart and Frances separated. He got into his boat with his well-worn charts to explore the coastline. She got into her car with her well-worn map to explore the neighborhoods. They met again for dinner, when Frances eluded Hart's perfunctory queries about her day and Hart lectured his wife about the nesting habits of the stormy petrel. Then after dinner they sat in the hideous living room, facing each other on the chintz couches. Hart lost himself in his seaman's lore, and Frances escaped to another planet.

The senior Drummonds could have gone on like this for the whole summer, but the schedule of their grandsons' day camp intervened. For some reason the administrators found it necessary to take four days off at the end of July, so Eleanor planned to bring the boys up to Weymouth. Frances seemed to have forgotten this when Eleanor mentioned the visit, which was unusual because she usually looked forward to seeing her grandsons. But maybe, Eleanor thought, hanging up the phone, Frances had been concentrating on something else. (It was Tirranion's search for the scarlet rune stone, as a matter of fact.)

Eleanor sighed and looked at the clock. It was only nine o'clock. The boys were in bed. The dishes were washed. There was a file folder of documents sitting on the desk and a stack of mail-order catalogs next to it. All of Eleanor's work shoes needed polishing, and the hem of her navy suit was coming down. She lay back on her pillows examining these alternatives with a complete lack of interest. The clock ticked; someone honked a horn outside.

She had been back in New York for nearly a month, and she was managing. In some respects, life was back to normal. She was used to her schedule again, accustomed to the routine of work and children and household chores. She had partially regained her sense of humor, even if it had acquired a slightly bitter edge. Certainly, propped up in bed on this hot July night, Eleanor could see the ridiculous side of her own— What was it? Stronger than malaise, but not quite depression. Eleanor nodded to herself. Staving off depression was a victory, anyway. Time was doing its job, and the memories of Venice were already less vivid. All in all, she was coping. But she could have coped more easily if George Sinclair would only leave her alone.

Eleanor sighed and pulled a small manila envelope from the drawer in her night table. She dumped the contents onto the bed: the postcard of San Marco, the glass eyes, a sketch of the lagoon drawn from the Torcello landing stage. He must have gone back there after she left, or else he had a phenomenal visual memory. There was a pink message slip in her secretary Teresa's childish handwriting: "George Sinclair Sends His Love." One evening when she came home she heard Sting singing "Every step you take . . ." on her answering machine.

What did it add up to? Eleanor wondered, picking up the

sketch gently in two fingers. She sighed. Her scheme for recovery from heartache had not covered sporadic, oblique communications from George. How was she supposed to respond to these things? Or *was* she supposed to respond? Did George have a plan? Was he working up to something? Or were these just random impulsive gestures? Eleanor put the sketch down and picked up the eyes. She held them so that they looked at her, and shook her head. George was screwing up her plans. It would have been a lot easier to get over him if he had stayed out of her life.

Eleanor dropped the eyes on the bed and rubbed her forehead. That was her resolve: to put George Sinclair out of her mind. Forget the man. Write him off.

But he wouldn't be written off. And his messages didn't merely jog Eleanor's memory. Each time she received a new one, she felt a completely unwelcome surge of hope.

Dozens of times a day, she heard Harry's voice say "He's crazy about you." Insidiously, a little voice from her own psyche echoed Harry's words. He wouldn't be sending these messages otherwise, would he? He must still like you. Be attracted to you. Want you. Eleanor always managed to shut off the voice before it told her, He must love you. That she was unwilling to hear.

Eleanor didn't want to hope. She didn't want even to *want*. She wanted to forget about the terrifying, intoxicating possibilities of a love affair. She wanted the messages to stop.

No. She really didn't. Making a face, she slid the eyes and the postcard and the sketch and the message slip back into the envelope. A word to Harry would stop George in his tracks. She could say, "Tell George to lay off, I never want to hear from him again," and that would be the end of that. She tucked the envelope back in the drawer, thinking sourly that she might as well be completely sentimental and tie it up in pink ribbon. Rescuing her from self-condemnation, the phone rang.

"What time are you going to Mom's?" asked Harry, without identifying himself.

"Driving up Thursday night after work," Eleanor answered. "Renting a car. Are you going up?"

"Not sure. I think so. I may go spend a night with Clara," Harry said. He paused. "How are you doing?"

Eleanor didn't answer right away. "Fine," she finally said. "I'm sort of dreading this weekend. Mom sounded odd on the phone."

"Really? Odd how?"

"Well, vague," Eleanor said. "Which is unlike her."

"I wouldn't read too much into a phone call," Harry said. "I'll see you when I see you."

He hung up and glared at George Sinclair, who was standing right next to him trying to hear. "Okay?"

George backed away until he was standing right next to one of Harry's silvery armchairs. He sat down suddenly and shrugged. "It was better than nothing. I've heard her answering machine message so often now that it doesn't even sound like her."

Harry pushed the phone across the counter that separated the kitchen from the dining area, then went to the stove to make coffee. In the sink lay the remains of his dinner with George: swordfish steaks and corn on the cob. George, uncharacteristically, had left an ear of corn unfinished. Harry looked across the room at his friend, who was sprawled on the chair with his chin against his chest. He noticed for the first time that George's face was looking a bit gaunt. "Are you pining away, George?" he asked lightly, scooping beans into the grinder.

"Pining," George answered, with a sigh and no hint of irony. "You know, I am. I can't work at all," he said, standing up and crossing to lean on the counter. "Everything I draw has Eleanor's face. This fresco commission is going to melt away if I can't produce something soon, but every time I start I keep thinking about your sister. I know I've been bugging you, calling every day, but believe me, it's not as often as I wish I could call. I dial your number and just hang up sometimes."

"I know," Harry said.

"You do?"

"I'm often at my desk, you know," Harry said, running water into the sink. "If the phone rings once and then stops, I do hear it. And if it begins to ring just once as a matter of habit after you come home from Italy with a broken heart, I draw my conclusions."

There was a saltshaker on the granite countertop. George slid it from his left hand to his right and sprinkled a few crystals of salt onto the polished granite. "You know I call Eleanor every day."

Harry turned off the water, startled. "You what?"

"I call Eleanor every day. At home, when I know she won't be there. I've sent her a few things. A sketch. A postcard." (He didn't feel up to explaining the glass eyes.)

"Every day?" Harry reiterated.

George nodded. "I don't send stuff every day. And I never talk to her. I left a message once with her secretary. And I've talked to the housekeeper, Luz. She's this very nice Spanish lady. I speak Italian to her."

"I know Luz," Harry said patiently.

"Oh, right, of course," George said. "You probably know Teresa, too. I don't know how Eleanor stands her; she's a sulky little bitch." He swept some salt crystals into a minuscule pile and looked up. "Eleanor hasn't told you?"

"No," Harry said. He stood immobile for a moment, with his hands on the faucets. "No, she hasn't mentioned it." He looked up. "Every day?"

"Every day. Sometimes I walk up there, just to be in her neighborhood."

Harry shook his head and got two coffee cups out of the cupboard. "You've got it bad, pal."

"I know," George agreed somberly. "I am completely helpless." He took a cup of coffee from Harry and sat on the sofa. "Do you think it's a good sign or a bad sign that she never told you I was calling her?"

Harry was pouring milk into a small Georg Jensen pitcher and didn't answer right away. He placed the pitcher on a tray along with his cup and brought it to the coffee table in front of the sofa. He spooned sugar into his coffee, and stirred it, and added milk. "You know, it might be a good sign," he said.

George leaned back, then leaned forward again. "You know, Harry," he said in a very soft voice, "I am getting desperate."

Harry looked at him carefully. This was interesting. This was what desperation looked like. "In what sense?" he asked.

"Well, I can't go on like this," George said. He shoved his hands through his hair and shook his head. "I mean, this is stupid. I'm spending all my time running around the city thinking up clever ways to get messages to her. I'm not working; I *can't* work. But I'm not getting anywhere. I am crazy about your sister, I am longing to see her again, I have fantasies of marrying her. But I can't just knock on her door and walk in. What about the boys? And I don't dare call her." He fell silent. "Listen to me. I don't dare call her. God, Harry, I'm afraid of her. That's what it boils down to." He rubbed his face, then took an enormous swallow of coffee.

Harry sat still, watching his friend. "Afraid of what?" he said. "She can't bite."

George shook his head, refusing to accept the levity. "I don't know, I'm just *paralyzed*. I'm afraid she'll tell me to go to hell. But I'm at the end of my rope. Pretty soon I'm going to have to give up and move on."

"No," Harry said, and was surprised to hear himself. "You can't do that."

"Why not?"

Harry thought. He stirred his coffee some more and tasted it. He knew he had a tendency to stand back from life, and he had never felt as intensely as George did now. But for all Harry's inclination to play the puppet master, he knew true emotion when he saw it. And he respected it. He looked over at George, who met his glance squarely. "It's the real thing, George. I mean, if you think Eleanor is the woman to make you happy, you have to pursue her until you can't go any further."

"Well, what am I supposed to do, accost her on Broadway at eight A.M. and propose?"

"No." Harry paused. "I have a better idea. It's kind of risky, but at this point, I don't think you have much to lose."

"Nothing at all," George agreed. "What's your plan?" In spite of his experience with Harry's schemes, George listened, and asked a few questions. In the end he agreed. It was chancy. But things couldn't be worse than they were.

When Eleanor woke up in the Weymouth house on the last Friday in July, she had trouble figuring out where she was. For the first night in weeks she had slept soundly and didn't remember any dreams, which lately had been the trying-desperately-to-finish-an-impossible-task variety.

It was a glorious day. As Eleanor got out of bed and walked to the window, she felt a moment's sympathy with her father. Sure, the house was hideous, but what a view! Long Island Sound fanned out before her, brilliantly blue. The small dark green islands tufted its surface and the north fork of Long Island lay like a blue finger on the horizon. As Eleanor stood at the window inhaling the fresh saline breeze, her father came out of the house wearing a terry-cloth bathrobe. He crossed the deck and walked out to the end of the dock, carrying a mug of coffee. He set the mug down carefully, took off the robe, and climbed down the ladder into the water. He struck out into the Sound, swimming in a straight line. Some distance from the shore, he turned onto his back and spouted like a whale, then swam back to the dock in his choppy, bent-armed crawl. Eleanor shook her head. In another mood she might have thought her father's ritualistic morning swim was funny. She might even have pulled on a bathing suit and joined him. She looked at the Speedo hanging from the doorknob and considered for a minute, but it didn't seem worth the effort, so she got dressed instead.

By the time she got downstairs, Hart was sitting at the table on the deck with a bowl of All-Bran, exuding the smugness of someone who has exercised before breakfast.

"Morning, Ellie," he said. "Water's fine today. A little cool, but refreshing."

She curbed her irritated impulse to snap at him. "How far can you swim without your coffee getting cold?" she asked.

"Fifty strokes," he answered, then looked up at her with a mouthful of cereal. "I do realize," he said when he'd swallowed, "that it's faintly ridiculous. But I like to take advantage of this," he said, gesturing at the dock. "What are your plans for the day?"

"We're taking Mom out to Farewell Island," said Toby,

standing in the doorway clutching a bowl, a gallon of milk, and a gigantic box of Cocoa Pebbles.

"Toby, where did you get those?" Eleanor said, grabbing the box.

"Out of the cupboard," Toby said, unconcerned.

"Did you buy these?" Eleanor said to her father.

"No, Frances does all the shopping," he answered, looking down at the front page of the newspaper.

"Did you buy these, Mom?" Eleanor asked her mother, who appeared in the door with a cup of coffee.

Frances sat down and took the box.

"Can't I have them back? It's *my* breakfast," Toby said.

"Goodness, I suppose I did," Frances said, examining the box as if it were the artifact of an unknown civilization. "Cocoa Pebbles. Do you really want to eat these, Toby?"

In answer her grandson seized the box and poured an enormous bowlful, then settled down to read the back with absolute concentration. Frances turned to Eleanor. "And what are your plans for the day?" she asked.

Eleanor looked at her mother suspiciously. "Mom, you know I don't let them eat that stuff," she said. "Why did you buy it?"

"Oh, I don't know, dear, I just wasn't thinking," Frances said. "It won't kill them."

Eleanor looked at her mother, who was sliding the second section of *The New York Times* out from under Hart's cereal bowl. "Just wasn't thinking" was unlike Frances. There hadn't been any sheets on the upstairs beds, either. And after dinner Frances, instead of sitting in the living room and chatting with Eleanor and Hart, had gone upstairs to read some weird sci-fi novel. It was bizarre: she was perfectly agreeable but somehow *not there*. Eleanor looked at Hart, happily devouring a bowl of Toby's Cocoa Pebbles. He seemed oblivious to the fact that Frances had turned into a zombie. The outward Frances was present, perfectly groomed and trim in blue seersucker shorts. But the Frances who always had to make sure the tuna salad had a squirt of lemon juice in it ("to cut the mayonnaise") or deplored her grandsons' devotion to GI Joe—the Frances who paid attention—seemed to have vanished.

Later Eleanor meditated on this as she steered the boat across the Sound. Simon stood next to her with a hand on the steering wheel while Toby sat in the bow, the self-appointed lookout. Harry was due to arrive sometime in the afternoon. What would he say about the latest twist in their parents' relationship? Could it be that they were, in the phrase common to magazine articles on love lives of the stars, "drifting apart"? They seemed to be getting along better, in one way. At least they weren't baiting each other. But didn't Hart care that Frances seemed to be in a world of her own?

"Island off the port bow!" Toby yelled, unnecessarily and inaccurately. Eleanor closed the throttle and let the boat drift to the beach.

"What's the tide, Toby? Can you tell?"

He peered down at the sand. "It's pretty high," he said, this time correctly. "Last time we came there was much more sand in front of those bushes."

"Okay," Eleanor said. "These are the rules. You stay where I can see you if you're going in the water. If you find anything sharp on the island, leave it there and come get me. Do you guys have watches on?"

"Yup."

"Okay. When we've beached the boat I'm going to put some more sun stuff on you—"

"But you already did!" Simon yelled. "I hate that stuff!"

"Nevertheless," his mother went on implacably, "I'm going to put more on. And the food stays with me." Eleanor slipped over the bow into the water, which was, as her father had insufferably said, refreshing.

In twenty minutes the boat was securely moored, Eleanor was settled in a folding chair by the beach plum bushes, and the boys had disappeared, though she could hear their voices and frequent crashing noises in the bushes. They were apparently building a fort. Eleanor looked down at the book she had brought, something she'd taken from the pile next to her mother's bed. *The Island Kingdom*, it was called. An hour later she had examined the fortress; helped Simon "swim"; rescued Toby, who couldn't turn around in the water and thought he was doomed to swim home; and read ten pages. She thought it was ridiculous, a poorly written saga of yet another battle between good and evil, studded with an invented vocabulary. The characters ate "triplak pie" and wore "gascards" instead of jerkins, but the weapons, which abounded in the opening pages of the book, went by their English names, no doubt so that readers could better imagine the mayhem.

When she glanced up from a heated duel in the common room of a mountainside inn, she noticed the sail of a small boat tacking toward the island from the shore. As it came closer, she thought she recognized the sail number of the dinghy that Clara Henschel kept at the Fenwick house for her younger guests to use. The boat came about and she was sure. It must be Harry, then. Typical of Harry to sail over from Clara's without worrying about how the boat was going to get back there or how he was going to get his car. She wondered if he'd brought overnight things with him in the boat. Maybe he was going to spend the night and sail back on Saturday. Or even Sunday. It might be nice to have the dinghy available, actually. The boys would enjoy it. She shaded her eyes to see if she could make out a duffel bag or something on board the boat. Then she froze. It wasn't Harry. There in Clara Henschel's dinghy, sailing toward her with the air of inevitability, was George Sinclair. She could barely make out his features, but she knew. That was George's hair. George's hand on the tiller. George's shoulders under the white T-shirt. Eleanor felt her mouth gaping open, and shut it.

In the instantaneous flood of emotions, Eleanor could identify one overwhelming feeling: chagrin at being caught unawares. In all of her fantasies about running into George somewhere in New York, Eleanor was well dressed and carefully groomed. But here she was, with her hair clumped all over her head, wearing nothing more than a wet piece of Lycra. It never occurred to Eleanor that George had seen her naked and expressed delight in her body. She was simply acutely aware of her hips and her thighs. And this feeling, half anticipation and half horror, that clutched her stomach and made her shiver.

She waited, sitting in her chair, while George with his

customary tidiness beached the boat and dropped the sail. She felt like Queen Victoria, enthroned on the sand, waiting for him to walk up the beach to her. But she had been in the corporate world long enough to hold instinctively to her position of advantage. Let George come to her.

He finally lifted an old wicker basket from the dinghy and walked toward her. He set it down carefully, then seated himself on the sand at her side. He gestured to it and said, "Peace offering. It's full of ritual sacrifices. I'm told that a young goat usually does the trick on these occasions."

Eleanor looked at him. He was pale and seemed thinner. "What am I supposed to say?" she asked in mild exasperation.

"Thank you very much, I've always wanted a young goat?" offered George.

"You know, I'm going to skip over all the how-did-you-get-here stuff, because I detect the interfering hand of my brother," said Eleanor. "I want to cut to the chase, as Harry no doubt says. Why are you here? And no more silliness about goats," she added sternly. "I know you're nervous."

George noted a faint maternal tone in her voice. "And if you weren't nervous you wouldn't be acting like a much-tried headmistress," he answered, with a tartness that was unusual in him. "I'm trying again, Ellie. Somehow I screwed up before and all I do is think about you, and yes, Harry came up with this idea. I couldn't think how else to approach you."

Eleanor watched for a moment as he sifted the sand by his knees. He plucked out an old cigarette filter and threw it into the bushes. She sighed. "I don't know. Is that why you sent me those things?"

George just nodded, with his eyes on the sand. Looking at his bowed head, just level with her shoulder, Eleanor felt a sudden rush of compunction. Maybe it was true. And if George was sincere, she was causing him a great deal of pain. Eleanor felt a new shame at the thought. She'd been so wrapped up in her own misery that she'd given no thought to George at all. Without thinking, she reached out to touch his hair. George leaned back slightly against her hand and turned to look at her.

"I'm sorry," Eleanor said quietly.

He turned his head further to kiss the palm of her hand, then reached up to take it between his own hands.

"I am, too," he said, searching her face. "I can see now how it must have looked to you—"

"No," Eleanor interrupted, shifting in her chair so that she was facing him. "I was irrational. You know, it's just that for some reason I couldn't stand the idea of having been a dupe." She reached out to clasp his hands with her own.

"I understand," George answered. "Can I explain to you how it really happened? I promise, it was all so *innocent*." He looked down and dug his feet deeper into the sand. "I know it's corny, but I wasn't even supposed to fall for you. Harry probably didn't imagine anything more than me helping you get your traveler's checks cashed or something."

Eleanor laughed, with a light, glorious feeling of relief. "I'm a pretty capable traveler, actually," she said, "and I think Harry probably believes I can cash my own traveler's checks."

Then, before George had time to reply, there was a crackle of twigs and a slithering noise behind her. Eleanor snatched her hand away, unwilling to have her sons catch her holding hands with this strange man. In a moment Toby emerged from behind the beach plum, scattering sand all over her legs. Before she had a chance to remonstrate, he was talking. "Hey! Mr. Sinclair! Mom, it's Mr. Sinclair! From school! Remember, I told you about him! I'm Toby Gray, remember me, sir? What are you doing here, sir? Whose boat is that?"

Eleanor froze. Her eyes widened, and she saw with something like horror the flush of embarrassment on George's face.

"This is true?" she said, in syntax deformed by stress.

George nodded and said hopelessly, "I was about to tell you."

In the following silence, Simon slid down next to his mother and put a hand on her shoulder. She tried to concentrate on the feeling of his hand on her skin. Often, in the days after Jared had left, Eleanor had been comforted by Simon's straightforward physical affection. Now she felt disoriented. It had been so close—she had believed George. Trusted him. Been ready to hope and look forward . . . and then bang! Betrayal again. She closed her eyes and slid an arm around Simon's small waist, burying her face momentarily against his sandy stomach. "Hi, Mr. Sinclair," piped his high voice over his mother's head. "I'm Simon Gray. I'll be in first grade next year."

"Of course, I remember both of you," George answered, getting to his feet. "That's your Aunt Clara's boat, Toby. Have you been in it before?"

Simon spotted the basket George had brought. "Oh, good, lunch!" he said. "What did you bring? We only have tuna fish because Gran didn't buy any peanut butter." He wriggled away from his mother and ran to the cooler that Eleanor had placed in the shade of the beach plum. "I'll trade you my tuna fish for whatever you've got," he offered, holding out a sandwich to George.

"What if I have something you don't like? Like sardines?"

"Oh, Simon will eat anything," Toby said. "But maybe if you have sardines we could use them for bait and try to catch something."

"I don't know if I'm staying," George protested, glancing at Eleanor. She was staring out at the water, with an expression of grief in her eyes that he knew he had caused. He ached to put his arms around her, to explain everything, to try to kiss some color back into her face. Toby tugged his hand, and George turned back to him. "I just came out here to check on something."

"But you have to stay," Simon said, looking up at George. "You brought lunch."

"It's up to your mother," George told the boys, watching Eleanor's frozen face.

"Please, Mom?" Simon asked, returning to his mother to drape an arm around her shoulder. The tuna sandwich oozed some mayonnaise from its wrapping onto her back.

"Why shouldn't he stay?" Toby asked, once again scenting inexplicable adult tension.

They were all looking at Eleanor. She looked back at them and made a painful, practical decision. If she sent George away now she would have to spend the next twenty-four hours explaining herself to her sons and to her parents, who would doubtless hear the story. Better to let George stay for another hour or two, however painful. And that would be the end of it. The *end,* Eleanor promised herself.

"No reason," Eleanor said to Toby, with a fairly good imitation of a smile.

George looked at Eleanor for an instant, appreciating that she was making a heartbreaking choice for her children's sake. Then he crouched down to the basket and took out a sandwich, offering it to Simon. "It's pâté. Do you still want it?"

As George and the boys bustled around setting out their picnic, Eleanor was silent. She helped her children, attempted to eat half of an apple, and did not speak to George. When the napkins and plastic bags and cups had been tidied away, the boys walked the few yards to the beach to spit their watermelon seeds into the water. George sat down again next to Eleanor.

"I honestly was going to tell you," he said. "Only we didn't get that far."

She turned her head to look at him with a searing gaze. "No doubt," she said dully.

"Eleanor, the job means nothing to me. I'll quit," he said.

"Don't bother."

"Is it the job, or the fact that I didn't tell you?" George went on, unheeding.

In reply, Eleanor stood up. "Mr. Sinclair," she said, in a quavering voice, "I am only barely in control of myself. I do not want to fall apart in front of my children. It doesn't do them any good. So would you please *shut up?*" The last two words were little more than a hoarse whisper. Eleanor turned on her heel and ran down the beach, running into the water and striking out in a fast crawl.

George reached into the picnic basket for his sketch pad and began to draw the boys, now intent on a sand castle. He kept an eye on Eleanor, wondering if she was going to stay in the water avoiding him. In a few minutes, she turned around and swam toward the shore. Quickly he turned over the page and drew her walking out of the water, Venus emerging from the waves. He turned the page over again as she approached.

She stood over him, wrapping a towel around her waist. "Can't you understand anything?" she said, in a low voice. "Can you think of a worse place to discuss our . . ." She cast about for a word. "Our *fling*, than in front of my children? Your *students?* I'm going to sleep," she said, and lay down elaborately on the towel, as far away from George as she could get.

He sat there for a while longer, filling in his drawing of Eleanor coming out of the water. Then he joined the boys in the sand, where they built an immense hole and filled it with hermit crabs, minnows, and an unlucky horseshoe crab.

The boys finally got thirsty, and since all the juice for the picnic had been consumed, they decided to go home. It was Toby who asked to go with George in the dinghy, and Eleanor, after judging the distance to the house, gave her permission for both boys to sail home with George. He watched with admiration as she buckled the unwilling boys into their life vests, shoved the Whaler down the sand into the water, and started the motor.

Though the sailboat was running downwind all the way to the Drummonds' house, George's trip was slower than Eleanor's, particularly since each boy got a chance to steer. George watched Eleanor speeding off across the waves and wondered if she was even going home, but the Whaler was bobbing at the dock when he got there, and he could see, off to his right, someone, Eleanor, swimming away as if sharks were after her. Harry was on the dock when George maneuvered the dinghy alongside, and George said, "Harry, can you show the boys how to cleat the boat securely? I need to cool off." He slipped into the water and struck out after Eleanor.

She was a good swimmer, but she was out of shape, and George had been on his college swim team. He had a long, powerful stroke that ate up water, and within a few minutes he was level with Eleanor. But she swam on, breathing only to the shore side. Maybe she didn't see him. He touched her heel, and she shrieked and sputtered to a stop.

She floated next to him, treading water furiously, wiping water from her eyes. "How dare you!" she shouted. "How dare you scare me? How dare you sneak up on me with the children there? How dare you tell me how miserable you've been? What the hell do I care, you . . . lout?"

George reached toward her, trying to clasp her shoulders.

"Stop it!" she screamed. "Don't touch me! Have you considered at any point what I might feel like in all of this? Has it occurred to you that I might be unhappy, too? That I might be *embarrassed*? That I might feel I'd been made a fool of? Don't you understand, George? It's bad enough that you're a friend of Harry's and he set you up with me. Can you really imagine that I'd have anything to do with one of the boys' *teachers*?"

"I've said I'll quit. I'd rather have you than that dumb job," he said. "Eleanor, if you've been unhappy, too, why can't we be together?"

"Did you think," Eleanor said, flinging a piece of seaweed away from her, "that I was unhappy about you? No, George," she went on. "I felt used, and I felt stupid, but I did not miss you."

George stopped paddling and sank slightly in the water. "You didn't?"

"No," said Eleanor, with a hard tone in her voice. "I didn't. And I wish you'd stop bothering me with your phone calls and weird postcards. I'm the laughingstock of my office and I'm getting afraid to open the mailbox."

"You mean that moron Teresa has been talking? You ought to fire her, you know; she's a mean little cow."

"Is that why I'm half-drowning out here in Long Island Sound?" Eleanor said, unwilling to be distracted. "Will you leave me alone, please? Will you?"

George looked at her. He was facing the sun, so he couldn't read her expression. Did she mean it? Could he have been wrong?

"You really mean it?" he asked, grabbing her hand beneath the surface of the water. "You want me to go away? For good?"

"Are you so conceited that you can't believe me?" she asked, once again pulling her hand from his. "Yes, I mean it, George Sinclair. I don't want anything more to do with you. And I'd better swim ashore now or I'm going to end up at Point Judith. Excuse me." She turned and began swimming against the tide toward the Drummonds' house.

George swam slowly alongside, occasionally turning over for

a few yards of backstroke. He knew she was tired, and the current was strong. He wanted to be sure she made it home. Once she got to the dock, though, he wouldn't even go into the house, but stayed outside with the boys until Harry appeared and drove him back to Clara's.

$$\textbf{14}$$

A week later, Hart was still ruminating about the peculiarity of the weekend. Although he was normally a cheerful man who enjoyed what life had to offer without worrying about what came next, his family's behavior had caused some faint unfamiliar stirrings of apprehension. First, there was Frances. Ordinarily a house full of guests, as she phrased it (never mind that they were her flesh and blood) occasioned a flurry of lists. Meals were planned in an intricate procession so that Sunday's lunch incorporated the leftovers from Friday dinner. Little nosegays were put into the bedrooms, amid much grumbling about having to buy cut flowers. And the local papers were scoured for activities that might entertain the grandchildren.

But for this weekend, Frances had roused herself from her fugue state only enough to make a very unsystematic trip to the supermarket on Friday, coming back with foods Hart had never seen before, like the cereal that had offended Eleanor, and frozen pizza.

All of this was merely novel and didn't worry Hart. He actually relished the chance to try Cocoa Pebbles and eat pizza with his fingers. But he had been shocked at the sight of Eleanor. Nobody had told Hart about the haircut, and the news wouldn't have made much impact in any case. But when he saw Eleanor's shorn head and haggard face, he winced with pity. There was obviously something terribly wrong.

Yet he couldn't find out what it was. He was by nature frank, and so was his daughter. Through Eleanor's twenties he had been something of a confidant to her, which gave him deep pleasure. They had even had several conversations after her divorce that made Hart feel comfortably helpful to his daughter.

But this, this evident pain, was something that gave him pause. There was something so ravaged in Eleanor's looks that he didn't feel able to simply say, as he had in the past, "Ellie, you look awful, what's up?" He tried to find out if Frances knew anything. Was one of the children secretly ill? Had Eleanor been fired? But Frances, cocooned in her alien self-absorption, merely said, "Oh, I imagine she's just short on sleep."

So Hart could only watch Eleanor with the puzzled concern of some large, dedicated dog. Then Harry came. Hart hoped Harry (who always knew everything) would be able to enlighten him about Eleanor's sorrow, but there was some clandestine emergency on Saturday afternoon. First Harry drove up to the house and put his bags in the downstairs bedroom. Then Eleanor came racing across the Sound in the Whaler without the children and barely bothered to cleat the boat to the dock before diving in and swimming off toward Rhode Island. Then some large friend of Harry's who apparently taught Toby and Simon at Avalon sailed up in Clara Henschel's boat with the children. He swam off after Eleanor, then came back and had an urgent muttered conversation with Harry that resulted in Harry's taking his bags out of the bedroom and driving back to Fenwick, leaving the little sailboat. Hart sat on the deck and watched the comings and goings in utter incomprehension. All he knew was that the emotional pitch of the household had suddenly reached near-hysteria and when Eleanor got out of the water her eyes were red. And not from the salt of Long Island Sound, either.

Finally on Monday Harry drove back up to Weymouth. He sailed the boat to Clara's and his father picked him up in Fenwick. Hart hadn't been a successful lawyer for years without becoming skilful at extracting information from unwilling sources. Once he had Harry safely buckled into the passenger seat of the Mercedes, the tale of Eleanor and George emerged.

When he knew the reason for his daughter's sadness Hart felt worse than ever. More helpless, less hopeful. After all, what can a father do about his adult daughter's broken heart? He didn't know this George Sinclair. He couldn't envision Eleanor having an affair in Venice. The whole thing made him feel out of date and useless.

He was mulling this over as he sat on an abandoned dock in Weymouth's harbor at seven-thirty the following Saturday morning. It was already hot. Haze shrouded the horizon and dulled the slanting gleam of the early sun. A solitary gull strutted at the end of the dock. Hart gently pulled in his line. The smooth whirring of the reel sounded loud in the early morning quiet. He inspected the lure dripping at the end of the line. It was the very latest thing from the tackle store, three hooks strung with shreds of opalescent Mylar. On seeing it, Frances had commented, "I didn't know fish could have bad taste." It was supposed to tickle the fancy of the up-to-date bluefish. With what he considered to be admirable aplomb, Hart cast the lure out into the harbor and began reeling in again.

Hart had noticed the fishing activity on the old dock when the Drummonds first moved to town. Right away it appealed to him as an activity of The People. The men who gathered there early in the morning or toward sunset looked to him like crusty exemplars of the old-fashioned Yankee virtues. He nosed around a little to find out how this game might be joined. Did he need a permit? What were they fishing for? What kind of bait was used? He even underwent the embarrassing experience of being taught to cast, in public, by the owner of the tackle shop.

It was a little disappointing to find that most of the putative crusty old Yankees were actually retired professional men, and the conversation of the three or four genuine Yankees consisted of platitudes or complaints, recycled at brief intervals. Before long Hart found himself gravitating to the end of the dock habitually occupied by the retired brokers and college presidents, who caught noticeably fewer fish than the locals. He was amused to find that one of them, a lean, dark-haired, spectacled man some twenty-five years younger than the rest who was introduced simply as "Chip," turned out to be the other half of Strong Harwood Realty.

Hart found this very interesting. He looked with wonderment at the man who could stand sharing a business with Margaret Harwood. He led carefully up to the subject one day, averring that she was "quite a personality." Chip Strong, who had never learned to be discreet, said cheerfully to his new acquaintance,

"She'd make a steamroller look subtle. And she's always trying to get men to marry her. But you've got to hand it to her, she moves property." He paused to cast, and said, "Frankly, I try to see as little of her as possible."

Chip Strong was a bachelor. He had never gotten around to marrying. Some people might have said he'd never gotten around to growing up. It was only a matter of chance that this, his fifth career, had proven profitable. He lived, as befitted a man in the real estate business, in a lovely house, but his domestic arrangements were eccentric. He slept on a futon in a ground-floor room and used another room as a closet, with his clothes hanging on racks. His kitchen counter was covered with appliances that performed only one task: he had a waffle iron, an electric juicer, a device to grill sandwiches, a popcorn popper, an ice-cream maker, and an immense black Italian coffee machine that dispensed espresso, cappuccino, and regular coffee, provided you pressed the correct buttons. (Chip was one of the few proud owners of the coffeemaker who could actually force it to make coffee.) He boasted that he only used his stove a couple of times a year, though his electricity bill was astronomical.

Chip became Hart Drummond's best friend in Weymouth. Hart admired Chip's free and easy approach to the world, but took consolation in his own more comfortable lifestyle. Chip Strong's weird house made Hart feel that all those late nights at the firm and all those tense moments with Frances had paid off in his own accustomed level of well-being.

It was already a joke between them that Hart was a seasoned fisherman. It intrigued Hart that people could have different fishing styles. He, it turned out, was a methodical and thorough angler. He read up on the ecology of the Sound and the habits of the common bluefish (his usual prey). He studied lures and spinners and rarely strayed into unconventional choices. But Chip was a maverick and paid no heed to common practice. One morning he came out with a bucket of night crawlers, fat disgusting worms that he thought might appeal to the blues. They appealed to *something*: every time Chip pulled up his hook the worms were gone, but he never caught anything.

Hart was now preparing to cast again when he heard footsteps on the dock behind him. "Any luck?" said the unmistakable reedy voice of Chip Strong. (It was one of his peculiarities that he generally sang alto in the Episcopal church choir.)

"No, it's too hot. Or too sunny," said Hart, with all the expertise acquired in his month of fishing.

"Don't you believe it," answered Chip, setting down a large cooler. "Blues love hot weather. What in the world is that on your line?"

Hart proudly held out his gaudy lure. Chip took it gingerly between two fingers. "Very nice," he said. "The last time I saw this it was a pair of earrings at Woolworth's."

"Frances thought it was tacky, too," Hart said, unperturbed. "I think it's kind of diverting."

"Original, certainly," rejoined Chip, attaching a flickering mirrored lure to his line. "Where were you last weekend? I caught a four-pounder, but there weren't any witnesses."

"And you probably threw it back, too," Hart said. He had quickly adapted to the ritual banter about fish caught or not caught.

"Nope. Took it home and filleted it. Then I froze some and gave some to Mrs. Frazer next door."

"You filleted it yourself?" asked Hart.

"Sure. It's not hard, if your knife is sharp enough."

"How do you do it?"

"Oh, it's just like filleting a trout when you eat it in a restaurant," Chip said airily. "Of course, you have to cut off the head and gut it first. Then you slide the knife along the backbone and lift the backbone off. Piece of cake."

"The couple of fish I've caught, we've had them filleted at the fish market," Hart offered. It seemed paltry and unmanly somehow.

"Don't bother. You can do it yourself. And then, get this, you cook them in the dishwasher!"

"What? Frances always puts them under the broiler. I think," Hart added. Actual cooking was something of a mystery to him. "I don't think I could persuade her to cook in the dishwasher."

"Well, you should try. You get some heavy-duty tinfoil, and

you slather the fish with mayonnaise, and you put it on the top rack of the dishwasher sealed up tight, and you run the dry cycle. Works like a charm, I promise you. And you don't use any gas."

Hart didn't listen to the last part. He knew Chip well enough by now to make allowances for his reluctance to light his stove. Frances would never, he was sure, cook anything in the dishwasher. But filleting the fish—that was appealing. He saw himself skilfully wielding a razor-sharp knife, lifting away the backbone with a swift, sure motion. He almost forgot the reel in his hand, until he felt some unmistakable resistance on the end of the line.

Three minutes later, an eighteen-inch fish lay flapping in Chip Strong's cooler, and Hart was reattaching his successful lure to his line. "Have you got another one of those that I could try?" asked Chip.

"I can afford to be generous," Hart said expansively. "They're in my bag." Maybe Frances could be persuaded to try that dishwasher trick after all.

Ignorant of her culinary fate, Frances was getting dressed. It was hard to find something in her closet that would be cool yet presentable. What the day really required was a sleeveless full-skirted dress in some dark Madras plaid that wouldn't show the wrinkles. But, thought Frances wryly, flicking the neat row of hangers, the day for sleeveless dresses had long since passed her by, even if you could still get or wear dark Madras. She found a long full skirt in a bandanna print and decided it would do. She was only going to look at another house, anyway.

Except that this time she was hopeful. As she pulled on a white shirt and found a pair of gold shell-shaped earrings, Frances allowed herself to run through the ad again in her mind. "Mint Cond. Victorian," it said. "In same family for 80 years. Beautiful gardens, 3 br. 2 bath. For Sale by Owner." The house was in Madison, a town she'd grown to appreciate. It was south of Route 1, which Hart should find appealing since it would be closer to the beach. The price seemed fair for that kind of property. Frances's study of the real estate pages had given her a sense of the market, though of course you couldn't tell anything until you actually saw the place. So Frances was heading off to the open house.

On one level, Frances knew she shouldn't be banking on this house. It was silly to get excited about the second house she'd seen by herself. She also knew that real-estate ads were not to be taken literally. But mere owners seemed to be less guileful than real-estate agents. If this ad said the house was in mint condition, wasn't that a term that meant specific things? Polished floors and the original brass hardware? Deep bathtubs with ball and claw feet? And "beautiful gardens." You wouldn't mention them if you weren't proud of them. Frances allowed herself to picture a wide perennial border, full of irises and peonies. Well, not in July. Snapdragons, then. Gardens, plural. A rock garden, full of wonderful little alpines? Maybe, Frances thought, maybe even roses. Without admitting as much to Hart, Frances had hated leaving her roses in Chester. She had devoted so much time and attention to them that it felt like abandonment. Could there be a rose garden at this house?

Frances tried to quell her anticipation as she drove down I-95 to Madison. Nobody bought the second house they looked at. It might be ghastly. Sometimes these Victorians were on very small lots. What if the neighbors had a huge dog or played loud music? What if the owners had put up hideous wallpaper? But wouldn't "Mint Condition" rule that out?

As Frances pulled up to the designated address, she could see no immediate flaws. The house was a classic mansard-roofed Victorian with a front porch. On either side of the steps bloomed a row of hydrangeas, each shrub weighed down with huge clusters of blue blossoms. Frances tried to be open-minded. She might not like hydrangeas, but she had to admit, these were healthy. And they were in period. In fact, you could look on them as a good sign. The Victorians loved their hydrangeas. Maybe that meant "Mint Condition" would include original stained glass.

A placard on the lawn (neatly trimmed) said OPEN HOUSE TODAY in neat but amateurish writing. As Frances walked past it, the screen door opened.

Immediately Frances's heart sank. The woman standing there

with a welcoming smile on her face was probably eighty, though clearly a fit and active eighty. She was wearing a flowered blouse over teal-green knitted pants, and comfortably squashy beige sandals. Instinctively Frances knew that this was not someone to whom "Mint Condition" meant original stained glass. The woman on the porch held out her hand and smiled. "Are you here for the open house? I'm so glad you're our first visitor. Bill and I were so worried about this. But it'll be easy to show you around. You look like a nice person and I'm sure you'll love our house. I'm Virginia McCarthy."

Frances, whose manners never failed her, shook hands and smiled. "Frances Drummond. Thank you. Yes, I was so interested to read about your gardens."

"Would you like to see them first? Why don't we go look at them now and then Bill can show you around inside?"

"No, no, Virginia, we agreed, first the interior, then the gardens," boomed a voice from the dark hall. "Lead up to it, you know."

"Oh, fine, I just thought since this lady was our first—"

"No, Virginia, we'll stick to what we planned," said the voice. A very tall man in a white short-sleeved dress shirt and dark pants stepped onto the porch. "Virginia does most of the gardening, so she wants to show off her babies, don't you? I'm Bill McCarthy. My parents bought this house before I was born and I grew up here along with my five sisters. Can't imagine what it'll be like to move out, but our daughter in New Jersey wants us closer to her and I can see her point," he said, flourishing the cane he'd held behind him. "Come on in, Mrs. Drummond."

"This is the hall," Virginia McCarthy said brightly.

Frances looked around. "Yes," she agreed. "I see." Her eye strayed to the fireplace in the living room. It had been filled in with what appeared to be plastic brick.

"We don't use the fireplace," Virginia said. "It got to be too much trouble to have it cleaned, and the bird's nests were a terrible problem, so we just covered it over. Bill had some of that nice brick paneling left over from the kitchen." She advanced into the living room and gestured. "Now, you'll see, everywhere in the house, Bill has been making improvements."

He had obviously worked hard. The walls were covered with knotty pine paneling. The ceiling, which should have been some twelve feet from the floor, had been dropped to eight with acoustic tile. Shallow shelving made of the knotty pine displayed an extensive collection of china teacups, while a huge glass-fronted cabinet (also obviously crafted by Bill) contained hundreds of commemorative teaspoons.

"Bill's mother started collecting those teaspoons on her honeymoon back in 1906," Virginia said proudly. "When she passed on and left it to me, I kept adding to it."

Frances's first glance into the living room had told her all she needed to know. Her hopes were dashed and she felt stupid. Naive. She felt as if she'd been taken in, not by the McCarthys' advertisement, but by her own assumptions. Harry and Eleanor had both, in tiresome stages of their youth, accused her of leading a sheltered life. She couldn't deny it, though she failed to see the fault. Most people she knew, certainly her friends, saw life as she did. They shared values and they shared tastes. What was wrong with that?

What was wrong with that, Frances realized as she looked at the rows of silvery spoons, was that she'd forgotten about other tastes. In a moment of unusual perception, Frances understood that Bill McCarthy had inherited a house he didn't much like. Its high ceilings and fireplaces made it hard to heat, the size of the rooms and the stairs were inconvenient, but it was the house he'd grown up in. So he kept it and did what he could to turn it into the 1940s-style Colonial that he really would have preferred. For the first time Frances grasped that maintaining a Victorian house in the style she took for granted, with its parquet floor polished and its slate roof restored—this required a great deal that she also took for granted. Money, time, and the education to appreciate it.

She turned away from the spoons and sighed. A series of photographs framed in green velvet caught her eye. Four girls and two boys in caps and gowns faced her. "Our children," said Bill McCarthy. "We had these done when they graduated from high school. This one here, Monica"—he pointed to a brunette with a perky expression—"is the one who's after us to sell the house and move."

"Come and see the dining room, Mrs. Drummond," Virginia said. "Bill put down a new linoleum floor in there. I was so tired of waxing the old wood, you know." Frances followed her and looked at the gold-flecked black and white tiles. She glanced around the walls, which had been paneled over with dark fake wood.

For a moment, Frances was speechless. She wanted more than anything to simply flee, to leave the McCarthys looking after her in surprise and to drive as fast as she could back to—but the thought stopped there. To what? To the Wrong House? It wouldn't offer much comfort. Neither would Hart. She could barely explain to herself why she was finding this experience so upsetting. Hart would never understand. And besides, she didn't want to hurt the McCarthys' feelings. The thought surprised her, but she welcomed it. These were nice people, hard-working people who were very proud of their house. Frances knew she was wasting her time and probably theirs, but she couldn't bring herself to be rude. She looked again at the floor and said, with all the tact she could muster, "That's a very elegant choice."

"I thought so, too," said Virginia. "Mary Pat—that's our eldest—thought it looked like a bathroom, but I told her she'd get used to it and she has. The last time she was here—she lives in Bristol—she said, 'Mom, I didn't think I'd ever like that linoleum but I'm coming around to it.' And now she's thinking of putting some in her kitchen, she doesn't really have a dining room, it's more an eat-in-kitchen."

The appliances in the kitchen were all mustard-colored, or, as the manufacturers called them in the 1960s, "Harvest Gold." One entire wall was faced with the plastic brick that Frances had seen in the fireplace. The bedrooms upstairs had also been renovated by Bill. The materials varied from room to room. One had white paneling and wall-to-wall carpet, one had reddish-stained pine and brick-patterned linoleum. Several rooms sported clever features invented by Bill, like a built-in sewing cabinet for Virginia (who had made all the curtains) or a window seat that held extra bedding. There wasn't a surface in the house, not a wall or a ceiling or a floor, that hadn't been re-covered by Bill in some substance Frances despised. Bill's improvements ruined the proportions of every room, and Virginia's curtains, all sewn from man-made fibers for ease of upkeep, struck Frances as perfectly hideous.

Nevertheless, she behaved heroically. She complimented Bill on his cleverness and practicality. She admired Virginia's invisible hemstitching. At no point did she betray her despair. When they went out to look at the gardens, a pair of oblong beds packed with zinnias and marigolds, she mentioned her own garden in Chester.

"But you don't live in New Jersey now?" Bill said. "I thought your car had Connecticut plates."

"Yes," Frances said. "We moved up to Weymouth earlier this summer. We bought a modern house, but to tell you the truth, I don't like it. I've always lived in an older house and I can't get used to the one we're in. And it doesn't have a garden. I miss that terribly."

"Oh, you must," Virginia said sympathetically. "I always find such consolation in a garden. No matter what's gone wrong, there's always something in the garden that's going *right*, don't you think?"

"Unless the raccoons have been around," Bill said. "You wouldn't believe, we never used to have them here so close to the water, but they've been coming across Route 1 in the last few years, they're a terrible pest."

"We used to have them in Chester," Frances said, "but what really bothered me more was the year we had a possum. It got into the garage and Hart, my husband, was away, and I was afraid to try to catch it. My son finally trapped it in a carpetbag. Well, I should be going." She turned to the McCarthys and found herself saying, "I don't know if I'll be back. I don't know if I can persuade my husband to consider moving. I've been looking at houses on my own because he isn't really interested at this point."

"I've noticed men don't care so much about where they live," Virginia McCarthy said, nodding. "Bill here is an exception. I'll bet your husband's just happy as a clam in that house. Well, I'll tell you what— Oh, look Bill, there's someone else driving up!" She pointed to a white BMW pulling up behind Frances's car. "You go greet them, Bill, I'll be right there. Here, Mrs. Drummond, I feel so badly for you without a garden, I want to cut you some flowers. Just let me get my clippers off the porch," she said. And before Frances had a chance to protest, Virginia had clipped a tight little bunch of zinnias. "Here, dear. Now you run home and get these in water. Good luck with the house, dear. I hope your husband comes around."

"Good luck to you," Frances said, and hesitantly patted Virginia on the arm. It wasn't the sort of thing she normally did, but she was so touched by this woman's warmth that something beyond the norm seemed required. "I'm sure you'll find a buyer who will appreciate all the work you've put into the house." And she managed to get to the car and drive away without blinking.

But the moment she was out of sight, Frances pulled over and turned off the engine, then buried her head in her arms.

Resentment and anger had carried her a long way that summer, and she had tried to keep self-pity at bay. She had not always been successful, but she congratulated herself on this, at least: she had not whined much. Yet the unexpected sympathy from this nice, brave woman cracked Frances's composure.

She didn't cry: on the whole, Frances wasn't a weeper. After taking a few deep breaths she sat with her head bowed until her hands, still gripping the steering wheel, grew numb. Then she sat up straight and rubbed her eyes. She touched the petals of one bright pink zinnia lying on the passenger seat. And she started the car to drive home.

Why, Frances wondered, had she been able to say so frankly to a perfect stranger what she could not express to Hart? "I miss my garden terribly." Was that such an awful admission? It was worrying about Hart's answer that stopped her from saying such things, Frances realized. Would he snap at her? Accuse her of not being a good sport? No, Frances decided, he would probably suggest again that she get to work and start a garden on the grounds of the Wrong House. As if soil and wind and sun made no difference. What she knew she would not get from Hart was the easy sympathy that Virginia McCarthy showed her.

She drove home in stony-faced glumness. The roads were full of families driving to the beach in heavily laden cars. Children squirmed in backseats and brandished water guns out windows. Frances barely noticed. Automatically she got off I-95 at the Weymouth exit and drove through town. She noticed Hart's car parked in front of Chip Strong's house. It didn't seem to matter. It didn't cross her mind to wonder what he was up to. All Frances wanted to do at that point was to flee, somehow. To go up to one of the guest bedrooms in the Wrong House and close the door. To retreat from the world.

When she got to the house she noticed a square of paper fluttering on the front door. As she put the key into the lock she read it: "Frances: sorry about mess. Back soon."

Incurious, she pulled it off the door and crumpled it up. Mess could hardly bother her now. Besides, the living room was as neat as ever. Automatically, without putting down her purse, Frances went into the kitchen to get a glass of iced tea.

She stopped on the threshold, shocked out of her reverie and gasping. The kitchen was covered with blood.

There was a paper bag on the floor next to the sink. Leaking from its bottom and its damp, dark creases was a sinister red ooze, which Hart had stepped in and tracked to the door. On the counter lay an immense fish. Its head had been hacked off roughly and lay with the huge bulbous eye staring at Frances. Entrails spilled from its stomach like jumbled-up knitting, smearing blood on the white cabinets. A red-streaked butcher knife lay next to it. Though the open window over the sink was screened, two huge flies buzzed and fumbled over the fish.

As Frances stood there frozen in horror, an enormous gull landed on the windowsill with a clattering rush of wings. It pecked at the screen with its vast yellow beak and shrieked, then pecked again.

Frances bolted. It was too much. The gull, the flies, the fish, the blood, the day, the bunch of zinnias—it was all too much for her suddenly. Her sense of duty and her self-control caved in. She ran upstairs and vomited in the brown marble bathroom.

Then with shaky hands, feeling light-headed, she scrabbled some underwear and a nightgown into a bag along with her reading glasses and Arden eye cream. She seized *The Hills of Maragon* from beside her bed. She ran back down the stairs, threw her bag in the car, and sped away, leaving the house wide open. When Hart returned ten minutes later with the filleting knife borrowed from Chip Strong, he didn't even know she'd been there. Been, and left. It was only when she called him from New York later that afternoon that he found out she wouldn't be cooking his fresh-caught, home-filleted bluefish for him, in the dishwasher or otherwise.

15

Neither of the Drummonds realized at first that Frances had left Hart. When she called him from a room at the Yale Club, Frances omitted to tell her husband precisely where she was or when she was coming home, but a little effort on Hart's part would have tracked her down. He didn't feel the effort was necessary, since she had indicated only that she'd gone to New York on the spur of the moment. This was unusual but not unprecedented, and Hart took advantage of her absence to cook the bluefish in the dishwasher and furthermore to throw it away after a few bites, since it turned out to be disgusting.

But after three days, Hart opened his closet to find that he had no clean shirts. "Frances!" he bellowed automatically, then checked himself, feeling silly. Right. Frances wasn't there. He stopped himself from moving toward the phone. He couldn't reach her anyway. That was odd, now that he thought of it. She hadn't told him where she was.

He sat down on the bed. His momentary curiosity about his wife's whereabouts was eclipsed by a more urgent dilemma. How could he get clean shirts? How did Frances get them? Should he try to call her for instructions? Hart looked at the phone by the bed. She was probably at the Yale Club, anyway. All it would take was a quick call. But maybe he could manage by himself. Show her. Why not? Anybody could do laundry.

So Hart started. He gathered six oxford-cloth shirts from the hook on the back of his closet where he hung them when they were dirty. It crossed his mind as he did this that Frances sent his shirts out, because they always reappeared in his drawers neatly pressed and wrapped around cardboard. Well, that was just a detail. He could iron them when he was done.

He managed to load them into the washer successfully. Three kinds of laundry detergent stood on the shelf above the washer and Hart, being systematic, read the labels of each one. They made the whole process remarkably clear. There was even a spray can of starch, which no doubt he would use to iron his shirts once they were clean.

He measured out the prescribed capful of Tide and pressed the buttons on the washer, which started up with a gratifying *whoosh*. He was very interested in the bottle of Downy and couldn't resist adding a measure of it as well. Feeling resourceful, he went off to eat breakfast.

The shirts came out of the washer looking fine. He loaded them into the dryer. This was a snap. Was this the kind of thing housewives complained about? And Frances had a cleaning lady, too! It hardly seemed necessary.

It was pleasant on the deck, since a cool front had moved in, pushing away the humidity. The Sound was glittering again and the Whaler bobbed lightly at the dock. Hart read a long article in *The New York Times* about beach erosion and shoreline real-estate values. He went upstairs to shave, and ran the dishwasher when he came back downstairs. Then he thought about going to the market. Hard to know what to buy if he didn't know when Frances was coming back. Maybe he should just stock up on staples.

So Hart drove off jauntily to the supermarket, where his delight in novelty was further gratified. He arrived home toward noon with four bags of groceries that included a jar of tiny pickled ears of corn, a box of meatless chili con carne mix, three flavors of Rice-A-Roni (on sale), and, as a symbol of rebellion, whole milk (Frances always bought skim).

He remembered the shirts as he was unpacking, so once all of his purchases were safely stowed, he set up the ironing board. He plugged in the iron and filled it with water from the plastic bottle, as he recalled having seen Mrs. Wilucki do. Then he opened the dryer and took out the first shirt.

It was wrinkled. That was to be expected. Cotton wrinkled in the dryer. He spread it out on the ironing board. He touched the iron with the tips of his fingers, also as he'd seen Mrs. Wilucki do. The woman clearly had skin like a horse's hoof, he thought, shaking his burned fingers. Now the spray starch.

He lined up one of the sleeves straight on the ironing board. He sprayed. He ran the iron over the sleeve. It flattened a little. He turned it over. Oh. The iron had set some wrinkles on the other side of the sleeve. Shake them out. Iron again, more carefully this time. Ooops. No spray. He sprayed. Turned the sleeve over again. Hadn't he ironed that side once? He ironed it again.

Hart stood the iron on end and picked up the shirt. He gave it a good hard flap. Maybe the sleeves were extra hard because they were two layers of cloth. He'd start on something easier, like the front. He laid the front panel of the shirt carefully on the ironing board and sprayed. He lowered the iron, which slid pleasantly along the fabric, leaving a smooth wake. The buttons were in the way. Hart nosed the iron gently between them, reasoning that the placket would cover those wrinkly bits anyway. It didn't look too bad. He stood the iron on end again and held the shirt up.

What was this? Hadn't he just ironed that part? It was all rumpled again. Hart frowned and lay the shirt back down. Dammit, maybe not enough starch. He sprayed again and checked the temperature on the iron. Probably wasn't hot enough. He goosed up the heat and ironed again. Better. He even slapped the iron down a little and rammed it between the buttons with more force. Clearly this was a shirt to be reckoned with. Stood to reason. Brooks Brothers made them to stand up to all kinds of wear and tear. You probably had to show them who was boss.

Hart flipped the shirt over and smoothed the back on the board. The two front halves and the sleeves hung down. He sprayed and enjoyed the hiss as the iron hit the foam of starch on the cotton. That pleat on the back was a little hard to manage, though. How were you supposed to make it line up? Was there a specific technique for this? Hart carefully set down the iron on end again and lifted the shirt to see how the pleat hung. He turned it around again just to admire his handiwork on the front.

"Goddamn!" Somehow the front of the shirt, which had been

submissively flat and fresh-looking only moments ago, had rumpled up again. What was it with this shirt? The damn thing was insubordinate. With irritation, Hart lay it down again and reattacked the front panel with a considerable thump on the ironing board. He knocked over the bottle of distilled water and knelt down carefully to get it. Wouldn't do to jostle the ironing board from beneath and get clobbered with a hot iron. Gingerly, avoiding the cord, he straightened up. Put down the water bottle. Lifted the iron, which he had left resting on the shirt. Contemplated the neat ocher imprint left by the hot iron squarely on the front of his best white shirt. Shut his eyes and swore loud and long.

Hart put away the iron after neatly emptying out the water, as he'd seen Mrs. Wilucki do. He collapsed the ironing board and slid it into the closet. And he drove back into the village to take his shirts to the cleaner, where someone he'd never seen looked at an inscrutable mark on the collar and said, "Okay, Mr. Drummond, starched and boxed, we'll deliver them next week."

When he got home the phone was ringing. It was Harry. "Hi, Dad, how are you?"

"Fine," Hart said. "Fine. Weather's changed; we've got a nice breeze. And I caught a couple of huge blues the other day in the harbor."

"Casting from the dock?" Harry asked. "What kind of lure?" He couldn't have cared less, but he was fond of his father.

"Something with little dangling pearly strips on it. Weird-looking, but the fish like it."

"That sounds good. You'll have to let me have a try next time I'm out. Listen, is Mom there? I wanted to ask her something about Eleanor's birthday."

"Ah, no, she's not."

"Oh. Okay, when will she be back? I'm going to be out, but I can call later."

"Um, I'm not really sure."

"Well, roughly. Where'd she go?"

"Actually, she's in New York. For a couple of days. Shopping, she said."

"Oh." Pause. "Okay, I'll try to reach her here. Is she at the Yale Club?"

"Um, yes. I think so. Yes."

"But you're not sure?" Harry said, suddenly attentive to the shade of doubt in his father's voice.

"Well, I just assumed so, I didn't really ask her. Listen, I have to go. Talk to you soon," Hart said, and hung up.

Harry raised his eyebrows at the phone and reached for the phone book. That was odd. Well, maybe not. Frances did come to New York to shop occasionally, and she did routinely stay at the Yale Club. So maybe Hart wouldn't ask where she was going; maybe he'd just assume.

Harry dialed the Yale Club and asked for Mrs. Drummond's room. "I'm sorry, Mrs. Drummond isn't here anymore," answered a voice.

"She isn't?" Harry said, puzzled. "When did she leave?"

"Just a moment." Pages flipped audibly. "Yesterday," said the voice.

"She did?"

"Yes. Can I help you with anything else?"

"No, thank you," Harry said, hanging up the phone. He dialed his father's number.

"Dad, she's not there," he said without preamble.

"Where? Who?" Hart answered, confused. He had been making a sandwich out of turkey bologna and dill pickle chips, a delicate operation.

"Mom. She's not at the Yale Club. She left yesterday."

"Well, I don't know where she is, then," Hart answered, sounding irritated. "Don't worry about it. She'll call in and I'll have her call you."

"Dad, how long is she going to be in the city, do you know? Maybe we can have lunch."

"I don't know, Harry," said his father impatiently. "You'll have to ask her that. Bye."

This made Harry very suspicious. Neither of his parents was the type for open-ended plans. Or spur-of-the-moment trips, for that matter. Harry got up from his desk and turned off his air conditioner. The hum suddenly seemed annoying.

218

He sat down again at his desk and turned his back on the bright blue screen of his computer. He dialed Eleanor's number at work. "Eleanor Gray," she said, picking up the receiver on the first ring.

"What happened to Teresa? How come you're answering your own phone?" Harry asked, diverted from his purpose.

"Oh, Lord, Teresa quit because I gave her a bad review. And she told the head of personnel—excuse me, human resources—that I was a terrible boss because I was so insecure about my children that I made her cram much too much work into too small a time. Or something like that; I wasn't really listening. So they're having some kind of procedure and I'm being reviewed, if you can believe it. And for the moment all they'll give me is a temp and she's too frightened to handle the phones. Every time I ask her to do something she hyperventilates. I'll tell you, it's grand around here," Eleanor finished wearily.

"Well, you're going to love this, too, El," Harry said, wondering for an instant if he should even tell her. After all, why give his poor sister anything more to worry about?

"What?" Eleanor asked, her voice suddenly sharpening. "If it's anything about George Sinclair I don't want to hear it," she said.

"No," Harry said quickly to distract her, "it's Mom and Dad. Mom seems to have gone astray."

"What does that mean?"

"Dad doesn't know where she is."

"How can he not know where she is?" Eleanor asked impatiently. "Where could she be?"

"Well, she's here in New York somewhere. But Dad thought she was staying at the Yale Club. Only I just called there and she isn't, she left yesterday."

Eleanor was silent. Harry could almost feel her thinking. "That is a little odd," she finally conceded. "I don't like it much. She's been so weird all summer. Do we know she's really here?"

"We know she *was*," Harry said. "She could be in Timbuktu by now."

"Mmm. Not Timbuktu," Eleanor said. "Not Mom."

"I know. But anywhere west of the Danube and north of the equator."

"Realistically," Eleanor said.

"Realistically," Harry said, "I'm going to call Clara. On a hunch."

"Okay. Well, realistically, you let me know. I'd just as soon not worry about Mom right now, so tell me what you find out," Eleanor said, and hung up. But she stared at the telephone for a full three minutes afterward, trying to convince herself it was all going to be all right.

Twenty-four hours earlier, the object of all this discussion had been seated in the cafeteria at the Museum of Modern Art, sipping tea and staring out the window, thinking how happy she was. Life, for the first time in several months, seemed, well, *attractive*. Fun. Packed—there was really no other word—with enticing opportunities. Frances glanced at her watch and drained her teacup. She didn't want to be late to her next activity, a lecture on old roses at the New York Horticultural Society. She stood up and stretched discreetly, feeling remarkably alert and interested in her surroundings. As she walked up Fifth Avenue, she studied the sari-clad woman in front of her. Exactly how did that thing stay up? Were they allowed to use safety pins? The woman was quite plump. There was a small but definite bulge of flesh between the skirt and that sort of blouse thing. But really, Frances conceded, it looked right. All of that flowing fabric wouldn't suit a lean frame. As she passed the plate-glass window of an airline office, Frances could see her own silhouette dimly reflected by the dark interior. She looked with approval at her new haircut. That was one thing you certainly couldn't get in Weymouth, she thought. She'd had her hair done there once and had to wash out the tight curls the minute she got home.

Really, some things about New York were marvelous, Frances went on thinking as she settled into her folding chair at the Horticultural Society. Hart always fussed about the noise and the air and the crime. But if you cared about, well, civilization, Frances thought, nothing beat New York. Hart didn't care much about civilization. He would probably have enjoyed living in some remote village in Newfoundland.

Frances wondered for a moment how he was getting on. He wasn't quite as helpless as many men of his age. She knew he wouldn't starve. But he probably wasn't very comfortable. She smiled momentarily. Hart had always claimed that he could live happily in Army barracks. He always told her, when she complained about cooking, for instance, that she could just serve him tuna fish and he'd be happy. Well, his affection for tuna fish was probably being tested.

Although she was extremely interested in old roses, Frances found the lecturer very irritating. He was an older man with a nasal voice and a pedantic way of pronouncing foreign languages, especially the French names of roses. His slides were grainy, and he spent far too much time describing a horrific drive to the Dutch palace of Het Loo, and not enough, for Frances's taste, on cultivation practices. About twenty minutes into the lecture, she stood up and walked out. As she stepped over the feet of the woman at the end of the row, she heard a whisper: "What a good idea. I think I'll come, too." The two women paused in the doorway onto West 58th Street, blinking in the bright afternoon light. Frances's companion, a pleasant-looking gray-haired woman in a simple suit, said, "Thank you. I've never actually walked *out* of anything before. It's rather thrilling!"

Frances smiled. "Neither have I, now that I think of it. It always seems so rude. But that awful man was really unbearable."

"Yes, he was," the other woman said. "Well, enjoy your afternoon!" And she walked briskly up Fifth Avenue.

After a moment's thought, Frances headed downtown, walking just fast enough not to get jostled in the crowd. Now what? It was Tuesday afternoon. She'd planned on going to an early movie after the lecture. But now . . . she looked at her watch. Well, maybe it would make sense to head back to the Yale Club and look in at the New York Public Library on the way. There was an exhibit of Audubon prints there, and Frances had never been in the place.

Then maybe a nap. Or the movie. Or dinner at the Oyster Bar, that would be nice. Though on second thought, fish— For a moment Frances didn't know why the thought of fish disturbed her, then she remembered the carnage in the kitchen of the Wrong House. No, not the Oyster Bar. Still, dinner somewhere that someone else had cooked, eaten off plates that someone else would wash. It was such bliss to be free of housework for a change. Not that she found it so onerous, Frances reminded herself. Not usually. Not in Chester, anyway, when there was something to take pride in. Keeping the house running in Chester had been a real pleasure, an achievement, Frances realized. Even if Hart didn't appreciate it, Frances felt that in some way the house itself did. It was a house that expected an orderly linen closet and gleaming brass andirons. The Wrong House didn't need as much care, it was true. She hardly ever dusted, and Mrs. Wilucki did all the vacuuming. But there was no point in trying to make it into something it wasn't. The Wrong House was utilitarian. It wasn't civilized.

Frances was so distracted by her thoughts that she turned left automatically at East 43rd Street, and it wasn't until she opened the door of the Yale Club that she remembered about the Audubon prints. She looked at her watch and shrugged. That was the beauty of having nothing particular to do. It didn't matter if you got it done or not. She collected her key at the desk and was surprised to hear the telephone ringing as she opened the door to her room. With great composure, Frances answered it. She couldn't imagine how anyone had gotten her number, but it didn't seem to matter. In fact, the caller was Clara, who had apparently tracked her down by ESP.

"Silly to spend all that money at that club," Clara said. "If you want to stay in New York, go to my house. It's open. Beatriz is there. She can cook for you, she'd love to have something to do."

"Aunt Clara, how did you find . . . ?" Frances began, but stopped. "Witchcraft, I suppose."

"Right. No questions asked. Go ahead. It's a nicer neighborhood, anyway."

Frances hesitated. The house was on East 73rd Street. It *was* a nicer neighborhood. She looked around her impersonal room, with the window that couldn't be opened and the view of the Pan Am Building. "You might as well be really comfortable," Clara's voice said. "You'll have the place to yourself."

"Well, thank you, Aunt Clara," Frances said. "If you're sure I won't be bothering anyone."

"Not at all. I'd rather have someone in the house anyway. Go on up there tomorrow morning, I'll let Beatriz know. What do you want for lunch? She'll have it ready."

"Goodness, is that how you really live?" Frances said, momentarily startled.

"Of course it is. What did you think, child, that I mess around in the kitchen myself? One more thing. Do you mind if they find out where you are?"

"They? You mean Hart and the children? Oh, no. I don't want them worrying. I suppose I should let them know."

"When they want you they'll track you down," Clara answered. "If anyone calls me, then, I'll tell them?"

"Oh, yes, that would be fine," Frances said. "Thank you."

"Not at all. Tell me what's happening when you feel like it," Clara answered, and hung up.

Eleanor was busier than usual and rather grateful for this. She knew that, if it did nothing else, hard work distracted you from your troubles. It also, if you were lucky, provided you with some tangible successes. Eleanor had been an attorney long enough to know that, especially in trusts and estates, the triumphs weren't flamboyant. You had to take pride in a well-crafted document or in convincing a stubborn widow that you knew how to shelter her money from the IRS. The settlement of the Gast accounting was satisfying in a more dramatic way. Charlie Winter's client had evidently decided to play ball. At a deeply satisfying meeting, Charlie, without cowboy boots or bolo tie, had been obliged to tell Eleanor that Russell Berk recognized his responsibilities and would make restitution to the Gast estate. So Eleanor, trying not to smirk, laid out her requirements, which Charlie then had to accept. His expression of meekness almost made up to Eleanor for the rude crack he had made about her haircut. And as she took the E train back to the office, she was able to reflect with grim satisfaction that at least she could still manage her job. And the boys were fine. And her hair was growing out. In fact, if you had asked Eleanor, that second week in August, how she was weathering the episode of George Sinclair, she would have told you curtly that she had put it behind her. If there was a certain joylessness to her demeanor, few people besides her family perceived it.

One of them, however, was her friend Sophy.

Sophy had known Eleanor since college. Sophy had memories of a girl whose earnestness and sense of responsibility were leavened by a sense of humor and an unexpected irreverent streak. She hadn't seen much of either characteristic in months, and this worried her. Something had to be done. She wanted Eleanor to visit a psychic.

Eleanor had laughed this off at first. Sophy was, she felt, prone to fall for silly trends. She had eaten macrobiotic food for a while, then practiced Transcendental Meditation. After that came a flirtation with the cult of some Eastern swami, then, in an abrupt about-face, devout attendance at an Episcopal church in the Village where they used home-baked seven-grain bread for Communion. Reliance on a psychic, though new, was not surprising.

But Sophy bristled at the suggestion that this was another passing fad. "He's just *helpful*, Ellie. You wouldn't believe what he sees. I know you think I'm a crackpot, but honestly, Frank is very practical."

Eleanor still didn't see how a practical psychic named Frank was going to make her life easier or more pleasant. So Sophy had resorted to force, emotionally speaking. For Eleanor's thirty-ninth birthday, she gave her friend a session with Frank.

Eleanor knew she was beaten, but tried to make difficulties anyway. When could she see him? She was so busy. His office—could psychics have offices?—was so hard to get to. Sophy countered by stating that Frank had a session free on Thursday, August 13, and she would baby-sit for Toby and Simon. And furthermore that nobody else in New York found the Upper East Side hard to get to.

So the day after Harry realized his mother had gone astray, Eleanor took the Lexington Avenue IRT to 86th Street and walked a few blocks to a modern apartment building with a doorman in the lobby. She wondered, as she asked for Frank Gerson, if the doorman knew the nature of his business. Did a stream of anxious-looking people come asking for him? Was this going to be a professional office like a shrink's, with a discreet waiting room?

Eleanor realized, as she took the elevator to the fourteenth floor, that her interest in the details of Frank's real estate arrangements was just a cover for anxiety. As she rang his bell and listened for answering footsteps, she tried to put her finger on just what she was anxious about. What could she have to hide? What could this man tell her that she didn't want to know?

When he opened the door, she thought she had pressed the wrong doorbell. He was small and slim, with very short curly hair and horn-rim glasses. He wore khakis and an eggplant-colored polo shirt, and his feet were bare. Eleanor felt that, at least, was a psychic touch.

"Come in, come in," he said, a little irritably. "We don't all wear turbans and big earrings, you know."

Eleanor felt taken aback. Had he read her mind? Well, he was supposed to, wasn't he? She took a few steps into the bland, beige living room, trying to decide where to leave her briefcase. There was an abstract painting over a fireplace and two armless sofas upholstered in ivory tweed.

"Just leave it there," Frank said, gesturing to a low bench by the door. "And come sit over here, please." He was sitting at a square table, where two chairs faced each other.

Eleanor sat down. There were three packs of ordinary playing cards on the table, the kinds with the bicycle rider on the back. Two were red, one navy blue. Frank picked up the pack closest to him and began to shuffle with startling dexterity.

"Sophy said you were in trouble and that you didn't want to come. You don't really believe I can see anything, do you?" Frank said. He had a slightly fussy manner, like a much older man, though he was probably in his early forties.

"Well," said Eleanor apologetically, "no."

"So you're humoring your friend."

"That's basically it," Eleanor said. "I hope I won't waste your time."

"My time has been paid for," Frank said disconcertingly. "What you should worry about is yours. Here, choose three cards." He fanned out the pack. Eleanor pulled out the three of clubs, the seven of clubs, and the six of spades. She laid them on the table.

Frank swept them up and shuffled again. "You should give your brother a little more credit. He's not a child anymore, you know. Just because you were precociously responsible doesn't mean that he's irresponsible. You know, he might be really helpful in this flap with your parents."

Eleanor sat still, eyes wide. "How do you know this stuff?" she blurted out.

"That's the gift, Eleanor," he said, with a slight smile. "I know things about people. For instance, it doesn't take a lot of insight to see that you're a very unhappy woman right now." He was shuffling again, laying out a square of cards faceup. "What can you expect from life? That's the big question, isn't it?" He glanced up at her, suddenly sympathetic. "Is it more than just the day in, day out stuff? Your job, your children—two, I think?"

Eleanor nodded.

"Yes," Frank said, sweeping up the cards again, tapping and squaring off the pack. "The children aren't a concern. You know and I know that they're grand. And your work is manageable, too. It's everything else, isn't it?" He laid out a single row of cards, facedown now. His hand hovered over them, pausing. Then he tapped one. "Turn it over, please."

Eleanor did. It was the king of hearts.

"That's really just a card trick," Frank said, satisfied. "I tell you that to gain your trust. If you had been a different kind of person I would have used the king to start talking about the man. But I knew right away. No, I know you don't want to talk about him," Frank went on, shuffling again. He put the pack of cards aside and picked up the blue pack.

Studying Eleanor's face, he fanned the cards. "You *know*

you're making a terrible mistake," he said calmly. "There is nothing substantial standing in your way. He's a good man. Are you listening? A good man. I don't often get to say this to people. He's honest and passionate. You'll have to learn to fight."

He looked down at the cards, which he had apparently forgotten, and put them aside. Eleanor said tightly, "What do you mean, learn to fight?"

"Well, fight to get him. Fight your pride. Which is stupid anyway, you don't need it. Fight your worst nature, if I may put it that way. Determination can be a fault, you know. You're just being obstinate." He looked up at her. "I've lost you, haven't I? This is something you don't want to hear." He shrugged. "Sometimes I hate being a messenger. Let's look at something else."

Eleanor took a deep breath and tried to relax her shoulders. She rubbed her forehead and watched as Frank laid cards in a pyramid.

"Yes, you feel better. But I have to warn you, he's taking up a great deal of room, that man. What's his name?"

"George," Eleanor said.

"George isn't leaving much space, is he?" Frank said. "What's going on with your parents? Someone's having a second childhood. Or both of them. You know the rift is not very deep," Frank said, frowning at the cards. "But it could still go either way if they aren't careful."

"What could go either way?" Eleanor asked, startled at this turn in the conversation.

"They may get back together and they may not," Frank said, plucking cards one by one from the pyramid. "The situation's not dissimilar to yours. Emotional connection clouded by a lot of pride and stubbornness."

"What do you mean, get back together?" Eleanor asked.

"She's left him," Frank said, surprised in turn. "Didn't you know?"

"Well, she's in New York for a visit," Eleanor protested, "but she hasn't *left* him." She paused, disturbed. "At least that's not the story Dad's telling."

"Goodness, what a strange family," Frank responded, shaking

his head. "Of course they're pretending it isn't what it looks like. WASPs," he said, with disapproval. "I try not to make judgments, but really, what a group for masking things." He paused and looked at Eleanor again. "Don't be their go-between. Don't let your brother do it, either. They have to communicate directly." He pulled another card from the pyramid and looked at it quizzically. "Whatever that may mean for them. Not what it means for you, I know."

By now Eleanor was relaxing, though her mind was reeling with Frank's advice. Her mother had left her father? The rift wasn't deep, but it could go either way? What was she supposed to do about this?

"No, there's nothing for you to do," Frank's voice broke into her thoughts. "They're grown up. They have a history. You and your brother can't manage their relationship. Manage yours instead. Listen, Eleanor. I know what you dream of. I do. I see all that yearning for a richer life. You tell yourself you can't be lonely because you're so busy. You've fooled yourself into thinking you're self-sufficient.

"Let me tell you a little more about George. You are the woman of his dreams. He wants the kind of life you lead. He appreciates you. You're an unusual woman, Eleanor. You must know by now that you intimidate people. George is not afraid of you. He sees through you. He knows the tenderness inside. He would be loyal and protective." The cards were lying on the table, unregarded, as Frank spoke.

"You would quarrel," he went on. "That would be hard for you because he has a temper and so do you, though you may not know it. George would ask a great deal of you. And he is an artist, he is in some ways a slave to his art, and he will have to be careful with the competing claims. He will neglect you sometimes. This you need to know." Frank suddenly looked down and picked up the cards. "That's all. That's all about him. There isn't much left." He shuffled more slowly, then paused before laying out the cards in a circle. Meditatively, he eased three cards from the circle and placed them faceup in the center.

"This is by way of being a card trick, too. I sometimes have odd bits of images or information left over," he said, in a voice that had lost its urgency. "For instance, keep your hair short. The long hair aged you." He tapped the second card. "Hire an older woman for your next secretary." The third card made him pause. He looked up at Eleanor, his face doubtful.

"What?" she said, suddenly tired. "I don't think I can handle much more."

"I hesitate to tell you this," he said. "It may turn you against everything I've already said, and you need help, even if you don't take mine."

"Go ahead," Eleanor said. "I'll try not to let it weigh too heavily."

Frank sighed and flipped the card onto the table faceup. It was a joker. "I don't know what it's doing here; I always take them out of the pack," he said. "I have a very strong and very strange image in my mind. Something you will see in the near future."

"What?" Eleanor said. "Enough of the mystery, just tell me," she urged, a little irritated.

Frank took a deep breath. "I see a boat on the floor of a house," he said apologetically.

Eleanor looked at him incredulously. "Are you ever wrong about those things?"

"Not that I know of," Frank said. "It puzzles me, too. When it happens, let me know. There must be some explanation." He looked at his watch. "I think you should go home. This is a very short session, but I don't think you are ready to hear more." He picked up the cards and laid them aside. "You haven't gotten your money's worth. I owe you more time. If you want to come back I'd be glad to see you. I realize how unlikely that is."

Eleanor dimly realized that he was being generous, and thanked him, but she couldn't wait to get away.

When she got home, Sophy had put the boys to bed and was waiting with eager questions. What had he said? Wasn't he brilliant? What did he think about George? (Despite Sophy's loyalty to Eleanor, she felt her friend had thrown away a great opportunity by being so cold to George.)

Eleanor, naturally, didn't want to talk about George. In fact, she found Frank's news about her family disturbing enough to put George out of her mind completely. Sophy, who was at her best in a crisis, met this news with genuine concern and tactfully vanished so that Eleanor could call Harry.

But Harry wasn't home. Next Eleanor called her father, who was blandly obstructive. No, Frances wasn't there. No, he wasn't quite sure where she was staying or when she would be coming back. He'd tell her that Eleanor had called, though, of course. Oh, yes, he was doing fine, good night.

It wasn't possible to press further. Eleanor couldn't ask her father, "Has Mom left you?" Even less could she tell him where she'd gotten that idea. She had a moment's amusement at the idea of his incredulous reaction and wondered, as she sat down to read the newspaper, about Frank's reliability. He had been very convincing, until he got to the boat on the floor.

16

From the moment she stepped into Clara's house, Frances felt at home. Better than that. Soothed, somehow. Relaxed. It wasn't just a matter of luxury, though that played a part. Frances deeply enjoyed having Beatriz cook delicate little meals for her. And after her first two attempts to clear the table, which clearly embarrassed Beatriz, she realized it was kinder to let the woman do her job, and simply walked away from the table.

But there was something more than that, Frances thought, as she sat in the living room on Thursday night. She got up from the silk-covered sofa and crossed the room to study the picture over the fireplace. It was a little Sisley of the Seine under snow, painted in a subdued palette with beautiful feathery brushwork. Frances turned her back to it and scanned the rest of the room. It had been decorated in the 1940s in a grand Francophile style, with gilded tables and brocade upholstery in a predominantly sea-green shade. Frances walked over to the table next to the sofa, where a miniature portrait stood on a tiny easel. She picked it up and studied the merry face of the woman in powdered hair and a hoop skirt. There was potpourri in a big Chinese export porcelain bowl. The room was silent except for the ticking of the mantel clock. Frances put the miniature back down and let her eyes rove around the room. The taste wasn't quite hers: a bit more formal, more luxurious than what she would have chosen. But impeccable, and comfortable, and beautiful. That was it. It was simply beautiful.

She walked out into the hall, where a single lamp shone on a marble-topped table. The ceiling was high; the stairs formed an elegant curve. From here she could hear the occasional hiss of a car passing on the street below, or footsteps clipping by on the sidewalk. She crossed the hall and walked into the library. The streetlight outside shone into the dark room, picking out the glossy sheen of a celadon vase on the mantel and the gilded bronze trim on a writing table. She stepped into the room, watching her shadowy reflection in the mirror over the mantel.

Anywhere you went in the house, there was something beautiful to look at. Frances sat down in a wing chair, running her fingers lightly over the velvet arms. She glanced around in the dark and wondered why the house felt so benign to her. Was it just because it was so pretty?

Maybe she needed that. Maybe she needed to have beautiful things around her. Maybe that was why the Wrong House had been so awful.

Hart would have pointed out that Long Island Sound was beautiful, and he was right. It was. But it wasn't the same thing, Frances thought. Hart had always been more moved by nature than she had. A forest was all very well in its way, but Frances preferred a garden.

Frances leaned back, resting her head on the tall chair-back. This was new to her, this kind of speculation. She hadn't given much thought before to what she might need from life. Probably, she thought with a flash of insight, because she'd had it. Her life before the Wrong House had provided what she needed. Funny how you could never tell what that was until it was gone, she thought, and got up from the velvet chair.

"We live and learn," she said aloud in the quiet room, and walked back across the hall to the living room.

The next day, she called Harry.

"Good morning, Harry, I gather from Clara that you've been trying to reach me," said his mother's voice, perfectly composed.

"Well, yes, Mom, I have," Harry said, walking with his cordless phone back to the dining room table and his half-finished breakfast. "Where the hell have you been? We've all been worried sick!"

"You knew where I was, though. Didn't you talk to Clara?"

"We weren't worried that you were lying on a slab at

Bellevue," Harry said, provoked into vulgarity. "What is going on?"

"What do you mean, what is going on?"

"Don't be obtuse, Mom," Harry said. "Have you left Dad? Don't you understand that we're *worried?*"

"Oh, no," said his mother's voice, surprised. "Where did you get that idea?"

Harry paused. Eleanor's psychic suddenly didn't seem to be a very credible source. "Well, Mom, what does it look like? You waltz out of the house with no warning and you won't tell Dad when you're coming back, what are we supposed to conclude?"

"That I'm taking a spur-of-the-moment vacation," Frances said crisply.

"I see. And when is this vacation going to be over?" Harry asked.

"It's not clear," Frances, said, less confidently.

"Sounds like a trial separation to me," Harry said, a little cruelly. "Mom, do you have a clue? Eleanor's already a zombie and the idea that you and Dad might be splitting up is just too much for her. Dad is wandering around that house completely helpless; he can barely feed himself."

Frances's voice sighed. "I'm not worried about your father. He knows how to defrost. I'll give Ellie a call now."

"Well, look, Mom," Harry said, suddenly hesitant. "Can we see you? Or are you taking a vacation from us, too?"

"No, I'd love to see you. Why don't we have dinner tomorrow night? Do you want to come up here?"

"Okay," Harry said. "I'll do that." But when he hung up he stared for a long time at his coffee cup, feeling rotten. Blunt as he'd been, he hadn't been able to tell his mother the most important thing. That he was worried, and hurt, and didn't want his parents to split up. The whole thing made him feel vulnerable as a child again.

When she talked to him later that morning, Eleanor tried to soothe her brother. "I agree it's alarming," she said. "But it's been a rough six months for her. Maybe she's just licking her wounds or something."

Harry snorted.

"Yes, but you know," Eleanor went on, "Mom's so private. Maybe this is just her way of sorting things out. Look, we know she's alive and well, and both she and Dad seem to think there's nothing wrong."

"But you know what worries me?" Harry said. "This makes it too easy for them to stop communicating. I mean, if there's something wrong between them, Mom walking out isn't going to help."

Eleanor hitched the phone more comfortably between her shoulder and ear and dangled a paper-clip chain. "We're just looking at this differently. Maybe it's a boy/girl thing. I agree that this is a crisis in their marriage, but I think they *are* communicating. You're the expert on semiotics, Harry. Mom's telling Dad she's fed up. She could never say so in so many words."

"But what about Dad?" Harry asked. "Don't you feel sorry for him?"

"Sorry for him?" Eleanor asked, as if it were a new idea. "No. He's probably looking on this as a big adventure. I think the whole thing will be good for them in the end."

"If it isn't the end now," Harry said darkly. But he was actually reassured.

Hart had indeed looked on Frances's absence as an adventure at first. The debacle with the shirts was the first hint that it might be less than perfectly jolly. As the week went on, other clues intruded.

The impatiens in the window boxes died. They hadn't been exactly flourishing, but Frances had faithfully watered and nipped off dead leaves. Hart didn't know you had to do this, and by the time he finally got the hose out it was too late. They had yellowed and withered and wouldn't come back.

He couldn't figure out how many scoops of coffee to put in the coffeepot. It took a week of experimentation to get a brew he could stomach.

Laundry was an incredible bore. He shrank three pairs of khakis and bleached spots in two polo shirts. He thought the sheets should probably be changed but couldn't be bothered.

234

Making the meals got onerous, too. Day in, day out. Hart got fed up with trying to really cook and fell back on cans and frozen meals. He would have eaten more often in the Weymouth Diner, but he was beginning to get questions.

Joan Failey called. Could he and Frances come for dinner next week? Hart said he thought so, Frances wasn't there, but he'd have her check the calendar. He got off the phone fast.

Some lady from the Garden Club called. Would Frances be interested in a trip to Newport in September? Hart gulped and said she probably would.

Mrs. Wilucki wanted instructions on cleaning the chintz slipcovers; Mrs. Drummond had said they needed to be done. Hart looked curiously at the sofas and couldn't see why. He told Mrs. Wilucki that Mrs. Drummond had decided the slipcovers could wait. After that he kept examining them for signs of dirt and kept his nightly beer away from them.

The worst moment came when, on a gray Saturday morning, Margaret Harwood cornered Hart by the dairy case in the supermarket.

"Hart!" she cried, as if he were her long-lost brother. She had on a magenta velour jogging suit which was particularly unfortunate from behind. "I've been meaning to call you and Frances. It was so nice of you all to invite me and Guy over the other night. I enjoyed that so much!" Her face darkened momentarily. "That Guy! Why, you wouldn't believe . . . Did you know he drank?"

Hart said, trying to edge away, "Well, he was there for drinks."

"No, I mean *drank!* My word, we got stopped by the police on the way back from Essex, and they did that test on him, you know where you breathe into the balloon? And then they typed his driver's license into the computer? And we had to sit in the police station for hours, oh, I was so humiliated!" she said, without lowering her voice a bit. Then, with a visible effort, she brightened up. "So how are you and Frances doing? You still interested in buying a Victorian? I've got something coming onto the market real soon if you are."

Hart surreptitiously tried to draw his shopping cart into a

retreating position. The wheels, however, were hooked on the wheels of her cart, which contained mostly jugs of diet soda and Weight Watchers frozen meals. He hoped she wouldn't notice the orange Stouffer's boxes in his. "I hadn't really given it much thought," he said, without meeting her bold glance.

"Chip tells me you've been fishing a lot," she said, tapping her nails on the handle of his cart. "You bringing Frances lots of fish to cook?"

"Um, yes, if you'll excuse me," he muttered, and gestured toward the checkout. "I need to . . ."

But she merely wheeled her cart around and followed him down the aisle. "I'm on my way out, too," she said. "Listen, I've been meaning to call to get you and Frances over for dinner. I'm not really much of a cook, but I always like to throw a piece of fish on the grill. Maybe we could cook something you'd caught, wouldn't that be fun?"

Frantically Hart scanned the checkout lines. Each one was obstructed by carts mounded high with food. The cashiers were all turning boxes and cans over and over, vainly trying to persuade the scanning machines to register the prices. The customers leaned on their carts hopelessly, leafing through magazines, waiting for the millennium. Margaret Harwood was right behind Hart. Suddenly panic overcame him. What if she named a specific date and he had to say Frances wouldn't be available? What if she started to pry information from him in that overpowering way she had? What if she found out that Frances was gone and he didn't know when she'd be back? God knew what she'd make him tell her. She'd probably extract the story of the mirror over the bed! "Sorry, I just realized . . . forgot . . . I need to get," he babbled, and wheeled his cart around.

As he disappeared up the baby food aisle he heard Margaret's voice floating after him, "Don't forget about dinner! I'll call Frances!"

Hart got home safely that day with most of what he needed (though he did have to go out again for milk). But he was beginning to feel harassed. He didn't know how to handle this.

It was extremely awkward. The situation made him feel helpless in a puzzling and somehow unfair way. He didn't know what attitude to take toward these people. And the only person he could ask, the only person he *wanted* to ask, was the very person who was responsible for it.

On the one hand, what did Frances want him to say? What line should he take? Was she on vacation? Was she coming back? And when? Could he make plans? Plans for the two of them? Did she want to go to Newport in September? Did she want Joan Failey knowing she was in New York? Any day now her friends were going to start talking. Gossiping. He'd heard it often enough to know how it would go: "Have you heard about Hart and Frances? Oh, well . . ." with lots of lowered voices and raised eyebrows. Next the harpies would be calling him up, and how could he fend them off?

He wanted to know what his wife had in mind. But there was more to it than that. He wanted her advice. Her advice about herself. Hart got that far in his thinking and realized he was being absurd. Yet at the same time, he'd put his finger on something.

Here he was, having wife troubles. He had to admit it. That was what all this was about. But the person he usually asked for advice in his troubles was—his wife. There wasn't anybody else.

He was out on the boat as this thought came to him. It was sunset, the time of day that somehow needed filling when Frances was gone. He'd put his dinner in the oven and taken a beer and the kitchen timer for a little spin in the Whaler. The water was choppy and the sky an unhelpful gray. The hushed sense of calm that usually fell on the Sound at that hour was missing.

From the shore, the house looked welcoming. The lights glowed yellow from the kitchen and the living room. Hart sighed.

He was really at a loss. Apparently he'd failed Frances in some way. But he couldn't figure out what that was. Okay, he'd dragged his feet on finding a new house. There was no getting around that.

But he liked this house. Granted, it was ugly. And their furniture looked funny in it.

Could their marriage be breaking up over a house?

Hart sighed and turned the boat for home. He wished he could ask Frances. As he covered the boat, he felt a few drops of rain and ran inside before the storm broke.

It was a sudden squall blowing up from the southeast, a dramatic end to a day of heavy dampness. In Fenwick the big old trees began to sway suddenly, tossing their topmost branches and showing the silvery undersides of their leaves. Enthroned upstairs on her four-poster bed, Clara Henschel took note of this and called down on the house intercom.

In the octagonal morning room, George Sinclair picked up the house phone. "George, dear, there's quite a squall moving in. Would you get Sarge and check the windows? And could you just run down to the boathouse to make sure it's all closed up?"

"No problem," George said, glancing out the window. "I'll do it right now." He put down his charcoal pencil and went to the kitchen to find Sarge.

This, George felt with some amusement, was typical Clara, a canny combination of prudence, generosity, and selfishness. While he and Sarge scurried around in the rain slamming windows and hooking shutters, Clara would huddle up there in her boudoir reading the memoirs of Madame de Sévigné, confident that her property would be safe from the storm. Of course, you couldn't expect a ninety-three-year-old woman to close her own windows, George recognized. But it was particularly characteristic of Clara to surround herself with people who could. Either because that was their job or because they were somehow in her debt.

George had not paid much attention to Clara on the morning when he and Harry had borrowed her boat. He had been so tense about the upcoming meeting with Eleanor that he had completely missed Harry's whispered explanation to Clara. But when the two men came back dejected, Clara had virtually ordered them to stay the night and recount the Eleanor saga.

The story interested Clara. She listened both to what was said and to what went unsaid. She watched George carefully and liked what she saw. It wasn't clear yet how she could intervene, but she intended to try.

Her opportunity came the next morning. George had left his

238

sketchbook lying on the huge round front-hall table. Clara, ever curious, had discovered it when she came down for breakfast. She leafed through it, pausing at the picture of Toby and Simon on the beach. She glanced at the drawing of Eleanor emerging from the waves and felt suddenly as if she were prying.

Clara didn't tell George she'd looked at his pictures, but when he came downstairs, she made a proposition. She had always hated the color of the morning-room walls. Did he ever do murals? Would he consider doing a mural for her? On his usual terms, of course, the subject up to him.

George agreed on the spot. He liked this commanding little woman and he sensed that she might be able to help him. He wasn't working well in New York; maybe the change of scene would do him good. At the very least, he might hear news of Eleanor through Clara.

He had gone back to New York for a few days to finish the Italian restaurant commission, which had been reduced to a few panels of decorative painting and some fancy lettering. Then he had returned to Fenwick to study the room and the light and his patron.

George's idea was to paint an allegory of Clara Henschel's life. The room was well suited to an episodic approach; each panel of the octagon could represent an important event. Clara's birth, debut, and three marriages would each occupy a wall. The two windows would be surrounded with foliage, George thought. And maybe he'd paint a kind of trompe l'oeil trophy arrangement on the back of the door, with a cane and a fan and a straw hat and bunches of peonies.

When he proposed this, Clara was delighted and entered happily into the planning. It was her idea to introduce vignettes of her various houses in the background of each panel, and she urged George to include portraits of her parents and husbands. "After all," she said, "it will be very boring to just look at me all the time. And my guests will get the impression that I'm completely egotistical."

"That wouldn't do, would it?" George said with a straight face.

"No, it wouldn't," Clara answered, "even if it is the truth.

What a pity we can't put in my funeral. Do you suppose it would be sacrilegious to paint the Assumption of Clara Henschel? I love the idea of seeing myself seated on a rather firm cloud, wafting up to the heavens."

"Tastefully arrayed in classical draperies?" George asked.

"Mmm . . . No, I think my Chanel lace dress. Can you paint lace?"

"In a sort of Goyaesque manner, yes."

"That should do. Though I think the Assumption is a little presumptuous," Clara said regretfully. "It might spoil my actual chances of getting into heaven."

They both laughed at this and felt pleased with themselves.

So George had become an established member of the Fenwick household. He had dinner each night with Clara and made free use of the dock, the boat, and the library (which had been assembled in the 1950s and concentrated on the works of Anya Seton and Paul Gallico). He made a couple of trips to New York for supplies and research, gave his agent Clara's telephone number, and planned to stay in Fenwick for the remainder of the summer.

When Harry arrived for dinner at Clara's New York house the next night, he looked sharply at his mother to see if she seemed different in any way. As they sat in the library before dinner, and later when they were seated in Clara's ground-floor dining room, he kept shooting glances at her when he thought she wouldn't notice. Actually, she looked wonderful. She appeared more focused and alert than she had at any time that summer. Gradually, Harry became aware that she was also privately amused at something. Her face showed a hint of a secretive smile. Finally, when they went back upstairs to the living room to drink coffee, she said gently, "Harry, please stop staring at me. Is there spinach stuck in my teeth or something?"

"No," Harry said. "I guess I'm just trying to get used to this new idea of you and Dad." He sank back into his armchair and sighed. "It's unnerving. Here I am, a grown man, and I'm completely flipped out by your leaving Dad."

"Honey, I haven't left him. I'm just taking a vacation," Frances said patiently. "Are you going to have any of this? Beatriz made these cookies specially for you."

Harry sat up. "Of course I am. Milk in the coffee. What's in them?"

"Ground almonds, sugar, and egg whites. When I went out this afternoon something in the kitchen was making a horrible racket and I think it was Beatriz grinding the almonds." Frances handed Harry the plate. "Would you like to know where I went?"

"Of course, Mom," Harry said, taking a cookie and examining it. "She's really quite a cook, isn't she?"

"Yes." Harry was looking so carefully at the cookie that he

didn't notice the distinct gleam of humor on his mother's face. She poured coffee for him and placed the cup and saucer on the table near him. Then she picked up a book lying on the sofa cushion next to her. A slim brochure slid out, and she opened it. By now Harry was watching her.

"What's that?"

"Well, this afternoon I found myself in the neighborhood of Sotheby's. And I went in, just on a whim. And I ended up buying something."

There was nothing immediately surprising in this. Frances had occasionally bought things at auction for the Chester house. Harry himself had acquired his bed and several chairs at William Doyle. What did seem odd was the notion that Frances had purchased anything for the Wrong House. What would you buy: a Naugahyde sectional sofa?

"What did you buy, Mom?" Harry asked, beginning to feel unaccountably cheerful.

"Well, that's the thing, Harry," his mother answered ruefully. "I honestly don't know what came over me. You know I'm a careful shopper." This was true. Frances was not the kind of auctiongoer who got carried away by adrenaline and overbid, or bid on things she hadn't intended to buy.

"Yes," Harry said encouragingly. "So this time . . ."

"So this time," his mother took up the tale, "I walked in and there was a sale in progress in the Arcade, you know, the second-string stuff."

"The junk," Harry offered.

"Well, that's not quite fair, you remember I got those dessert plates for Eleanor there—"

"Right, Mom. So this time . . ." prompted Harry again.

"Well, I walked in and I had no intention of buying, you know, but I signed in anyway and . . ." Frances paused to fold back the brochure. "Mind you, I hadn't even looked at any of the lots beforehand."

"Mom, cut to the chase," said Harry. "What have you done?"

"Well, dear," his mother said wryly, "I bought an armoire."

"An armoire," Harry repeated flatly.

"Yes. Massive. It's six feet tall," Frances said. "Here, lot thirty-seven." She held out the brochure.

" 'Victorian mahogany armoire,' " Harry read out loud. " 'Circa 1860. Rococo revival, with scrolling outline and bracket feet. Fifteen hundred to three thousand dollars.' "

"It went for much less," Frances said. "I suppose it was too big for most people."

"And what are you going to do with it?" Harry asked.

"I'm not really sure," Frances said tranquilly. "Would you like it?"

Harry looked down at the brochure in his hand. " 'Six feet tall, four feet wide, almost two feet deep'? It wouldn't fit in my front door." He looked sharply at her. "You couldn't get it into the new house, either."

"No," his mother agreed. "Do you think Eleanor would like it?"

"No," Harry said, "somehow I don't. You've gone and bought some expensive firewood, Mom."

Frances shrugged. "We'll see," she said. "I may have to store it for a while."

Harry stared at her. This was not the woman he'd seen merely two weeks ago, drifting around the Weymouth house in a daze. There was a quality in her that he hadn't seen in quite some time. Levity, maybe. Here she had just acquired what seemed to be nothing more than an albatross, and her reaction was not regret, not anxiety, but amusement.

"Why is it funny?" he asked her suddenly.

"Why is what funny?"

"Why do you think this armoire is so hilarious? Is it lined with Mickey Mouse shelf paper or something?"

Frances sipped her coffee and considered. "No," she said. "It's actually a very ordinary piece of furniture, but when I saw it I really felt I had to have it. And then afterward, you know, when they started talking about shipping it, I realized."

"Realized what?" Harry said, watching her narrowly.

"Realized what you just said," she answered, with a delighted smile. "That it wouldn't fit into the new house. And then I realized why I'd bought it. It's for the *next* house."

"The next house," Harry repeated blankly.

"Mm," his mother said, sipping coffee. "The house I'm going to find. A house that the armoire would suit, or fit into." Frances looked over at Harry, who seemed to be having trouble following her. "Maybe it seems weird, dear, but I promise you, *I* understand what I mean."

Harry put down his coffee cup and rubbed his eyes. "Okay. I guess I should realize by now that there's no fathoming human behavior."

"No," his mother agreed. "I don't think there is." And Harry had to be content with that. But he would have been more encouraged if he had seen his mother with the Sunday newspapers two mornings later. She read the front section and flipped through the magazine with particular attention to fashion (a special section on Ralph Lauren's latest nautical looks) and food (recipes involving fresh tomatoes). Then she took the real-estate section to Clara's desk, got out a red pen, and began to read carefully. The time had come. Her vacation was over.

Frances had spent the summer trying to be something she wasn't. A relaxed person who could adapt to anything. An informal type of gal, who put her feet up on the furniture. An outdoorsy woman. Someone who made friends easily. Who took life as it came.

She had failed. Her sense of inadequacy had deepened through July. She had neither adapted to the Wrong House nor lived up to one of her cardinal rules of life, which was to put a pleasant face on things. This had made her increasingly passive and self-absorbed, to the extent that even Hart (who was exploring new territories of self-absorption himself that summer) noticed.

All along, however, Frances felt that the Wrong House was a key. It had taken on a personality in her mind, the personality of a large, friendly, but extremely unattractive dog. It wanted to please, but was physically repulsive. It had, metaphorically speaking, huge muddy paws, horrible breath, and strings of rubbery drool trailing from its fangs. Frances actually felt a little sorry for the house. It needed owners who would love it, who would cherish the antler chandeliers and put back the swinging doors to the kitchen and luxuriate in the brown-marble bathroom. And she and Hart needed a house they could love, too. Winter would come and the Old Man of the Sea would have to put the Whaler on blocks in the backyard, and then what was he going to do? Devise ever more garish lures for intellectually subnormal fish? Play chess against himself? Stare out the window hoping to see a black-backed cormorant (or whatever it might be, Frances didn't care)? He would go stir-crazy.

Except that it wasn't going to happen that way. Frances was determined that by the end of Daylight Savings Time, the Wrong House would be full of mover's cartons and the Drummonds would have a new home.

So she began by scanning the real-estate ads. There were very few listings worth bothering with, but they gave her the names of agents. She made a list and picked up the phone to call.

Curiously, Frances noticed that this time around she had no hesitation placing these calls. She marveled at how simple it was. "My name is Frances Drummond. I'm looking for a house on the eastern Connecticut shore and I wonder what you have that I could look at. I'm specifically interested in Victorian houses, three bedrooms, not a lot of land. . . . Yes, I can come up on Tuesday. . . ." Before noon, she had scheduled three full days of house hunting and felt a glow of satisfaction. It occurred to her, as she went out to buy file folders and a clipboard for this project, that part of her problem that summer had been that she simply hadn't had enough to do.

On Tuesday morning she took an early train to New Haven and reclaimed her car. Then she drove up to Stonington and spent the morning looking at houses.

The real-estate agent told a colleague afterward that he had taken Mrs. Drummond to every prewar house for sale in the town of Stonington, but that she was incredibly hard to please. That afternoon, in Noank, she told the broker firmly that she didn't want to see anything built later than 1920, with fewer than three bedrooms, on a plot bigger than two acres. He was so awestruck that he could only think of three houses to show her, and none of them was acceptable.

She spent that night at a motel in Mystic that had a fax machine. She made a few phone calls late in the afternoon and used the hour before dinner leafing through the faxes of listings that the next day's broker had sent her. As Harry would have said, she was on a roll.

The Drummond family had seen Frances in this mode before. When she got her heart set on something, she was implacable. Harry always said that Eleanor at her most efficient was only a shadow of their mother, and Eleanor agreed. There was something superb about Frances intent on a mission. She would ride smoothly over all obstacles with a small smile, never wavering from good manners and always closer to her goal. She was organized, thorough, and tireless, a courteous juggernaut.

Her driving around the coast during July had almost convinced her that Hart was right about Weymouth. The other towns just weren't quite suitable. Essex was too far up the river, besides being too touristy. Lyme would get very dull in the winter. Madison was a little too big, Stonington a little too self-consciously quaint. Frances was purposely conscientious about looking at houses in other towns, but she had nearly made up her mind. A mediocre house in Weymouth would be better than a jewel somewhere else. And she realized that a mediocre house might be her fate. Somehow she had come to grips with this. Anything was better than the Wrong House.

On Wednesday she got as far south as Essex. In two days she had seen fifteen houses and there were only four listing sheets left for consideration in her file folders. The other houses she dismissed out of hand. Early on Thursday morning, from her room at the Griswold Inn in Essex, Frances called Chip Strong.

Chip was padding around innocently in his knee-length plaid bathrobe, tending to the coffee machine and the sandwich maker and the juicer (breakfast was a particularly machine-intensive meal), when the phone rang. When Frances identified herself, he gulped.

"Listen, Chip," Frances went on, ignoring his audible consternation, "I need you to do something for me." (She deliberately left him no room for refusal.)

"Oh, of course, Frances," he said, aware that his voice was actually squeaking. "What can I do?"

"Well, it may not be easy. I think you know about the mix-up with the house we bought, how it wasn't the one we wanted?"

Chip nodded, then realized she couldn't see him, and said, "Yes." He noticed smoke coming from the sandwich maker and tried to stretch the cord far enough to turn it off. He could just barely flip the switch with the tips of his fingers, but he had to take the receiver away from his ear, and he lost part of what Frances was saying. As he listened again, he heard:

". . . but not with Margaret Harwood. I know you have to work with her, Chip, but I just couldn't stand it. Do you understand?"

"Oh, I do," Chip said. "Only I didn't catch the beginning, I'm sorry. You want to do what without Margaret?"

"Look at houses, Chip," Frances's voice came patiently down the line. Goodness, what else would she want to do with him? "You do have some for sale?"

"Oh, yes. Yes." Chip nodded. The coffee was ready, and he grabbed a mug and poured half a cupful. The refrigerator was out of reach of the phone. He didn't dare try the stretching maneuver again to get some milk.

"Well, look, Chip, could we do it Saturday morning, then? First thing? By then I will have looked at every other three-bedroom Victorian on the market north of Guilford, so I'll have a good basis for comparison. It won't cut into your fishing too much, will it?" Frances said, enjoying a flash of malice.

"No, no, of course not," Chip said. "But maybe we could meet here, at my house, instead of the office. If you want to keep away from Margaret."

"That's fine," Frances answered. "Oh, and don't tell Hart."

Chip gulped. He had never been good at keeping secrets. "All right. Saturday, nine o'clock?"

"Fine. Thank you so much," Frances said sweetly, and hung up. If she had known how alarming Chip Strong found her, she would have been tickled pink.

Frances Drummond on the phone was one thing, Chip found on Saturday morning. Frances Drummond in the flesh was even more imposing.

Until that morning Chip had heard about Frances from Hart and had formed an image of her as a kind of middle-aged neurasthenic, drifting around with a book in her hand and refusing to cook bluefish in the dishwasher. In fact, both times he'd been to the house to go out in Hart's boat, she had been reading on one of the sofas and hadn't even bothered to get up to greet him. So this crisp, opinionated woman came as something of a surprise.

She strode into his house and glanced around, taking in the futon on the floor of the parlor and the racks in the center of the other living room. For the first time in months, Chip was reminded that the arrangement was unusual, and he furtively inspected the baseboards for dust kitties as he led Frances into the kitchen. She glanced at the array of machinery on the counter, but didn't comment.

"Would you like coffee?" Chip asked. "I've just made a pot."

"Thank you, that would be nice," Frances said, and sat down at the kitchen table.

Chip placed a handful of listings next to her and went over to the counter. He turned around and glanced at her, then, ignoring the mugs in the dish drainer, reached into a cupboard. From the back he brought a pink lusterware cup and saucer, which he filled carefully with coffee and put in front of her.

Frances looked up at him when she saw the cup. "This is pretty, thank you." She smiled at him, and Chip began to feel less alarmed.

Frances made short work of the listings. "No. No. No; we saw this one with Margaret, it's a terrible dump. They should drop the price by about forty thousand. No, Chip, I really mean Victorian. Hmm. This is interesting." She put one aside and sipped the coffee. "This is very good coffee," she said, and he suddenly felt she might be human. "I've been living in motels for three days and drinking awful weak stuff."

"Thank you. I use a Gaggia and transfer the coffee right into a thermos. It stays fresh amazingly well," he told her earnestly.

Frances blinked. There didn't seem to be an answer to that. She looked down at the pile in front of her. "What about this one? Where is it?" she asked, holding out a listing.

Chip took it. "If you go up Main Street in the other direction, it's right on the corner. You've probably never noticed it because of the trees."

Frances took the sheet back and looked at the picture. "Probably. Horrible old hemlocks. We'll look at that one. Why is it so cheap?"

"Needs work, as they say," Chip told her. "Cosmetic, mostly. Pair of old sisters lived there and went to a nursing home a few months ago, then died within a week of each other. It's pretty depressing."

"Depressing!" Frances snorted. "It's amazing how many people live in depressing houses, isn't it?" She leafed through more listings, putting most of them in the discard pile. "Your house is pretty."

"Thank you," Chip said, a bit unnerved.

"Do you ever use the upstairs rooms?"

"Mostly for storage," Chip said. The floor· of one of the bedrooms was covered with obsolete kitchen appliances that Chip kept "just in case."

Frances nodded, apparently satisfied. She looked again at the listing sheet in her hand, then passed it to him. It showed a rambling stone-clad mansion with turrets and crenellations. "Only six bedrooms in this whole house? What else is in there?"

"Billiard room, library, music room. And you know, those dressing room suites that were so popular a few years ago."

Frances looked interested. "I don't want to buy it, but can we see it anyway?"

"Of course," Chip said. "You're the buyer. Only, can we go soon? Because if Margaret should happen to be driving by and see you with me, she's going to create an unholy fuss. She thinks you and Hart are her personal property."

"I don't know how Hart feels about it," Frances said, "but I find the idea very disturbing. Let's go."

They saw the castle first. Chip was impressed when Frances said, "There's a house like this outside of Essex that just sold to a rock star. This house has the same combination of pretentious public spaces and good security. Have you thought about cobroking it with someone in New York?" Chip hadn't.

The next house was an outside chance. It was the carriage house for a big place that had been built by a very prosperous mill owner in the late nineteenth century. The house itself was still owned by his descendants, but they had decided to sell off the carriage house, which had been long since converted to a guest house.

Frances took one encompassing look around the living room and said slowly, "It's very charming, isn't it?" The big arched doors that had given access to the carriages were painted jade green, while the rest of the batten boards were dark. The low beamed ceiling was whitewashed, and the whole effect was cheerful and quirky. The kitchen and bathrooms were all brand-new, and Chip assured Frances that the wiring and heating were new as well. The bedrooms, however, were disappointing. "It stands to reason we'd have to sleep in the stalls, I suppose," was Frances's comment when she saw the first one. The master bedroom was a bit larger (having been carved out of two stalls and the former tack room), but what had felt cozy in the living room suddenly, to Frances, seemed slightly oppressive. The lot, screened from the big house by a tall white fence, was virtually unlandscaped. And there was no garage.

"Still," Frances said as they drove away, "it is very attractive. And the price is fair, I think, don't you?"

"Yes," Chip agreed. "For what you're getting, it's fair."

"What about the next place?" Frances continued. "It's the one with the hemlock trees? The price is just the same."

"Yes," Chip answered cautiously. Experience had taught him to be noncommittal with customers. "You'd get a lot more house for the same money."

"But . . ." Frances added for him.

He nodded. "You'll see."

She did see. They parked on the gravel driveway at the side of the lot. As Frances stepped out of the car she noticed a patch of crabgrass thrusting its way up through the granite chips. She bent down to pull up a large clump and tossed it into the bushes that bordered the lot.

The large slates that formed the walkway to the side door were uneven, pushed out of true by frosts and thaws and possibly by the spreading roots of a very large maple that stood back from the house. Luxuriant topknots of grass sprouted between the cracks in the slates.

"We'll go in by the side door," Chip said, studying a ring of keys. "I've never been able to get the front door open."

The porch sagged slightly, though an attempt had been made to shore it up with raw, unpainted two-by-fours. Frances looked at the peeling dark green paint and said, "Chip, this looks like a waste of time. The place is falling to rack and ruin."

"No," he answered, a bit surprised at his temerity, "It's not as bad inside. I think you should see it, Frances." And he added cannily, "For comparison."

Of course. For comparison. She wouldn't actually consider living in a place that looked so ramshackle. Frances was reassured. "All right."

The door opened after a tussle with the lock, and Chip and Frances found themselves in a gloomy hall. Straight ahead of them, cracks of light outlined the front door.

"What do you want to see first?" Chip asked. "Kitchen or parlor?"

"Save the best for last," Frances answered.

"Okay. Here's the kitchen." They turned left into a big room that looked like a stage set for a movie about the Depression. An ancient gas stove dominated one side of the room while a huge deep double sink took up most of another wall. On a vinyl-covered table in the center stood an old wooden Lazy Susan laden with a napkin caddy, ketchup bottle, salt and pepper shakers, and a few prescription pill bottles. Frances prodded the mottled green linoleum with one toe. "Estate sales are so gloomy, aren't they?" she remarked. "I get the idea."

Chip led her out through a swinging door into the dining

room. The walls had been covered with a gold-on-white star-patterned paper, while the floor featured a lush purplish wall-to-wall carpet. But the ceilings were high and there was a handsome marble fireplace. Frances didn't say anything. There were two parlors at the front of the house, both with floor-to-ceiling windows giving onto the front porch. These, too, had fireplaces.

Frances paused in the hall. "Chip, can we possibly get that front door open? I really can't see anything in the gloom."

So he tried several keys until one grudgingly penetrated the keyhole, and tugged and swore a little until one half of the double front door swung inward. Frances crossed the hall to look at the edge of the other door, where inset levers shot bolts into the doorframe. She pulled on the levers to release the door and opened it. The space between the wooden door and the outer glass door was dusty and furred with cobwebs, as if the door hadn't been opened in decades.

Seen in the full light from outdoors, the hall had real elegance. The stairs, with turned balusters and a sinuous handrail painted gray-green, curved gracefully up to a landing where an arched niche looked out. Just the right place, Frances thought, for a big vase full of lilacs. But she wasn't really considering the house, she remembered. The wallpaper featured massive grayish cabbage roses on a kind of baroque trelliswork, and though the oyster-gray paint on the walls up to the chair rail was flat and scuffed, the paper seemed to be intact. The floor was a handsome parquet, popping up in places.

She led the way upstairs. On the landing, a door led off to the right. She looked at Chip.

"Attic. Servant's bedroom. Back stairs," he said. She turned to the left, where the staircase led to an upstairs hall. There were four bedrooms, all large cubes with marble fireplaces and twelve-foot ceilings. Two had bay windows with window seats. One had a built-in mirror over the fireplace. In all of them the paint was peeling, the windows were cloudy with dust, the doors stuck or hung crooked on their hinges. The bathroom floors were old linoleum curling up at the corners, and the tubs had greenish streaks running from the taps.

In every corner of the house neglect had done its damage. Doors lacked doorknobs. Lights switched on with frayed pieces of string. Patches of carpet samples skidded over gouges in the parquet floors. Rust crept over medicine cabinets. Paint scaled off the tall old radiators. Ganglia of extension cords snaked along the baseboards. For years nothing had been done to maintain the original beauty of the house. The two old women living there had hidden what could be hidden and added ugly little conveniences like the plastic laundry rack standing on a towel in a corner of one of the bathrooms.

Frances gestured to this and said, "Chip, if you really want to sell this house, you should get rid of things like that."

"I can't," he said uncomfortably. "It's an estate sale and I'm not allowed to move anything."

Frances shot him an impatient look. She picked up the rack and collapsed it, then whisked the towel off the floor. Several many-legged insects scuttled off toward the safety of the wainscoting as she said, "I just tripped over it. It was a safety hazard. Honestly, Chip, who's to know how the poor old dears left their house? If you could just sneak in with some Windex early on a Sunday morning you'd do a lot to make it more salable."

She stalked out of the bathroom into the bedroom, where a yellowed roller blind hung askew at one window. "Look," she said with irritation, unhooking the roller from the window. "Do the heirs really want this old blind, circa 1949?" She picked up a half-empty box of Kleenex from the bedside table. "Or *this?*" She waved a *TV Guide* in front of him. "Or this? Look, Chip, this has the date on it. Any sharp buyer is going to look at this *TV Guide*, see the date, December, and realize that the house has been empty and probably on the market for months. Your average buyer will deduce that the property is not moving and will make you a laughable offer. Or won't offer at all. Meanwhile, the estate is still paying taxes. The estate is going to have to heat the house or have the pipes drained this winter. Preferably heat the house, because you'll never sell a house that's freezing cold, even if you *do* assure the buyers that the furnace works. The sooner the house sells and the better the price, the happier the estate will be. In fact, you might *even* recoup the cost of that box of Kleenex for them, if you can just spruce the place up a little and sell it sooner instead of later." Frances slapped the *TV Guide* down on top of the old RCA television, where it raised a cloud of dust from an old lace bureau scarf. She stepped forward to finger the lace and said, in a completely different tone of voice, "This is good lace, by the way."

"Is it?" Chip answered, paying no attention. He was looking around the room as if seeing it for the first time. "I suppose you're right. I never thought about it that way. I mean, the place does have potential."

"Of course it does," Frances said, turning to leave the room. "I'm sorry to fly off the handle like that, but really, you could be marketing this place much better." She started down the stairs. "I want to see the yard."

The yard was just as dispiriting. The hemlocks had crowded around the house, squeezing out the somewhat anemic plantings of mountain laurel and andromeda. Facing the road a weedy row of privet bushes had once been intended as a hedge, but years had passed since they'd seen a pruning. The grass all over was patchy and thin, with crabgrass getting the better of the fescue and rye in most places.

Behind the house, a pair of sunken oblongs indicated where the lawn had once been dug up for beds, but only a few leggy phlox and one lonely snapdragon poked their stiff leaves through the grass. In a lonely little circle near the back porch, blossoms nodded on a couple of scrawny rosebushes. Frances surveyed the rest of the yard, then crossed to the bushes, where she gently bent the stems and turned over the leaves.

"Those roses need attention," she said, coming back to Chip.

"But—" he started.

"I know, I know," she cut him off. "Do you have a pair of scissors or anything in the car? I know! Wait a minute."

She went back into the house and came back out with a pair of pruning shears and a can of some kind of spray.

"What are you doing?" Chip answered, hoping he wouldn't feel obligated to stop her.

"I found these on that shelf over the washing machine,"

Frances said. "Just where they were left. I am going to prune those poor roses and give them a quick spray for aphids, then we can go. Believe me, the next time you bring someone here, they'll look a lot better." And with obvious skill, she snipped the longest shoots off the bushes. When she had finished she took the shears and spray back into the house. Then she picked a rosebud from the pile of flowers on the ground and brought it over to Chip.

"Here, let's dress you up for the rest of the day," she said, tucking the yellow bud into the buttonhole of his jacket. "Makes you look very festive," she said, standing back. "All right, I've seen enough, shall I help you close up?"

Chip leaned down to sniff the rose. Even though the bud was tightly furled, it had a rich scent. "Amazing how they survive," he said, walking into the house behind Frances.

"Roses are amazing," Frances agreed quietly. "That's a Jacqueminot, a strain that was very popular a hundred years ago until the American Beauty was hybridized. A couple of the bushes out there are quite valuable." She walked down the hall to the front door and swung the two panels shut, carefully shooting the bolts into the doorframe. She paused for a minute under the crystal chandelier that hung from the ceiling, looking up at its balls and drops in the shadowy room. Chip waited for her by the back door.

"So are you interested?" he asked as he locked the door. Turning around, he surprised a softer look on her face than he'd seen yet.

"Yes," she said, meeting his gaze with a rueful smile. "Defying all common sense, I am."

18

Frances went back to New York trying not to yield to the feeling of exhilaration that kept welling up, an almost physical sensation around her heart. It was just a house. It needed a great deal of work, inside and out. The cosmetic details had been sorely neglected, and who knew what the infrastructure of the house was like? It could have termites. It almost certainly needed rewiring. The plumbing might be falling apart, too. It would cost quite a bit to have those hemlocks cut down and hauled away.

But there was something there. Frances had felt it. She wouldn't have said she was imaginative, and she didn't believe in auras or anthropomorphizing objects. But that house had dignity. It held itself apart from the extension cords and the cracked linoleum and the exposed shanks of doorknobs. Frances could imagine how it had looked in 1880, and how it could look now, with the right care. Care she wanted to give it. And, she thought wryly, the armoire would look perfect in the upstairs hall.

The difficulty was going to be selling this house to Hart. Because he could grow to love it, too, Frances felt sure of that. But he would have to be convinced.

Her first move, when she got back to Clara's house in New York, was to call the engineer whose name Chip had given her. His report would be essential. Could he do it quickly? Of course. That was routine. He promised to have the report in Chip Strong's office in a week.

Next, a contractor. Frances wanted ammunition. She wanted to be able to say to Hart, "It will take twenty-five thousand dollars to put in a new kitchen and ten thousand to do all the floors." And she wanted to be able to say to Chip Strong, "It will cost us seventy-five thousand to make the place livable; the price is much too high." Chip had given her the name of a contractor who would probably be able to give her rough figures for general renovation, so she called him. And a landscape architect, to find out about getting rid of the hemlocks. And, as an afterthought, digging a long bed for a perennial border.

Since it was Saturday, Frances knew she had been lucky to get the engineer at home. She had left messages on the answering machines of the contractor and landscaper. When the phone rang later that evening, she thought it might be one of them returning her call. To her surprise, it was an unfamiliar voice.

"Mrs. Drummond," the man said, "my name is George Sinclair. We met briefly at your house a couple of weeks ago, I'm a friend of Harry's. . . ." He paused here, his voice on an inquiring note, to allow her to say she remembered him.

"Oh, yes," Frances said, frowning. She vaguely remembered hearing about some friend of Harry's, but didn't recall having actually seen him. It had been that weekend Eleanor was there.

"I'm calling at Clara Henschel's suggestion," the man went on, a bit hesitant. "I've been staying with her at Fenwick, and I'm doing a mural in the house. It's going to be a series of panels about her life. The thing is, I'd like to be able to see some of her scrapbooks, because I want to incorporate certain things into the panels. Portraits of her husbands, that kind of thing," he said, sounding more confident. "Clara told me the scrapbooks are in her New York house. And she suggested that I call you to see if I could come over and see some of them. She said I could bring anything I needed back to Fenwick. Would that be all right with you?"

"Yes, of course," Frances said, intrigued. "What a wonderful idea. She has dozens of books; it may take you quite a while. When did you want to come?"

"Well," the voice said, a bit apologetically, "I'm in New York for just a couple of days, so as soon as possible, really. Would any time Monday be convenient?"

"Yes," Frances said, "Monday's fine. In the morning? Around ten?"

"Fine. I have the address. I'll see you then," said George Sinclair. And he hung up the phone.

Frances went back to the coffee-table book about privately held châteaux in France that she was leafing through. The house was quiet around her. Beatriz had gone out, and Frances sat in the velvet wing chair in the library. The casement windows overlooked the garden, and Frances could occasionally hear a phone's ring or a voice from an apartment across the way. Though music didn't interest her much, Frances had tuned the radio to a classical station, and a string quartet played in the background in a muted, civilized kind of way.

It came as a surprise when Clara's phone rang again. Frances let it ring twice before picking it up. "Hello?"

"Frances, what is this about a house?" came Hart's voice, blustering down the phone cord.

"Oh," she said, "hello. You've been talking to Chip Strong. I told him not to tell you. Did he tell you where I was, too?"

"Yes," snapped Hart. "I'm at his house now, talking on a pay phone, if you can believe such a thing," he went on in a lower tone of voice. "He thinks it keeps his phone bills down."

"Goodness!" Frances said, fascinated. "I didn't notice that when I was there. Isn't it the strangest place? Have you been upstairs?"

"Oh, yes," Hart said, indifferent, "it looks like the Salvation Army. But listen!" His voice grew louder as he remembered why he was calling. "Chip says he showed you a house yesterday!"

"Several, actually. I asked him not to tell you," Frances said, "because I wanted to surprise you with a fait accompli. But I suppose he just blurted it out, didn't he?"

"More or less," Hart said. "He seemed so nervous that I asked him what his guilty secret was and he turned purple and told me."

Frances sighed. "I might have known. Well, do you want to see them, too, then?" Some canny instinct prompted her to add, "You see, I thought I could save you time by screening them, so to speak. Weeding out the worst ones."

"Oh," Hart said, sounding a bit mollified. "Well. That's

probably a good idea." Then the blustering tone came back into his voice. "But why are you even looking at houses?"

"Hart, I can't live in that house on the water, you know that," Frances said, with the patience of a nursery school teacher.

"Well, can't you let it wait until the end of the summer?" he answered.

"Why?" asked his wife in a reasonable tone. There was a long pause as Hart examined this. Then a series of clicks came, punctuated with some muffled swearing. "Damn. Running out of money. Listen, can you call me back?"

"I don't really want to run up a big bill on Clara's phone," Frances said in the same patient tone. "I'm getting an engineer's report . . ." But she couldn't finish. The line went dead.

Three minutes later the phone rang again. Again Frances calmly put a marker in her book and reached for the receiver. Expecting to hear her husband's voice, she said sweetly, "Yes?"

"Mom? Is that you?" It was Harry, sounding confused.

"Oh, Harry! Goodness, such excitement tonight," his mother said. "I thought New York was supposed to be dead on summer weekends, but the phone hasn't stopped ringing!"

"Was one of the calls from George Sinclair?"

"Yes, Harry, who is he? He says I met him this summer, but I don't think I did."

Harry sighed. "He is a friend of mine and he was only there for a few minutes—remember, with Clara's boat? I may not have even introduced you. The thing is, Mom, Eleanor had an affair with him in Venice. And he's in love with her and I swear she's in love with him, but she won't see him."

Frances put the book on the floor. "What? What is all this? Eleanor in love? How did I miss this?"

Harry didn't answer right away. "It's a long story, Mom. Do you want to hear it on the phone, or can I come and tell you in person?"

"I think you'd better come up here," said Frances.

"I'll hop in a cab and be there in fifteen minutes," he answered, and hung up.

Frances laid *Private Châteaux of the Loire* carefully on a table and went down to the kitchen to make a pot of decaf coffee. As she arranged a few almond cookies on a plate, the phone rang again. "You're running late?" she said.

"No," came Hart's exasperated voice, "I'm not running late, I had to borrow a roll of quarters from Chip and then your phone was busy, what are you *up* to?"

"Up to?" Frances exclaimed in annoyance. "I'm not up to anything. I was talking to my son and yours on the phone, which I suppose I am permitted to do."

"No, no, about the house," Hart said, suddenly sounding weary.

"I'm not up to anything," Frances answered, trying to be calm. "I am trying to find a place to live."

"You have a place to live," Hart said. "Here, with me."

"No," Frances said, very quietly. "I really am sorry, Hart. I just can't. Not in that horrible house."

There was a long pause. Frances could hear music coming faintly from the background. Jazz, it sounded like. "I feel like you're railroading me," Hart said finally.

Frances stood in the quiet white kitchen, considering. The coffeepot made its bubbling noises behind her, indicating that the brewing cycle was finished. She turned to get coffee cups from the cupboard. "Maybe I am," she answered. "But it seemed like the only way to get things moving."

"But what if I hate the house?" Hart answered. "It looks like a real dog from the outside."

"We looked at several houses."

"But Chip said there was one you really liked."

Frances sighed. "I thought these people were supposed to be discreet."

"Not Chip," Hart said, with some satisfaction. "Not with me."

"Well, then," Frances admitted, "there was one house with more potential than the others."

"Right. It looks like something the Addams Family would live in."

"It does," Frances conceded. "It needs a lot of work. But the price is reasonable and as I said, it has potential."

"But if I hate it?"

"Nobody can force you to live in it," Frances said lightly. Upstairs the doorbell rang. "I have to go. Harry's here."

"Wait, Frances, when are you coming back?"

"I don't know," his wife said, as the doorbell pealed again. "I'll talk to you during the week." And she hung up without saying good-bye.

Upstairs on the doorstep, Harry had turned his back to the house and was looking at the streetlight's yellowish glow filtering through the thick leaves of the plane trees. When Frances opened the door, she noticed that he looked tired. She kissed his cheek as he walked past her.

"I've made some coffee," she said. "I'll bring it into the library."

"I'll help you," Harry said. "Or, for heaven's sake, why carry it upstairs? We can just sit down here."

"Clara has all these rooms, why not use them?" came his mother's voice from the refrigerator, where she was reaching for a carton of milk.

"I suppose," Harry said, giving up. His mother shot him a sharp glance, and the look of defeat on his face wrung her heart.

"I spoke to your father just now," she said.

"Oh?" Harry looked up.

"We're looking at a house next week." She finished pouring milk into Clara's little silver pitcher. "There, you can carry that up."

"Where?" Harry asked when he was settled on a loveseat in the library.

"Weymouth. I don't know that Hart will be interested; it needs a lot of work." Frances looked across at Harry. "It's been quite a summer, hasn't it?"

He sighed. "I'll be glad as hell when it's over," he said. "I don't know why I mind so much about you and Dad, Eleanor doesn't seem very bothered, but I guess she's got enough on her plate anyway. And I feel horrible about that, too. I feel incredibly responsible for causing two people I love a great deal of pain."

"How did I miss this?" Frances said. "That's what I want to know. Why didn't I know that Eleanor was so unhappy?"

Harry looked embarrassed. "Well, you've been . . . I mean . . . you were a little . . ." His eyes searched the shadowed cornice above the bookshelves. "Abstracted. Distracted. Something. This summer."

Frances nodded. "True." She was silent for a few moments. "Yes. Well, that's over. So tell me about Ellie. If this man George is in love with her and she's in love with him, I don't see where the problem lies."

"Well, you know how stubborn she is," Harry began, with relief. Frances settled back to listen.

George Sinclair knew that he had more than the usual share of social confidence. But even he was apprehensive about meeting Eleanor's mother. How much would she know? Would she hate him on sight? Would she talk to him about Eleanor? Would she look like her daughter? That weekend up in Weymouth, they had not actually laid eyes on each other, since George didn't go inside the house. Alluding to their meeting was just a polite fiction, and he assumed she had taken it as such. Were they going to maintain the further polite fiction that they knew nothing more about each other? George, in his anxiety, had tried to reach Harry, but his friend's answering machine was on and even George's pleading ("Please pick up, Harry, I'm about to go meet your mother and I'm terrified") didn't earn a response.

And now, walking down this impeccable block, past pretty row houses that looked as spanking clean as circus ponies, George felt an urge to flee, coupled with the compulsion to forge ahead and meet Eleanor's mother.

The gleaming brass doorbell produced a peal somewhere in the house. After a minute, the door was opened by a pretty middle-aged woman in an apricot-colored uniform with an apron.

"Mr. Sinclair? Mrs. Drummond is in the library. I will take you up."

George had an impression of oak paneling lining the stairs and a beautiful little watercolor hanging above a French console table before he was ushered into a small room overlooking the garden.

A tall blond woman was rising from a love seat, holding out her hand to him.

George searched her fine-boned face for a resemblance to Eleanor and couldn't find it. But her navy linen dress looked like something Eleanor might have chosen. And as she sat down again, he noticed her square, competent-looking hands and felt a twinge of sadness. Eleanor had her mother's hands.

Frances's hands were spread out, at the moment, on two tall stacks of leather-bound photograph albums, and Frances Drummond was saying, "I don't know exactly what you're looking for, but I have to admit, I'm fascinated by the whole idea and I'd love to help."

George collected his thoughts and faced Eleanor's mother. "You know the morning room in her house in Fenwick, I assume?" Frances nodded. "I'm doing each of the walls as a separate compositional element. Birth, debut, marriage. Marriages," he amended, stressing the final syllable.

"All the occasions when a lady has her name in the paper," Frances said helpfully.

"Exactly," George answered. "She suggested putting in the various houses she's lived in, too, as a kind of architectural background. I gather some of them were pretty grand. And I'm thinking of putting in the husbands themselves. I'd like to look at her wedding pictures, if I can, because the dresses should be accurate. And any other attributes. Animals? Horses or pet monkeys or anything? Cars or boats?"

Frances nodded. "I see. Clara was really a friend of my mother's first," she said. "She was Madame de Montpolignac when I was little. Mummy used to tell me about her life; I loved hearing the stories," she said, lifting a pile of albums onto the floor. "Her first husband, Buzzy Sterling, had a cottage at Newport. I think that would be ideal. As I recall, it's part of Salve Regina College now, but there should be a few shots of it. Here, you look," she said, handing a stack of albums to George. "Look for the albums with 'C.L.S.' on the cover. The initials change with each marriage."

They soon found albums full of photographs from her first

marriage. There was the Newport cottage, a vast limestone palace modeled after the Petit Trianon. There was the yacht, a rakish two-masted schooner called *Clair de Lune*. Groups of beauties in knitted bathing suits and sleekly waved hair lounged under striped tents. There were several Dorothy Wilding studio shots of Clara languid in gleaming satin, her left arm weighed down with bracelets and three white plumes at the back of her head.

"Her court presentation," Frances said, handing the album to George. "Maybe you can fit this in somewhere."

George put the album open on the floor. "I hadn't really thought this out very carefully. I don't have anything to put the pictures in, and I don't want to carry the albums up to Fenwick."

"Do you need the originals? Or could you do with xeroxes?"

"The originals would be best. And I hate to xerox old photographs anyway," George said. "It doesn't do them any good."

Frances considered. "Would a box do? We can probably find a flat box somewhere."

George nodded. "Especially if we could find some tissue paper, just to protect them a bit more."

Frances went back to the albums, impressed. Whatever else George Sinclair might be, he was thoughtful.

"Oh, look, here she is as a widow!" George said enthusiastically. "Doesn't she look wonderful?" Frances moved around to look over his shoulder. There indeed was Clara, in black from head to foot, about to get into an immense Daimler.

"How like Clara to put that in her album," Frances said dispassionately. "You'd think she was the widowed Queen of England, wouldn't you, with that veil?

"It was probably the best role of her life," Frances went on, going back to sit on the love seat. "She wore deepest widow's black for her first husband until she married de Montpolignac. I think even then she would have liked to be married in black, but decided it was unseemly. At least she admitted that she only wore it because it was so becoming."

"Have you gotten to the album of her wedding to Al Markson?" George asked.

"This should be it," Frances said, sliding a blue album across to him. She paused and said deliberately, "Eleanor was there."

"Ah," George said, a long sighing breath. He looked out the window. Somewhere in a nearby building someone was playing a clarinet extremely well. The notes bubbled smoothly up and down like water in a fountain. He held the album closed on his lap and looked down at his hands on it. There was a stubborn residue of green paint under his thumbnail. He felt limp, somehow, like a punctured balloon. "Harry told you?"

Frances nodded. "He feels terrible."

George looked away from her, then stood up and walked to the window. "He shouldn't. He's not entirely responsible. I managed things badly myself." He turned back to Frances, but she couldn't quite read the expression on his backlit face. "Why is she doing this, Mrs. Drummond?" he asked, with pain in his voice.

Frances looked down. "She's a very obstinate girl," she answered. "She always has been. When she feels that she's being pushed, she digs in her heels. That may be part of it. I really don't know what to say. Harry and I talked about this last night for quite a while."

"I have no pride, you know," George said. "I would try again if I thought it would help. But I can't keep this up much longer. Hoping. She was very definite last time."

Frances looked up then and saw a bleak, faraway look on his face. She barely knew this young man, but she felt great pity for him. And if he felt like this, what must Eleanor be going through?

"What a waste," she said softly to herself.

"Isn't it?" George said, suddenly coming to kneel on the floor next to her. "Why should two people who care about each other—and I know she does," he interrupted himself, "no matter what she says—be kept apart for silly superficial reasons?"

"Harry said she's angry because he set you up. And didn't tell her you worked at Avalon. Is that right?"

"I think that's it," George said, shrugging. "We've never actually discussed this rationally."

"Well, you know, dear," Frances said, laying a hand on his shoulder, "I think the truth is that Eleanor is scared stiff. You represent something she wants so much that she's afraid to reach out for it. Or so it seems to me," Frances finished, surprised at herself. "I don't usually indulge in pop psychology, but my daughter has had a difficult few years." She sat back on the love seat and looked at George. "This sounds like a cliché from an English novel, but would you like a cup of tea?"

19

When George indicated to Frances that he was ready to give up on Eleanor, he was exaggerating only slightly. When Eleanor had flung herself away from him in the Piazza San Marco he had been angry and disappointed. But he hadn't really felt that things were over. His curious way of keeping in touch with her had been another one of his instinctive choices. He wanted Eleanor to know that he wasn't giving up. He wanted her to have the sense that she was on his mind. He wanted to be on *her* mind. He hoped that his occasional one-way contacts might create a sense of mystery. Ultimately, George wanted Eleanor to feel he was wooing her.

But the tactic had taken its toll. The price was complete preoccupation with Eleanor. He looked back on the month of July and remembered only thinking about her. Painting badly, if at all. Dialing her phone number many times daily. Roving the streets of New York with little offerings for her. At the time he had relished doing this; it had kept her image breathing in front of him. But now, walking home from his visit to Frances, carrying a box of photographs of Clara Henschel, George felt he had made a terrible mistake. While he had become obsessed with this woman, she had only felt hounded. All of the efforts that he had thought would charm her had merely deepened her resistance. He had made himself miserable and, according to her mother, had made her even more miserable. The very idea wrung George's heart.

And it was all such a waste. George found himself standing at a stoplight on Lexington Avenue, shaking his head and saying out loud, "Such a waste." The blond woman next to him on the sidewalk gave him a curious glance and edged away. It was sad, really. Almost tragic. Because of whatever it was that held her back, Eleanor wasn't going to let this love affair happen. George had a brief fantastic image of himself and Eleanor on their wedding day, Eleanor radiant with flowers in her hair, leaning over to kiss him. He closed his eyes on the picture, wrenched with pain.

Frances had discouraged him from trying to change Eleanor's mind. The prudent sober path now would probably be to try to forget her. But there was one more thing . . . one more argument, one more plea, George wasn't quite sure what it was. One more gesture, anyway, that he needed to make. Something else that he wanted her to have, regardless of what happened afterward.

His apartment had never been very appealing in the summer. Though a breeze from the Hudson sometimes wormed its way in through the tiny bathroom window, George found the treeless blocks of Tribeca oppressive in August. On Church Street the discount stores offered tables of pawed-over underwear and flimsy plastic child-sized chairs and pirated videos of slasher movies. The milky sunlight was everywhere, oozing beneath awnings and into alleys that were usually shadowed. As he pushed open the front door of his building, the shaft of light that followed him in slashed across an airy broth of dust motes and shreds of feathers from the novelty shop on the first floor.

The loft was stuffy and a thin fog of dust lay everywhere. George put down the package of Clara's pictures and opened the window onto the street, knowing it would not draw in a fresh breeze.

He collapsed for a moment onto his sofa, which belched a cloud of dust into the sunlight. With his head on one scrolled arm and his feet hanging over the other, George lay looking up at the grimy pressed-tin ceiling and contemplated his bitter fate.

He had played his cards wrong. It was obvious now. There might have been a window, if he could only have judged it, an interval when Eleanor would have listened to him. When her first anger had faded, but before he blew everything by confronting her in Weymouth. After that, of course, it was hopeless. George pressed his palms against his eyes to shut out the light.

Was it possible that you could screw up something so important by simple misjudgment? Shouldn't there be a special dispensation for good intentions? Or was he really at fault? Had he just been a coward? At first he hadn't wanted to expose himself to Eleanor's anger, George admitted to himself. Hence the one-sided contact.

Then it had come to seem like the correct strategy. Gentle, soothing. A reassuring approach. George sat up. Had he convinced himself of this just so he wouldn't have to risk confronting Eleanor? He got up and ambled into the kitchen. Who knew, anyway? Who knew what folly lurked in the hearts of lovelorn painters?

He opened the refrigerator door and blinked at the cool, humming brightness inside. There was a small globular bottle of Orangina on the top shelf. George took it out and absentmindedly unscrewed the cap. He took it over to the painting area and began packing charcoal and brushes and sketch pads into a duffel bag, taking occasional swigs from the bottle. When the bag was nearly full, he threw in some clothes and books. As he crossed the loft with an armful of shirts, he glanced at his answering machine and flicked the switch to turn it off. If he was going to spend all of August in Fenwick, he might as well leave the machine off. He had given Clara's number to everyone who would need it. He wedged the shirts into the duffel bag and went back for some underwear. Then he glanced at his watch and realized that, if he wanted to make his train, he'd have to leave. So neat, organized George Sinclair zipped his bags shut, picked up Clara's pictures and a brown-paper parcel that stood by his desk, and walked out of his loft, leaving an open window and half-drunk bottle of Orangina.

He took a cab up to the Upper West Side and had the driver wait while he left the parcel with Eleanor's doorman. Then the taxi took him to the train station at 125th Street, where he caught the 2:35 to New Haven. As the train swept through the leafy suburbs of Westchester and Fairfield County, he looked out the window numbly, with a pained expression on his face.

*   *   *

269

It was an expression that would have been familiar to Eleanor, though it sat differently on her face. A certain immovability, a tension between the eyebrows, an inability to smile. Resignation had not, as Eleanor hoped, become acceptance. She ached. All day, from waking to sleeping, she was aware of emotional bruises. She wept easily and her temper was shocking and she couldn't find energy for the most mundane activities. On the weekends when the boys were at Jared's she lay on her bed with the air conditioner on, dozing or trying to work or reading magazines whose contents she promptly forgot.

The worst of it was that the children had noticed. Toby taxed her with crabbiness and clowned around, trying to get her to smile. Aware that her maternal power to thwart him was at a low ebb, he made constant inroads on routine discipline. He wouldn't go to bed, he wouldn't clean up his room, he talked back to her, daring her (urging her, in an oblique childish way) to crack down and restore the norm. He wore her down. Simon, meanwhile, became heartbreakingly clingy. He whined and wrapped his arms around her as she put him on the bus in the morning. When she came home at night he threw himself at her and nuzzled her neck like a baby.

Eleanor knew what the boys' behavior meant. They sensed her pain and knew that something else had usurped their place at the center of her emotions. She knew that if she could snap out of this depression, the boys would be back to normal in a week.

But it wasn't the kind of depression you could snap out of, she thought bitterly as she walked past her doorman that Monday night. It was the kind of depression that you climbed out of an inch at a time, with a lot of backsliding.

"Mrs. Gray," the doorman said, "wait, I have a package for you." He disappeared into his little cubby. Eleanor waited, unconcerned. It was probably something Toby had sent away for from a cereal box. But the doorman came back with a sizable brown paper parcel, and Eleanor's eyes flew to her name, written in a familiar elegant handwriting on the front.

"Thank you, Eddie," she said, trying to sound composed. But as she went up alone in the elevator she studied her name, written in George's handwriting. It was a picture; she could feel the hard outline of the frame through the paper. As the elevator stopped on her floor, she considered tearing the paper off. But caution conquered curiosity. Whatever it was, Eleanor knew, it was going to be upsetting. Better wait until the children were in bed. So when she opened the door and heard Simon calling out "Mommy! Mommy!" she leaned the package by the front hall table and tried to forget it.

It wasn't until three hours later that the children were asleep, the dishes done, the lunches made, the clothes laid out for the next day. Eleanor went to the front hall to bolt the door. She turned out the lights in the living room. Then she bent down in the dark, her fingers finding the package right away. She carried it to her bedroom, loosening the tape as she went. She lay it down on her bed and took the paper off.

The tears, as she had known they would, welled up. She pressed a fist to her mouth as it pulled into a grimace. When the first tear splashed onto the glass protecting the picture, she didn't even wipe it off.

It was a pencil sketch of Toby and Simon at the beach. On the far right, George had drawn the leaves of the beach plum and a few grasses and a hillock of sand. Off on the horizon floated the Connecticut shore, with a faraway sail to mark the distance. And in the center, Toby knelt in a few inches of water, placing a shell on the battlement of his sand castle. Simon stood watching, intent on Toby's task, holding a forgotten bucket of water in his right hand.

It was just a pencil sketch. George had used no color, no ink, though he must have gone over the picture later, Eleanor thought, to refine the various textures. Toby's hair, sleek as a seal's fur. The little quivering leaves of the beach plum. The glassy water around Simon's ankles. Even the gleaming, sandy skin of the boys' arms and chests.

Blinking hard and smearing the tears out of her eyes with the back of a hand, Eleanor turned the picture over. On the brown paper of the back, nothing but the framer's seal. She turned it over again and looked at the margin of the picture. George had merely signed and dated it. She smoothed out the paper it had come wrapped in. All it said was her name. There was no other message.

No other message, thought Eleanor, no message but the one in the picture. She sat on the bed, holding it in her lap. George had chosen to have the sketch matted in a sunny yellow. The frame itself was golden wood with a pretty flamelike grain. Bird's-eye maple, Eleanor thought. There was just a thread of gilding on the frame, next to the glass. It had been beautifully done.

Eleanor inched backward on the bed until she was leaning against the pillows, with the picture propped up on her knees. What more could a woman want? she thought to herself. What more could a woman want from life than a man like George Sinclair? A man who knew the way to her heart. Thoughtful. Sensitive. A man whom, moreover, she liked. Enjoyed. And open; a man who had been willing to *pursue* her. To let her know how much he wanted her.

But a man, Eleanor told herself grimly, who had also been underhanded. Who had hidden important facts from her. It wasn't just that he taught at the boys' school. Eleanor knew that a romance with one of their teachers would create a flap, but, as George himself had pointed out, his job wasn't important to him. He could leave Avalon, and she could weather a certain amount of gossip. And it wasn't just that he was one of Harry's friends. Harry knew some interesting people. And Harry was himself a good person, even if his judgment was lousy.

It wasn't these aspects of George's identity that bothered Eleanor so much, she told herself. It was the fact that he had hidden them. It made Eleanor angry. She felt like a dupe. It also made her worry. What else might still be hidden?

She put the picture aside and straightened out her legs. What had Frank Gerson said? "You don't need that pride"? Still, what did he know, with his boats on living room floors? (She *had* hired a new secretary, a woman in her forties who had a sense of humor and a great memory. Frank had been right about that.)

Pride. Was that what was holding her back? Concentrating hard, Eleanor thought about it. Could she admit she'd been wrong? She tried to imagine it: apologizing. It didn't seem difficult. That wasn't the problem.

But if pride wasn't the problem, what was? She got up and pulled her nightgown from beneath the pillows.

Eleanor would have laughed at the very idea, but one of her great virtues was courage. Hart had often watched her as a child, wringing her hands at the side of the pool and then doing a flip off the diving board. Or silent at breakfast before an audition, then getting a part in a play. Fear, for Eleanor, had never been a reason to turn away from something. Later in life, when the most frightening things she faced were emotional, she charted the same course. And she had found, through trial and error, that a steely honesty with herself was the wisest strategy. In the first year after the divorce, she had often resorted to a kind of emotional surgery, mentally poking and prodding until she found the sources of her pain. The guilt. The anger. The sense of inadequacy. The deep-seated conviction that if she had only been different, her children's father would still live with them.

In the calmer years that followed, she had no need to plumb her own depths. Life was an exhausting logistical battle, but it had its satisfactions and if they were temperate, that was enough for Eleanor. She didn't ask for emotional peaks, knowing all too well the valleys that came with them.

Yet here she was, staring at herself in the mirror as she brushed her teeth, in, as she told herself, a veritable Slough of Despond. Because of George Sinclair.

Who hadn't given up.

There he was, hers if she would only reach out a hand. Why could she not reach out a hand?

Eleanor spat and rinsed out her mouth. She turned off the light and padded back into the bedroom. And asked herself, with a sudden clarity, What is it I am afraid of?

Betrayal.

Nothing less. The answer came with a rush, and a spurt of tears, and excruciating memories of loss and pain. Of Jared walking out the door as she held a screaming infant Simon, with Toby crying at her knees and her own tears pouring silently down her face. As she sat on the side of her bed Eleanor felt the tears again, and the ache in her throat, and remembered the desolation. More than a body could bear. She shook her head, still crying. More than anyone could bear twice.

She sniffed, and mopped her face and blew her nose. So that was it. She was simply afraid. She was afraid George would leave her. It really didn't have anything to do with the minor deceptions he'd practiced in Venice. Well, maybe it did, she thought, maybe she was worried that a man who had tried to fool her from the first would simply never stop. But honesty seemed to be George's natural style. She remembered that moment in bed in Venice: "This is too important to me to be sloppy about." That was the real George, Eleanor believed. The subterfuges were an aberration. Had to be an aberration. Didn't they?

So she was scared. She pulled her legs into bed and dragged the sheet up over her. She laid the picture of her sons on the other side of the big bed and turned out her lamp. Once burned, twice shy. Nothing like living your life by a cliché.

Chip Strong was nervous. He had arrived at the Main Street house on his bicycle and had forgotten to take his bicycle clips off, so he stood on the sidewalk leafing through the engineer's report with his khakis bunched up around his ankles. Frances, who had skimmed the engineer's report first, checked her watch. Hart, punctual to a fault, would be along in moments.

Frances admitted to herself that she was a little anxious, too. She had dithered over her clothes that morning and checked her bag three times for the train schedule. It had proved impossible to get estimates from a contractor or landscaper; Frances now realized she'd been a bit naive in that hope. But the engineer's report was good, better than she had expected. And the contractor could wait. The important thing now was handling Hart.

Frances had wondered how she would feel when she saw the house again. Would it look better than she'd remembered? Worse? Would its drawbacks, the hemlock trees and the linoleum and the sagging blinds, look like insuperable obstacles? Or things that could be fixed? She hadn't been prepared for the surge of affection she felt when she saw the mansard roof come into view between the feathery treetops.

But Frances had learned from her mistakes that summer, and she told herself not to be emotional. Or at least to be as unemotional as possible. A brisk, offhand attitude was the way to approach this.

So when Hart drove up, Frances was brisk and offhand. She offered her cheek for her husband to kiss and didn't tell him, though the words were on the tip of her tongue, that he needed a haircut. They got right down to business.

The first thing Hart noticed was the propped-up porch. He knelt and knocked on the latticework that supported the stairs behind the two-by-fours. "Rotten," he said. "It's all rotten. Have to be replaced."

"Yes," Frances said. "I had an engineer look it over. There's quite a bit of work to be done."

Hart straightened up. "You got an engineer's report?" he said, surprised. "How did you know about that?"

"We had one for the Shore Road house," Frances replied calmly. "I've been doing my research."

And how, Chip Strong silently said to himself, and handed the report to Hart. Hart glanced at him, apparently noticing his fishing crony for the first time. Unable to articulate his irritation, he merely glared.

Hart's eyes ran down the first page, and he flipped through the rest of it quickly. Frances didn't want to appear to be hanging on to the engineer's words, so she gently took the key ring from Chip's hand and unlocked the side door.

She went in and threw wide the front doors, propping open the glass outer doors to get some air and light into the place. Glancing around at the flowered wallpaper and the dusty chandelier, she felt doubt. There was such a stifling old-lady aura about the whole house. Could it be eradicated? Did she and Hart have the energy for it? Wasn't this instead a house for a young couple who would strip the walls themselves and live on pizza and popcorn while they did so?

"It's depressing, Frances," said Hart querulously as he came to stand by her in the front hall. "I can't imagine what you see in it."

"Possibilities, I suppose," she said. "I must see it as a diamond in the rough. A connoisseur's house. Look," she said, turning into the parlor on the right. "The proportions are wonderful."

Hart walked into the parlor and stood with his hands in his pockets, looking up at the parlor ceiling, where a dusty cobweb floated gently in the corner, disturbed by the unfamiliar current of air from outdoors. He didn't say a word, but walked back out into the hall, where he knelt and poked at a piece of the parquet that came right up in his hand.

"I know," Frances said. "It's probably not for us. What this house needs is really competent owners. Who are good with their hands and have a sense of history. It could be put in really beautiful shape, but it's an enormous job. We aren't the people to do it. Still, you might as well come see the rest while you're here."

Frances's little speech was not calculated. While she knew that selling Hart the house would be difficult, she had no subtle plan in mind. She wanted Chip to take him to the carriage house as well, to demonstrate that she was broad-minded and would consider a range of options. It was important that Hart not feel, as he had put it, "railroaded."

But what she had done instinctively, with all the skill of forty years of marriage, was appeal to Hart's personal myth. Hart believed *he* was competent, a can-do kind of guy. A man thoroughly at home with the more arcane elements of a workshop. A man who could learn to fish and tie flies with the best of them. So Frances's dismissive comment about what the house required was a direct challenge to his image of himself. She thought the house demanded owners who would know how to fix it up? Who would that be, if not Hart Drummond? After all, look at all the work he'd put into the Chester house. Had Frances forgotten that? He had an impulse to catch up to his wife as she climbed the stairs and remind her of the way he'd restored the mahogany pocket doors, stripped them and put on new brass hardware and replaced them on their tracks. Surely there was nothing more complex than that in this house.

He noticed the niche at the head of the stairs and tapped the wall with his knuckles. Good sound plaster. The linoleum on the bathroom floors was revolting. All of the bathrooms would probably need complete tiling. There was no point in taking historical fidelity into the john with you. In one of the bedrooms he stooped down to look up the fireplace, which was predictably enough a black cavern.

"Do they look clean?" Frances asked politely.

"I can't tell, it's all dark," her husband answered. They looked at each other. "Naturally," Hart said, and smiled wryly.

Frances smiled back. "Naturally," she agreed.

Chip Strong, who witnessed this exchange, began to get confused. Of course, the situation confused him anyway. If Frances had left Hart, why were they buying a house together? And if they were buying a house together, why weren't they living together? Chip knew that the refinements of married life were a closed book to him, but this situation seemed positively Oriental in its refinement. And incomprehensibility.

Chip trailed along behind Frances and Hart as they went through the rest of the house. He didn't dare open his mouth to do his usual real estate agent spiel, since he felt that he would somehow be stepping on someone's toes. Or interfering in this odd relationship. Anyway, Frances was doing just fine. In fact, she was doing extremely well, Chip thought. Discreetly pointing out the best features. Frankly admitting to the drawbacks, a tactic that Chip had always thought made buyers trust you.

They were by now out in the yard, looking up at the house. The mansard part of the roof was covered with beautiful old scalloped slates, many of which were loose or cracked. "Those slates would be hell to replace," Hart said.

Frances nodded. "Is there anything you can use instead? Shingle?"

"No," Hart said, shaking his head. "Nothing else looks right." He turned his gaze on the offending hemlocks. "How much to get those trees out of here?" he asked his wife.

"I couldn't get a landscaper's estimate in time," she admitted. "They're big, old trees, though. Many thousands, I'd imagine."

Hart turned to look at the rest of the yard. At the back of the lot, a hundred yards from the house, was a small garage. "We'd have to expand that for two cars," Hart pointed out.

Frances looked at him. "Well," she said, trying to be brisk and offhand, "let's go look at the other place, and we can decide afterward what to do next."

"Let me just go look at the garage," Hart said. "Might as well be thorough while I'm here."

Frances watched him cross the lawn with Chip and come back a few minutes later dusting his hands, with an expression of suppressed glee.

"There's a workshop in there," he told her as they walked to the car. "Beautifully laid out. Tons of space. I don't know how they managed it."

"That's nice," Frances said in a temperate tone. But inwardly she rejoiced. Behind Hart's back, she winked at Chip. As he clambered onto his bicycle, he was more confused than ever.

Hart hated the carriage house. He thought it was corny and too Laura Ashley-ish, and he objected strongly to sleeping in a former stall. "What if I get asthma, Frances?" he said.

"You've never wheezed an instant in your life," she said. "I doubt you'll start at the advanced age of sixty-six." But he wasn't to be convinced. The conversion had been done shoddily. He hated Sheetrock and mistrusted the sleek Italian kitchen fixtures. The lighting, all artfully recessed next to the oak beams, drove him crazy, with all of its sliding dimmer switches.

Finally Frances interrupted one of his complaints and said, "Hart, I just don't understand you. This is a perfectly nice house, much nicer than that thing on Shore Road, and you can only find fault with it. What is the matter with you?"

Hart looked at her, taken aback, and didn't answer for a moment.

"There are dimmer switches in that house," Frances reminded him.

Hart lifted his hands in the age-old gesture of puzzlement. "Damned if I know," he said. "This place just rubs me the wrong way."

"Well, now you know how I feel about Shore Road," Frances

said tartly. "I'm going to have to catch a train back to the city, so maybe we can decided what to do next."

"Oh, fine," Hart said, abashed. "I don't need to see any more anyway." So they went outside to find Chip, who had given up on them completely and was sitting against a wall with his face lifted to the sun, thinking about fish.

When Eleanor woke up the morning after she'd received George's picture, she felt different. Both better and worse. She was calm, but there was a hollow, fearful feeling in the pit of her stomach. Before she was completely awake she knew she had to do something she dreaded. When her eyes opened she remembered what it was.

Eleanor was not a woman who relied much on clothes, but a few items in her closet were vested with some emotional weight. Her party dress, of course, had festive vibes, and she relied on her sharpest suit as armor for difficult days in the office. And there was a dress that, with a blazer, could just pass as business-like, a soft checked cotton with a high waist and a long skirt. It felt as reassuring as a nightgown. When Eleanor found herself pulling it over her head, she acknowledged that some crisis had arrived. She felt that she would need every ounce of comfort available because today was the day she would talk to George Sinclair.

She chased the boys through their morning routine with a degree of absent-mindedness that made Toby even wilder than ever. She put them on the van to camp, then bought her newspaper and went down into the subway station on Broadway, unconscious of the morning rush hour around her.

She tried to concentrate on *The New York Times* as the express train roared its way toward Wall Street, but she found herself staring blankly at the below-the-fold story of intrigue in national beauty pageants. She folded the paper and tucked it under her arm. If she couldn't concentrate on beauty pageants, the lead stories on health insurance and Middle East conflict weren't going to interest her, either.

All she could think about was what to say to George Sinclair.

Hi. How are you? I got the picture. I really love it. Umm . . . Then what? Can we talk? I need to see you. No, how about, I'd like to see you? That sounded like asking for a date. Eleanor frowned so fiercely that a boy seated directly in front of her shut his mouth and stopped popping his bubble gum.

It was no good. By the time the train pulled into the station, Eleanor's stomach was sour with anxiety and she still didn't know what she was going to say to George. Nevertheless, her first action when she marched into her office was to look up his number in the phone book. It seemed odd, actually not to know it; but there he was, Sinclair George on Reade Street. She dialed the number, standing at her desk with her back to the door, looking out onto the sparkling water of New York Harbor. It was only nine-thirty. He would be there.

But he wasn't. The phone rang and rang. No answering machine picked up, and Eleanor was so puzzled by this (didn't everyone in Manhattan have an answering machine?) that she dialed the number again to be sure. Eight rings. She shrugged. No doubt he'd gone out for coffee.

At intervals for the rest of the day, Eleanor called his number. By noon she knew it by heart. Nothing changed. It just rang and rang.

She took the boys out for pizza that night and called again after they were in bed. Still no answer.

Eleanor's family had spent the previous month reminding each other how stubborn she was, and they were right. A little resistance was all it took to make Eleanor really sink her teeth into something. Now it was the disappearance of George Sinclair. Having decided that she needed to talk to George, she wanted to start right away. Get it over with. If you decide you must, for moral or emotional reasons, jump off a cliff, you don't want to hang around on the edge for days. The fact that the cliff (or George) seemed to have vanished into a mist only made Eleanor more determined.

Harry would know where George was. Eleanor considered calling him.

Impossible. Harry would guess why she wanted to know. She

could grit her teeth and call George, but not under the interested gaze of her baby brother.

So then who? Who would know where he was? His dealer, only she didn't know his full name. André something. Not a help.

Eleanor looked at her watch. It wasn't even ten. She had only been trying to reach the man for twelve hours. He was probably just out for the day.

But he wasn't there the next day. Or the next.

It was August, Eleanor told herself. People went away in August. Especially people like artists. For the whole month, sometimes. To hip places like Provence or Berlin. (Here Eleanor checked herself. She had never actually heard of anyone going to Berlin for August.) If you were gone for the whole month you might not turn on your answering machine. Maybe George had one of those old-fashioned machines that you couldn't call into from outside. There were any number of reasons he might not be there. Still Eleanor kept calling. As the week trickled past, her anxiety faded. By Thursday she no longer expected anyone to answer the phone. But doggedly, three times a day, Eleanor dialed George's number. Less than ever did she know what she would say to him. But talk to him she felt she must.

$$\left(20\right)$$

The laws of hospitality required that Hart, having eaten dinner at Chip Strong's house, invite Chip Strong over to dinner at the Wrong House. When the date had been set, Hart felt that it was comfortably distant, but sooner than he would have liked, it arrived. In fact, it was the day after Hart had seen the Main Street house with Frances.

There was one welcome aspect to this. Chip had seemed to be on the best of terms with Frances. Hart even felt that a less highly sophisticated man than himself might feel a bit jealous of Chip Strong. He didn't plan to bring this up, but he did intend to pump Chip about Frances's intentions, after plying his guest with food and wine. It was the plying part that was turning out to be harder than it looked.

By now Hart was aware of his housekeeping limitations, which were at their most pronounced in the kitchen. He ate a lot of boiled eggs and Campbell's Chunky Soup and grilled Velveeta sandwiches which formed a nice blistery skin under the broiler. This did not seem festive enough for Chip. So Hart had bought a chicken. Surely roasting a chicken was simple enough. And there were Frances's cookbooks, too.

He allowed a generous margin of time for the preparations and began to unwrap the chicken at three o'clock, looking regretfully out the window at the brisk breeze teasing the sparkling waves. He washed the chicken as directed by *The Joy of Cooking*, hating the dank feel of the flesh and the way the paper towels clung to the pimply-looking yellow skin. But a concentrated search did not produce the roasting pan. He could find nothing more appropriate than a soufflé dish, and after an attempt to cram the bird into its porcelain circumference, he gave up and called Frances at Clara's house in New York.

"Hi," he said tentatively when she answered the phone.

"Oh. Hi," she answered, noncommittally, then waited.

"Listen," Hart said, a few seconds after the silence became noticeable, "I'm cooking a chicken here. And I can't find the roasting pan."

"Oh," Frances said. "No, you wouldn't be able to. It's actually in the closet in that little bedroom down there. I couldn't find room for it in the kitchen cabinets."

"Oh," Hart said, enlightened. "Is that where the ice bucket is?"

"Yes," Frances said. "And some other stuff I don't think you will have missed. A stockpot, for instance."

"Hold on," Hart told her, and put the phone on the counter while he searched the closet. He came back holding the roasting pan and the ice bucket.

"I might have wanted the blender," he said reproachfully as he picked up the receiver again.

"Well, now you know where it is," Frances answered. "What are you planning on roasting?"

"I told you, I have this chicken. Here's another thing, Frances, this cookbook talks about a rack. Do you have a rack?"

"No, I make a little snake out of tinfoil and sit the chicken in that. Don't undercook it; you'll get salmonella."

"I will? How will I know?"

"I don't know exactly. High fever and the trots, I think."

"No, the chicken. How will I know it's done?"

"Make sure the meat isn't pink anywhere. Did you get one of the ones with the little pop-up button?"

"I don't know," Hart said, frowning. "How can I tell?"

"You look at it," she said patiently. "The button's on the breast. The white meat. But what I was going to say was, don't trust it. Sometimes they pop up when the white meat is done but the dark meat is still bloody on the bone. Don't eat it that way."

"Okay," Hart said, examining his chicken. "Oh, and how do I truss it?"

"Who's coming for dinner?" Frances's voice came back in what was apparently a non sequitur.

"What does that matter? Chip Strong."

"Chip won't notice if it's been trussed. Don't bother." She paused. "Is that all?"

"Well . . ." Hart said, plopping the chicken back into the soufflé dish. He twirled the phone cord in his left hand. "What about next weekend? It's Labor Day weekend. I think Eleanor was planning on coming up."

"Oh," Frances said, and Hart could tell from her voice that this was a new idea.

"It's only a weekend," Hart said.

"I know, but . . . remember the dimmer switches," she said.

"Is it the dimmer switches, or is it me?" Hart found himself asking. "Because I miss you, Frances. I'm bored. I don't have anybody to talk to."

"You have Chip Strong," she couldn't resist saying.

"Frances," Hart said, with a warning tone in his voice. "You know what I mean."

"I know," she said, subdued.

"And I need you. I wanted to ask you for advice about *us*," he said. "It made me realize that I count on you."

There was silence from Frances's end of the phone. "Are you still there?"

"Yes," she said. "I'm taking it all in." She paused. "I'll think about it," she said. "I'll call you tomorrow or the next day. And we need to talk about that house. Do you want to have a contractor look at it? Or just keep looking?"

"I'll think about that," Hart said, untwisting himself from the phone cord, which had managed to encircle him completely.

"Okay. Good luck with the chicken," Frances said, and hung up.

Being a real belt-and-suspenders type, Hart managed to overcook the chicken into a desiccated state just short of incineration. Fortunately he had bought a can of cranberry jelly, which made the stringy meat just barely palatable.

Chip Strong didn't seem to notice much about the food, but he did take a strong interest in the six-pack of Miller in the

284

refrigerator. They ate outside on the deck, and between chewing the tough chicken and swatting at gnats, they were kept pretty busy. Hart kept waiting for an opening to talk about Chip's perfidy with Frances, but Chip nattered on defensively about fishing and Margaret Harwood's latest broken heart. Finally, as he plunked two bowls of ice cream on the table, Hart said, "What is all this with you and Frances anyway?"

"Oh, good, Heath Bar Crunch," said Chip, looking at the bowl. "I never buy this at home because I eat all the Heath Bars out and then there are all these cartons of mangled ice cream left." He took a bite. "I'm glad you mentioned Frances," he went on, swallowing. "I didn't know how to bring her up. She's quite a woman, you know?"

"I know," Hart said dryly, looking out to sea. A seagull dived at the surface of the water, coming up with a few inches of flapping fish.

Chip looked at Hart surreptitiously. "But you know what's weird?" he said. "The first time I took her to see that house on Main Street, I thought she really liked it. And then when the three of us saw it together, she . . . well, I thought maybe she was pretending not to like it. To make you like it more. If you see what I mean."

Hart turned to Chip, who was excavating a chunk of toffee from the ice cream. "You mean you think she was pretending not to like it, even though she really did?"

Chip nodded, chewing.

"Thinking that I would be better disposed to the house if she made light of it?"

Chip swallowed and nodded again. "She even winked at me."

"She *winked* at you?" It was a sprightly, waggish gesture, completely unlike Frances.

"So you think she was basically trying to manipulate me into buying that house on Main Street, is that what you're saying?"

"More or less," Chip answered, wiping his mouth carefully. He watched Hart, curious to know how his friend would take this. Hart merely looked down at his bowl of melting ice cream and started eating. But Chip thought he could detect a smile, and was puzzled. "You're not annoyed with her?" he asked.

Hart shook his head. He was definitely smiling. "She knows me pretty well," he said, and there was no mistaking the tone of pride in his voice.

Hart's phone call amused Frances, but in another way she found it rather poignant. That was Hart for you, always game, willing to try whatever was required of him. She knew he had invited Chip for dinner out of a sense of obligation. And he was cooking a chicken because it seemed like company food.

Frances was sitting in the garden behind the house, where a glass table and four chairs sat beneath an old fruit tree. It was the kind of crisp, dry day that made Frances feel it was a crime to be indoors. There would have been a lot to do in a garden on a day like this, but Clara's little city plot was planted with low-care pachysandra and a few sturdy yews. Nothing for Frances to do there.

It must be a beautiful day up in Weymouth. Frances could imagine how Main Street must look with the tall maples deeply green in the shade and the sun glaring off the white paint of the Methodist church. You'd be able to hear cicadas today, buzzing in unison and then stopping, mysteriously, all at once.

Frances looked down at the newspaper in front of her and tried to focus on it, but her mind kept going back to Hart. He missed her. She could feel her mouth curving into a smile at the thought. Imagine being so pleased by such a little thing. It reminded her of the early months of their courtship, when she was in Philadelphia working at the Art Museum and he was in New York. He never had been demonstrative; she'd grasped that about him right away, and welcomed it. He would never make a big fuss about things, but what he said you could believe. He'd written her letters in those days, just a page or less in his spiky handwriting. And she remembered the thrill the first time he'd written that he missed her.

Frances sat back in the chair and contemplated the scrap of blue sky she could see between the buildings on Clara's block. There had been a story in the newspaper that morning about someone they both knew. Actually, now that Frances thought about it, he had introduced them at a party in Vermont. Noble

Glenn, the brother of Frances's college roommate. In those days he'd been at the medical school of the University of Vermont. And here he was in a huge profile *The New York Times*, proclaiming the merits of alternative medicine. He'd written a book and now gave lectures about how some natural antibiotic found in many gardens had cured him of prostate cancer. The AMA naturally hated him and had kicked him out. There was a picture of him in the paper, in front of his big modern house in Santa Fe, wearing a ponytail and an earring.

Frances tore the page from the paper. Noble Glenn had been a self-righteous prig, and Hart would think this was funny. She folded it up to send to him, along with a listing for a house in Madison. She didn't really think it was a particularly interesting house. Hart, however, would understand what she meant by sending it: that she didn't have her heart set on the Main Street house, but was open to further ideas. And was planning on living with him again. That was the thing about being married for so long. You didn't have to spell everything out.

A marriage counselor might have told the Drummonds that they were putting themselves in a risky position. Their brief, businesslike meeting to look at houses had actually resulted in what could be construed as two challenges. Was Hart going to have a contractor look at the new house? And was Frances going to spend the weekend in Weymouth? Were both of them willing, in short, to make major concessions and retreat from their adversarial positions without prior negotiations?

They were. When Hart told his wife, as an irritated aside, that he needed her and missed her, she understood what had made her so unhappy that summer. She had felt superfluous. Her flight to New York had been a spontaneous escape from an unbearable situation, but it had brought Hart to what Frances thought of as his senses. He no longer took her for granted.

As for Hart, he might not have admitted that he ever *had*. Yet the recalcitrant shirts and the dry chicken and the many lonely evenings had ensured that henceforth he would appreciate his wife.

Frances had better internal resources than Hart did. She had not been lonely or uncomfortable in New York. She had managed just fine without her husband. But as she addressed the manila envelope to him at Shore Road, she realized that she was bored without him. Life was simply more interesting with Hart around. Even if all he did was tie flies all day. She liked him. She liked his point of view, his energy, his optimism. She missed him, too.

Of course, this all went unspoken. Frances called Hart the following day and told him that she would come to Weymouth for Labor Day weekend. He, in turn, told her that he was meeting three contractors at Main Street to get rough estimates, and didn't she think that a fairly plain tile would be fine for the bathrooms? By the end of the conversation, they were both quite pleased with themselves and with each other.

So was Harry, when he found out that his mother was going back to his father. He was in fact delighted, and celebrated by sketching out a new plot development involving the threatened divorce of the exiled king and queen of a small Balkan country (who ran a country inn in Sonoma County to pass the time) whose royalist movement has recalled them to assume the throne, rescuing the feisty little nation from chaos. It almost made up to him for the previous weeks when his family troubles had made it impossible for him to concentrate.

Eleanor took the happy news in stride, however. Her mother's little sabbatical had always made sense to her. Now that it was over, her parents would probably enjoy each other again. Eleanor could now stop worrying about them and devote more attention to her current preoccupation: the whereabouts of George Sinclair.

She was still calling George's number daily, usually several times, but without hope of reaching him. She had even sent him a terse little note asking him to call her. No result.

She didn't know what to think or how to feel about this. What did she expect to achieve by talking to George now? Even that wasn't clear. The terrible tension of the week after his visit to Weymouth had diminished. You couldn't live at such an emotional pitch. Maybe the most she hoped for now was simply a conclusion. What Sophy, the veteran of many hours of therapy, called "closure."

Distraction from George came in the unwelcome form of Eleanor's least favorite annual ritual: getting the boys ready for school. This involved hours of digging through boxes of Toby's hand-me-downs to find the sizes that would fit Simon and forcing Toby to try on the three pairs of khaki trousers that had finished school in a wearable condition. There followed a very expensive trip to the Gap and an even more more painful trip to the shoe store, after which Eleanor felt compelled to take the boys to the movies so that she wouldn't have to listen to them for at least an hour. After spending the entire eighty-two minutes of the film obsessing about George, she was happy enough to concentrate on their incessant jokes, questions, and demands for the rest of the evening.

On Monday the Gray boys went back to camp, having worn their mother out and decimated the balance of her checking account. Eleanor went back to her office with gratitude and automatically called George's number while she was checking her mail. She hung up after eight rings, feeling no disappointment. By now this had become merely habit, and whatever she felt about George was in a state of suspended animation.

Nobody in the Drummond family watched Monday night's news, which featured a short segment about a tropical storm brewing up in the Caribbean. By Tuesday the storm (named Albertine) had picked up some heft and was twirling its way toward the Florida coast. Hart, who watched the seven o'clock news when he wasn't out on the boat, took note of Albertine's path. When the hair-sprayed newscaster announced that the storm might conceivably reach the Northeast in a few days, he pricked up his ears. There was nothing Hart liked better than a hurricane.

Overnight Albertine got promoted to this status, and she changed her course. She spared Florida and skimmed past the Carolinas. She lingered out in the ocean, picking up speed and moisture. Poor little Bermuda was her first landfall and suddenly the entire East Coast began to pay attention as footage of massive waves and flattened trees moved up to the opening minutes of news broadcasts. Hurricane Albertine was headed in a direct path for Maryland. No, the New Jersey shore. No, she was still at sea. By Friday morning, she seemed to be aiming for New York.

New Yorkers pride themselves on their savvy and their coolness, yet there is nothing they enjoy more than a good crisis. Neighbors share water in a drought. They loan each other flashlights in a blackout. Blizzards, riots, and transit strikes unite New Yorkers against chaos. So in the hours when Albertine was spinning her way toward New York, a pleasant prepanic energy filled the air. Rumors flew. You should fill your bathtub in case the water got cut off. Buy candles. Buy canned food. Put crosses of tape on your windows (nobody knew why). Don't take a shower; don't turn on the TV. Get home while you can.

Getting home while you can is usually a large component of these New York panics. Down forty flights on the elevator, onto a subway or a commuter train, it's hard enough on a good day, impossible with a foot of snow on the ground. Or, as in this case, in sixty-mile-an-hour winds.

Because the wind had started blowing. Eleanor's office building was unmistakably swaying. The secretaries clutched each other in the hall with each gust, deliciously terrified. The wind made a keening noise that was somehow amplified by the steel bands framing the windows. Inside Eleanor's office she could barely make herself heard. By ten o'clock the rumors were feverish. The Stock Exchange was closing. The Long Island Railroad was putting on extra trains. People started fretting about their houses and their dogs. The managing partners consulted quickly and closed the firm.

During the morning flurry Eleanor's principal concern was Toby and Simon. Their day camp was sending them home, but there would be no one there. She couldn't get uptown by the time the bus dropped them off. She called Jadrancka. She called Luz. Finally, in desperation, she called Harry. Who agreed with alacrity to drive up to her apartment and meet the boys. But he said further, "I think we should go up to Weymouth."

"What? Why?" Eleanor said. "If anything, it's going to be worse there."

"Dad," Harry said. "In that house."

"Oh, Lord," Eleanor said, aghast. "I guess you're right. But if he's in danger won't they make him evacuate?"

"That's the point," Harry said. "If we get there in time, we can help. Think of all the stuff. The silver. Books. Pictures."

"Right. Okay," Eleanor said, suddenly decisive. "I'll meet you at the apartment. If you have time, pack bags for the boys. A change of clothes, toothbrushes. Simon's bear. They'll tell you."

Only after she'd hung up did Eleanor start to worry about the wisdom of taking her sons to Weymouth in the teeth of the hurricane. Folly, clearly. She'd do much better to keep them in her fortresslike apartment building in New York. But by the time she got home to communicate this change of heart to Harry, the boys were alight with excitement. A hurricane! Big waves, lashing wind, the prospect of wide-scale destruction! It took Eleanor just thirty seconds to assess the situation and decide that there was no point in resisting. There could be no real danger if they stayed away from the water during the peak of the storm.

An hour and a half later, as Harry's Land Rover battled its way up I-95 on the outskirts of New Haven, Eleanor's second thoughts became alarmist. To her right lay the wide expanse of New Haven Harbor, usually a calm sheet of water. Now it was lashed with whitecaps, heaving with six-foot swells. The Land Rover quivered under an extra-strong blast of wind.

"I wonder why this road isn't closed," Eleanor said rashly. "Aren't we in danger?"

"Danger? Danger!" yelped Simon in delight. "We're in danger!" he told Toby.

"No," Toby said disdainfully. "We aren't, are we, Uncle Harry?"

"No," said Harry. "Sorry, Simon. If we were, the road would be closed, but they're letting us drive on it."

Eleanor flinched as the car shuddered again, and Harry glanced over at her. "The door isn't going to fly open by itself," he said, noticing her death grip on the door's armrest.

"Never mind. This way I feel I'm doing my small part to keep us safe," retorted Eleanor. "I wish we'd get there. This is driving me crazy."

The conditions were actually rather fierce and Harry, though he knew enough not to tell Eleanor this, was surprised that the highway *was* still open. Rain was streaming down in a solid gray blanket and the slashing windshield wipers gave Harry only a momentary view of the road ahead of him. The Land Rover's high center of gravity meant that the car tilted quite noticeably in the worst gusts of wind, which were coming off the harbor with a ferocity Harry didn't like. He remembered that Simon got carsick and silently seconded Eleanor's wish that the trip were over.

Neither Harry nor Eleanor had given much thought to what would happen when they got to Weymouth, though Harry, when he saw New Haven Harbor, suspected that the Wrong House would already be evacuated. He was correct.

Hart had been eagerly watching the storm develop. The television was tuned to the local news station. He had his birding glasses out to examine the growing waves. And he tried to ready the house for the storm. He unearthed the big flashlight and put extra batteries on the counter. He dug a transistor radio from a closet and carefully tuned it to the news. Then he climbed into his foul-weather gear and went out to haul the porch furniture into the garage.

He could barely open the door against the force of the wind, which made the air outside seem like a solid wall. The door slammed shut after him as if pushed by a gigantic invisible hand. Hart bent down to pick up the table. It was a fairly light affair, made of plastic-coated tubular metal. As he crouched to lift it, the wind got beneath it and Hart could feel it alternately tugging and shoving, as if the tabletop were a rigid sail. Meanwhile, the rain was pelting down into his eyes and mouth and all over his hands, which were getting slippery. Hart struggled to the far edge of the deck and down the stairs. At the bottom he paused, setting the table down and wiping his eyes. For the first time, he began to worry. Was it possible that this storm was going to do some damage?

He got the table to the garage. He floundered back up onto the deck and managed to bring two chairs to safety. He looked at the chaise and reluctantly decided that he'd better go inside to rest before he tackled that. As he walked back into the house he glanced at the boat, tossing on the waves at the end of the dock. When he went back out he would have to be sure it was secured bow and stern.

Inside the house he stripped off his streaming raincoat and pants. His shirtsleeves were drenched to the elbows, and the rain had soaked right through the back and shoulders. His pants, meanwhile, were wet to the knee. He carefully hung the rain clothes in the downstairs bathroom and mopped the puddles from the floor so they wouldn't stain the wood. Pushing back a sense of defeat, Hart went upstairs to change his clothes.

He was in the master bedroom, watching the waves out the window as he pulled on a turtleneck and a dry pair of khakis, when the police car drove up. So he was unaware of the officer's presence until he heard the doorbell, instantly followed by a voice shouting up the stairs, "Hello? Anyone home?"

He came to the top of the stairs and saw, dripping onto his carefully mopped wood floor, a young man in a peaked hat and a long, black, shiny wet raincoat.

"Sorry to bother you, sir, but I have to ask you to leave your house," the young man said. "The storm is due to hit in a few hours and we're expecting very high water. The Red Cross has set up a shelter in the high school auditorium. I need to ask you to go along there right away."

Hart came partway down the stairs in his bare feet. "Who are you?"

"Sorry, sir. Officer Malory of the state police." He unbuttoned the top buttons of his raincoat and pulled aside the flap so that Hart could see the shield and name tag.

"Goodness," Hart said. "Evacuating! Can I secure a few things in the house first?"

"I'm afraid not, sir. I have to see you off the premises and I've got three other houses to get to before we can set up the roadblock. So I have to ask you to hurry."

"But . . ." Hart said, suddenly taking it in. "The house? I have to just leave the house wide open like this?"

The policeman looked around at the bay windows, opaque with the water rolling down them, and said, "I'm afraid so. I could help you close the shutters if you have any, but we can't stay any longer than that."

Hart came down to the bottom of the stairs and looked around the living room. It had a certain coziness in the face of the storm. All the lights were on. There were magazines on the end tables, and a book lay open on the window seat, next to the water-washed glass that still kept the storm at bay.

In a lull in the wind, the newscaster's voice momentarily spoke clearly from the TV. ". . . high tide at two o'clock, just as the storm is due to hit the coast. This means the experts are predicting eight- to ten-foot waves and tides six feet above normal. Coastal and low-lying areas are being evacuated . . ." The last words were drowned out by another shriek of wind.

Hart looked around the living room once more, wondering if he should feel sentimental.

"Sir . . ." said the policeman.

"I know," Hart said. "Just give me five minutes to pack a bag." And indeed, as he had promised, five minutes later he had packed a canvas holdall with his birding glasses, his favorite flies, a handful of family photographs in silver frames, and, at the last minute, a cribbage board and a couple of packs of cards. Ever methodical, he turned out the lights and locked the door as he left, recognizing the futility of the gesture.

The polite young policeman watched as he drove out of the driveway and toward town, then turned to go to the next house. By noon, all the waterfront houses were evacuated and Shore Road was blocked off by two sawhorses and three police cars, huddling together against the rain.

Hart had a basically practical nature. He regretted that he hadn't been more careful about the house. Maybe, with a little foresight, he would have been able to nail plywood over the windows and get some of the smaller furniture upstairs. Even with tides six feet above normal, the second floor might stay dry. But the living room, Hart realized, was more or less doomed. Good-bye to the chintz sofas. And the plaid curtains and the antler chandelier. But maybe it was also good riddance. After all, there was that new house they were looking at. And he'd never really liked those flowery sofas. As he turned into the parking lot of the Weymouth High School, Hart was already thinking about insurance. Maybe Margaret Harwood was right. Maybe, after all of this, they would end up with "a free summer on the water." As he got out of his car, sheltering the cribbage board and cards beneath his raincoat, he wondered where his wife was.

21

Hart had imagined Frances to be secure in Clara's New York house, perhaps watching the storm reporting on TV, or possibly even ignoring it altogether. He could picture her sitting serenely on one of Clara's silk sofas, reading something civilized and occasionally glancing out the window at the maelstrom.

But Hart did Frances an injustice. Ever since Albertine had been promoted to a hurricane, Frances had monitored the storm's progress. And when it began to look as if she would hit Connecticut, Frances made her plans. She awoke early Friday morning and turned on the news. What she heard was enough. She went down to the kitchen, where she found Beatriz and explained that she would be gone for a few days. She drank a cup of coffee standing up and took a cab to Penn Station, where she caught the Amtrak train to Boston.

As the train made its way up the coast, Frances peered out the cloudy Plexiglas windows for clues about the storm's potential. In Westport the tracks followed the path of a lagoon. On a tiny island at the center of the lagoon perched a small house, accessible only by boat at high tide. Frances craned eagerly to see how the little house was weathering the storm, but the wind-lashed rain on the train windows obscured the view. It all looked merely wet.

On her last trip up to Connecticut Frances had tried a new procedure. She left her car in a small garage near the station in Old Saybrook. The garage owner charged less than New Haven's municipal parking authorities, and the Amtrak train was faster that the commuter train to New Haven. So on the day of the hurricane she crammed her rain hat onto her head and clutched her long raincoat and walked the few blocks to the garage, wondering with each step how Hart was managing with the house.

The train trip had been mildly enjoyable, since the train, though buffeted, felt secure. The drive from Old Saybrook was terrifying. Frances kept to Route 1, reasoning that the road would be sheltered from the wind by the trees that lined it. But by the time she turned into Weymouth she knew the trees were going to start falling and that she had been lucky to get so far before the winds got worse.

Weymouth looked empty. The stores were all closed. No cars were on the street. Chip Strong's house was closed up tight, shutters over the windows. As Frances drove slowly through the village, she began to wonder. Where was everyone? She had come to Weymouth to help Hart secure the house against the storm. She might hate the house, but there were some good things in it and it seemed only fair to help Hart take care of them. Whatever that might entail. (Frances did realize that there was only so much that a couple in their sixties could do when it came to moving furniture around. She had already mentally sacrificed the big chintz sofas.) But Weymouth seemed to be a ghost town. She turned down Main Street and saw, with a jolt, the police blockade at Shore Road.

Frances was not an imaginative woman, and she had never wasted much time on morbid worries, but when she saw the cars pulled up nose to nose, with their roof lights flashing, horrible fantasies flooded her mind. Electrical lines down, Hart pinned beneath them. A massive tidal wave that had swept her husband out to sea. Hart's legs crushed by a fallen tree. As she drew to a stop, she knew she was clutching the steering wheel hard, and a shaky, quivery current of alarm ran through her body. One of the police car doors opened and a young man ran over to her car window. When she rolled it down the rain blew in all over her face and shoulders.

"Sorry, ma'am, I can't let you go down there," said the policeman.

"But I live there, my house is there," Frances said, aware she was talking too fast. "My husband is there. At 751 Shore Road."

"No, he isn't, ma'am," he said. "We evacuated the entire road an hour ago. They're all in the high school gym. I'm sure you'll find him there, ma'am."

She didn't answer him immediately, but looked at him for a minute longer as the news sank in. He'd been evacuated. He was in the high school gym. Frances realized she was beaming at the officer and remembered to thank him as she rolled up her window.

Before she reversed her car, Frances paused and looked out over the marsh, where acres of beige marsh grass usually ran down to the Sound. Today a wide stretch of the grass was covered with heaving leaden water, crashing in sizable waves on the yet-uncovered grasses. A vague recollection of high September tides (neap tides? mean tides? full moons? Something like that) flashed through her mind; then she closed her eyes. She realized that her heart was still pounding and she patted herself gently on the chest with an unconsciously ladylike gesture.

Hart was all right. She wasn't going to spend the rest of her days regretting this stupid flap over the house. Suddenly Frances felt a flood of affection for Hart. Thinking of his warmth, his reliability, his patience, Frances put the car in gear and drove slowly and carefully to Weymouth High School.

She was still alight with relief and rekindled fondness when she walked into the gym at Weymouth High. The Red Cross had set up a number of tables against the walls. Children played under the basketball hoops, and along one wall there was a table covered with huge coffee percolators and trays of sandwiches. Frances stood in the doorway and scanned the room. There, sitting at one of the tables with Chip Strong, was Hart. They were playing cards. As Chip looked at his hand, choosing his card, Hart glanced around the room. His eye caught Frances's.

She stood there at the end of the crowded room, tall and slender, innately elegant despite her dripping raincoat and sodden hat. Her composure was complete. She took off her hat and shook her head slightly, like a seabird settling its feathers after landing in the surf. Hart surprised Chip by putting down his cards and getting up from the table without a word.

She had come. He didn't know how, but she was there. For better, for worse, Hart thought. In sickness and in floods, or some such nonsense. Loyal and true. In that moment he loved his wife with a fierceness that surprised him. Would have surprised everyone, perhaps, but her.

He threaded through the crowd, reaching her in a moment. He reached out and clasped her in a bear hug, holding her tight for a moment until he felt the rain from her coat soak through his shirt. He pulled back quickly, looking in dismay at the wet marks on his chest and arms.

"I thought the whole point was to keep dry," Frances said with a sidelong smile.

Hart looked at her and shrugged. He reached down and took her hand after setting her wet rain hat at a rakish angle on his own head.

Chip looked up at the approaching apparition of Hart, ridiculous with his wife's hat on his head, and Frances, calm and collected as ever. Hart was beaming as if he had just caught a very large fish. It occurred to Chip that the look on Hart's face might somehow be connected with Frances's appearance on the scene, but that seemed far-fetched, especially when she sat down and said, "Who's winning?" as casually as if she had merely come downstairs after checking her hair in an bedroom mirror.

"Hart is," Chip said. "I never was any good at cards. I can't remember to count. I'd happily give you my hand," he said, holding out the cards.

"I brought my needlepoint," Frances said, slipping out of her coat, which Hart hung on the back of a nearby chair. "Since it looked as if we might be here for a while."

"I imagined you snug as a bug in New York," Hart said, sitting down. Chip noticed that he inched his chair closer to Frances's. "Do you want some coffee? What are you doing here?"

"No coffee, thanks. I came to help with the house," Frances explained, unfolding her needlepoint canvas.

"But you hate the house," Hart protested.

Frances lay the canvas on the table and looked at Hart. "I do. But I thought about you trying to get it all safe for the storm, and I thought you might need help." She put a hand over Hart's for a moment.

"Well, I did," Hart said. "I didn't start early enough. I feel terrible, Frances, you know we're bound to lose a lot, if I'd thought about it I could have put something over the windows—"

"You mean you left the windows unprotected?" Chip broke in. "Those bay windows? You realize—"

"Never mind, Chip," Frances interrupted in turn. "You know, Hart, I think I would like a cup of coffee, if you don't mind. And maybe a sandwich, too. Thank you," she said, as he stood up.

The minute he was out of hearing, she turned to Chip. "Look," she said, "you heard him. He feels terrible. He did what he could and it wasn't enough. Please don't go on about it."

Chip looked at Frances for a moment, then nodded. "Okay," he said. "What's the needlepoint for? Is that a chair cushion or a pillow?"

So when Hart came back, Chip was telling Frances about his aunt's petit-point rug that had taken her twenty years to finish. Hart set down Frances's coffee and sandwich and laid out a hand of solitaire.

Half an hour later, when Harry's Land Rover pulled into the parking lot and its passengers struggled through the rain to the gymnasium door, Simon called out "There's Gran's car," pointing to a blue Mercedes barely visible behind a pickup truck.

"I don't think so," Eleanor said. "Gran's in New York. Now come *on*, Simon, I'm getting drenched!" she called, holding out her hand.

"But I'm *sure* it's Gran's car," he told her, as they walked into the gym, "it has that flower sticker in the back window, you know the one Gran has, from the Garden Club?" he went on. "Look, I told you! There's Gran!" And Simon was off, running across the gym floor to his grandparents, closely followed by Toby.

The boys vanished instantly into the crowd, but Eleanor and Harry hung back for a moment, surveying the scene. Most of the tables were full now, and the noise was deafening. The whole place smelled like coffee and wet wool. Someone's dog rushed up and thrust its nose against Eleanor's crotch, then skittered back across the gym floor after a tattered yellow tennis ball before Eleanor had time to swat it away. Toward the back of the room a baby set up a wail and was quickly echoed by three other babies in different parts of the room.

"Have you ever noticed how babies always cry like that in stereo?" Harry asked idly. "Especially on airplanes. What's Mom doing here?"

Eleanor raised her eyebrows. "I don't understand anything anymore," she muttered to the air, and began to make her way through the crowd to her parents.

It was an unexpectedly pleasant afternoon. Somehow the coffee and sandwiches were supplemented with hot soup and baskets of fruit. One of the evacuees was a kindergarten teacher who organized the children into a series of exhausting games. Periodically people would venture as far as the glass-doored vestibule beyond the gym to look outside and report back on the weather. There were radios all over, tuned to the news, which endlessly reiterated the report of high winds, high tides, high waves. As the storm reached its peak, even the solid cinder-block walls of the gym vibrated. But the feeling was one of shelter rather than threat.

Harry and Eleanor sat with their parents, unable to ask anything more than the most superficial questions. ("How did you get here, Mom?" instead of "What are you doing here?" and "How was the drive?" rather than "Are you going to stay with Dad now?") Hart told them the story of his evacuation, managing to make it sound as if he, an elderly cripple, had been forcibly ejected from his ancestral homestead by a sneering, goose-stepping officer of the state. They played hearts and gin rummy and cribbage. Every now and then Eleanor got up to check on the boys, who thought the whole thing was a marvelous adventure.

When she came back to the table, Harry was laying out a deck of cards for clock solitaire. As his hand moved swiftly around the circle, Eleanor's eyes widened and she exclaimed, "Oh, my goodness! The boat! The boat on the living room floor!" Then she clapped a hand over her mouth and sat down.

"What are you talking about?" Harry asked, watching her as

his hands went on laying out the cards. "What boat on what living room floor?"

"I don't know exactly," Eleanor said, embarrassed now. "I mean . . ." She took a breath and glanced around at her mother, her father, and her brother. They were all staring at her.

"For my birthday Sophy sent me to a psychic," she explained hurriedly. "I didn't really want to go, but she made me. He said he saw an image of a boat on the living room floor. And just now, when I saw Harry with the cards . . . Frank used a pattern like that. And I thought . . ." She looked up. "Dad, could the Whaler end up on the floor of the house?"

Hart scratched the back of his neck, calculating. "With the tide and the wind . . ." He shrugged. "It could. I guess a wave could fling it right through the bay window." He frowned. "I don't know about the dimensions. It would probably fit."

"Pretty funny if we get back to the house and it's sitting there on the sofas," Harry said.

"Frank said on the floor," Eleanor corrected him absentmindedly.

"So what else did he tell you?" Harry asked. "Tall dark stranger in your future?"

Eleanor threw her brother a look of loathing and walked away from the table.

"Don't tease your sister," Frances said calmly. "You're being unusually thoughtless."

"Oh, Lord, George!" Harry said, and stopped dealing for a minute. He put the cards down. "Am I ever going to stop feeling like a heel about that?" he asked his mother.

Frances only sighed. "Yes, of course you are. All you did was set it in motion."

Harry looked down at the solitaire and played a card, then got up from the table and went to join his sister, who was standing at the door of the vestibule, looking out.

"Look, it's the eye of the storm," she said as Harry came to her side. The wind was slowing down and the rain visibly abating. Word spread, and soon the lobby was crowded. The trees ceased tossing and their leaves slowed to a quiet fluttering.

Soon someone opened a door, and everyone stepped out onto the glistening, rain-wet asphalt.

The quiet was eerie. You could hear water dripping from the building's gutters, but the birds were silent. For a few minutes, the sun even came out. "Is the hurricane over?" Simon asked, coming to his mother's side.

"No," she answered, putting a hand on his shoulder as he leaned against her. "This is called the eye. It's a peaceful time in the middle of the storm. Soon the wind will start blowing again."

Toby joined them, with Harry behind. "Harry says the wind will blow from the opposite direction. Is that true, Mom?"

"Yes," Eleanor said. "The hurricane is like a huge . . ." she hesitated. "Fried egg," she said, gesturing with her hands. "And the wind is the white part, blowing around and around, clockwise."

"Counterclockwise," Harry corrected her.

"Counterclockwise," Eleanor repeated, rolling her eyes. "Heaven forbid we should get this wrong. So look." She showed Toby her right fist and circled around it with her left hand. "This is us over here," she said, "and here is the wind going this way—"

"Mom," Toby said, having lost interest in her explanation, "what about Aunt Clara? Do you think she had to evacuate?"

"I don't know," Eleanor said, in the automatically soothing tone of the parent. "Maybe. But she has Sarge to help her. I'm sure she'll be all right."

"And George is there," Harry added to Toby, in the same reassuring tone. "You know, Mr. Sinclair." Then, in a mirror image of the gesture Eleanor had just used inside, he clapped his hand over his mouth as he met Eleanor's gaze.

"What's Mr. Sinclair doing there?" came Simon's question in an unworried treble voice.

"He's painting a picture on Aunt Clara's walls," Harry said, watching Eleanor. "He's staying with her for most of the summer."

As Eleanor heard these words she felt a flood of relief, a physical sensation, wash through her. He was at Clara's. He had been there all summer. He was not hiding from her, evading her calls, ignoring her letter. He didn't know. He didn't know.

Harry observed his sister as she took a deep breath and stood a little straighter. The lines in her face seemed to fade as he watched. And she looked him straight in the eye and said, "I've been trying to reach him."

"Why, Mom?" asked Toby.

"He sent me a wonderful picture of the two of you," Eleanor said, looking down at Toby. "He drew it that day on Farewell Island. I wanted to thank him for it."

Harry hesitated. "Among other things?" he suggested. "Not that I want to pry," he went on hurriedly.

"Not that you're in any position to," Eleanor reminded him, but there was good nature beneath the asperity. She looked up at the sky, which was darkening. The sun had already faded and the leaves were rushing again in the trees. "It's starting up again. Let's get back inside."

Inside the gym the general good feeling had taken on a slightly hilarious tinge. A piano had been uncovered on a corner of the stage, and the indefatigable kindergarten teacher was up there playing "Bingo" and "I've Been Working on the Railroad." Chip Strong, finally bored with losing card games to Drummonds, began building a card house with a great deal of help from Toby, who had a very light touch. Simon curled up on his mother's lap with his bear, tired now of the adventure and wishing for home. As she told him a story he fell asleep, so Eleanor just sat there, stroking his hair, thinking about nothing much at all.

By five o'clock, the storm had blown itself out. The gym began to empty as evacuees were told they could go back to their homes. Shore Road, however, was not considered safe. "Not for at least twenty-four hours," said the state trooper who brought the news. "There's still a lot of extra water out there. I can't even let anybody go look at the damage until after high tide tomorrow."

Hart and Frances took this news calmly and decided, in spite of Chip Strong's offer of his spare bedroom, to spend the night at a motel on Route 1 that was opening its doors to evacuees. As they gathered up the cribbage board and the cards and Simon's bear and Frances's needlepoint, Harry took his sister aside. He pressed the key to his car into her hands.

"Just go," he said. "I know I've interfered too much, but you have to go. He'll be there. I'll take care of the boys." Eleanor looked at her brother with her eyes welling and clutched the keys. She kissed him on the cheek and slipped out.

It was an eerie drive. The air was still wild, stirred up, as if currents had been set in motion that would not easily be stilled. The sky was white and opaque, but bright enough so that the trees cast shadows. Only a handful of drivers were out on the streets.

Afterward Eleanor couldn't fathom why she hadn't been stopped by the police. There were trees down everywhere, elms and oaks and even a beech, flat on the pavement or dizzily angled against other tree trunks. There must have been wires down; it stood to reason. Yet Eleanor always remembered it as a serene interval. She rolled down the windows of her brother's big car and listened to the birds begin again, tentatively, to chirp and sing. Soon there was a chorus, full-throated and strong, as if they were all reassuring themselves. Taking stock, taking attendance, after the storm.

There was half of an old elm down across Clara's drive. It was a pity, Eleanor thought, as she got out of the car. The tree must have been ailing; the trunk was split and rotten partway down. But half of the tree still stood. As she circled the trunk Eleanor glanced ahead to the house, suddenly worried. What if there had been damage there? What if they, too, had been evacuated? Would George even be there? And—what would he say?

The ground was sodden. Water welled up in her footprints and squelched around her feet. The grass was coated with a layer of leaves, twigs, and bark blown from the trees, all dark with water. Eleanor had to pick her way toward the house. Even when she had walked around the elm and gotten back onto the driveway, the footing was uneven. She stepped over a branch that caught her sweater, and it took nearly a minute for her trembling hands to release the yarn from the splintered wood.

And all the time, she was trying not to think. It was one of the hardest things she ever did, walking into Clara's house to see George. It took all of her courage to keep her feet moving. It was something that had to be done.

She didn't think about what to say, or about what he might answer. She simply knew she had to see him. Face-to-face.

She got her sweater untangled and went onward. The light was brightening as the clouds cleared away, and turning a deep gold. Somewhere there should be a tremendous rainbow.

Twigs and leaves littered the steps of the house, and a few shingles had blown off the roof to land in random squares on the lawn. Eleanor walked up the steps, looking at the windows masked with glossy green shutters. They gave the house an air of aloofness. Eleanor felt slightly ill.

She crossed the wide veranda and reached out to the door. Should she ring? What if Clara was asleep? That was just an excuse, Eleanor realized. She wanted to get this over with. No, she wanted it to have happened already. Maybe George wasn't there anyway. The thought made her put her hand on the doorknob. If George wasn't there she was going to have to screw her emotions up to the breaking point yet again. Get it over with.

The door swung open silently. Eleanor stepped into the big front hall, clotted with gloomy shadows. The shutters blocked out all light from the adjoining parlor and dining room, and nobody had turned on a lamp. It was spooky.

Eleanor stepped into the hall and took a few tentative steps. The house felt empty. Should she call out? She took a breath, but her voice wouldn't come. She walked silently forward, then stopped to listen again.

There. There was something. A tiny noise, a little click or something. Someone putting down a pencil. Down here on the first floor. In the morning room, behind a closed door.

Eleanor walked forward again and stopped with her hand on the door. She closed her eyes. He was in there. Before she had time to race silently back out of the house, she opened the door.

There, with his back to her, was George. He was crouched on the floor, brush in hand, gently touching white highlights onto the dozens of windows of Clara's French chateau. His T-shirt was covered with paint and a large smear of dirt, and his khakis seemed wet. He had tied a red bandanna over his hair.

Eleanor tried to speak. Nothing came out. She tried to breathe and a rattling sound came from her throat.

George turned around, startled, and dropped his brush. He stood up slowly. Eleanor thought irrelevantly how tall he was. She took a breath and clasped her hands together and tried again to speak.

She looked like a schoolgirl trying to repeat a memorized speech and stricken by panic. She had arrived out of the storm like an apparition and stood in front of George like a ghost laboring to produce words. George stepped over to her and put a hand on each shoulder.

"What? You don't have bad news, do you? Is everyone all right?"

Eleanor gulped and shook her head. "No. No, we're all fine. Harry told me you were here."

"Uh-huh," George said, trying to coax her voice back by speaking in a soothing tone. "Clara's been in Lenox for a few days, so she missed the storm." He paused. "Here, sit down." He pulled a rag off a canvas-draped chair and Eleanor sat, looking up at him with the same intent expression. "And your parents are all right? Your father, I mean? Is the house all right?"

Eleanor swallowed and coughed slightly. "We don't know. He was evacuated this morning. They're at a motel in Weymouth." She fell silent and looked down at the floor with her elbows on her knees.

George watched her for a moment, then stepped over to the wall to retrieve his fallen brush. He thrust it into a coffee can full of water, watching Eleanor all the while. She had gotten hold of the dropcloth on the chair and was fidgeting with the edge of the fabric, where the coarse threads were coming loose. The room was so quiet George thought he could hear her breathing.

He wanted to help her. There was something she wanted to say. But he stood there, hands at his side, trying not to acknowledge his dawning hope.

She took a deep breath and looked up. "I got your picture of

Toby and Simon. It was beautiful." She straightened up, still holding the dropcloth. "I tried to call you. I guess you were up here. I wrote a note."

"To say what?" George asked, in a voice that he managed to keep from shaking.

"That I needed to see you. I wanted to talk to you."

"Well, here I am," he said, as lightly as he could.

"I know," Eleanor said, and dropped her eyes again. "Harry drove me up here with the children. He gave me his car keys just now and told me to come."

"Maybe this time Harry was right," George said.

"I think he was right before," Eleanor said to her lap.

George stood still for a moment. Maybe he hadn't heard her. Slowly, he knelt on the floor next to her and sat back on his heels. "What do you mean?"

Eleanor's face was now level with his. "He was right, George. Harry was right. You were right. I've been trying to pretend this wasn't true, George, but I have fallen in love with you and if you don't want to have anything to do with me I am completely sympathetic but I had to say this and get it out of my system." She looked at him squarely, with a kind of weary finality.

In reply, George lifted a hand to her cheek. He ran his thumb over her cheekbone, cupping her jaw with his palm. "Now neither of us has to," he murmured as she turned her head to kiss his palm.

"Has to what?" she asked.

"Get the other one out of his system." He reached forward to put his arms around her, chair and all. "It would have been such a waste." Her head rested on his shoulder, and her arms came up around his back. He felt the bandanna being pulled off.

"You don't like my head scarf?" he asked the corner of her neck closest to his lips.

"I like your hair better," she said, and ran a hand through it.

"I miss yours," he said, pulling away from her to look. "I like the wood sprite look, but I miss the lush locks."

"Oh, well," Eleanor said, self-consciously pulling a curl. "It was a . . ." she rolled her eyes. "I don't know, some weird impulse."

George sat back on his heels, assessing her. "Turn your head that way?" he said. "Look out the window." Eleanor looked out the window obligingly.

"Do you remember the card I sent you? Now you look like a David," he announced, and leaped to his feet. He pulled her up with him. "I want to paint you as the Empress Josephine, in an enormous pearl tiara." Eleanor giggled and blushed. "God, Eleanor, I am so *happy!*" He backed away from the chair into a clear part of the room. "I want to waltz around with you. I want to waltz right out of this room and around and around in that gloomy hall until we fall down with dizziness! I feel like I should hire the largest brass band I can find to march down the Post Road in front of you and me, nodding and smiling graciously on an enormous heart-shaped float studded with roses. Oh, Eleanor, I do love you, too," he finally subsided, and kissed her.

Eventually George took Eleanor back to the Sound View Motel and stayed to eat pizza on the wide motel beds with the Drummond family. Harry, seeing his sister incandescent with happiness, felt vindicated. He felt he had crafted a splendid happy ending for a real-life soap opera.

Frank Gerson's image of the boat on the living room floor turned out to be perfectly accurate. When Hart and Frances opened the door, the Whaler lay beached between the two sofas, with the shards of the coffee table beneath it. A remarkable selection of flotsam had been deposited by the hurricane and Frances and Hart spent several days in rubber boots, peeling starfish from the curtains and unhooking seaweed from the antler chandelier. The house reeked.

The damage wasn't profound, though. The house was unlivable, but once the windows were replaced and the walls repainted, the wiring renewed and the appliances repaired, it would be habitable. Only the barn siding was permanently damaged: the salt water had darkened it so that there was a flood marker halfway up the stairs.

Builders and contractors in Weymouth were overwhelmed with work, but Hart managed to find a man who came down from East Haddam to do the repairs. He expressed admiration for the house, and Hart offered facetiously to sell it. Soon they worked out a splendid deal that permitted the contractor to renovate to his own taste (which was clean and angular and improved the place immensely) and allowed the Drummonds to save several thousand dollars by not listing the house at all through Strong Harwood. Margaret Harwood was irate, but Chip was delighted for his friends and offered them his house to stay in while they renovated the Main Street house.

They turned him down, of course (Frances was unnerved by his cooking methods) and camped in successive rooms of Main Street. Though they had professionals for the big jobs, Hart did as much of the fine work as he could. He spent much of the fall and winter stripping the banister (which turned out to be mahogany), hunting for antique doorknobs, and cleaning the marble fireplaces. Frances helped him as much as she could, but there were other demands on her time.

In the middle of September, Chip Strong astonished Frances by asking her to join his firm. He felt she had good taste, an intuitive grasp of real estate transactions, and a soothing sales personality. With some misgivings, Frances began going to the office to learn the business, which she found fascinating. She was also, to her surprise, a brilliant saleswoman. She never could learn to hide her disdain for postwar builder's houses, but her real enthusiasm for older homes clinched many a deal. And when Margaret Harwood departed suddenly for Florida in pursuit of a retired concrete magnate, Chip and Frances ran the office very cozily together. Hart even became a kind of unofficial restoration consultant for them. Since summer was the busy period for Weymouth real estate, Frances didn't get as much time for her garden as she would have liked, but she told Hart with a nearly straight face that she was now putting off gardening for her retirement.

George and Eleanor married at Christmas. Eleanor wore almond-colored velvet and George wore a blue blazer and a look of incredible pride. Toby and Simon behaved like princes and were delighted to have another grown-up in their lives whose principal job was to pay attention to them. George quit teaching at Avalon and sold his loft to set up a much cheaper studio in

Washington Heights. Eleanor didn't find that her life was any less complicated once she was remarried. It took several months for her hair to grow out to a graceful length, and she had to get it cut frequently so it wouldn't look merely shaggy. Toby still dawdled in the morning and she still had trouble managing her wardrobe. George helped, though, by shopping with her, cooking, and keeping her warm at night. Among their wedding presents were an antique sleigh bed from George's parents, a little Van Dongen drawing from Clara Henschel, and an electric doughnut maker from Chip Strong.

Harry's confident management of his sister's love life went to his head a bit and he gave a few friends unsolicited advice on romantic endeavors. George felt Harry should have a taste of his own medicine and invited him to dinner with a columnist from an art magazine, whom Harry afterward characterized as "a humorless Bride of Art." Everyone noticed how often he danced with Eleanor's friend Sophy at the wedding.

In time the summer of the Wrong House became a Drummond family story. It could be told to illustrate Frances's perfectionism or Hart's ability to ignore the unpleasant. Frances hated hearing the story. She hated being reminded how dreadful that summer had been and how badly she had behaved. But she never could imagine how else she might have gotten through it all.